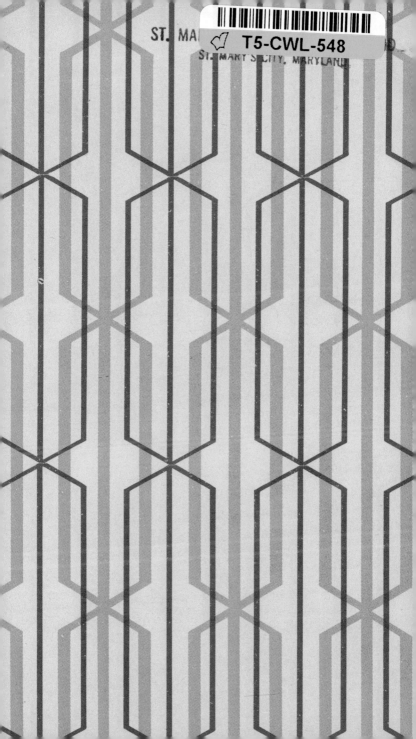

# CONDENSED NOVELS
## AND STORIES

# CONDENSED NOVELS
## AND STORIES

BY

BRET HARTE

*Short Story Index Reprint Series*

## BOOKS FOR LIBRARIES PRESS
### FREEPORT, NEW YORK

First Published 1882
Reprinted 1970

STANDARD BOOK NUMBER:
8369-3549-7


LIBRARY OF CONGRESS CATALOG CARD NUMBER:
75-122716


PRINTED IN THE UNITED STATES OF AMERICA

# CONTENTS.

## STORIES.

## CONDENSED NOVELS.

*Contents.*

*STORIES.*

# The Story of a Mine.

## CHAPTER I.

### WHO SOUGHT IT.

IT was a steep trail leading over the Monterey Coast Range. Concho was very tired, Concho was very dusty, Concho was very much disgusted. To Concho's mind there was but one relief for these insurmountable difficulties, and that lay in a leathern bottle slung over the *machillas* of his saddle. Concho raised the bottle to his lips, took a long draught, made a wry face, and ejaculated—

"Carajo!"

It appeared that the bottle did not contain *aguardiente*, but had lately been filled in a tavern near Tres Pinos by an Irishman who sold bad American whisky under that pleasing Castilian title. Nevertheless Concho had already nearly emptied the bottle, and it fell back against the saddle as yellow and flaccid as his own cheeks. Thus reinforced, Concho turned to look at the valley behind him, from which he had climbed since noon. It was a sterile waste bordered here and there by arable fringes and *valdas* of meadow land, but in the main dusty, dry, and forbidding. His eye rested for a moment on a low white cloud-line on the eastern horizon, but so mocking and unsubstantial that it seemed to come and go as he gazed. Concho struck his forehead and winked his hot eyelids. Was it the Sierras or the cursed American whisky?

Again he recommenced the ascent. At times the half-worn, half-visible trail became utterly lost in the bare black out-crop of the ridge, but his sagacious mule soon found it again, until, stepping upon a loose boulder, she slipped and fell. In vain Concho tried to lift her from out the ruin of camp kettles, prospecting pans and picks; she remained quietly recumbent, occasionally raising her head as if to contemplatively glance over the arid plain below. Then he had recourse to useless blows. Then he essayed profanity of a secular kind, such as "Assassin," "Thief," "Beast with a pig's head," "Food for the bull's horns," but with no effect.

Then he had recourse to the curse ecclesiastic—

"Ah, Judas Iscariot! is it thus, renegade and traitor, thou leavest me, thy master, a league from camp, and supper waiting? Stealer of the Sacrament, get up!"

Still no effect. Concho began to feel uneasy; never before had a mule of pious lineage failed to respond to this kind of exhortation. He made one more desperate attempt—

"Ah, defiler of the altar! lie not there! Look!" he threw his hand into the air, extending the fingers suddenly. "Behold, fiend! I exorcise thee! Ha! tremblest! Look but a little now—see! Apostate! I—I—excommunicate thee—Mula!"

"What are you kicking up such a devil of a row down there for?" said a gruff voice from the rocks above.

Concho shuddered. Could it be that the devil was really going to fly away with his mule? He dared not look up.

"Come now," continued the voice, "you just let up on that mule, you d—d old Greaser. Don't you see she's slipped her shoulder?"

Alarmed as Concho was at the information, he could not help feeling to a certain extent relieved. She was lamed, but had not lost her standing as a good Catholic.

He ventured to lift his eyes. A stranger—an *Americano* from his dress and accent—was descending the rocks toward him. He was a slight-built man with a dark, smooth face, that would have been quite commonplace and inexpressive but for his left eye, in which all that was villanous in him apparently centred. Shut that eye, and you had the features and expression of an ordinary man; cover up those features, and the eye shone out like Eblis' own. Nature had apparently observed this too, and had, by a paralysis of the nerve, ironically dropped the corner of the upper lid over it like a curtain, laughed at her handiwork, and turned him loose to prey upon a credulous world.

"What are you doing here?" said the stranger after he had assisted Concho in bringing the mule to her feet, and a helpless halt.

"Prospecting, Señor."

The stranger turned his respectable right eye toward Concho, while his left looked unutterable scorn and wickedness over the landscape.

"Prospecting, what for?"

"Gold and silver, Señor; yet for silver most."

"Alone?"

"Of us there are four."

The stranger looked around.

"In camp—a league beyond," explained the Mexican.

"Found anything?"

"Of this—much." Concho took from his saddle-bags a lump of greyish iron ore, studded here and there with star points of pyrites. The stranger said nothing, but his eye looked a diabolical suggestion.

"You are lucky, friend Greaser."

"Eh?"

"It *is* silver."

"How know you this?"

"It is my business. I'm a metallurgist."

"And you can say what shall be silver and what is not."

"Yes—see here!" The stranger took from his saddle-bags a little leather case containing some half-dozen phials. One, enwrapped in dark-blue paper, he held up to Concho.

"This contains a preparation of silver."

Concho's eyes sparkled, but he looked doubtingly at the stranger.

"Get me some water in your pan."

Concho emptied his water bottle in his prospecting pan and handed it to the stranger. He dipped a dried blade of grass in the bottle, and then let a drop fall from its tip in the water. The water remained unchanged.

"Now throw a little salt in the water," said the stranger.

Concho did so. Instantly a white film appeared on the surface, and presently the whole mass assumed a milky hue.

Concho crossed himself hastily, "Mother of God, it is magic!"

"It is chloride of silver, you darned fool."

Not content with this cheap experiment, the stranger then took Concho's breath away by reddening some litmus paper with the nitrate, and then completely knocked over the simple Mexican by restoring its colour by dipping it in the salt water.

"You shall try me this," said Concho, offering his iron ore to the stranger; "you shall use the silver and the salt."

"Not so fast, my friend," answered the stranger. "In the first place this ore must be melted, and then a chip taken and put in shape like this; and that is worth something, my Greaser cherub. No, sir, a man don't spend all his youth at Freiburg and Heidelberg to throw away his science gratuitously on the first Greaser he meets."

"It will cost—eh—how much!" said the Mexican eagerly.

"Well, I should say it would take about a hundred dollars and expenses to—to—find silver in that ore. But once you've got it there, you're all right for tons of it."

"You shall have it," said the now excited Mexican. "You shall have it of us—the four! You shall come to our camp and shall melt it—and show the silver and—enough! Come," and in his feverishness he clutched the hand of his companion as if to lead him forth at once.

"What are you going to do with your mule?" said the stranger.

"True, Holy Mother! what, indeed?"

"Look yer," said the stranger, with a grim smile, "she won't stray far, I'll be bound. I've an extra pack-mule above here; you can ride on her, and lead me into camp, and to-morrow come back for your beast."

Poor honest Concho's heart sickened at the prospect of leaving behind the tired servant he had objurgated so strongly a moment before, but the love of gold was uppermost. "I will come back to thee, little one, to-morrow, a rich man. Meanwhile, wait thou here, patient one. *Adios*, thou smallest of mules, *Adios!*"

And seizing the stranger's hand he clambered up the rocky ledge until they reached the summit. Then the stranger turned and gave one sweep of his malevolent eye over the valley.

Wherefore, in after years, when their story was related, with the devotion of true Catholic pioneers, they named the mountain " *La Cañada de la Visitacion del Diablo*," "The Gulch of the Visitation of the Devil," the same being now the boundary lines of one of the famous Mexican land grants.

## CHAPTER II.

### WHO FOUND IT.

CONCHO was so impatient to reach the camp and deliver his good news to his companions that more than once the stranger was obliged to command him to slacken his pace. "Is it not enough, you infernal Greaser, that you lame your own mule, but you must try your hand on mine? Or am I to put Jinny down among the expenses?" he added with a grin and a slight lifting of his baleful eyelid.

When they had ridden a mile along the ridge they began to descend again toward the valley. Vegetation now sparingly bordered the trail, clumps of chimisal, an occasional Manzanita bush, and one or two dwarfed "buckeyes" rooted their way between the interstices of the black-grey rock. Now and then, in crossing some dry gully worn by the overflow of winter torrents from above, the greyish rock gloom was relieved by dull red and brown masses of colour, and almost every overhanging rock bore the mark of a miner's pick. Presently, as they rounded the curving flank of the mountain, from a rocky bench below them, a thin ghost-like stream of smoke seemed to be steadily drawn by invisible hands into the invisible ether. "It is the camp," said Concho gleefully; "I will myself forward to prepare them for the stranger;" and before his companion could detain him he had disappeared at a sharp canter around the curve of the trail.

Left to himself, the stranger took a more leisurely pace, which left him ample time for reflection. Scamp as he was, there was something in the simple credulity of poor Concho that made him uneasy. Not that his moral consciousness was touched, but he feared that Concho's companions might, knowing Concho's simplicity, instantly suspect him of trading upon it. He rode on in a deep study. Was he reviewing his past life? A vagabond by birth and education, a swindler by profession, an outcast by reputation, without absolutely turning his back upon respectability, he had trembled on the perilous edge of criminality ever since his boyhood. He did not scruple to cheat these Mexicans, they were a degraded race ; and for a moment he felt almost an accredited agent of progress and civilisation. We never really understand the meaning of enlightenment until we begin to use it aggressively.

A few paces farther on four figures appeared in the now gathering darkness of the trail. The stranger quickly recognised the beaming smile of Concho, foremost of the party. A quick glance at the faces of the others satisfied him that, while they lacked Concho's good humour, they certainly did not surpass him in intellect. " Pedro " was a stout vaquero. " Manuel " was a slim half-breed and ex-convert of the Mission of San Carmel, and " Miguel " a recent butcher of Monterey. Under the benign influences of Concho that suspicion with which the ignorant regard strangers died away, and the whole party escorted the stranger—who had given his name as Mr. Joseph Wiles—to their camp-fire. So anxious were they to begin their experiments that even the instincts of hospitality were forgotten, and it was not until Mr. Wiles—now known as " Don José "—sharply reminded them that he wanted some " grub," that they came to their senses. When the frugal meal of *tortillas, frijoles,* salt pork, and chocolate was over, an oven was built of the dark red rock brought from the ledge before them, and an earthenware jar, glazed by some peculiar local process, tightly fitted over it, and packed with clay and sods. A fire was speedily built of pine boughs continually brought from a wooded ravine below, and in a few moments the furnace was in full blast. Mr. Wiles did not participate in

these active preparations, except to give occasional directions between his teeth, which were contemplatively fixed
over a clay pipe as he lay comfortably on his back on the
ground.   Whatever enjoyment the rascal may have had in
their useless labours he did not show it, but it was observed
that his left eye often followed the broad figure of the ex-
vaquero, Pedro, and often dwelt on that worthy's beetling
brows and half-savage face.   Meeting that baleful glance
once Pedro growled out an oath, but could not resist a
hideous fascination that caused him again and again to
seek it.

The scene was weird enough without Wiles' eye to add
to its wild picturesqueness.   The mountain towered above
—a heavy Rembrandtish mass of black shadow—sharply
cut here and there against a sky so inconceivably remote
that the world-sick soul must have despaired of ever reaching so far, or of climbing its steel-blue walls.   The stars
were large, keen, and brilliant, but cold and steadfast.   They
did not dance nor twinkle in their adamantine setting.   The
furnace fire painted the faces of the men an Indian red,
glanced on brightly coloured blanket and *serapé*, but was
eventually caught and absorbed in the waiting shadows of
the black mountain, scarcely twenty feet from the furnace
door.   The low, half-sung, half-whispered foreign speech of
the group, the roaring of the furnace, and the quick, sharp
yelp of a *coyote* on the plain below, were the only sounds
that broke the awful silence of the hills.

It was almost dawn when it was announced that the ore
had fused.   And it was high time, for the pot was slowly
sinking into the fast-crumbling oven.   Concho uttered a
jubilant " God and Liberty," but Don José Wiles bade him
be silent and bring stakes to support the pot.   Then Don
José bent over the seething mass.   It was for a moment
only.   But in that moment this accomplished metallurgist

Mr. Joseph Wiles, had quietly dropped a silver half dollar into the pot!

Then he charged them to keep up the fires and went to sleep—all but one eye.

Dawn came with dull beacon fires on the near hill-tops, and far in the east, roses over the Sierran snow. Birds twittered in the alder fringes a mile below, and the creaking of waggon wheels—the waggon itself a mere fleck of dust in the distant road—was heard distinctly. Then the melting-pot was solemnly broken by Don José, and the glowing incandescent mass turned into the road to cool.

And then the metallurgist chipped a small fragment from the mass and pounded it, and chipped another smaller piece and pounded that, and then subjected it to acid, and then treated it to a salt bath which became at once milky, and at last produced a white something—*mirabile dictu !*— two cents' worth of silver !

Concho shouted with joy, the rest gazed at each other doubtingly and distrustfully ; companions in poverty, they began to diverge and suspect each other in prosperity. Wiles' left eye glanced ironically from the one to the other.

" Here is the hundred dollars, Don José," said Pedro, handing the gold to Wiles with a decidedly brusque intimation that the services and presence of a stranger were no longer required.

Wiles took the money with a gracious smile and a wink that sent Pedro's heart into his boots, and was turning away, when a cry from Manuel stopped him. " The pot—the pot —it has leaked ! look ! behold ! see ! "

He had been cleaning away the crumbled fragments of the furnace to get ready for breakfast, and had disclosed a shining pool of quicksilver !

Wiles started, cast a rapid glance around the group, saw

in a flash that the metal was unknown to them, and then said quietly—

"It is not silver."

"Pardon, Señor; it is, and still molten."

Wiles stooped and ran his fingers through the shining metal.

"Mother of God! what is it then, magic?"

"No, only base metal." But then Concho, emboldened by Wiles' experiment, attempted to seize a handful of the glittering mass, that instantly broke through his fingers in a thousand tiny spherules, and even sent a few globules up his shirt sleeves, until he danced around in mingled fear and childish pleasure.

"And it is not worth the taking?" queried Pedro of Wiles.

Wiles' right eye and bland face were turned toward the speaker, but his malevolent left was glancing at the dull red-brown rock on the hill-side.

"No!"—and, turning abruptly away, he proceeded to saddle his mule.

Manuel, Miguel, and Pedro, left to themselves, began talking earnestly together; while Concho, now mindful of his crippled mule, made his way back to the trail where he had left her. But she was no longer there. Constant to her master through beatings and bullyings, she could not stand incivility and inattention. There are certain qualities of the sex that belong to all animated nature.

Inconsolable, footsore, and remorseful, Concho returned to the camp and furnace, three miles across the rocky ridge. But what was his astonishment on arriving to find the place deserted of man, mule, and camp equipage. Concho called aloud. Only the echoing rocks grimly answered him. Was it a trick? Concho tried to laugh. Ah—yes—a good one —a joke—no—no—they *had* deserted him! And then poor Concho bowed his head to the ground, and, falling on his face, cried as if his honest heart would break.

The tempest passed in a moment; it was not Concho's nature to suffer long nor brood over an injury. As he raised his head again·his eye caught the shimmer of the quicksilver—that pool of merry antic metal that had so delighted him an hour before. In a few moments Concho was again disporting with it; chasing it here and there, rolling it in his palms, and laughing with boylike glee at its elusive freaks and fancies. "Ah, sprightly one—skipjack— there thou goest—come here. This way—now I have thee, little one—come *muchacha*—come and kiss me," until he had quite forgotten the defection of his companions. And even when he shouldered his sorry pack he was fain to carry his playmate away with him in his empty leathern flask.

And yet I fancy the sun looked kindly on him as he strode cheerily down the black mountain side, and his step was none the less free nor light that he carried with him neither the silver nor the crime of his late comrades.

## CHAPTER III.

### WHO CLAIMED IT.

THE fog had already closed in on Monterey and was now rolling, a white, billowy sea, above, that soon shut out the blue breakers below. Once or twice in descending the mountain Concho had overhung the cliff and looked down upon the curving horseshoe of a bay below him, distant yet many miles. Earlier in the afternoon he had seen the gilt cross on the whitefaced Mission flare in the sunlight, but now all was gone. By the time he reached the highway of the town it was quite dark, and he plunged into the first *fonda* at the wayside, and endeavoured to forget his woes and his weariness in *aguardiente*. But Concho's head ached, and his back ached, and he was so generally distressed that

he bethought him of a *medico*—an American doctor—lately
come into the town, who had once treated Concho and his
mule with apparently the same medicine and after the same
heroic fashion. Concho reasoned, not illogically, that if he
were to be physicked at all he ought to get the worth of his
money. The grotesque extravagance of life, of fruit and
vegetable, in California was inconsistent with infinitesimal
doses. In Concho's previous illness the Doctor had given
him a dozen 4-gr. quinine powders. The following day the
grateful Mexican walked into the Doctor's office—cured.
The Doctor was gratified until, on examination, it appeared
that to save trouble, and because his memory was poor,
Concho had taken all the powders in one dose. The
Doctor shrugged his shoulders and—altered his practice.

"Well," said Dr. Guild, as Concho sank down ex-
haustedly in one of the Doctor's two chairs, "what now?
Have you been sleeping again in the *tule* marshes, or
are you upset with commissary whisky? Come, have it
out."

But Concho declared that the devil was in his stomach,
that Judas Iscariot had possessed himself of his spine, that
imps were in his forehead, and that his feet had been
scourged by Pontius Pilate.

"That means 'blue mass,'" said the Doctor. And
gave it to him, a bolus as large as a musket ball and as
heavy.

Concho took it on the spot and turned to go.

"I have no money, Señor Medico."

"Never mind. It's only a dollar, the price of the
medicine."

Concho looked guilty at having gulped down so much
cash. Then he said timidly—

"I have no money, but I have got here that which is
fine and jolly. It is yours," and he handed over the

contents of the precious tin can he had brought with him.

The Doctor took it, looked at the shivering volatile mass, and said, "Why, this is quicksilver!"

Concho laughed, "Yes, very quick silver, so!" and he snapped his fingers to show its sprightliness.

The Doctor's face grew earnest. "Where did you get this, Concho?" he finally asked.

"It ran from the pot in the mountains beyond."

The Doctor looked incredulous. Then Concho related the whole story.

"Could you find that spot again?"

"*Madre de Dios*, yes. I have a mule there; may the devil fly away with her!"

"And you say your comrades saw this?"

"Why not?"

"And you say they afterwards left you—deserted you?"

"They did, ingrates!"

The Doctor arose and shut his office door. "Hark ye, Concho," he said, "that bit of medicine I gave you just now was worth a dollar. It was worth a dollar because the material of which it was composed was made from the stuff you have in that can—quicksilver or mercury. It is one of the most valuable of metals, especially in a gold-mining country. My good fellow, if you know where to find enough of it, your fortune is made."

Concho rose to his feet.

"Tell me, was the rock you built your furnace of, red?"

"Si, Señor."

"And brown."

"Si, Señor."

"And crumbled under the heat?"

"As to nothing."

"And did you see much of this red rock?"

" The mountain mother is in travail with it."

" Are you sure that your comrades have not taken possession of the mountain mother ? "

" As how ? "

" By claiming its discovery under the mining laws, or by pre-emption ? "

" They shall not."

" But how will you, singlehanded, fight the four ? for I doubt not your scientific friend has a hand in it."

" I will fight."

" Yes, my Concho ; but suppose I take the fight off your hands. Now, here's a proposition : I will get half a dozen *Americanos* to go in with you. You will have to get money to work the mine—you will need funds. You shall share half with them. They will take the risk, raise the money, and protect you."

" I see," said Concho, nodding his head and winking his eyes rapidly. " *Bueno !* "

" I will return in ten minutes," said the Doctor, taking his hat.

He was as good as his word. In ten minutes he returned with six original locaters, a board of directors, a president, secretary, and a deed of incorporation of the " Blue Mass Quicksilver Mining Co." This latter was a delicate compliment to the Doctor, who was popular. The President added to these necessary articles a revolver.

" Take it," he said, handing over the weapon to Concho, " take it ; my horse is outside ; take that, ride like h—l and hang on until we come ! "

In another moment Concho was in the saddle. Then the mining director lapsed into the physician.

" I hardly know," said Dr. Guild doubtfully, " if in your present condition you ought to travel. You have just taken a powerful medicine," and the Doctor looked hypo-critically concerned.

"Ah—the devil!" laughed Concho; "what is the quick-silver that is *in* to that which is *out?* Hoopa la! Mula!" and with a clatter of hoofs and jingle of spurs, he was presently lost in the darkness.

"You were none too soon, gentlemen," said the American alcalde, as he drew up before the Doctor's door; " another company has just been incorporated for the same location, I reckon."

"Who are they?"

" Three Mexicans : Pedro, Manuel, and Miguel, headed by that d—d cockeyed Sydney Duck, Wiles."

" Are they here?"

"Manuel and Miguel only. The others are over at Tres Pinos lally-gagging Roscommon and trying to rope him in to pay off their whisky bills at his grocery."

" If that's so we needn't start before sunrise, for they're sure to get roaring drunk."

And this legitimate successor of the grave Mexican alcaldes, having thus delivered his impartial opinion, rode away.

Meanwhile, Concho the redoubtable, Concho the fortu-nate, spared neither *riata* nor spur. The way was dark, the trail obscure and at times even dangerous, and Concho, familiar as he was with these mountain fastnesses, often regretted his surefooted "Francisquita." " Care not, O Concho," he would say to himself, " 'tis but a little while, only a little while, and thou shalt have another Francis-quita to bless thee. Eh, skipjack, there was fine music to thy dancing. A dollar for an ounce—'tis as good as silver, and merrier." Yet for all his good spirits he kept a sharp look-out at certain bends of the mountain trail; not for assassins or brigands, for Concho was physically courageous, but for the Evil One, who, in various forms, was said to lurk in the Santa Cruz Range, to the great discomfort of all true Catholics. He recalled the incident of Ignacio, a muleteer of the Franciscan Friars, who, stopping at the "Angelus" to repeat the "Credo," saw Luzbel plainly in the likeness of a monstrous grizzly bear, mocking him by sitting on his haunches and lifting his paws, clasped together, as if in prayer. Nevertheless, with one hand grasping his reins and his rosary, and the other clutching his whisky flask and revolver, he fared on so excellently that he reached the summit as the earlier streaks of dawn were outlining the far-off Sierran peaks. Tethering his horse on a strip of tableland, he descended cautiously afoot until he reached the bench, the wall of red rock, and the crumbled and dismantled furnace. It was as he had left it that morning; there was no trace of recent human visitation. Revolver in hand, Concho examined every cave, gully, and recess, peered behind trees, penetrated copses of buckeye and Manzanita, and listened. There was no sound but the faint soughing of the wind over the pines below him. For a while he paced backward and forward with a vague sense of being a sentinel, but his mercurial nature soon rebelled against this monotony, and soon the fatigues of the day began to tell upon him. Recourse to his whisky flask only made him the drowsier, until at last he was fain to lie down and roll himself up tightly in his blanket. The next moment he was sound asleep.

His horse neighed twice from the summit, but Concho heard him not. Then the brush crackled on the ledge above him, a small fragment of rock rolled near his feet; but he stirred not. And then two black figures were outlined on the crags beyond.

"St-t-t!" whispered a voice. "There is one lying beside the furnace." The speech was Spanish, but the voice was Wiles.

The other figure crept cautiously to the edge of the crag and looked over. "It is Concho, the imbecile," said Pedro contemptuously.

"But if he should not be alone, or if he should waken?"

"I will watch and wait. Go you and affix the notification."

Wiles disappeared. Pedro began to creep down the face of the rocky ledge, supporting himself by chimisal and brushwood.

The next moment Pedro stood beside the unconscious man. Then he looked cautiously around. The figure of his companion was lost in the shadow of the rocks above; only a slight crackle of brush betrayed his whereabouts. Suddenly Pedro flung his *serapé* over the sleeper's head, and then threw his powerful frame and tremendous weight full upon Concho's upturned face, while his strong arms clasped the blanket-pinioned limbs of his victim. There was a momentary upheaval, a spasm, and a struggle; but the tightly-rolled blanket clung to the unfortunate man like cerements.

There was no noise, no outcry, no sound of struggle. There was nothing to be seen but the peaceful, prostrate figures of the two men darkly outlined on the ledge. They might have been sleeping in each other's arms. In the black silence the stealthy tread of Wiles in the bush above was distinctly audible.

Gradually the struggles grew fainter. Then a whisper from the crags—

"I can't see you. What are you doing?"

"Watching!"

"Sleeps he?"

"He sleeps!"

"Soundly?"

"Soundly."

"After the manner of the dead?"

"After the fashion of the dead!"

The last tremor had ceased. Pedro rose as Wiles descended.

"All is ready," said Wiles; "you are a witness of my placing the notifications?"

"I am a witness."

"But of this one?" pointing to Concho. "Shall we leave him here?"

"A drunken imbecile—why not?"

Wiles turned his left eye on the speaker. They chanced to be standing nearly in the same attitude they had stood the preceding night. Pedro uttered a cry and an impreca. tion, "Carramba! Take your devil's eye from me! What see you? Eh—what?"

"Nothing, good Pedro," said Wiles, turning his bland right cheek to Pedro. The infuriated and half-frightened ex-vaquero returned the long knife he had half drawn from its sheath, and growled surlily—

"Go on, then! But keep thou on that side and I will on this." And so, side by side, listening, watching, distrustful of all things, but mainly of each other, they stole back and up into those shadows from which they might have been evoked.

A half hour passed, in which the east brightened, flashed, and again melted into gold. And then the sun came up haughtily, and a fog that had stolen across the summit in the night arose and fled up the mountain side, tearing its white robes in its guilty haste, and leaving them fluttering from tree and crag and scar. A thousand tiny blades, nestling in the crevices of rocks, nurtured in storms, and rocked by the trade-winds, stretched their wan and feeble arms toward him; but Concho the strong, Concho the brave, Concho the lighthearted, spake not nor stirred.

## CHAPTER IV.

### WHO TOOK IT.

THERE was persistent neighing in the summit.  Concho's horse wanted his breakfast.

This protestation reached the ears of a party ascending the mountain from its western face.  To one of the party it was familiar.

"Why, blank it all, that's Chiquita.  That d—d Mexican's lying drunk somewhere," said the President of the B. M. Co.

"I don't like the look of this at all," said Dr. Guild, as they rode up beside the indignant animal.  "If it had been an American it might have been carelessness, but no Greaser ever forgets his beast.  Drive ahead, boys; we may be too late."

In half an hour they came in sight of the ledge below, the crumbled furnace, and the motionless figure of Concho, wrapped in a blanket, lying prone in the sunlight.

"I told you so—drunk," said the President.

The Doctor looked grave, but did not speak.  They dismounted and picketed their horses.  Then crept on all fours to the ledge above the furnace.  There was a cry from Secretary Gibbs, "Look yer.  Some fellar has been jumping us, boys.  See these notices."

There were two notices on canvas affixed to the rock, claiming the ground, and signed by Pedro, Manuel, Miguel, Wiles, and Roscommon.

"This was done, Doctor, while your trustworthy Greaser locater—d—n him—lay there drunk.  What's to be done now?"

But the Doctor was making his way to the unfortunate

cause of their defeat lying there quite mute to their re-
proaches.   The others followed him.

The Doctor knelt beside Concho, unrolled him, placed
his hand upon his waist, his ear over his heart, and then
said—

"Dead."

"Of course.   He got medicine of you last night.   This
comes of your d—d heroic practice."

But the Doctor was too much occupied to heed the
speaker's raillery.   He had peered into Concho's protu-
berant eye, opened his mouth, and gazed at the swollen
tongue, and then suddenly rose to his feet.

"Tear down those notices, boys, but keep them.   Put
up your own.   Don't be alarmed, you will not be interfered
with, for here is murder added to robbery."

"Murder!"

"Yes," said the Doctor excitedly, "I'll take my oath on
any inquest that this man was strangled to death.   He was
surprised while asleep.   Look here."   He pointed to the
revolver still in Concho's stiffening hand, which the murdered man had instantly cocked, but could not use in the
struggle.

"That's so," said the President, "no man goes to sleep
with a cocked revolver.   What's to be done?"

"Everything," said the Doctor.   "This deed was committed within the last two hours ; the body is still warm.
The murderer did not come our way, or we should have
met him on the trail.   He is, if anywhere, between here and
Tres Pinos."

"Gentlemen," said the President with a slight prepara-
tory and half-judicial cough, "two of you will stay here and
stick!   The others will follow me to Tres Pinos.   The law
has been outraged.   You understand the Court!"

By some odd influence the little group of half-cynical,

half-trifling, and wholly reckless men had become suddenly
sober, earnest citizens. They said, " Go on," nodded their
heads, and betook themselves to their horses.

" Had we not better wait for the inquest and swear out
a warrant ? " said the Secretary cautiously.

" How many men have we ? "

" Five ! "

" Then," said the President, summing up the Revised
Statutes of the State of California in one strong sentence ;
" then we don't want no d—d warrant."

## CHAPTER V.

### WHO HAD A LIEN ON IT.

IT was high noon at Tres Pinos. The three pines from
which it gained its name, in the dusty road and hot air,
seemed to smoke from their balsamic spires. There was
a glare from the road, a glare from the sky, a glare from
the rocks, a glare from the white canvas roofs of the few
shanties and cabins which made up the village. There was
even a glare from the unpainted red-wood boards of Roscommon's grocery and tavern, and a tendency on the warp-
ing floor of the veranda to curl up beneath the feet of the
intruder. A few mules, near the watering-trough, had shrunk
within the scant shadow of the corral.

The grocery business of Mr. Roscommon, although ade-
quate and sufficient for the village, was not exhausting nor
overtaxing to the proprietor ; the refilling of the pork and
flour barrel of the average miner was the work of a brief
hour on Saturday nights, but the daily replenishment of the
average miner with whisky was arduous and incessant.
Roscommon spent more time behind his bar than his
grocer's counter. Add to this the fact that a long shed-

like extension or wing bore the legend, "Cosmopolitan Hotel, Board or Lodging by the Day or Week. M. Roscommon," and you got an idea of the variety of the proprietor's functions. The "hotel," however, was more directly under the charge of Mrs. Roscommon, a lady of thirty years, strong, truculent, and goodhearted.

Mr. Roscommon had early adopted the theory that most of his customers were insane, and were to be alternately bullied or placated, as the case might be. Nothing that occurred, no extravagance of speech or act, ever ruffled his equilibrium, which was as dogged and stubborn as it was outwardly calm. When not serving liquors, or in the interval while it was being drunk, he was always wiping his counter with an exceedingly dirty towel, or, indeed, anything that came handy. Miners, noticing this purely perfunctory habit, occasionally supplied him slyly with articles inconsistent with their service—fragments of their shirts and underclothing, floursacking, tow, and once with a flannel petticoat of his wife's, stolen from the line in the backyard. Roscommon would continue his wiping without looking up, but yet conscious of the presence of each customer. "And it's not another dhrop ye'll git, Jack Brown, until ye've wiped out the black score that stands agin ye." "And it's there ye are, darlint, and it's here's the bottle that's been lukin' for ye sins Saturday." "And fwhot hev ye done with the last I sent ye, ye divil of a M'Corkle, and here's me back that's bruk entoirely wid dipping intil the pork barl to give ye the best sides— and ye spending yur last cint on a tare into Gilroy. Whist! and if it's fer foighting ye are, boys, there's an illigant bit o' sod beyant the corral, and its maybe meself 'll come out wid a shtick and be sociable."

On this particular day, however, Master Roscommon was not in his usual spirits, and when the clatter of horses hoofs before the door announced the approach of strangers, he absolutely ceased wiping his counter, and looked up, as Dr. Guild, the President and Secretary of the new company, strode into the shop.

"We are looking," said the President, "for a man by the name of Wiles, and three Mexicans known as Pedro, Manuel, and Miguel."

"Ye are?"

"We are!"

"Faix, and I hope ye'll foind 'em. And if ye'll git from em the score I've got agin 'em, darlint, I'll add a blessing to it."

There was a laugh at this from the bystanders, who, somehow, resented the intrusion of these strangers.

"I fear you will find it no laughing matter, gentlemen," said Dr. Guild a little stiffly, "when I tell you that a murder has been committed, and the men I am seeking within an hour of that murder put up that notice signed by their names," and Dr. Guild displayed the paper.

There was a breathless silence among the crowd as they eagerly pressed around the Doctor. Only Roscommon kept on wiping his counter.

"You will observe, gentlemen, that the name of Roscommon also appears on this paper as one of the original locaters."

"And sure, darlint," said Roscommon without looking up, if ye've no better ividince agin them boys then you have forninst me, it's home ye'd bether be riding to wanst. For it's meself as hasn't sturred fut out of the store the day and noight—more betoken as the boys I've sarved kin testify."

"That's so, Ross," chorused the crowd; "we've been running the old man all night."

"Then how comes your name on this paper?"

"Oh, murdher! will ye listin to him, boys. As if every

felly that owed me a whisky bill didn't come to me and say, 'Ah, Misther Roscommon,' or 'Moike,' as the case moight be, sure it's an illigant sthrike I've made this day, and it's meself that has put down your name as an original locater, and yer fortune's made, Mr. Roscommon, and will yer fill me up another quart for the good luck betune you and me. Ah, but ask Jack Brown over yan if it isn't sick that I am of his original locations."

The laugh that followed this speech, and its practical application, convinced the party that they had blundered, that they could obtain no clue to the real culprits here, and that any attempt by threats would meet violent opposition. Nevertheless the Doctor was persistent.

"When did you see these men last?"

"When did I see them is it? Bedad, what with sarvin' up the liquor and keeping me counters dry and swate I never see them at all."

"That's so, Ross!" chorused the crowd again, to whom the whole proceeding was delightfully farcical.

"Then I can tell you, gentlemen," said the Doctor stiffly, "that they were in Monterey last night, that they did not return on that trail this morning, and that they must have passed here at daybreak."

With these words, which the Doctor regretted as soon as delivered, the party rode away.

Mr. Roscommon resumed his service and counterwiping. But late that night, when the bar was closed and the last loiterer summarily ejected, Mr. Roscommon, in the conjugal privacy of his chamber, produced a legal-looking paper. "Read it, Maggie, darlint; for it's meself never had the larnin' nor the parts."

Mrs. Roscommon took the paper.

"Shure, it's law papers, making over some property to yis. O Moike! ye havn't been spekilating!"

" Whist ! and fwhotz that durty grey paper wid the sales and flourishes ? "

" Faix, it bothers me intoirely. Shure it oin't in English."

" Whist ! Maggie, it's a Spanish grant ! "

" A Spanish grant ? O Moike, and what did ye giv for it ? "

Mr. Roscommon laid his finger beside his nose and said softly, " Whishky ! "

## CHAPTER VI.

### HOW A GRANT WAS GOT FOR IT.

WHILE the Blue Mass Company, with more zeal than discretion, were actively pursuing Pedro and Wiles over the road to Tres Pinos, Señores Miguel and Manuel were comfortably seated in a *fonda* at Monterey, smoking cigarritos and discussing their late discovery. But they were in no better mood than their late companions, and it appeared from their conversation that in an evil moment they had sold out their interest in the alleged silver mine to Wiles and Pedro for a few hundred dollars, succumbing to what they were assured would be an active opposition on the part of the *Americanos*. The astute reader will easily understand that the accomplished Mr. Wiles did not inform them of its value as a quicksilver mine, although he was obliged to impart his secret to Pedro as a necessary accomplice and reckless coadjutor. That Pedro felt no qualms of conscience in thus betraying his two comrades may be inferred from his recent direct and sincere treatment of Concho ; and that he would, if occasion offered or policy made it expedient, as calmly obliterate Mr. Wiles— that gentleman himself never for a moment doubted.

" If we had waited but a little he would have given more, this cockeye ! " regretted Manuel querulously.

" Not a *peso*," said Miguel firmly.

" And why, my Miguel ? Thou knowest we could have worked the mine ourselves."

" Good, and lost even that labour. Look you, little brother. Show to me now the Mexican that has ever made a *reál* of a mine in California. How many, eh ? None ! Not a one. Who owns the Mexican's mine, eh ? *Americanos !* Who takes money from the Mexican's mine ? *Americanos.* Thou remembrest Briones, who spent a gold mine to make a silver one ? Who has the lands and house of Briones ? *Americanos !* Who has the cattle of Briones ? *Americanos !* Who has the mine of Briones ? *Americanos !* Who has the silver Briones never found ? *Americanos !* Always the same ! Forever ! Ah ! carramba ! "

Then the Evil One evidently took it into his head and horns to worry and toss these men—comparatively innocent as they were—still further, for a purpose. For presently to them appeared one Víctor Garcia, whilom a clerk of the Ayuntemiento, who rallied them over *aguardiente,* and told them the story of the quicksilver discovery, and the two mining claims taken out that night by Concho and Wiles. Whereat Manuel exploded with profanity and burnt blue with sulphurous malediction ; but Miguel, the recent ecclesiastic, sat livid and thoughtful. Finally came a pause in Manuel's bombardment, and something like this conversation took place between the cooler actors—

Miguel (thoughtfully). When was it thou didst petition for lands in the valley, friend Victor ?

Victor (amazedly). Never ! It is a sterile waste. Am I a fool ?

Miguel (softly). Thou didst. Of thy Governor, Micheltorena. I have seen the application.

Victor (beginning to appreciate a rodential odor). *Si !*
I had forgotten. Art thou sure it was in the valley ?

Miguel (persuasively). In the valley and up the *falda.**

Victor (with decision). Certainly. Of a verity—the
*falda* likewise.

Miguel (eyeing Victor). And yet thou hadst not the
grant. Painful is it that it should have been burned with
the destruction of the other archives by the *Americanos* at
Monterey.

Victor (cautiously, feeling his way). *Possiblemente.*

Miguel. It might be wise to look into it.

Victor (bluntly). As why ?

Miguel. For our good and thine, friend Victor. We
bring thee a discovery ; thou bringest us thy skill, thy
experience, thy government knowledge — thy Custom-
House paper.†

Manuel (breaking in drunkardly). But for what ? We
are Mexicans. Are we not fated ? We shall lose. Who
shall keep the *Americanos* off ?

Miguel. We shall take *one* American in ! Ha ! seest
thou ? This American comrade shall bribe his courts, his
*corregidores.* After a little he shall supply the men who
invent the machine of steam, the mill, the furnace, eh ?

Victor. But who is he—not to steal ?

Miguel. He is that man of Ireland, a good Catholic at
Tres Pinos.

Victor and Manuel (omnes). Roscommon ?

* *Falda,* or *valda, i.e.,* that part of the skirt of a woman's robe
that breaks upon the ground, and is also applied to the final slope of a
hill, from the angle that it makes upon the level plain.

† Grants, applications, and official notifications, under the Spanish
Government, were drawn on a stamped paper known as Custom-
House paper

Miguel. Of the same. We shall give him a share for the provisions, for the tools, for the *aguardiente*. It is of the Irish that the *Americanos* have great fear. It is of them that the votes are made, that the President is chosen. It is of him that they make the alcalde in San Francisco. And we are of the Church, like him.

They said "*Bueno*" all together, and for the moment appeared to be upheld by a religious enthusiasm—a joint confession of faith that meant death, destruction, and possibly forgery, as against the men who thought otherwise.

This spiritual harmony did away with all practical consideration and doubt. "I have a little niece," said Victor, "whose work with the pen is marvellous. If one says to her, 'Carmen, copy me this, or the other one'—even if it be copperplate—look you it is done, and you cannot know of which is the original. *Madre de Dios!* the other day she makes me a rubric * of the Governor, Pio Pico—the same, identical. Thou knowest her, Miguel. She asked concerning thee yesterday."

With the embarrassment of an underbred man, Miguel tried to appear unconcerned, but failed dismally. Indeed, I fear that the black eyes of Carmen had already done their perfect and accepted work, and had partly induced the application for Victor's aid. He, however, dissembled so far as to ask—

"But will she not know?"

"She is a child."

"But will she not talk?"

"Not if I say nay, and if thou—eh, Miguel?"

This bit of flattery—which, by the way, was a lie, for Victor's niece did not incline favourably to Miguel—had

---

* The Spanish "rubric" is the complicated flourish attached to a signature, and is as individual and characteristic as the handwriting.

its effect. They shook hands over the table. "But," said Miguel, "what is to be done must be done now." "At the moment," said Victor, "and thou shalt see it done. Eh! Does it content thee? then come!"

Miguel nodded to Manuel. "We will return in an hour; wait thou here."

They filed out into the dark, irregular street. Fate led them to pass the office of Dr. Guild at the moment that Concho mounted his horse. The shadows concealed them from their rival, but they overheard the last injunctions of the President to the unlucky Concho.

"Thou hearest?" said Miguel, clutching his companion's arm.

"Yes," said Victor. "But let him ride, my friend; in one hour we shall have that that shall arrive *years* before him," and with a complacent chuckle they passed unseen and unheard until, abruptly turning a corner, they stopped before a low adobe house.

It had once been a somewhat pretentious dwelling, but had evidently followed the fortunes of its late owner, Don Juan Briones, who had offered it as a last sop to the three-headed Cerberus that guarded the *El Refugio* Plutonian treasures, and who had swallowed it in a single gulp. It was in a very bad case. The furrows of its red-tiled roof looked as if they were the results of age and decrepitude. Its best room had a musty smell; there was the dampness of deliquescence in its slow decay, but the Spanish Californians were sensible architects, and its massive walls and partitions defied the earthquake thrill, and all the year round kept an even temperature within.

Victor led Miguel through a low anteroom into a plainly furnished chamber, where Carmen sat painting.

Now Mistress Carmen was a bit of a painter, in a pretty little way, with all the vague longings of an artist, but without, I fear, the artist's steadfast soul. She recognised beauty and form as a child might, without understanding their meaning, and somehow failed to make them even interpret her woman's moods, which surely were nature's too. So she painted everything with this innocent lust of the eye—flowers, birds, insects, landscapes, and figures —with a joyous fidelity, but no particular poetry. The bird never sang to her but one song, the flowers or trees spake but one language, and her skies never brightened except in colour. She came out strong on the Catholic saints, and would toss you up a cleanly-shaven Aloysius, sweetly destitute of expression, or a dropsical, lethargic Madonna that you couldn't have told from an old master, so bad it was. Her faculty of faithful reproduction even showed itself in fanciful lettering, and latterly in the imitation of rubrics and signatures. Indeed, with her eye for beauty of form she had always excelled in penmanship at the Convent, an accomplishment which the good Sisters held in great repute.

In person she was *petite*, with a still unformed girlish figure, perhaps a little too flat across the back, and with possibly a too great tendency to a boyish stride in walking. Her brow, covered by blueblack hair, was low and frank and honest; her eyes, a very dark hazel, were not particularly large, but rather heavily freighted in their melancholy lids with slipping passion ; her nose was of that unimportant character which no man remembers ; her mouth was small and straight, her teeth white and regular. The whole expression of her face was piquancy that might be subdued by tenderness or made malevolent by anger. At present it was a salad in which the oil and vinegar were deftly combined. The astute feminine reader will of course understand that this is the ordinary superficial masculine criticism, and at once make up her mind both as to the char

acter of the young lady and the competency of the critic.
I only know that *I* rather liked her. And her functions
are somewhat important in this veracious history.

She looked up, started to her feet, levelled her black
brows at the intruder, but at a sign from her uncle, showed
her white teeth and spake.

It was only a sentence, and a rather common-place one
at that ; but if she could have put her voice upon her canvas she might have retrieved the Garcia fortunes. For it
was so musical, so tender, so sympathising, so melodious,
so replete with the graciousness of womanhood, that she
seemed to have invented the language. And yet that
sentence was only an exaggerated form of the "How d'ye
do," whined out, doled out, lisped out, or shot out from the
pretty mouths of my fair countrywomen.

Miguel admired the paintings. He was struck particularly with a crayon drawing of a mule—" Mother of God !
it is the mule itself—observe how it will not go." Then
the crafty Victor broke in with, " But it is nothing to her
writing ; look, you shall tell to me which is the handwriting
of Pio Pico," and from a drawer in the secretary he drew
forth two signatures. One was affixed to a yellowish paper,
the other drawn on plain white foolscap. Of course Miguel
ook the more modern one with lover-like gallantry. " It
is this is genuine ! " Victor laughed triumphantly, Carmen
echoed the laugh melodiously in childlike glee, and added,
with a slight toss of her piquant head, " It is mine ! " The
best of the sex will not refuse a just and overdue compliment from even the man they dislike. It's the principle
they're after, not the sentiment.

But Victor was not satisfied with this proof of his niece's
skill. " Say to her," he demanded of Miguel, " what name
thou lik'st and it shall be done before thee here." Miguel
was not so much in love but he perceived the drift of

Victor's suggestion, and remarked that . the rubric of Governor Micheltorena was exceedingly complicated and difficult. "She shall do it!" responded Victor, with decision.

From a file of old departmental papers the Governor's signature and that involved rubric, which must have cost his late Excellency many youthful days of anxiety, was produced and laid before Carmen.

Carmen took her pen in her hand, looked at the brownish looking document and then at the virgin whiteness of the foolscap before her. "But," she said, pouting prettily, "I should have to first paint this white paper brown. And it will absorb the ink more quickly than that. When I painted the San Antonio of the Mission San Gabriel, for Father Acolti, I hád to put the decay in with my oils and brushes before the good Padre would accept it."

The two scamps looked at each other. It was their supreme moment. "I think I have," said Victor, with assumed carelessness, "I think I have some of the old Custom-House paper." He produced from the secretary a sheet of brown paper with a stamp. "Try it on that."

Carmen smiled with childish delight, tried it, and produced a marvel! "It is as magic," said Miguel, feigning to cross himself.

Victor's rôle was more serious : he affected to be deeply touched; took the paper, folded it and placed it in his breast. "I shall make a good fool of Don José Castro," he said, "he will declare it is the Governor's own signature, for he was his friend; but have a care, Carmen! that you spoil it not by the opening of your red lips. When he is fooled I will tell him of this marvel—this niece of mine, and he shall buy her pictures. Eh, little one?" and he gave her the avuncular caress, *i.e.*, a pat of the hand on either cheek, and a kiss. Miguel envied him, but cupidity out-generaled Cupid, and presently the conversation flagged, until a convenient recollection of Victor's—that himself and comrade were due at the Posada del Toros at 10 o'clock —gave them the opportunity to retire.

But not without a chance shot from Carmen. " Tell to me," she said, half to Victor and half to Miguel, " what has chanced with Concho? He was ever ready to bring to me flowers from the mountain, and insects and birds. Thou knowest how he would sit, O my uncle, and talk to me of the rare rocks he had seen, and the bears and the evil spirits, and now he comes no longer, my Concho! How is this? Nothing evil has befallen him, surely?" and her drooping lids closed half-pathetically.

Miguel's jealousy took fire. " He is drunk, Señorita, doubtless, and has forgotten not only thee, but mayhap his mule and pack! It is his custom, ha! ha!"

The red died out of Carmen's ripe lips, and she shut them together with a snap like a steel purse. The dove had suddenly changed to a hawk; the child-girl into an antique virago; the spirit hitherto dimly outlined in her face, of some shrewish Garcia ancestress, came to the fore. She darted a quick look at her uncle, and then, with her little hands on her rigid hips, strode with two steps up to Miguel.

" Possibly, O Señor Miguel Dominguez Perez (a profound courtesy here), it is as thou sayest. Drunkard Concho may be ; but drunk or sober, he never turned his back on his friend—or—(the words grated a little here)—his enemy."

Miguel would have replied, but Victor was ready. " Fool," he said, pinching his arm, "'tis an old friend. And—and—the application is still to be filled up. Are you crazy?"

But on this point Miguel was not, and with the revenge of a rival added to his other instincts, he permitted Victor to lead him away.

On their return to the *fonda* they found Master Manuel too far gone with *aguardiente*, and a general animosity to the average *Americano*, to be of any service. So they worked alone, with pen, ink and paper, in the stuffy, cigarrito-clouded back room of the *fonda*. It was midnight, two hours after Concho had started, that Miguel clapped spurs to his horse for the village of Tres Pinos, with an application to Governor Micheltorena for a grant to the "Rancho of the Red Rocks," comfortably bestowed in his pocket.

## CHAPTER VII.

### WHO PLEAD FOR IT.

THERE can be little doubt the Coroner's jury of Fresno would have returned a verdict of "death from alcoholism," as the result of their inquest into the cause of Concho's death, had not Dr. Guild fought nobly in support of the law and his own convictions. A majority of the jury objected to there being any inquest at all. A sincere juryman thought it hard that whenever a Greaser pegged out in a sneakin' kind o' way, American citizens should be taken from their business to find out what ailed him. "'Spose he was killed," said another, "thar ain't no time this thirty year he weren't, so to speak, just sufferin' for it, ez his nat'ral right ez a Mexican." The jury at last compromised by bringing in a verdict of homicide against certain parties unknown. Yet it was understood tacitly that these unknown parties were severally Wiles and Pedro; Manuel, Miguel, and Roscommon proving an unmistakable *alibi*. Wiles and Pedro had fled to Lower California, and Manuel, Miguel, and Roscommon deemed it advisable, in the then excited state of the public mind, to withhold the forged application and claim from the courts and the public comment. So that for a year after the murder of Concho and the flight of his assassins "The Blue Mass Mining Company" remained in undisturbed and actual possession of the mine, and reigned in their stead.

But the spirit of the murdered Concho would not down any more than that of the murdered Banquo, and so wrought, no doubt, in a quiet, Concho-like way, sore trouble with the "Blue Mass Company." For a great Capitalist and Master of Avarice came down to the mine and found it fair, and taking one of the Company aside, offered to lend his name and a certain amount of coin for a controlling interest, accompanying the generous offer with a suggestion that if it were not acceded to he would be compelled to buy up various Mexican mines and flood the market with quicksilver to the great detriment of the "Blue Mass Company," which thoughtful suggestion, offered by a man frequently alluded to as one of "California's great mining princes," and as one who had "done much to develop the resources of the State," was not to be lightly considered, and so, after a cautious nonconsultation with the Company, and a commendable secrecy, the stockholder sold out. Whereat it was speedily spread abroad that the great Capitalist had taken hold of "Blue Mass," and the stock went up and the other stockholders rejoiced—until the Great Capitalist found that it was necessary to put up expensive mills, to employ a high salaried superintendent, in fact, to develop the mine by the spending of its earnings, so that the stock quoted at 112 was finally saddled with an assessment of $50 per share. Another assessment of $50 to enable the superintendent to proceed to Russia and Spain and examine into the workings of the quicksilver mines there, and also a general commission to the gifted and scientific Pillageman to examine into the various component parts of quicksilver, and report if it could not be manufactured from ordinary sandstone by steam or electricity, speedily brought the other stockholders to their senses. It was at this time that the good fellow " Tom," the serious-minded " Dick," and the speculative but fortunate " Harry," brokers of the Great Capitalist, found it convenient to buy up, for the Great Capitalist aforesaid, the various other shares at great sacrifice.

I fear that I have bored my readers in thus giving the tiresome details of that ingenuous American pastime, which my countrymen dismiss in their epigrammatic way as the " freezing-out process." And lest any reader should question the ethics of the proceeding, I beg him to remember that one gentleman accomplished in this art was always a sincere and direct opponent of the late Mr. John Oakhurst, gambler.

But for once the Great Master of Avarice had not taken into sufficient account the avarice of others, and was suddenly and virtuously shocked to learn that an application for a patent for certain lands, known as the " Red Rock Rancho," was about to be offered before the United States Land Commission. This claim covered his mining property. But the information came quietly and secretly, as all of the Great Master's information was obtained, and he took the opportunity to sell out his clouded title and his proprietorship to the only remaining member of the original " Blue Mass " Company, a young fellow of pith, before many-tongued rumour had voiced the news far and wide. The blow was a heavy one to the party left in possession. Saddled by the enormous debts and expenses of the Great Capitalist, with a credit now further injured by the defection of this lucky magnate, who was admired for his skill in anticipating a loss, and whose relinquishment of any project meant ruin to it, the single-handed, impoverished possessor of the mine, whose title was contested and whose reputation was yet to be made—poor Biggs, first secretary and only remaining officer of the "Blue Mass Company," looked ruefully over his books and his last transfer, and, sighed! But I have before intimated that he was built of good stuff, and that he believed in his work—which was well —and in himself, which was better, and so, having faith even as a grain of mustard seed, I doubt not he would have been able to remove that mountain of quicksilver beyond the over-lapping of fraudulent grants. And, again, Providence—having disposed of these several scamps—raised up to him a friend. But that friend is of sufficient importance to this veracious history to deserve a paragraph to himself.

The Pylades of this Orestes was known of ordinary mortals as Royal Thatcher. His genealogy, birth and education are, I take it, of little account to this chronicle, which is only concerned with his friendship for Biggs and the result thereof. He had known Biggs a year or two previously; they had shared each other's purses, bunks, cabins, provisions and often friends, with that perfect freedom from obligation which belonged to the pioneer life. The varying tide of fortune had just then stranded Thatcher on a desert sand-hill in San Francisco, with an uninsured cargo of Expectations, while to Thatcher's active but not curious fancy it had apparently lifted his friend's bark, over the bar in the Monterey mountains, into an open quicksilver sea. So that he was considerably sur-prised on receiving a note from Biggs to this purport——

"DEAR ROY,—Run down here and help a fellow. I've too much of a load for one. Maybe we can make a team and pull 'Blue Mass' out yet.                                               BIGSEY."

Thatcher, sitting in his scantily furnished lodgings, doubtful of his next meal and in arrears for rent, heard this Macedonian cry as St. Paul did. He wrote a promissory and soothing note to his landlady, but fearing the "sweet sorrow" of a personal parting, let his collapsed valise down from his window by a cord, and by means of an economical combination of stage riding and pedestrianism, he presented himself, at the close of the third day, at Biggs' door. In a few moments he was in possession of the story; half an hour later in possession of half the mine, its infelix past and its doubtful future, equally with his friend.

Business over, Biggs turned to look at his partner. "You've aged some since I saw you last," he said. "Starvation luck, I 'spose. I'd know your eyes, old fellow, if I saw them among ten thousand, but your lips are parched and your mouth's grimmer than it used to be." Thatcher smiled to show that he could still do so, but did not say, as he might have said, that self-control, suppressed resentment, disappointment and occasional hunger had done something in the way of correcting Nature's obvious mistakes, and shutting up a kindly mouth. He only took off his threadbare coat, rolled up his sleeves, and saying, "We've got lots of work and some fighting before us," pitched into the "affairs" of the Blue Mass Company on the instant.

## CHAPTER VIII.

### OF COUNSEL FOR IT.

MEANWHILE Roscommon had waited. Then, in Garcia's name and backed by him, he laid his case before the Land Commission, filing the application (with forged indorsements) to Governor Micheltorena, and alleging that the original grant was destroyed by fire. And why?

It seemed there was a limit to Miss Carmen's imitative

talent. Admirable as it was, it did not reach to the reproduction of that official seal, which would have been a
necessary appendage to the Governor's grant. But there
were letters written on stamped paper by Governor Micheltorena, to himself, Garcia and to Miguel, and to Manuel's
father, all of which were duly signed by the sign manual
and rubric of Mrs.-Governor-Micheltorena-Carmen-de-Haro.
And then there was "parol" evidence and plenty of it;
witnesses who remembered everything about it—namely,
Manuel, Miguel, and the all-recollecting De Haro; here
were details, poetical and suggestive; and Dame-Quicklyish,
as when his late Excellency, sitting, not "by a sea-coal
fire," but with aguardiente and cigarros, had sworn to him,
the ex-ecclesiastic Miguel, that he should grant and had
granted Garcia's request. There were clouds of witnesses,
conversations, letters and records, glib and pat to the
occasion. In brief, there was nothing wanted but the
seal of his Excellency. The only copy of that was in the
possession of a rival school of renaissant art and the restor-
ation of antiques, then doing business before the Land
Commission.

And yet the claim was rejected! Having lately recom-
mended two separate claimants to a patent for the same
land, the Land Commission became cautious and conservative.

Roscommon was at first astounded, then indignant, and
then warlike—he was for an "appale to onst!"

With the reader's previous knowledge of Roscommon's
disposition this may seem somewhat inconsistent; but there
are certain natures to whom litigation has all the excitement
of gambling, and it should be borne in mind that this was
his first lawsuit. So that his lawyer, Mr. Saponaceous
Wood, found him in that belligerent mood to which counsel
are obliged to hypocritically bring all the sophistries of

their profession. "Of course you have your right to an appeal, but calm yourself, my dear sir, and consider. The case was presented strongly, the evidence overwhelming on our side, but we happened to be fighting *previous decisions of the Land Commission that had brought them into trouble;* so that if Micheltorena had himself appeared in Court and testified to his giving you the grant it would have made no difference—no Spanish grant had a show then, nor will it have for the next six months. You see, my dear sir, the Government sent out one of its big Washington lawyers to look into this business, and he reported frauds, sir, frauds, in a majority of the Spanish claims. And why, sir; why? He was bought, sir, bought—body and soul—by the Ring!"

"And fwhot's the Ring?" asked his client, sharply.

"The Ring is—ahem! a combination of unprincipled but wealthy persons to defeat the ends of justice."

"And sure, fwhot's the Ring to do wid me grant as that thaving Mexican gave me as the collatherals fer the bourd he was owin' me? Eh, mind that now!"

"The Ring, my dear sir, is the other side. It is—ahem! always the Other Side."

"And why the divil haven't we a Ring too? And ain't I payin' ye five hundred dollars—and the divil of Ring ye have—at all, at all? Fwhot am I payin' ye fur, eh?"

"That a judicious expenditure of money," began Mr. Wood, "outside of actual disbursements, may not be of infinite service to you I am not prepared to deny—but "——

"Look ye, Mr. Sappy Wood, it's the 'appale' I want, and the grant I'll have, more betoken as the old woman's har-rut and me own is set on it entoirely. Get me the land and I'll give ye the half of it—and it's a bargain!"

"But, my dear sir, there are some rules in our profession —technical though they may be "——

"The divil fly away wid yer profession.   Shure is it better nor me own?   If I've risked me provisions and me whisky, that cost me solid goold in Frisco, on the thafe Garcia's claim, bedad ! the loikes of ye can risk yer law."

"Well," said Wood, with an awkward smile, "I suppose that a deed for one half, on the consideration of friendship, my dear sir, and a dollar in hand paid by me, might be reconcilable."

"Now it's talkin' ye are.   But who's the felly we're foighten, that's got the Ring?"

"Ah, my dear sir, it's the United States," said the lawyer, with gravity.

"The States ! the Government is it?   And is't that ye'r afeard of?   Sure it's the Gov'ment that I fought in me own counthree, it was the Gov'ment that druv me to Ameriky, and is it now that I'm goin' back on me principles?"

"Your political sentiments do you great credit," began Mr. Wood.

"But fwhot's the Gov'ment to do wid the appale?"

"The Government," said Mr. Wood significantly, "will be represented by the District Attorney."

"And who's the spalpeen?"

"It is rumoured," said Mr. Wood, slowly, "that a new one is to be appointed.   *I*, myself, have had some ambition that way."

His client bent a pair of cunning but not overwise grey eyes on his American lawyer.   But he only said, "Ye have, eh?"

"Yes," said Wood, answering the look boldly, "and if I had the support of a number of your prominent countrymen, who are so powerful with *all* parties—men like *you*, my dear sir—why I think you might in time become a Conservative, at least more resigned to the Government."

Then the lesser and the greater scamp looked at each

other, and for a moment or two felt a warm, sympathetic, friendly emotion for each other, and quietly shook hands.

Depend upon it there is a great deal more kindly human sympathy between two openly confessed scamps than there is in that calm, respectable recognition that you and I, dear reader, exhibit when we happen to oppose each other with our respective virtues.

"And ye'll get the appale?"

"I will."

And he DID! And by a singular coincidence, got the District Attorneyship also. And with a deed for one half of the "Red Rock Rancho" in his pocket, sent a brother lawyer in court to appear for his client, the United States, as against *himself*, Roscommon, Garcia *et al.* Wild horses could not have torn him from this noble resolution. There is an indescribable delicacy in the legal profession which we literary folk ought to imitate.

The United States lost! Which meant ruin and destruction to the Blue Mass Company, who had bought from a paternal and beneficent Government lands which didn't belong to it. The Mexican grant, of course, antedated the occupation of the mine by Concho, Wiles, Pedro, *et al.*, as well as by the "Blue Mass Company," and the solitary partners, Biggs and Thatcher. More than that, it swallowed up their improvements—it made Biggs and Thatcher responsible to Garcia for all the money the Grand Master of Avarice had made out of it. Mr. District Attorney was apparently distressed, but resigned. Messrs. Biggs and Thatcher were really distressed and combative.

And then, to advance a few years in this chronicle, began real litigation with earnestness, vigour, courage, zeal and belief on the part of Biggs and Thatcher, and technicalities, delay, equivocation and a general Fabian-like policy on the part of Garcia, Roscommon, *et al.* Of all these tedious processes I note but one, which for originality and audacity of conception appears to me to indicate more clearly the temper and civilisation of the epoch. A subordinate officer of the District Court refused to obey the mandate ordering a transcript of the record to be sent up to the United States Supreme Court. It is to be regretted that the name of this Ephesian youth, who thus fired the dome of our constitutional liberties, should have been otherwise so unimportant as to be confined to the dusty records of that doubtful court of which he was a doubtful servitor, and that his claim to immortality ceased with his double-fee'd service. But there still stands on record a letter by this young gentleman arraigning the legal wisdom of the land, which is not entirely devoid of amusement or even instruction to young men desirous of obtaining publicity and capital. Howbeit the Supreme Court was obliged to protect itself by procuring the legislation of his functions out of his local fingers into the larger palm of its own attorney.

These various processes of law and equity, which, when exercised practically in the affairs of ordinary business, might have occupied a few months' time, dragged, clung, retrograded or advanced slowly during a period of eight or nine years. But the strong arms of Biggs and Thatcher held Possession, and, possibly by the same tactics employed on the other side, arrested or delayed ejectment, and so made and sold quicksilver, while their opponents were spending gold, until Biggs, sorely hit in the interlacings of his armour, fell in the lists, his cheek growing waxen and his strong arm feeble, and finding himself in this sore condition, and passing, as it were, made over his share in trust to his comrade, and died. Whereat, from that time henceforward, Royal Thatcher reigned in his stead.

And so, having anticipated the legal record, we will go back to the various human interests that helped to make it up.

To begin with Roscommon. To do justice to his later conduct and expressions, it must be remembered that when he accepted the claim for the "Red Rock Rancho," yet unquestioned, from the hands of Garcia, he was careless, or at least unsuspicious of fraud. It was not until he had experienced the intoxication of litigation that he felt, some-how, that he was a wronged and defrauded man, but with the obstinacy of defrauded men, preferred to arraign some one fact or individual as the impelling cause of his wrong, rather than the various circumstances that led to it. To his simple mind it was made patent that the "Blue Mass Company" were making money out of a mine which he claimed, and which was not yet adjudged to them. Every dollar they took out was a fresh count in this general indictment. Every delay toward this adjustment of rights —although made by his own lawyer—was a personal wrong. The mere fact that there never was or had been any *quid pro quo* for this immense property—that it had fallen to him for a mere song—only added zest to his struggle. The possibility of his losing this mere speculation affected him more strongly than if he had already paid down the million he expected to get from the mine. I don't know that I have indicated as plainly as I might that universal preference on the part of mankind to get something from nothing, and to acquire the largest return for the least possible expenditure, but I question my right to say that Roscommon was much more reprehensible than his fellows.

But it told upon him as it did upon all whom the spirit of the murdered Concho brooded—upon all whom Avarice alternately flattered and tortured. From his quiet gains in his legitimate business, from the little capital accumu-ated through industry and economy, he lavished thousands on this chimera of his fancy. He grew grizzled and worn over his self-imposed delusion; he no longer jested with his customers, regardless of quality or station or importance; he had cliques to mollify, enemies to placate, friends to reward. The grocery suffered; through giving food and lodgment to clouds of unimpeachable witnesses before the Land Commission and the District Court, "Mrs. Ros." found herself losing money. Even the bar failed; there was a party of Blue Mass employees who drank at the opposite *fonda* and cursed the Roscommon claim over the liquor. The calm, mechanical indifference with which Roscommon had served his customers was gone. The towel was no longer used after its perfunctory fashion; the counter remained unwiped; the disks of countless glasses marked its surface, and indicated other pre-occupation on the part of the proprietor. The keen grey eye of the claimant of the Red Rock Rancho was always on the lookout for friend or enemy.

Garcia comes next: that gentleman's inborn talent for historic misrepresentation, culminated unpleasantly through a defective memory; a year or two after he had sworn in his application for the Rancho, being engaged in another case, some trifling inconsistency was discovered in his statements, which had the effect of throwing the weight of evidence to the party who had paid him most, but was instantly detected by the weaker party. Garcia's pre-eminence as a witness, an expert and general historian, began to decline. He was obliged to be corroborated, and this required a liberal outlay of his fee. With the loss of his credibility as a witness bad habits supervened. He was frequently drunk, he lost his position, he lost his house, and Carmen, removed to San Francisco, supported him with her brush.

And this brings us once more to that pretty painter and innocent forger, whose unconscious act bore such baleful fruit on the barren hill-sides of the Red Rock Rancho, and also to a later blossom of her life, that opened, however, in kindlier sunshine.

## CHAPTER IX.

### WHAT THE FAIR HAD TO DO ABOUT IT.

THE house that Royal Thatcher so informally quitted in his exodus to the promised land of Biggs, was one of those over-sized, under-calculated dwellings conceived and erected in the extravagance of the San Francisco builder's hopes, and occupied finally to his despair. Intended originally as the palace of some inchoate Californian Aladdin, it usually ended as a lodging-house in which some helpless widow, or hopeless spinster, managed to combine respectability with the hard task of bread-getting. Thatcher's landlady was one of the former class. She had unfortunately survived not only her husband, but his property, and living in some deserted chamber, had, after the fashion of the Italian nobility, let out the rest of the ruin. A tendency to dwell upon these facts gave her conversation a peculiar significance on the first of each month. Thatcher had noticed this with the sensitiveness of an impoverished gentleman. But when, a few days after her lodger's sudden disappearance, a note came from him containing a draft in noble excess of all arrears and charges, the widow's heart was lifted, and the rock smitten with the golden wand gushed beneficence, that shone in a new gown for the widow, and a new suit for "Johnny," her son, a new oil-cloth in the hall, better service to the lodgers, and, let us be thankful, a kindlier consideration for the poor little black-eyed painter from Monterey, then dreadfully behind in her room rent. For, to tell the truth, the calls upon Miss de Haro's scant purse by her uncle had lately been frequent, perjury having declined in the Monterey market, through excessive and injudicious supply, until the line of demarcation between it and absolute verity was so finely drawn that Victor Garcia had remarked that "he might as well tell the truth at once and save his soul, since the devil was in the market!"

Mistress Plodgitt, the landlady, could not resist the desire to acquaint Carmen de Haro with her good fortune. "He was always a friend of yours, my dear—and I know him to be a gentleman that would never let a poor widow suffer; and see what he says about you!" Here she produced Thatcher's note and read: "Tell my little neighbour that I shall come back soon to carry her and her sketching-tools off by force, and I shall not let her return until she has caught the black mountains and the red rocks she used to talk about, and put the Blue Mass Mill in the foreground of the picture I shall order."

What is this, little one? Surely, Carmen, thou needst not blush at this, thy first grand offer. Holy Virgin! Is it of a necessity that thou shouldst stick the wrong end of thy brush in thy mouth, and then drop it in thy lap? Or was it taught thee by the good Sisters at the convent to stride in that boyish fashion to the side of thy elders and snatch from their hands the missive thou wouldst read? More of this we would know, O Carmen—smallest of brunettes— speak, little one, even in thine own melodious speech, that I may commend thee and thy rare discretion to my own fair countrywomen.

Alas! neither the present chronicler nor Mistress Plodgitt got any further information from the prudent Carmen, and must fain speculate upon certain facts that were already known.

Mistress Carmen's little room was opposite to Thatcher's,

and once or twice, the doors being open, Thatcher had a glimpse across the passage of a black-haired head and a sturdy, boyish little figure in a great blue apron, perched on a stool before an easel, and, on the other hand, Carmen had often been conscious of the fumes of a tobacco pipe penetrating her cloistered seclusion, and had seen across the passage, vaguely enveloped in the same nicotine cloud, an American Olympian, in a rocking-chair, with his feet on the mantel-shelf. They had once or twice met on the staircase, on which occasion Thatcher had greeted her with a word or two of respectful yet half-humorous courtesy —a courtesy which never really offends a true woman, although it often piques her self-aplomb by the slight assumption of superiority in the humorist. A woman is quick to recognise the fact that the great and more dangerous passions are always *serious*, and may be excused it in self-respect she is often induced to try if there be not somewhere under the skin of this laughing Mercutio the flesh and blood of a Romeo. Thatcher was by nature a defender and protector; weakness, and weakness alone, stirred the depths of his tenderness—often, I fear, only through its half humorous aspects—and on this plane he was pleased to place women and children. I mention this fact for the benefit of the more youthful members of my species, and am satisfied that an unconditional surrender, and the complete laying down at the feet of Beauty of all strong masculinity, is a cheap Gallicism that is untranslatable to most women worthy the winning. For a woman *must* always look up to the man she truly loves—even if she has to go down on her knees to do it.

Only the masculine reader will infer from this that Carmen was in love with Thatcher; the more critical and analytical feminine eye will see nothing herein that might not have happened consistently with friendship. For

Thatcher was no sentimentalist; he had hardly paid a compliment to the girl—even in the unspoken but most delicate form of attention. There were days when his room door was closed; there were days succeeding these blanks when he met her as frankly and naturally as if he had seen her yesterday. Indeed on those days following his flight the simple-minded Carmen, being aware—heaven knows how—that he had not opened his door during that period, and fearing sickness, sudden death, or perhaps suicide, by her appeals to the landlady, assisted unwittingly in discovering his flight and defection. As she was for a few moments as indignant as Mrs. Plodgitt, it is evident that she had but little sympathy with the delinquent. And besides, hitherto she had known only Concho—her earliest friend—and was true to his memory—as against all *Americanos*, whom she firmly believed to be his murderers.

So she dismissed the offer and the man from her mind, and went back to her painting—a fancy portrait of the good Padre Junipero Serra, a great missionary, who, haply for the integrity of his bones and character, died some hundred years before the Americans took possession of California. The picture was fair but unsaleable, and she began to think seriously of sign-painting, which was then much more popular and marketable. An unfinished head of San Juan de Bautista, artificially framed in clouds, she disposed of to a prominent druggist for $50, where it did good service as exhibiting the effect of four bottles of " Jones' Freckle Eradicator," and in a pleasant and unobtrusive way revived the memory of the saint. Still she felt weary and was growing despondent, and had a longing for the good Sisters and the blameless lethargy of conventual life, and then——

He came !

But not as the Prince should come, on a white charger,

to carry away this cruelly abused and enchanted damsel. He was sun-burned, he was bearded " like the pard ; " he was a little careless as to his dress, and preoccupied in his ways.    But his mouth and eyes were the same, and when he repeated in his old frank, half-mischievous way the invitation of his letter, poor little Carmen could only hesitate and blush.

A thought struck him and sent the colour to his face. Your gentleman born is always as modest as a woman. He ran downstairs, and seizing the widowed Plodgitt, said hastily—

" You're just killing yourself here.    Take a change. Come down to Monterey for a day or two with me, and bring Miss De Haro with you for company."

The old lady recognised the situation.    Thatcher was now a man of vast possibilities.    In all maternal daughters of Eve there is the slightest bit of the chaperone and match-maker.    It is the last way of reviving the past.

She consented, and Carmen De Haro could not well refuse.

The ladies found the Blue Mass Mills very much as Thatcher had previously described it to them, "a trifle rough and mannish."    But he made over to them the one tenement reserved for himself, and slept with his men, or more likely under the trees.    At first Mrs. Plodgitt missed gas and running water, and the several conveniences of civilisation, among which I fear may be mentioned sheets and pillow cases; but the balsam of the mountain air soothed her neuralgia and her temper.    As for Carmen, she rioted in the unlimited license of her absolute freedom from conventional restraint and the indulgence of her childlike impulses.    She scoured the ledges far and wide alone ; she dipped into dark copses and scrambled over sterile patches of chimisal, and came back laden with the spoil of buckeye blossoms, Manzanita berries and laurel. But she would not make a sketch of the Blue Mass Company's mills on a Mercator's projection; something that could be afterwards lithographed or chromoed, with the mills turning out tons of quicksilver through the energies of a happy and picturesque assemblage of miners—even to please her *padrone*, Don Royal Thatcher. On the contrary, she made a study of the ruins of the crumbled and decayed Red Rock furnace, with the black mountain above it, and the light of a dying camp fire shining upon it and the dull red excavations in the ledge. But even this did not satisfy her until she had made some alterations, and when she finally brought her finished study to Don Royal she looked at him a little defiantly. Thatcher admired honestly and then criticised a little humorously and dishonestly. " But couldn't you, for a consideration, put up a signboard on that rock with the inscription, ' Road to the Blue Mass Company's new mills to the right,' and combine business with art ? That's the fault of you geniuses. But what's this blanketed figure doing here, lying before the furnace ? You never saw one of my miners there—and a Mexician, too, by his *serapé !* " " That," quoth Mistress Carmen coolly, " was put in to fill up the foreground ; I wanted something there to balance the picture." " But," continued Thatcher, dropping into unconscious admiration again, " it's drawn to the life. Tell me, Miss De Haro, before I ask the aid and counsel of Mrs. Plodgitt, who is my hated rival and your lay figure and model ? " " Oh," said Carmen, with a little sigh, " it's only poor Concho." " And where is Concho ? " (a little impatiently.) " He's dead, Don Royal." " Dead ? " " Of a verity — very dead — murdered here by your countrymen." " I see—and you knew him ? " " He was my friend."

"Oh !"

" Truly."

" But " (wickedly), " isn't this a rather ghastly advertisement—outside of an illustrated newspaper—of my property ? "

" Ghastly, Don Royal.   Look you, he sleeps."

" Ay " (in Spanish), " as the dead."

Carmen—(crossing herself hastily)—"After the fashion of the dead."

They were both feeling uncomfortable.   Carmen was shivering.   But being a woman and tactful, she recovered her head first.   " It is a study for myself, Don Royal ; I shall make to you another."   And she slipped away, as she thought, out of the subject and his presence.

But she was mistaken : in the evening he renewed the conversation.   Carmen began to fence, not from cowardice or deceit, as the masculine reader would readily infer, but from some wonderful feminine instinct that told her to be cautious.   But he got from her the fact, to him before unknown, that she was the niece of his main antagonist, and being a gentleman, so redoubled his attentions and his courtesy that Mrs. Plodgitt made up her mind that it was a foregone conclusion, and seriously reflected as to what she should wear on the momentous occasion.   But that night poor Carmen cried herself to sleep, resolving that she would hereafter cast aside her wicked uncle for this good-hearted *Americano,* yet never once connected her innocent penmanship with the deadly feud between them.   Women—the best of them—are strong as to collateral facts, swift of deduction, but vague as children are to the exact statement or recognition of premises.   It is hardly necessary to say that Carmen had never thought of connecting any act of hers with the claims of her uncle, and the circumstance of the signature she had totally forgotten.

The masculine reader will now understand Carmen's confusion and blushes, and believe himself an ass to have thought them a confession of original affection. The feminine reader will, by this time, become satisfied that the deceitful minx's sole idea was to gain the affections of Thatcher. And really I don't know who is right.

Nevertheless she painted a sketch for Thatcher—which now adorns the Company's office in San Francisco—in which the property is laid out in pleasing geometrical lines, and the rosy promise of the future instinct in every touch of the brush. Then, having earned her "wage," as she believed, she became somewhat cold and shy to Thatcher. Whereat that gentleman redoubled his attentions, seeing only in her presence a certain *méprise*, which concerned her more than himself. The niece of his enemy meant nothing more to him than an interesting girl—to be protected always—to be feared, never. But even suspicion may be insidiously placed in noble minds.

Mistress Plodgitt, thus early estopped of match-making, of course put the blame on her own sex, and went over to the stronger side—the man's.

"It's a great pity gals should be so curious," she said, *sotto voce*, to Thatcher, when Carmen was in one of her sullen moods. "Yet I 'spose it's in her blood. Them Spaniards is always revengeful—like the Eyetalians."

Thatcher honestly looked his surprise.

"Why, don't you see, she's thinking how all these lands might have been her uncle's but for you. And instead of trying to be sweet and "—— here she stopped to cough.

"Good God!" said Thatcher in great concern, "I never thought of that." He stopped for a moment and then added with decision, "I can't believe it; it isn't like her."

Mrs. P. was piqued. She walked away, delivering, however, this Parthian arrow: "Well, I hope *'taint nothing worse.*"

Thatcher chuckled, then felt uneasy. When he next met Carmen she found his grey eyes fixed on hers with a curious, half-inquisitorial look she had never noticed before. This only added fuel to the fire. Forgetting their relations of host and guest, she was absolutely rude. Thatcher was quiet but watchful ; got the Plodgitt to bed early, and under cover of showing a moonlight view of the " Lost Chance Mill," decoyed Carmen out of ear-shot, as far as the dismantled furnace.

" What is the matter, Miss De Haro ; have I offended you ? "

Miss Carmen was not aware that anything was the matter. If Don Royal preferred old friends, whose loyalty of course he knew, *who were above speaking ill against a gentleman in his adversity*—(O Carmen ! fie !) if he preferred *their* company to *later friends*—why—(the masculine reader will observe this tremendous climax and tremble)—why she didn't know why *he* should blame *her.*

They turned and faced each other. The conditions for a perfect misunderstanding could not have been better arranged between two people. Thatcher was a masculine reasoner. Carmen a feminine feeler—if I may be pardoned the expression. Thatcher wanted to get at certain facts, and argue therefrom. Carmen wanted to get at certain feelings and then fit the facts to them.

" But I am *not* blaming you, Miss Carmen," he said gravely. " It *was* stupid in me to confront you here with the property claimed by your uncle and occupied by me, but it was a mistake—no ! (he added hastily)—it was not a mistake. You knew it and I didn't. You overlooked it before you came, and I was too glad to overlook it after you were here."

" Of course," said Carmen, pettishly, " I am the only one to be blamed. It's like you *men !* " (Mem. She was just fifteen, and uttered this awful *resumé* of experience just as if it hadn't been taught to her in her cradle.)

Feminine generalities always stagger a man. Thatcher said nothing. Carmen became more enraged.

" Why did you want to take Uncle Victor's property, then ? " she asked triumphantly.

" I don't know that it is your uncle's property."

" You—don't—know ? Have you seen the application with Governor Micheltorena's indorsement ? Have you heard the witnesses ? " she said passionately.

" Signatures may be forged and witnesses lie," said Thatcher, quietly.

" What is it you call ' forged ? ' "

Thatcher instantly recalled the fact that the Spanish language held no synonym for " forgery." The act was apparently an invention of *El Diable Americano.* So he said, with a slight smile in his kindly eyes—

" Anybody wicked enough and dexterous enough can imitate another's handwriting. When this is used to benefit fraud we call it ' forgery.' I beg your pardon—Miss De Haro, Miss Carmen—what is the matter ? "

She had suddenly lapsed against a tree, quite helpless, nerveless, and with staring eyes fixed on his. As yet an embryo woman, inexperienced and ignorant, the sex's instinct was potential ; she had in one plunge fathomed all that his reason had been years groping for.

Thatcher saw only that she was pained, that she was helpless ; that was enough. " It is possible that your uncle may have been deceived," he began, " many honest men have been fooled by clever but deceitful tricksters, men and women "——

" Stop ! *Madre de Dios!* WILL YOU STOP ? "

Thatcher for an instant recoiled from the flashing eyes and white face of the little figure that had, with menacing

and clenched baby fingers, strode to his side.   He stopped.
"Where is this application—this forgery?" she asked.
"Show it to me!"

Thatcher felt relieved, and smiled the superior smile of
our sex over feminine ignorance.   "You could hardly
expect me to be trusted with your uncle's vouchers.   His
papers of course are in the hands of his counsel."

"And when can I leave this place?" she asked, passionately.

"If you consult my wishes you will stay, if only long
enough to forgive me.   But if I have offended you, unknow-
ingly, and you are implacable"——

"I can go to-morrow, at sunrise, if I like?"

"As you will," returned Thatcher, gravely.

"Gracias, Señor."

They walked slowly back to the house.   Thatcher with
a masculine sense of being unreasonably afflicted, Carmen
with a woman's instinct of being hopelessly crushed.   No
word was spoken until they reached the door.   Then
Carmen suddenly, in her old, impulsive way, and in a
childlike treble, sang out merrily, "Good-night, O Don
Royal, and pleasant dreams.   *Hasta Mañana.*"

Thatcher stood dumb and astonished at this capricious
girl.   She saw his mystification instantly.   "It is for the
old Cat!" she whispered, jerking her thumb over her
shoulder in the direction of the sleeping Mrs. P.   "Good-
night—go!"

He went to give orders for a *peon* to attend the ladies
and their equipage the next day.   He awoke to find Miss
De Haro gone, with her escort, towards Monterey.   And
without the Plodgitt.

He could not conceal his surprise from the latter lady.
She, left alone—a not altogether unavailable victim to the
wiles of our sex—was embarrassed.   But not so much that

she could not say to Thatcher : " I told you so—gone to
her uncle . . . To tell him *all !* "

" All.   D—n it, *what* can she tell him ? " roared Thatcher,
stung out of his self-control.

"Nothing, I hope, that she should not," said Mrs. P.,
and chastely retired.

She was right.   Miss Carmen posted to Monterey, running her horse nearly off its legs to do it, and then sent back
her beast and escort, saying she would rejoin Mrs. Plodgitt
by steamer at San Francisco.   Then she went boldly to the
law office of Saponaceous Wood, District Attorney and
whilom solicitor of her uncle.

With the majority of masculine Monterey Miss Carmen
was known and respectfully admired, despite the infelix
reputation of her kinsman.   Mr. Wood was glad to see her,
and awkwardly gallant.   Miss Carmen was cool and business-like ; she had come from her uncle to " regard " the
papers in the Red Rock Rancho case.   They were instantly
produced.   Carmen turned to the application for the grant.
Her cheek paled slightly.   With her clear memory and
wonderful fidelity of perception she could not be mistaken.
*The signature of Micheltorena was in her own handwriting !*

Yet she looked up to the lawyer with a smile :   " May I
take these papers for an hour to my uncle ? "

Even an older and better man than the District Attorney
could not have resisted those drooping lids and that gentle
voice.

" Certainly."

" I will return them in an hour."

She was as good as her word, and within the hour dropped
the papers and a little courtesy to her uncle's legal advocate, and that night took the steamer to San Francisco.

The next morning Victor Garcia, a little the worse for the
previous night's dissipation, reeled into Wood's office.   " I

have fears for my niece, Carmen. She is with the enemy,' he said thickly. " Look you at this."

It was an anonymous letter (in Mrs. Plodgitt's own awkward fist), advising him of the fact that his niece was bought by the enemy, and cautioning him against her.

" Impossible," said the lawyer, " it was only last week she sent thee $ 50."

Victor blushed, even through his ensanguined cheeks, and made an impatient gesture with his hand.

" Besides," added the lawyer coolly, " she has been here to examine the papers at thy request, and returned them of yesterday."

Victor gasped—" And—you—you—gave them to her?"

" Of course!"

" All? Even the application and the signature?"

" Certainly—you sent her."

" Sent her? The devil's own daughter?" shrieked Garcia. " No! A hundred million times, no! Quick, before it is too late. Give to me the papers."

Mr. Wood reproduced the file. Garcia ran over it with trembling fingers, until at last he clutched the fateful document. Not content with opening it and glancing at its text and signature, he took it to the window.

" It is the same," he muttered with a sigh of relief.

" Of course it is," said Mr. Wood sharply. " The papers are all there. You're a fool, Victor Garcia!"

And so he was. And, for the matter of that, so was Mr. Saponaceous Wood, of counsel.

Meanwhile Miss De Haro returned to San Francisco and resumed her work. A day or two later she was joined by her landlady. Mrs. P. has too large a nature to permit an anonymous letter, written by her own hand, to stand between her and her demeanour to her little lodger. So she coddled her and flattered her, and depicted in slightly ex-

aggerated colours the grief of Don Royal at her sudden departure. All of which Miss Carmen received in a demure-
kitten-like way, but still kept quietly at her work. In due
time Don Royal's order was completed ; still she had leisure
and inclination enough to add certain touches to her
ghastly sketch of the crumbling furnace.

Nevertheless, as Don Royal did not return, through'
excess of business, Mrs. Plodgitt turned an honest penny
by letting his room, temporarily, to two quiet Mexicans,
who, but for a beastly habit of cigarrito smoking which
tainted the whole house, were fair enough lodgers. If
they failed in making the acquaintance of this fair countrywoman, Miss De Haro, it was through that lady's preoccu-
pation in her over work, and not through their ostentatious
endeavours.

"Miss De Haro is peculiar," explained the politic Mrs.
P. to her guests, "she makes no acquaintances, which I
consider bad for her business. If it had not been for me
she would not have known Royal Thatcher, the great
quicksilver miner—and had his order for a picture of his
mine ! "

The two foreign gentlemen exchanged glances. One
said, "Ah, God ! this is bad," and the other, "It is not possible ! " and then, when the landlady's back was turned,
introduced themselves with a skeleton key into the then
vacant bedroom and studio of their fair countrywoman,
who was absent sketching. "Thou observest," said Mr.
Pedro, refugee, to Miguel, ex-ecclesiastic, "that this *Americano* is all powerful, and that this Victor, drunkard as he
is, is right in his suspicions."

"Of a verity, yes," replied Miguel, "thou dost remember
it was Jovita Castro who, for her *Americano* lover, betrayed
the Sobriente claim. It is only with us, my Pedro, that
Mexican spirit, the real God and Liberty, yet lives ! "

They shook hands nobly and with sentimental fervour, and then went to work, *i.e.*, the rummaging over of the trunks, drawers and portmanteaus of the poor little painter, Carmen De Haro, and even ripped up the mattress of her virginal cot. But they found not what they sought.

" What is that yonder on the easel, covered with a cloth?' said Miguel; "it is a trick of these artists to put their valuables together."

Pedro strode to the easel and tore away the muslin curtain that veiled it; then uttered a shriek that appalled his comrade and brought him to his side.

"In the name of God," said Miguel hastily, " are you trying to alarm the house?"

The ex-vaquero was trembling like a child. "Look," he said hoarsely, "look, do you see? It is the hand of God," and fainted on the floor!

Miguel looked. It was Carmen's partly finished sketch of the deserted furnace. The figure of Concho, thrown out strongly by the camp fire, occupied the left foreground. But to balance her picture she had evidently been obliged to introduce another: the face and figure of Pedro, on all fours, creeping toward the sleeping man.

## CHAPTER X.

### WHO LOBBIED FOR IT.

It was a midsummer's day in Washington. Even at early morning, while the sun was yet level with the faces of pedestrians in its broad, shadeless avenues, it was insufferably hot. Later the avenues themselves shone like the diverging rays of another sun—the Capitol—a thing to be feared by the naked eye. Later yet it grew hotter, and then a mist arose from the Potomac, and blotted out the blazing

arch above, and presently piled up along the horizon de-
lusive thunder-clouds, that spent their strength and substance
elsewhere and left it hotter than before.   Towards evening
the sun came out invigorated—having cleared the heavenly
brow of perspiration, but leaving its fever unabated.

The city was deserted.   The few who remained apparently buried themselves from the garish light of day in some
dim cloistered recess of shop, hotel or restaurant, and the
perspiring stranger, dazed by the outer glare, who broke in
upon their quiet, sequestered repose, confronted collarless
and coatless spectres of the past with fans in their hands,
who, after dreamily going through some perfunctory business,
immediately retired to sleep after the stranger had gone.
Congressmen and Senators had long since returned to their
several constituencies with the various information that the
country was going to ruin, or that the outlook never was more
hopeful and cheering, as the tastes of their constituency
indicated.   A few Cabinet officers still lingered, having by
this time become convinced that they could do nothing
their own way, or indeed in any way but the old way, and
getting gloomily resigned to their situation.   A body of
learned, cultivated men, representing the highest legal
tribunal in the land, still lingered in a vague idea of earning
the scant salary bestowed upon them by the economical
founders of the Government, and listened patiently to the
arguments of Counsel, whose fees for advocacy of claims
before them would have paid the life income of half the
bench.   There was Mr. Attorney General and his assistants
still protecting the Government's millions from rapacious
hands, and drawing the yearly public pittance that their
wealthier private antagonists would have scarce given as a
retainer to their junior counsel   The little standing army
of departmental employees—the helpless victims of the most
senseless and idiotic form of discipline the world has known

—a discipline so made up of Caprice, Expediency, Cowardice and Tyranny that its reform meant Revolution, not to be tolerated by legislators and lawgivers, or a Despotism in which half a dozen accidentally chosen men interpreted their prejudices or preferences as being that Reform. Administration after Administration and Party after Party had persisted in their desperate attempts to fit the youthful colonial garments, made by our fathers after bygone fashion, over the expanded limits and generous outline of a matured nation. There were patches here and there, there were grievous rents and holes here and there, there were ludicrous and painful exposures of growing limbs everywhere, and the Party in Power and the Party out of Power could do nothing but mend and patch, and revamp and cleanse and scour, and occasionally, in the wildness of despair, suggest even the cutting off the rebellious limbs that persisted in growing beyond the swaddling clothes of its infancy.

It was a capital of Contradictions and Inconsistencies. At one end of the Avenue sat the responsible High Keeper of the Military Honour, Valour and Warlike Prestige of a Great Nation, without the power to pay his own troops their legal dues until some selfish quarrel between Party and Party was settled. Hard by sat another secretary, whose established functions seemed to be the misrepresentation of the nation abroad by the least characteristic of its classes—the politicians—and only then when they had been defeated as politicians, and when their constituents had declared them no longer worthy to be even *their* representatives. This National Absurdity was only equalled by another, wherein an Ex-Politician was for four years expected to uphold the honour of a flag of a great nation over an ocean he had never tempted, with a discipline the rudiments of which he could scarcely acquire before he was removed, or his term of office expired, receiving his orders from a superior officer as ignorant of his special duties as himself, and subjected to the revision of a Congress cognisant of him only as a politician. At the further end of the Avenue was another department, so vast in its extent and so varied in its functions that few of the really Great Practical Workers of the land would have accepted its responsibility for ten times its salary, but which the most perfect Constitution in the World handed over to men who were obliged to make it a stepping stone to future preferment. There was another department, more suggestive of its financial functions from the occasional extravagances or economies exhibited in its pay-rolls—successive Congresses having taken other matters out of its hands—presided over by an official who bore the title and responsibility of the Custodian and Disburser of the Nation's Purse, and received a salary that a bank president would have sniffed at. For it was part of this Constitutional Inconsistency and Administrative Absurdity that in the matter of Honour, Justice, Fidelity to Trust, and even Business Integrity, the official was always expected to be the superior of the Government he represented. Yet the crowning Inconsistency was that, from time to time, it was submitted to the sovereign people to declare if these various Inconsistencies were not really the perfect expression of the most perfect Government the world had known. And it is to be recorded that the unanimous voices of Representative, Orator and Unfettered Poetry were that it was.

Even the public press lent itself to the Great Inconsistency. It was as clear as crystal to the journal on one side of the Avenue that the country was going to the dogs unless the *spirit* of the fathers once more reanimated the public; it was equally clear to the journal on the other side of the Avenue that only a rigid adherence to the *letter* of the fathers would save the nation from decline. It was obvious to the first-named journal that the "letter" meant Government patronage to the other journal; it was potent to that journal that the "Shekels" of Senator X. really animated the spirit of the fathers. Yet all agreed it was a great and good and perfect government—subject only to the predatory incursions of a hydra-headed monster known as a "Ring." The Ring's origin was wrapped in secrecy, its fecundity was alarming; but although its rapacity was preternatural, its digestion was perfect and easy. It circumvolved all affairs in an atmosphere of mystery; it clouded all things with the dust and ashes of distrust. All disappointment of place, of avarice, of incompetency or ambition, was clearly attributable to it. It even permeated private and social life : there were Rings in our kitchen and household service ; in our public schools, that kept the active intelligences of our children passive; there were Rings of engaging, handsome, dissolute young fellows, who kept us moral but unengaging seniors from the favours of the Fair ; there were subtle, conspiring Rings among our creditors, which sent us into bankruptcy and restricted our credit. In fact, it would not be hazardous to say that all that was calamitous in public and private experience was clearly traceable to that combination of power in a minority over weakness in a majority—known as a "Ring."

Haply there was a body of demigods, as yet uninvoked, who should speedily settle all that. When Smith of Minnesota, Robinson of Vermont, and Jones of Georgia, returned to Congress from those rural seclusions, so potent with information and so freed from local prejudices, it was understood, vaguely, that great things would be done. This was always understood. There never was a time in the history of American politics when, to use the expression of the journals before alluded to, "the present session of Congress" did not "bid fair to be the most momentous in our history," and did not, as far as the facts go, leave a vast amount of unfinished important business lying hopelessly upon its desks, having "bolted" the rest as rashly and with as little regard to digestion or assimilation as the American traveller has for his railway refreshment.

In this capital, on this languid midsummer day, in an upper room of one of its second rate hotels, the Honourable Mr. Pratt C. Gashwiler sat at his writing-table. There are certain large, fleshy men with whom the omission of even a necktie or collar has all the effect of an indecent exposure. The Honourable Mr. Gashwiler, in his trousers and shirt, was a sight to be avoided by the modest eye. There were such palpable suggestions of vast extents of unctuous flesh in the slight glimpse offered by his open throat, that his *dishabille* should have been as private as his business. Nevertheless, when there was a knock at his door he unhesitatingly said, " Come in ! "—pushing away a goblet crowned with a certain aromatic herb with his right hand, while he drew towards him with his left a few proof slips of his forthcoming speech. The Gashwiler brow became, as it were, intelligently abstracted.

The intruder regarded Gashwiler with a glance of familiar recognition from his right eye, while his left took in a rapid survey of the papers on the table, and gleamed sardonically.

" You are at work, I see," he said apologetically.

" Yes," replied the Congressman, with an air of perfunctory weariness—" one of my speeches. Those d—d printers make such a mess of it, I suppose I don't write a very fine hand."

If the gifted Gashwiler had added that he did not write a very intelligent hand, or a very grammatical hand, and that his spelling was faulty, he would have been truthful, although the copy and proof before him might not have borne him out. The near fact was, that the speech was composed and written by one Expectant Dobbs, a poor retainer of Gashwiler, and the honourable member's labour as a proof-reader was confined to the introduction of such words as " Anarchy," " Oligarchy," " Satrap," " Palladium " and " Argus-eyed," in the proof, with little relevancy as to position or place, and no perceptible effect as to argument.

The stranger saw all this with his wicked left eye, but continued to beam mildly with his right. Removing the coat and waistcoat of Gashwiler from a chair, he drew it towards the table, pushing aside a portly, loud-ticking watch—the very image of Gashwiler—that lay beside him, and resting his elbows on the proofs, said—

" Well ? "

" Have you anything new ? " asked the Parliamentary Gashwiler.

" Much ! a woman ! " replied the stranger.

The astute Gashwiler, waiting further information, concluded to receive this fact gaily and gallantly. " A woman ?—my dear Mr. Wiles—of course ! The dear creatures," he continued, with a fat, offensive chuckle, "somehow are always making their charming presence felt. Ha ! Ha ! A man, sir, in public life becomes accustomed to that sort of thing, and knows when he must be agreeable —agreeable, sir, but firm ! I've had my experience, sir— my *own* experience,"—and the Congressman leaned back in his chair, not unlike a robust St. Anthony, who had withstood one temptation to thrive on another.

" Yes," said Wiles impatiently, " but d—n it, she's on the *other side.*"

" The other side ! " repeated Gashwiler vacantly.

" Yes. She's a niece of Garcia's. A little she-devil."

" But Garcia is on our side," rejoined Gashwiler.

" Yes ; but she is bought by the Ring."

" A woman," sneered Mr. Gashwiler, " what can she do with men who won't be made fools of? Is she so hand- some ? "

" I never saw any great beauty in her," said Wiles, shortly, "although they say that she's rather caught that d—d Thatcher, in spite of his coldness. At any rate she is his *protégée*. But she isn't the sort you're thinking of, Gash- wiler. They say she knows or pretends to know something about the grant. She may have got hold of some of her uncle's papers. Those Greasers were always d—d fools, and if he did anything foolish, like as not he bungled or didn't cover up his tracks. And with his knowledge and facilities too ! Why if I'd "—but here Mr. Wiles stopped to sigh over the inequality of fortune that wasted oppor- tunities on the less skilful scamp.

Mr. Gashwiler became dignified. " She can do nothing with us," he said potentially.

Wiles turned his wicked eye on him. " Manuel and Miguel, who sold out to our man, *are* afraid of her. They were our witnesses. I verily believe they'd take back every- thing if she got after them. And as for Pedro, he thinks she holds the power of life and death over him."

" Pedro ! Life and death—what's all this ? " said the astonished Gashwiler.

Wiles saw his blunder, but saw also that he had gone too far to stop. " Pedro," he said, " was strongly suspected of having murdered Concho, one of the original locaters."

Mr. Gashwiler turned white as a sheet, and then flushed again into an apoplectic glow. " Do you dare to say," he began as soon as he could find his tongue and his legs, for in the exercise of his congressional functions these extreme members supported each other, " do you mean to say," he stammered in rising rage, " that you have dared to deceive an American lawgiver into legislating upon a measure con- nected with a capital offence ?   Do I understand you to say, sir, that murder stands upon the record—stands upon the record, sir—of this cause to which, as a representative of Remus, I have lent my official aid ?   Do you mean to say that you have deceived my constituency, whose sacred trust I hold, in inveigling me to hiding a crime from the Argus eyes of Justice ? "   And Mr. Gashwiler looked towards the bell-pull as if about to summon a servant to witness this outrage against the established judiciary.

" The murder, if it *was* a murder, took place before Garcia entered upon this claim or had a footing in this court," returned Wiles blandly, " and is no part of the record."

" You are sure it is not spread upon the record ! "

" I am.   You can judge for yourself."

Mr. Gashwiler walked to the window, returned to the table, finished his liquor in a single gulp, and then with a slight resumption of dignity, said—

" That alters the case."

Wiles glanced with his left eye at the Congressman.   The right placidly looked out of the window.   Presently he said quietly, " I've brought you the certificates of stock ; do you wish them made out in your own name ? "

Mr. Gashwiler tried hard to look as if he were trying to recall the meaning of Wiles' words.   " Oh !—ah !—umph ! —let me see—Oh yes, the certificates—certainly !   Of course you will make them out in the name of my secretary, Mr. Expectant Dobbs.   They will perhaps repay him for the extra clerical labour required in the prosecution of your claim.   He is a worthy young man.   Although not a public officer, yet he is so near to me that perhaps I am wrong in permitting him to accept a fee for private interests. An American representative cannot be too cautious, Mr. Wiles. Perhaps you had better have also a blank transfer. The stock is, I understand, yet in the future. Mr. Dobbs, though talented and praiseworthy, is poor; he may wish to realise. If some—ahem! some *friend*—better circumstanced should choose to advance the cash to him and run the risk—why it would only be an act of kindness."

"You are proverbially generous, Mr. Gashwiler," said Wiles, opening and shutting his left eye, like a dark lantern, on the benevolent representative.

"Youth, when faithful and painstaking, should be encouraged," replied Mr. Gashwiler. "I lately had occasion to point this out in a few remarks I had to make before the Sabbath school reunion at Remus. Thank you, I will see that they are—ahem—conveyed to him. I shall give them to him with my own hand," he concluded, falling back in his chair, as if the better to contemplate the perspective of his own generosity and condescension. Mr. Wiles took his hat and turned to go. Before he reached the door Mr. Gashwiler returned to the social level with a chuckle—

"You say this woman, this Garcia's niece, is handsome and smart?"

"Yes."

"I can set another woman on the track that'll euchre her every time!"

Mr. Wiles was too clever to appear to notice the sudden lapse in the Congressman's dignity, and only said, with his right eye—

"Can you?"

"By G—d I *will*, or I don't know how to represent Remus."

Mr. Wiles thanked him with his right eye, looked a dagger with his left. "Good," he said, and added persuasively : "Does she live here ?"

The Congressman nodded assent. "An awfully handsome woman—a particular friend of mine !" Mr. Gashwiler here looked as if he would not mind to have been rallied a little over his intimacy with the fair one, but the astute Mr. Wiles was at the same moment making up his mind, after interpreting the Congressman's look and manner, that he must know this fair incognito if he wished to sway Gashwiler. He determined to bide his time.

The door was scarcely closed upon him when another knock diverted Mr. Gashwiler's attention from his proofs. The door opened to a young man with sandy hair and anxious face. He entered the room deprecatingly, as if conscious of the presence of a powerful being, to be supplicated and feared. Mr. Gashwiler did not attempt to disabuse his mind. "Busy, you see," he said shortly, "correcting your work !"

"I hope it is acceptable !" said the young man, timidly.

"Well—yes—it will do," said Gashwiler, "indeed I may say it is satisfactory on the whole," he added with the appearance of a large generosity, "quite satisfactory."

"You have no news, I suppose," continued the young man with a slight flush, born of pride or expectation.

"No, nothing as yet." Mr. Gashwiler paused as if a thought had struck him.

"I have thought," he said finally, "that some position—such as a secretaryship with me—would help you to a better appointment. Now, supposing that I make you my private secretary, giving you some important and confidential business. Eh ?"

Dobbs looked at his patron with a certain wistful, doglike expectancy, moved himself excitedly on his chair seat in a peculiar canine-like anticipation of gratitude, strongly suggesting that he would have wagged his tail if he had had one. At which Mr. Gashwiler became more impressive.

"Indeed, I may say I anticipated it by certain papers I have put in your charge and in your name, only taking from you a transfer—that might enable me to satisfy my conscience hereafter in recommending you as my—ahem—private secretary. Perhaps as a mere form you might now, while you are here, put your name to these transfers, and, so to speak, begin your duties at once."

The glow of pride and hope that mantled the cheek of poor Dobbs might have melted a harder heart than Gashwiler's. But the Senatorial toga had invested Mr. Gashwiler with a more than Roman stoicism towards the feelings of others, and he only fell back in his chair in the pose of conscious rectitude as Dobbs hurriedly signed the paper.

"I shall place them in my portman-tell," said Gashwiler, suiting the word to the action, "for safe keeping. I need not inform you, who are now, as it were, on the threshold of official life, that perfect and inviolable secrecy in all affairs of State"—Mr. G., here motioned toward his portmanteau as if it contained a treaty at least—"is most essential and necessary."

Dobbs assented; "Then my duties will keep me with you here?" he asked doubtfully.

"No—no," said Gashwiler, hastily; then, correcting himself, he added: "that is—for the present—no!"

Poor Dobbs' face fell. The near fact was that he had lately had notice to quit his present lodgings in consequence of arrears in his rent, and he had a hopeful reliance that his confidential occupation would carry bread and lodging with it. But he only asked if there were any new papers to make out.

"Ahem! not at present; the fact is that I am obliged to give so much of my time to callers—I have to-day been obliged to see half-a-dozen—that I must lock myself up and say 'Not at home' for the rest of the day."

Feeling that this was an intimation that the interview was over, the new private secretary, a little dashed as to his near hopes, but still sanguine of the future, humbly took his leave.

But here a certain Providence, perhaps mindful of poor Dobbs, threw into his simple hands—to be used or not, if he were worthy or capable of using it—a certain power and advantage. He had descended the staircase, and was passing through the lower corridor, when he was made the unwilling witness of a remarkable assault.

It appeared that Mr. Wiles, who had quitted Gashwiler's presence as Dobbs was announced, had other business in the hotel, and in pursuance of it had knocked at room No. 90. In response to the gruff voice that bade him enter, Mr. Wiles opened the door and espied the figure of a tall, muscular, fiery-bearded man extended on the bed, with the bed-clothes carefully tucked under his chin and his arms lying flat by his side.

Mr. Wiles beamed with his right cheek, and advanced to the bed as if to take the hand of the stranger, who, however, neither by word nor sign, responded to his salutation.

"Perhaps I'm intruding?" said Mr. Wiles blandly.

"Perhaps you are," said Red Beard drily.

Mr. Wiles forced a smile on his right cheek, which he turned to the smiter, but permitted the left to indulge in unlimited malevolence. "I wanted merely to know if you have looked into that matter?" he said meekly.

"I've looked into it and round it, and across it and over it and through it," responded the man gravely, with his eyes fixed on Wiles.

"And you have perused all the papers?" continued Mr. Wiles.

"I've read every paper, every speech, every affidavit, every decision, every argument," said the stranger, as if repeating a formula.

Mr. Wiles attempted to conceal his embarrassment by an easy, right-handed smile, that went off sardonically on the left, and continued, "Then I hope, my dear sir, that, having thoroughly mastered the case, you are inclined to be favourable to us?"

The gentleman in the bed did not reply, but apparently nestled more closely beneath the coverlids.

"I have brought the shares I spoke of," continued Mr. Wiles insinuatingly.

"Hev you a friend within call?" interrupted the recumbent man gently.

"I don't quite understand!" smiled Mr. Wiles. "Of course any name you might suggest"——

"Hev you a friend—any chap that you might waltz in here at a moment's call?" continued the man in bed. "No? Do you know any of them waiters in the house? Thar's a bell over yan!" and he motioned with his eyes towards the wall, but did not otherwise move his body.

"No," said Wiles, becoming slightly suspicious and wrathful.

"Mebbe a stranger might do? I reckon thar's one passin' in the hall. Call him in—he'll do!"

Wiles opened the door a little impatiently, yet inquisitively, as Dobbs passed. The man in bed called out, "O stranger!" and as Dobbs stopped, said, "Come 'yar."

Dobbs entered a little timidly, as was his habit with strangers.

"I don't know who you be—nor care, I reckon," said the stranger. "This yer man"—pointing to Wiles—"is

Wiles. I'm Josh Sibblee of Fresno, Member of Congress from the 4th Congressional District of Californy. I'm jist lying here, with a derringer into each hand—jist lying here kivered up and holdin' in on'y to keep from blowin' the top o' this d—d skunk's head off. I kinder feel I can't hold in any longer. What I want to say to ye, stranger, is that this yer skunk—which his name is Wiles—hez bin tryin' his d—dest to get a bribe onto Josh, and Josh, outo respect for his constituents, is jist waitin' for some stranger to waltz in and stop the d—dest fight "——

"But, my dear Mr. Sibblee, there must be some mistake," said Wiles earnestly.

"Mistake? Strip me!"

"No! no!" said Wiles hurriedly, as the simple-minded Dobbs was about to draw down the coverlid.

"Take him away," said the Honourable Mr. Sibblee, "before I disgrace my constituency. They said I'd be in jail 'afore I get through the session. Ef you've got any humanity, stranger, snake him out, and pow'ful quick too."

Dobbs, quite white and aghast, looked at Wiles and hesitated. There was a slight movement in the bed. Both men started for the door, and the next minute it closed very decidedly on the member from Fresno.

## CHAPTER XI.

### HOW IT WAS LOBBIED FOR.

THE Honourable Pratt C. Gashwiler, M.C., was of course unaware of the incident described in the last chapter. His secret, even if it had been discovered by Dobbs, was safe in that gentleman's innocent and honourable hands, and certainly was not of a quality that Mr. Wiles, at present, would have cared to expose. For, in spite of Mr. Wiles' discomfiture, he still had enough experience of character to know that the irate member from Fresno would be satisfied with his own peculiar manner of vindicating his own personal integrity, and would not make a public scandal of it. Again, Wiles was convinced that Dobbs was equally implicated with Gashwiler, and would be silent for his own sake. So that poor Dobbs, as is too often the fate of simple but weak natures, had full credit for duplicity by every rascal in the land.

From which it may be inferred that nothing occurred to disturb the security of Gashwiler. When the door closed upon Mr. Wiles he indited a note, which, with a costly but exceedingly distasteful bouquet—re-arranged by his own fat fingers, and discord and incongruity visible in every combination of colour—he sent off by a special messenger. Then he proceeded to make his toilet—an operation rarely graceful or picturesque in our sex, and an insult to the spectator when obesity is superadded. When he had put on a clean shirt, of which there was grossly too much, and added a white waistcoat, that seemed to accent his rotundity, he completed his attire with a black frock coat of the latest style, and surveyed himself complacently before a mirror. It is to be recorded that, however satisfactory the result may have been to Mr. Gashwiler, it was not so to the disinterested spectator. There are some men on whom "that deformed thief, Fashion," avenges himself by making their clothes appear perennially new. The gloss of the tailor's iron never disappears; the creases of the shelf perpetually rise in judgment against the wearer. Novelty was the general suggestion of Mr. Gashwiler's full dress—it was never his *habitude*—and "Our own Make," "Nobby," and the "Latest Style, only $ 15," was as patent on the legislator's broad back as if it still retained the shopman's ticket.

Thus arrayed, within an hour he complacently followed the note and his floral offering. The house he sought had been once the residence of a foreign ambassador, who had loyally represented his government in a single unimportant treaty, now forgotten, and in various receptions and dinners, still actively remembered by occasional visitors to its *salon*, now the average dreary American parlour. " Dear me," the fascinating Mr. X. would say, " but do you know, love, in this very room I remember meeting the distinguished Marquis of Monte Pio," or perhaps the fashionable Jones of the State Department instantly crushed the decayed friend he was perfunctorily visiting, by saying, " 'Pon my soul, *you* here—why the last time I was in this room I gossiped for an hour with the Countess de Castenet in that very corner." For with the recall of the aforesaid Ambassador the mansion had become a boarding-house, kept by the wife of a departmental clerk.

Perhaps there was nothing in the history of the house more quaint and philosophic than the story of its present occupant. Rogar Fauquier had been a departmental clerk for forty years. It was at once his practical good luck and his misfortune to have been early appointed to a position which required a thorough and complete knowledge of the formulas and routine of a department that expended millions of the public funds. Fauquier, on a poor salary, diminishing instead of increasing with his service, had seen successive Administrations bud and blossom and decay, but had kept his position through the fact that his knowledge was a necessity to the successive chiefs and employees. Once it was true that he had been summarily removed by a new Secretary, to make room for a camp follower, whose exhaustive and intellectual services in a political campaign had made him eminently fit for anything, but the alarming discovery that the new clerk's knowledge of grammar and etymology was even worse than that of the Secretary himself, and that, through ignorance of detail, the business of that department was retarded to a damage to the Government of over half a million of dollars, led to the reinstatement of Mr. Fauquier—*at a lower salary.* For it was felt that something was wrong somewhere, and as it had always been the custom of Congress and the Administration to cut down salaries as the first step to reform, they made of Mr. Fauquier a moral example. A gentleman born, of somewhat expensive tastes, having lived up to his former salary, this change brought another bread-winner into the field, Mrs. Fauquier, who tried, more or less unsuccessfully, to turn her old Southern habits of hospitality to remunerative account. But as poor Fauquier could never be prevailed upon to present a bill to a gentleman, Sir, and as some of the scions of the best Southern families were still waiting for, or had been recently dismissed from a position, the experiment was a pecuniary failure. Yet the house was of excellent repute and well patronised ; indeed, it was worth something to see old Fauquier sitting at the head in his ancestral style, relating anecdotes of great men now dead and gone, interrupted only by occasional visits from importunate tradesmen.

Prominent among what Mr. Fauquier called his "little family," was a black-eyed lady of great powers of fascination, and considerable local reputation as a flirt. Nevertheless, these social aberrations were amply condoned by a facile and complacent husband, who looked with a lenient and even admiring eye upon the little lady's amusement, and to a certain extent lent a tacit indorsement to her conduct. Nobody minded Hopkinson; in the blaze of Mrs. Hopkinson's fascinations he was completely lost sight of. A few married women with unduly sensitive husbands, and several single ladies of the best and longest standing, reflected severely on her conduct. The younger men of course admired her, but I think she got her chief support from old fogies like ourselves. For it is your quiet, self-conceited, complacent, philosophic, broad-waisted *pater-familias* who, after all, is the one to whom the gay and giddy of the proverbially impulsive, unselfish sex owe their place in the social firmament. We are not inclined to be captious; we laugh at as a folly what our wives and daughters condemn as a fault; our " withers are unwrung," yet we still confess to the fascinations of a pretty face. We know, bless us, from dear experience, the exact value of one woman's opinion of another; we want our brilliant little friend to shine; it is only the moths who will burn their two-penny immature wings in the flame! And why should they not? Nature has been pleased to supply more moths than candles! Go to !—give the pretty creature— be she maid, wife or widow, a show! And so, my dear sir, while *materfamilias* bends her black brows in disgust, we smile our superior little smile, and extend to Mistress *Anonyma* our gracious indorsement. And if Giddiness is grateful, or if Folly is friendly—well, of course, *we* can't help that. Indeed it rather proves our theory.

I had intended to say something about Hopkinson, but really there is very little to say. He was invariably good-humoured. A few ladies once tried to show him that he really ought to feel worse than he did about the conduct of his wife, and it is recorded that Hopkinson, in an excess of good-humour and kindliness, promised to do so. Indeed the good fellow was so accessible that it is said that young De Lancy of the Tape Department confided to Hopkinson his jealousy of a rival, and revealed the awful secret that he (De Lancy) had reason to expect more loyalty from his (Hopkinson's) wife. The good fellow is reported to have been very sympathetic, and to have promised De Lancy to lend whatever influence he had with Mrs. Hopkinson in his favour. "You see," he said explanatorily to De Lancy, "she has a good deal to attend to lately, and I suppose has got rather careless—that's women's ways. But if *I* can't bring her round I'll speak to Gashwiler—I'll get him to use his influence with Mrs. Hop. So cheer up, my boy, *he'll* make it all right."

The appearance of a bouquet on the table of Mrs. Hopkinson was no rare event; nevertheless Mr. Gashwiler's was not there. Its hideous contrasts had offended her woman's eye—it is observable that good taste survives the wreck of all the other feminine virtues—and she had distributed it to make *boutonnières* for other gentlemen. Yet when he appeared she said to him hastily, putting her little hand over the cardiac region—

"I'm so glad you came. But you gave me *such* a fright an hour ago."

Mr. Gashwiler was both pleased and astounded. "What have I done, my dear Mrs. Hopkinson?" he began.

"Oh, don't talk," she said sadly. "What have you done? indeed! Why, you sent me that beautiful bouquet. I could not mistake your taste in the arrangement of the flowers—but my husband was here. You know his jealousy. I was obliged to conceal it from him. *Never*—promise me now—*never* do it again."

Mr. Gashwiler gallantly protested.

"No! I am serious! I was so agitated; he must have seen me blush."

Nothing but the gross flattery of this speech could have clouded its manifest absurdity to the Gashwiler consciousness. But Mr. Gashwiler had already succumbed to the girlish half-timidity with which it was uttered. Nevertheless, he could not help saying—

"But why should he be so jealous now? Only day

before yesterday I saw Simpson of Duluth hand you a nose-gay right before him!"

"Ah," returned the lady, "he was outwardly calm *then*, but you know nothing of the scene that occurred between us after you left."

"But," gasped the practical Gashwiler, "Simpson had given your husband that contract—a cool fifty thousand in his pocket!"

Mrs. Hopkinson looked as dignifiedly at Gashwiler as was consistent with five feet three (the extra three inches being a pyramidal structure of straw-coloured hair), a frond of faint curls, a pair of laughing blue eyes and a small belted waist. Then she said, with a casting down of her lids—

"You forget that my husband loves me." And for once the minx appeared to look penitent. It was becoming, but as it had been originally practised in a simple white dress, relieved only with pale blue ribbons, it was not entirely in keeping with beflounced lavender and rose-coloured trim-mings. Yet the woman who hesitates between her moral expression and the harmony of her dress is lost. And Mrs. Hopkinson was *victrix* by her very audacity.

Mr. Gashwiler was flattered. The most dissolute man likes the appearance of virtue. "But graces and accom-plishments like yours, dear Mrs. Hopkinson," he said oleaginously, "belong to the whole country." Which, with something between a courtesy and a strut, he endeav-oured to represent. "And I shall want to avail myself of all," he added, "in the matter of the Castro claim. A little supper at Welcker's, a glass or two of champagne, and a single flash of those bright eyes, and the thing is done."

"But," said Mrs. Hopkinson, "I've promised Josiah that I would give up all those frivolities, and although my con-science is clear, you know how people talk! Josiah hears it. Why, only last night, at a reception at the Patagonian

Minister's, every woman in the room gossiped about me because I led the German with him. As if a married woman, whose husband was interested in the Government, could not be civil to the representative of a friendly power?"

Mr. Gashwiler did not see how Mr. Hopkinson's late contract for supplying salt pork and canned provisions to the army of the United States should make his wife susceptible to the advances of foreign princes, but he prudently kept that to himself. Still, not being himself a diplomate, he could not help saying—

"But I understood that Mr. Hopkinson did not object to your interesting yourself in this claim, and you know some of the stock"——

The lady started, and said—

"Stock! Dear Mr. Gashwiler, for heaven's sake don't mention that hideous name to me. Stock! I am sick of it! Have you gentlemen no other topic for a lady?"

She punctuated her sentence with a mischievous look at her interlocutor. For a second time, I regret to say that Mr. Gashwiler succumbed. The Roman constituency at Remus, it is to be hoped, were happily ignorant of this last defection of their great legislator. Mr. Gashwiler instantly forgot his theme—began to ply the lady with a certain bovine-like gallantry, which, it is to be said to her credit, she parried with a playful, terrier-like dexterity, when the servant suddenly announced, "Mr. Wiles."

Gashwiler started. Not so Mrs. Hopkinson, who, however, prudently and quietly removed her own chair several inches from Gashwiler's.

"Do you know Mr. Wiles?" she asked pleasantly.

"No! That is, I—ah—yes, I may say I have had some business relations with him," responded Gashwiler, rising.

"Won't you stay?" she added pleadingly. "Do!"

Mr. Gashwiler's prudence always got the better of his gallantry. "Not now," he responded, in some nervousness. "Perhaps I had better go now, in view of what you have just said about gossip. You need not mention my name to this-er—this—Mr. Wiles." And with one eye on the door and an awkward dash of his at the lady's fingers, he withdrew.

There was no introductory formula to Mr. Wiles' interview. He dashed at once *in medias res.* "Gashwiler knows a woman that, he says, can help us against that Spanish girl who is coming here with proofs, prettiness, fascinations and what not? You must find her out."

"Why?" asked the lady laughingly.

"Because I don't trust that Gashwiler. A woman with a pretty face and an ounce of brains could sell him out; ay, and *us* with him."

"Oh, say *two* ounces of brains. Mr. Wiles, Mr. Gashwiler is no fool."

"Possibly, except when your sex is concerned, and it is very likely that this woman is his superior."

"I should think so," said Mrs. Hopkinson with a mischievous look.

"Ah, you know her, then?"

"Not so well as I know him," said Mrs. H., quite seriously. "I wish I did."

"Well, you'll find out if she's to be trusted! You are laughing—it is a serious matter! This woman "——

Mrs. Hopkinson dropped him a charming courtsey and said—

"*C'est moi!*"

## CHAPTER XII.

### A RACE FOR IT.

ROYAL THATCHER worked hard. That the boyish little painter who shared his hospitality at the "Blue Mass" mine should afterward have little part in his active life, seemed not inconsistent with his habits. At present the mine was his only mistress, claiming his entire time, exasperating him with fickleness, but still requiring that supreme devotion of which his nature was capable. It is possible that Miss Carmen saw this too, and so set about with feminine tact, if not to supplement, at least to make her rival less pertinacious and absorbing. Apart from this object she zealously laboured in her profession, yet with small pecuniary result, I fear. Local art was at a discount in California. The scenery of the country had not yet become famous; rather it was reserved for a certain Eastern artist, already famous, to make it so, and people cared little for the reproduction, under their very noses, of that which they saw continually with their own eyes and valued not. So that little Mistress Carmen was fain to divert her artist soul to support her plump little material body, and made divers excursions into the region of ceramic art, painting on velvet, illuminating missals, decorating china, and the like. I have in my possession some wax-flowers—a startling fuchsia, and a bewildering dahlia— sold for a mere pittance by this little lady, whose pictures lately took the prize at a foreign exhibition, shortly after she had been half-starved by a California public, and claimed by a California press as its fostered child of genius.

Of these struggles and triumphs Thatcher had no knowledge, yet he was perhaps more startled than he would own to himself, when, one December day, he received this despatch :

"Come to Washington at once. Carmen de Haro."

"Carmen de Haro!" I grieve to state that such was the pre-occupation of this man, elected by fate to be the hero of the solitary amatory episode of this story, that for a moment he could not recall her. When the honest little figure that had so manfully stood up against him, and had proved her sex by afterwards running away from him, came back at last to his memory, he was at first mystified and then self-reproachful. He had been, he felt vaguely, untrue to himself. He had been remiss to the self-confessed daughter. of his enemy. Yet why should she telegraph to him, and what was she doing in Washington ? To all these speculations, it is to be said to his credit, that he looked for no sentimental or romantic answer. Royal Thatcher was naturally modest and self-depreciating in his relations to the other sex, as indeed most men, who are apt to be successful with women, generally are—despite a vast degree of superannuated bosh to the contrary. In the half-dozen women who are startled by sheer audacity into submission, there are scores who are piqued by a self-respectful patience. And where a woman has to do half the wooing, she generally makes a pretty sure thing of it.

In his bewilderment Thatcher had overlooked a letter lying on his table. It was from his Washington lawyer. The concluding paragraph caught his eye—"Perhaps it would be well if you came here yourself; Roscommon is here, and they say there is a niece of Garcia's, lately appeared, who is likely to get up a strong social sympathy for the old Mexican. I don't know that they expect to prove anything by her, but I'm told she is attractive and clever, and has enlisted the sympathies of the delegation." Thatcher laid the letter down a little indignantly. Strong men are quite as liable as weak women are to sudden inconsistencies on any question they may have in common. What right had this poor little bud he had cherished—he was quite satisfied now that he had cherished her, and really had suffered from her absence—what right had she to suddenly blossom in the sunshine of power, to be, perhaps, plucked and worn by one of his enemies. He did not agree with his lawyer that she was in any way connected with his enemies; he trusted to her masculine loyalty that far. But here was something vaguely dangerous to the feminine mind—position, flattery, power. He was almost as firmly satisfied now that he had been wronged and neglected as he had been positive a few moments before that he had been remiss in his attention. The irritation, although momentary, was enough to decide this strong man; he telegraphed to San Francisco, and having missed the steamer, secured an overland passage to Washington; thought better of it, and partly changed his mind an hour after the ticket was purchased—but, manlike, having once made a practical step in a wrong direction, he kept on rather than admit an inconsistency to himself. Yet he was not entirely satisfied that his journey was a business one. The impulsive, weak little Mistress Carmen had evidently scored one against the strong man.

Only a small part of the present great transcontinental railway at this time had been built, and was but piers at either end of a desolate and wild expanse as yet unbridged. When the overland traveller left the rail at Reno, he left, as it were, civilisation with it, and until he reached the Nebraska frontier, the rest of his road was only the old emigrant trail traversed by the coaches of the Overland Company. Excepting a part of "Devil's Cañon," the way was unpicturesque and flat, and the passage of the Rocky Mountains, far from suggesting the alleged poetry of that region, was only a reminder of those sterile distances of a level New England landscape. The journey was a dreary monotony, that was scarcely enlivened by its discomforts, never amounting to actual accident or incident, but utterly destructive to all nervous tissue. Insanity often super-vened. "On the third day out," said Hank Monk, driver, speaking casually but charitably of a "fare"—"on the third day out, after axing no end of questions and getting no answers, he took to chewing straws that he picked outer the cushion, and kinder cussin' to hisself. From that very day I knew it was all over with him, and I handed him over to his friends at 'Shy Ann,' strapped to the back seat, and ravin' and cussin' at Ben Holliday, the gent'manly proprietor." It is presumed that the unfortunate tourist's indignation was excited at the late Mr. Benjamin Holliday, then the proprietor of the line—an evidence of his insanity that no one who knew that large-hearted, fastidious, and elegantly cultured Californian, since allied to foreign nobility, will for a moment doubt.

Mr. Royal Thatcher was too old and experienced a mountaineer to do aught but accept patiently and cynically his brother Californian's method of increasing his profits. As it was generally understood that any one who came from California by that route had some dark design, the victim received little sympathy. Thatcher's equable tem-perament and indomitable will stood him in good stead, and helped him cheerfully in this emergency. He ate his scant meals, and otherwise took care of the functions of his weak human nature, when and where he could, without grumbling, and at times earned even the praise of his driver by his ability to "rough it." Which "roughing it," by the way, meant the ability of the passenger to accept the incompetency of the company. It is true there were times when he regretted that he had not taken the steamer,

but then he reflected that he was one of a Vigilance
Committee, sworn to hang that admirable man, the late
Commodore William H. Vanderbilt, for certain practices
and cruelties done upon the bodies of certain steerage
passengers by his line, and for divers irregularities in their
transportation. I mention this fact merely to show how
so practical and stout a voyager as Thatcher might have
confounded the perplexities attending the administration
of a great steamship company with selfish greed and
brutality, and that he, with other Californians, may not
have known the fact, since recorded by the Commodore's
family clergyman, that the great millionaire was always
true to the hymns of his childhood.

Nevertheless Thatcher found time to be cheerful and
helpful to his fellow passengers, and even to be so far
interesting to " Yuba Bill," driver, as to have the box seat
placed at his disposal. " But," said Thatcher, in some
concern, " the box seat was purchased by that other gentleman in Sacramento. He paid extra for it, and his name's
on your way-bill !" " That," said Yuba Bill, scornfully,
" don't fetch me even ef he'd chartered the whole shebang.
Look yar, do you reckon I'm goin' to spile my temper by
setting next to a man with a game eye. And such an eye !
Gewhillikins ! Why, darn my skin, the other day when we
war watering at Webster's, he got down and passed in front
of the off-leader—that yer *pinto* colt that's bin accustomed
to injins, grizzlies and buffalo, and I'm blest ef, when her
eye tackled his, ef she didn't jist git up and rar 'round, that
I reckoned I'd hev to go down and take them blinders off
from *her* eyes and clap 'em on his." " But he paid his
money and is entitled to his seat," persisted Thatcher.
"Mebbe he is—in the office of the kempeny," growled
Yuba Bill, " but it's time some folks knowed that out in
the plains I run this yer team myself." A fact which was

self-evident to most of the passengers. "I suppose his authority is as absolute on this dreary waste as the captain of a ship's in mid-ocean," explained Thatcher to the baleful-eyed stranger. Mr. Wiles—whom the reader has recognised—assented with the public side of his face, but looked vengeance at Yuba Bill with the other, while Thatcher, innocent of the presence of one of his worst enemies, placated Bill so far as to restore Wiles to his rights. Wiles thanked him. "Shall I have the pleasure of your company far?" Wiles asked insinuatingly. "To Washington," replied Thatcher frankly. "Washington is a gay city during the session," again suggested the stranger. "I'm going on business," said Thatcher bluntly.

A trifling incident occurred at Pine Tree Crossing which did not heighten Yuba Bill's admiration of the stranger. As Bill opened the double-locked box in the "boot" of the coach—sacred to Wells, Fargo & Co.'s Express and the Overland Company's treasures—Mr. Wiles perceived a small, black morocco portmanteau among the parcels. "Ah, you carry baggage there too?" he said sweetly. "Not often," responded Yuba Bill shortly. "Ah, this then contains valuables?" "It belongs to that man whose seat you've got," said Yuba Bill, who, for insulting purposes of his own, preferred to establish the fiction that Wiles was an interloper, "and ef he reckons, in a sorter mixed kempeny like this, to lock up his portmantle, I don't know who's business it is. Who?" continued Bill, lashing himself into a simulated rage, "who, in blank, is running this yer team? Hey? Mebbe you think, sittin' up thar on the box-seat, you are. Mebbe you think you kin see 'round corners with that thar eye, and kin pull up for teams 'round corners, on down grades, a mile ahead?" But here Thatcher, who with something of Launcelot's concern for Modred, had a noble pity for all infirmities, interfered so sternly that Yuba Bill stopped.

On the fourth day they struck a blinding snow storm while ascending the dreary plateau that henceforward for six hundred miles was to be their road bed. The horses, after floundering through the drift, gave out completely on reaching the next station, and the prospects ahead, to all but the experienced eye, looked doubtful. A few passengers advised taking to sledges, others a postponement of the journey until the weather changed. Yuba Bill alone was for pressing forward as they were. "Two miles more and we're on the high grade, whar the wind is strong enough to blow you through the windy and jist peart enough to pack away over them cliffs every inch of snow that falls. I'll jist skirmish round in and out o' them drifts on these four wheels, whar ye can't drag one o' them flat-bottomed dry goods boxes through a drift." Bill had a California whip's contempt for a sledge. But he was warmly seconded by Thatcher, who had the next best thing to experience, the instinct that taught him to read character, and take advantage of another man's experience. "Them that wants to stop kin do so," said Bill, authoritatively, cutting the Gordian knot, "them as wants to take a sledge can do so— thar's one in the barn. Them as wants to go on with me and the relay will come on." Mr. Wiles selected the sledge and a driver, a few remained for the next stage, and Thatcher, with two others, decided to accompany Yuba Bill. These changes took up some valuable time, and the storm continuing, the stage was run under the shed, the passengers gathering around the station fire, and not until after midnight did Yuba Bill put in the relays. "I wish you a good journey," said Wiles, as he drove from the shed as Bill entered. Bill vouchsafed no reply, but addressing himself to the driver, said curtly, as if giving an order for the delivery of goods, "Shove him out at Rawlings," passed contemptuously around to the tail-board of the sled and returned to the harnessing of his relay.

The moon came out and shone high as Yuba Bill once more took the reins in his hands. The wind, which instantly attacked them as they reached the level, seemed to make the driver's theory plausible, and for half a mile the road bed was swept clean and frozen h..rd. Farther on a tongue of snow extending from a boulder to the right, reached across their path to the height of two or three feet. But Yuba Bill dashed through a part of it, and by skilful manœuvring circumvented the rest. But even as the obstacle was passed the coach dropped with an ominous lurch on one side, and the off fore wheel flew off in the darkness. Bill threw the horses back on their haunches, but before their momentum could be checked the rear hind wheel slipped away, the vehicle rocked violently, plunged backwards and forwards, and stopped.

Yuba Bill was on the road in an instant with his lantern. Then followed an outbreak of profanity which I regret, for artistic purposes, exceeds that generous limit which a sympathising public has already extended to me in the explication of character. Let me state, therefore, that in a very few moments he succeeded in disparaging the characters of his employers, their male and female relatives, the coach builder, the station keeper, the road on which he travelled and the travellers themselves, with occasional broad expletives addressed to himself and his own relatives. For the spirit of this and a more cultivated poetry of expression, I beg to refer the temperate reader to the 3d chapter of Job.

The passengers knew Bill, and sat, conservative, patient and expectant. As yet the cause of the catastrophe was not known. At last Thatcher's voice came from the box-seat—

"What's up, Bill?"

"Not a blank linch-pin in the whole blank coach," was the answer.

There was a dead silence. Yuba Bill executed a wild war dance of helpless rage.

" Blank the blank *enchanted* thing to blank !"

(I beg here to refer the fastidious and cultivated reader to the only adjective I have dared transcribe of this actual oath which I once had the honour of hearing. He will, I trust, not fail to recognise the old classic *dæmon* in this wild Western objurgation.)

"Who did it?" asked Thatcher.

Yuba Bill did not reply, but dashed up again to the box, unlocked the "boot," and screamed out—

" The man that stole your portmantle—Wiles !"

Thatcher laughed—

" Don't worry about that, Bill. A 'biled' shirt, an extra collar and a few papers. Nothing more."

Yuba Bill slowly descended. When he reached the ground he plucked Thatcher aside by his coat sleeve—

" Ye don't mean to say ye had nothing in that bag ye waz trying to get away with?"

" No," said the laughing Thatcher frankly.

" And that Wiles warn't one 'o them detectives?"

" Not to my knowledge, certainly."

Yuba Bill sighed sadly and returned to assist in the replacing of the coach on its wheels again.

" Never mind, Bill," said one of the passengers sympathisingly, " we'll catch that man Wiles at ' Rawlings ' sure," and he looked around at the inchoate vigilance committee already " rounding into form " about him.

" Ketch him !" returned Yuba Bill derisively, " why we've got to go back to the station, and afore we're off agin he's pinted fur Clarmont on the relay we lose. Ketch him ! H—ll's full of such ketches !"

There was clearly nothing to do but to go back to the station to await the repairing of the coach. While this was being done Yuba Bill again drew Thatcher aside—

"I allers suspected that chap's game eye, but I didn't somehow allow for anything like this. I reckoned it was only the square thing to look arter things gen'rally, and 'specially your traps. So, to purvent troubil and keep things about 'ekal, ez he was goin' away, I sorter lifted this yer bag of hiz outer the tail-board of his sleigh. I don't know as its any ex-change or compensation, but it may give ye a chance to spot him agin, or him you. It strikes me as bein' far-minded and squar," and with these words he deposited at the feet of the astounded Thatcher the black travelling bag of Mr. Wiles.

"But, Bill—see here! I can't take this!" interrupted Thatcher hastily. "You can't swear that he's taken my bag—and—and—blank it all—this won't do, you know. I've no right to this man's things, even if"——

"Hold your hosses," said Bill gravely, "I ondertook to take charge o' your traps. I didn't—at least that d—d wall eyed—Thar's a portmantle. I don't know who's it is. Take it."

Half amused, half embarrassed, yet still protesting, Thatcher took the bag in his hands.

"Ye might open it in my presence," suggested Yuba Bill gravely.

Thatcher, half-laughingly, did so. It was full of papers and semi-legal looking documents. Thatcher's own name on one of them caught his eye; he opened the paper hastily and perused it. The smile faded from his lips.

"Well," said Yuba Bill, "suppose we call it a fair exchange at present."

Thatcher was still examining the papers. Suddenly this cautious, strong-minded man looked up into Yuba Bill's waiting face, and said quietly, in the despicable slang of the epoch and region—

"It's a go! Suppose we do."


## CHAPTER XIII.

### HOW IT BECAME FAMOUS.

YUBA BILL was right in believing that Wiles would lose no time at Rawlings. He left there on a fleet horse before Bill had returned with the broken-down coach to the last station, and distanced the telegram sent to detain him two hours. Leaving the stage road and its dangerous telegraphic stations, he pushed southward to Denver over the army trail, in company with a half-breed packer, crossing the Missouri before Thatcher had reached Julesburg. When Thatcher was at Omaha, Wiles was already in St. Louis, and as the Pullman car containing the hero of the "Blue Mass Mine" rolled into Chicago, Wiles was already walking the streets of the National Capital. Nevertheless he had time *en route* to sink in the waters of the North Platte, with many expressions of disgust, the little black portmanteau belonging to Thatcher, containing his dressing case, a few unimportant letters and an extra shirt, to wonder why simple men did not travel with their important documents and valuables, and to set on foot some prudent and cautious inquiries regarding his own lost carpet-bag and its important contents.

But for these trifles he had every reason to be satisfied with the progress of his plans. "It's all right," said Mrs. Hopkinson merrily, "while you and Gashwiler have been working with your 'stock' and treating the whole world as if it could be bribed, I've done more with that earnest, self-believing, self-deceiving and perfectly pathetic Ros-

common than all you fellows put together. Why I've told
his pitiful story and drawn tears from the eyes of senators
and cabinet ministers. More than that, I've introduced
him into society, put him in a dress coat—such a figure—
and you know how the best folk worship everything that is
*outré* as the sincere thing ; I've made him a complete success. Why, only the other night, when Senator Misnancy
and Judge Fitzdawdle were here, after making him tell his
story—which you know I think he really believes—I sang,
'There came to the beach a poor exile of Erin,' and my
husband told me afterwards it was worth at least a dozen
votes."

"But about this rival of yours—this niece of Garcia's ? "

"Another of your blunders—you men know nothing of
women. Firstly, she's a swarthy little brunette, with dots
for eyes, and strides like a man, dresses like a dowdy, don't
wear stays and has no style. Then she's a single woman
and alone, and although she affects to be an artist and has
Bohemian ways, don't you see she can't go into society without a chaperon or somebody to go with her. Nonsense."

"But," persisted Wiles, "she must have some power;
there's Judge Mason and Senator Peabody, who are constantly talking about her, and Dinwiddie of Virginia
escorted her through the Capitol the other day."

Mistress Hopkinson laughed. "Mason and Peabody
aspire to be thought literary and artistic, and Dinwiddie
wanted to pique *me !* "

"But Thatcher is no fool"——

"Is Thatcher a lady's man ? " queried the lady suddenly.

"Hardly, I should say," responded Wiles. "He pretends to be absorbed in his swindle and devoted to his
mine, and I don't think that even you "—he stopped with
a slight sneer.

"There, you are misunderstanding me again, and what is worse, you are misunderstanding your case. Thatcher is pleased with her because he has probably seen no one else. Wait till he comes to Washington and has an opportunity for comparison," and she cast a frank glance at her mirror, where Wiles, with a sardonic bow, left her standing.

Mr. Gashwiler was quite as confident of his own success with Congress. "We are within a few days of the end of the session. We will manage to have it taken up and rushed through before that fellow Thatcher knows what he is about."

"If it could be done before he gets here," said Wiles, "it's a reasonably sure thing. He is delayed two days— he might have been delayed longer." Here Mr. Wiles sighed ; if the accident had happened on a mountain road, and the stage had been precipitated over the abyss? What valuable time would have been saved and success become a surety. But Mr. Wiles' functions as an advocate did not include murder ; at least he was doubtful if it could be taxed as costs.

"We need have no fears, sir," resumed Mr. Gashwiler, "the matter is now in the hands of the highest tribunal of appeal in the country. It will meet, sir, with inflexible justice. I have already prepared some remarks"——

"By the way," interrupted Wiles infelicitously, "where's your young man—your private secretary—Dobbs?"

The Congressman for a moment looked confused. "He is not here. And I must correct your error in applying that term to him. I have never put my confidence in the hands of any one."

"But you introduced him to me as your secretary?"

"A mere honorary title, sir. A brevet rank. I might, it is true, have thought to repose such a trust in him. But I was deceived, sir, as I fear I am too apt to be when I permit my feelings as a man to overcome my duty as an American legislator. Mr. Dobbs enjoyed my patronage and the opportunity it gave me to introduce him into public life only to abuse it. He became, I fear, deeply indebted. His extravagance was unlimited, his ambition unbounded, but without, sir, a cash basis. I advanced money to him from time to time upon the little property you so generously extended to him for his services. But it was quietly dissipated. Yet, sir, such is the ingratitude of man that his family lately appealed to me for assistance. I felt it was necessary to be stern, and I refused. I would not for the sake of his family say anything, but I have missed, sir, books from my library. On the day after he . left two volumes of Patent Office reports and a Blue Book of Congress, purchased that day by me at a store on Pennsylvania avenue, were *missing*—missing! I had difficulty, sir, great difficulty in keeping it from the papers!"

As Mr. Wiles had heard the story already from Gashwiler's acquaintance, with more or less free comment on the gifted legislator's economy, he could not help thinking that the difficulty had been great indeed. But he only fixed his malevolent eye on Gashwiler and said—

"So he is gone, eh?"

"Yes."

"And you've made an enemy of him? That's bad."

Mr. Gashwiler tried to look dignifiedly unconcerned, but something in his visitor's manner made him uneasy.

"I say it's bad, if you have. Listen. Before I left here I found at a boarding-house where he had boarded, and still owed a bill, a trunk which the landlord retained. Opening it I found some letters and papers of yours, with certain memoranda of his, which I thought ought to be in *your* possession. As an alleged friend of his I redeemed the trunk by paying the amount of his bill, and secured the more valuable papers."

Gashwiler's face, which had grown apoplectically suffused as Wiles went on, at last gasped—" But you got the trunk and have the papers ? "

" Unfortunately no ; and that's why it's bad."

" But good God ! what have you done with them ? "

" I've lost them somewhere on the Overla Road."

Mr. Gashwiler sat for a few moments speechless, vacillating between a purple rage and a pallid fear. Then he said hoarsely—

" They are all blank forgeries—every one of them."

" Oh no ! " said Wiles, smiling blankly on his dexter side, and enjoying the whole scene malevolently with his sinister eye. " *Your* papers are all genuine, and I won't say are not all right, but unfortunately I had in the same bag some memoranda of my own for the use of my client, that, you understand, might be put to some bad use if found by a clever man."

The two rascals looked at each other. There is, on the whole, really very little " honour among thieves "—at least great ones—and the inferior rascal succumbed at the reflection of what *he* might do if he were in the other rascal's place. " See here, Wiles," he said, relaxing his dignity with the perspiration that oozed from every pore, and made the collar of his shirt a mere limp rag. " See here, *We* " —this first use of the plural was equivalent to a confession —" *we* must get them papers."

" Of course," said Wiles coolly, " if we *can*, and if Thatcher don't get wind of them."

" He cannot."

" He was on the coach when I lost them, coming East."

Mr. Gashwiler paled again. In the emergency he had

recourse to the sideboard and a bottle, forgetting Wiles. Ten minutes before, Wiles would have remained seated; but it is recorded that he rose, took the bottle from the gifted Gashwiler's fingers, helped himself *first* and then sat down.

" Yes, but, my boy," said Gashwiler, now rapidly changing situations with the cooler Wiles, "yes, but, old fellow," he added, poking Wiles with a fat fore-finger, "don't you see the whole thing will be up before he gets here."

" Yes," said Wiles gloomily, " but those lazy, easy, honest men have a way of popping up just at the nick of time. They never need hurry; all things wait for them. Why, don't you remember that on the very day Mrs. Hopkinson and me and you got the President to sign that patent, that very day one of them d—n fellows turns up from San Francisco or Australia, having taken his own time to get here; gets here about half an hour after the President had signed the patent and sent it over to the office, finds the right man to introduce him to the President, has a talk with him, makes him sign an order countermanding its issuance, and undoes all that has been done in six years in one hour."

"Yes, but Congress is a tribunal that does not revoke its decrees," said Gashwiler with a return of his old manner; " at least," he added, observing an incredulous shrug in the shoulders of his companion, " at least *during the session.*"

" We shall see," said Wiles, quietly taking his hat.

" We shall see, sir," said the member from Remus with dignity.

## CHAPTER XIV.

### WHO INTRIGUED FOR IT.

THERE was at this time in the Senate of the United States an eminent and respected gentleman, scholarly, orderly, honourable and radical—the fit representative of a scholarly, orderly, honourable and radical commonwealth. For many years he had held his trust with conscious rectitude, and a slight depreciation of other forms of merit, and for as many years had been as regularly returned to his seat by his constituency with equally conscious rectitude in themselves, and an equal scepticism regarding others. Removed by his nature beyond the reach of certain temptations, and by circumstances beyond even the knowledge of others, his social and political integrity was spotless. An orator and practical debater, his refined tastes kept him from personality, and the public recognition of the complete unselfishness of his motives and the magnitude of his dogmas, protected him from scurrility. His principles had never been appealed to by a bribe; he had rarely been approached by an emotion.

A man of polished taste in art and literature, and possessing the means to gratify it, his luxurious home was filled with treasures he had himself collected, and further enhanced by the stamp of his own appreciation. His library had not only the elegance of adornment that his wealth could bring and his taste approve, but a certain refined negligence of habitual use and the easy disorder of the artist's workshop. All this was quickly noted by a young girl who stood on its threshold at the close of a dull January day.

The card that had been brought to the Senator bore the name of "Carmen de Haro," and modestly, in the right-

hand corner, in almost microscopic script, the further description of herself as "Art..." Perhaps the picturesqueness of the name and its historic suggestion caught the
scholar's taste, for, when to his request, through his servant,
that she would be kind enough to state her business, she
replied as frankly that her business was personal to himself,
he directed that she should be admitted. Then, entrench-
ing himself behind his library table, overlooking a bastion
of books, and a *glacis* of pamphlets and papers, and
throwing into his forehead and eyes an expression of utter
disqualification for anything but the business before him, he
calmly awaited the intruder.

She came, and for an instant stood, hesitatingly, framing
herself as a picture in the door. Mrs. Hopkinson was
right—she had "no style," unless an original and half
foreign quaintness could be called so. There was a
desperate attempt visible to combine an American shawl
with the habits of a *mantilla*, and it was always slipping
from one shoulder, that was so supple and vivacious as to
betray the deficiencies of an education in stays. There
was a cluster of black curls around her low forehead, fitting
her so closely as to seem to be a part of the seal-skin cap
she wore. Once, from the force of habit, she attempted
to put her shawl over her head and talk through the folds
gathered under her chin, but an astonished look from the
Senator checked her. Nevertheless, he felt relieved, and,
rising, motioned her to a chair with a heartiness he would
have scarcely shown to a Parisian *toilleta*. And when, with
two or three quick, long steps, she reached his side, and
showed a frank, innocent, but strong and determined little
face, feminine only in its flash of eye and beauty of lip and
chin curves, he put down the pamphlet he had taken up somewhat ostentatiously, and gently begged to know her business.

I think I have once before spoken of her voice—an

organ more often cultivated by my fair countrywomen for singing than for speaking, which, considering that much of our practical relations with the sex are carried on without the aid of an opera score, seems a mistaken notion of theirs—and of its sweetness, gentle inflexion and musical emphasis. She had the advantage of having been trained in a musical language, and came of a race with whom catarrhs and sore throats were rare. So that in a few brief phrases she sang the Senator into acquiescence as she imparted the plain libretto of her business—namely, a "desire to see some of his rare engravings."

Now the engravings in question were certain etchings of the early great apprentices of the art, and were, I am happy to believe, extremely rare. From my unprofessional view they were exceedingly bad—showing the mere genesis of something since perfected, but dear, of course, to the true collector's soul. I don't believe that Carmen really admired them either. But the minx knew that the Senator prided himself on having the only "pot-hooks" of the great "A" or the first artistic efforts of "B"—I leave the real names to be filled in by the connoisseur—and the Senator became interested. For the last year two or three of these abominations had been hanging in his study, utterly ignored by the casual visitor. But here was appreciation! "She was," she added, "only a poor young artist, unable to purchase such treasures, but equally unable to resist the opportunity afforded her, even at the risk of seeming bold, or of obtruding upon a great man's privacy," &c., &c.

This flattery, which, if offered in the usual legal tender of the country, would have been looked upon as counterfeit, delivered here in a foreign accent, with a slightly tropical warmth, was accepted by the Senator as genuine. These children of the Sun are so impulsive! We, of course, feel a little pity for the person who thus transcends our standard of good taste and violates our conventional canons—but they are always sincere. The cold New Englander saw nothing wrong in one or two direct and extravagant compliments, that would have insured his visitor's early dismissal if tendered in the clipped metallic phrases of the commonwealth he represented.

So that in a few moments the black, curly head of the little artist and the white, flowing locks of the Senator were close together bending over the rack that contained the engravings. It was then that Carmen, listening to a graphic description of the early rise of Art in the Netherlands, forgot herself and put her shawl around her head, holding its folds in her little brown hand. In this situation they were, at different times during the next two hours, interrupted by five Congressmen, three Senators, a Cabinet officer, and a Judge of the Supreme Bench—each of whom were quickly but courteously dismissed. Popular sentiment, however, broke out in the hall.

"Well, I'm blanked, but this gets me." (The speaker was a Territorial delegate.)

"At his time o' life, too, lookin' over pictures with a gal young enough to be his grandchild. (This from a venerable official, since suspected of various erotic irregularities.)

"She don't handsome any." (The honourable member from Dakotah.)

"This accounts for his protracted silence during the session." (A serious colleague from the Senator's own State.)

"Oh, blank it all!" (*Omnes.*)

Four went home to tell their wives. There are few things more touching in the matrimonial compact than the superb frankness with which each confide to each the various irregularities of their friends. It is upon these sacred con-

fidences that the firm foundations of marriage rest un-
shaken.

Of course the objects of this comment, at least *one* of
them, were quite oblivious. "I trust," said Carmen timidly,
when they had for the fourth time regarded in rapt admiration an abominable something by some Dutch wood-
chopper, "I trust I am not keeping you from your great
friends"—her pretty eyelids were cast down in tremulous
distress—"I should never forgive myself. Perhaps it is
important business of the State?"

"Oh dear, no! *They* will come again—it's *their*
business."

The Senator meant it kindly. It was as near the perilous
edge of a compliment as your average cultivated Boston
man ever ventures, and Carmen picked it up, femininely,
by its sentimental end. "And I suppose *I* shall not
trouble you again?"

"I shall always be proud to place the portfolio at your
disposal. Command me at any time," said the Senator,
with dignity.

"You are kind. You are good," said Carmen, "and I—
I am but—look you—only a poor girl from California, that
you know not."

"Pardon me. I know your country well." And indeed
he could have told her the exact number of bushels of
wheat to the acre in her own county of Monterey, its voting
population, its political bias. Yet of the more important
product before him, after the manner of book-read men, he
knew nothing.

Carmen was astonished, but respectful. It transpired
presently that she was not aware of the rapid growth of the
silk-worm in her own district, knew nothing of the Chinese
question, and very little of the American mining laws.
Upon these questions the senator enlightened her fully.

"Your name is historic, by the way," he said pleasantly; "there was a Knight of Alcantara, a 'de Haro,' one of the emigrants with Las Casas."

Carmen nodded her head quickly, "Yes; my great-great-great-g-r-e-a-t grandfather!"

The Senator stared.

"Oh yes. I am the niece of Victor Castro, who married my father's sister."

"The Victor Castro of the Blue Mass Mine?" asked the Senator abruptly.

"Yes," quietly.

Had the Senator been of the Gashwiler type he would have expressed himself, after the average masculine fashion, by a long-drawn whistle. But his only perceptible appreciation of a sudden astonishment and suspicion in his mind was a lowering of the social thermometer of the room so decided that poor Carmen looked up innocently, chilled, and drawing her shawl closer around her shoulders.

"I have something more to ask," said Carmen, hanging her head—"it is a great, oh, a very great favour."

The Senator had retreated behind his bastion of books again, and was visibly preparing for an assault. He saw it all now. He had been, in some vague way, deluded. He had given confidential audience to the niece of one of the Great Claimants before Congress. The inevitable axe had come to the grindstone. What might not this woman dare ask of him? He was the more implacable that he felt he had already been prepossessed—and honestly prepossessed —in her favour. He was angry with her for having pleased him. Under the icy polish of his manner there were certain Puritan callosities caused by early straight-lacing. He was not yet quite free from his ancestor's cheerful ethics, that Nature, as represented by an Impulse, was as much to be restrained as Order represented by a Quaker.

Without apparently noticing his manner, Carmen went on, with a certain potential freedom of style, gesture and manner scarcely to be indicated in her mere words. "You know, then, I am of Spanish blood, and that, in what was my adopted country, our motto was, 'God and Liberty.' It was of you, sir—the great Emancipator—the apostle of that Liberty—the friend of the down-trodden and oppressed —that I, as a child, first knew. In the histories of this great country I have read of you, I have learned your orations. I have longed to hear you in your own pulpit deliver the creed of my ancestors. To hear you, of yourself, speak, ah! *Madre de Dios!* what shall I say—speak the oration eloquent to make the—what you call—the debate, that is what I have for so long hoped. Eh! Pardon —you are thinking me foolish—wild, eh—a small child —eh?"

Becoming more and more dialectical as she went on, she said suddenly, "I have you of myself offended. You are mad of me as a bold, bad child? Is it so?"

The Senator, as visibly becoming limp and weak again behind his entrenchments, managed to say, "Oh no!" then, "really!" and finally, "Tha-a-nks!"

"I am here but for a day. I return to California in a day, as it were to-morrow. I shall never—never hear you speak in your place in the Capitol of this great country?"

The Senator said, hastily, that he feared, he in fact was convinced, that his duty during this session was required more at his desk, in the committee work, than in speaking, &c., &c.

"Ah," said Carmen, sadly, "it is true, then, all this that I have heard. It is true that what they have told me—that you have given up the great party—that your voice is not longer heard in the old—what you call this—eh—the old *issues?*"

"If any one has told you that, Miss De Haro," responded the Senator, sharply, "he has spoken foolishly. You have been misinformed. May I ask who "——

"Ah!" said Carmen, "I know not! It is in the air! I am a stranger. Perhaps I am de-ceived. But it is of all. I say to them, When shall I hear him speak? I go day after day to the Capitol, I watch him—the great Emancipator—but it is of business, eh?—it is the claim of that one, it is the Tax, eh? it is the Impost, it is the Post office, but it is the great speech of Human Rights—*never*, NEVER. I say, 'How arrives all this?' And some say and shake their heads, 'never again he speaks.' He is what you call 'played'—yes, it is so, eh? 'played out.' I know it not—it is a word from Bos-ton perhaps? They say he has—eh, I speak not the English well—the party he has 'shaken,' 'shook'—yes—he has the Party 'shaken,' eh? It is right —it is the language of Boston, eh?"

"Permit me to say, Miss De Haro," returned the Senator, rising with some asperity, "that you seem to have been unfortunate in your selection of acquaintances, and still more so in your ideas of the derivations of the English tongue. The—er—the—er—expressions you have quoted are not common to Boston, but emanate, I believe, from the West."

Carmen De Haro contritely buried everything but her black eyes in her shawl.

"No one," he continued, more gently, sitting down again, "has the right to forecast from my past what I intend to do in the future, or designate the means I may choose to serve the principles I hold or the Party I represent. Those are *my* functions. At the same time, should occasion—or opportunity—for we are within a day or two of the close of the Session "——

"Yes," interrupted Carmen sadly, "I see—it will be

some business, some claim, something for somebody—ah !
*Madre de Dios*—you will not speak, and I "——

"When do you think of returning?" asked the Senator,
with grave politeness, "when are we to lose you?"

"I shall stay to the last—to the end of the Session," said
Carmen. "And *now* I shall go." She got up and pulled
her shawl viciously over her shoulders with a pretty pettishness, perhaps the most feminine thing she had done that
evening. Possibly, the most genuine.

The Senator smiled affably: "You do not deserve to
be disappointed in either case; but it is later than you
imagine; let me help you on the shorter distance with my
carriage; it is at the door."

He accompanied her gravely to the carriage. As it
rolled away she buried her little figure in its ample cushions
and chuckled to herself, albeit a little hysterically. When
she had reached her destination she found herself crying,
and hastily, and somewhat angrily, dried her eyes as she
drew up at the door of her lodgings.

"How have you prospered?" asked Mr. Harlowe, of
counsel for Royal Thatcher, as he gallantly assisted her
from the carriage. "I have been waiting here for two
hours; your interview must have been prolonged—that was
a good sign."

"Don't ask me now," said Carmen, a little savagely,
"I'm worn out and tired."

Mr. Harlowe bowed. "I trust you will be better
to-morrow, for we expect our friend, Mr. Thatcher."

Carmen's brown cheek flushed slightly. "He should
have been here before. Where is he? What was he
doing?"

"He was snowed up on the plains. He is coming as
fast as steam can carry him, but he may be too late."

Carmen did not reply.

The lawyer lingered. "How did you find the great New England Senator?" he asked, with a slight professional levity.

Carmen was tired, Carmen was worried, Carmen was a little self-reproachful, and she kindled easily. Consequently she said icily—

"I found him *a gentleman!*"

## CHAPTER XV.

### HOW IT BECAME UNFINISHED BUSINESS.

THE closing of the LXIX Congress was not unlike the closing of the several preceding Congresses. There was the same unbusiness like, impractical haste; the same hurried, unjust, and utterly inadequate adjustment of unfinished, ill-digested business, that would not have been tolerated for a moment by the sovereign people in any private interest they controlled. There were frauds rushed through; there were long-suffering, righteous demands shelved; there were honest, unpaid debts dishonoured by scant appropriations; there were closing scenes which only the saving sense of American humour kept from being utterly vile. The actors, the legislators themselves, knew it and laughed at it; the commentators, the Press, knew it and laughed at it; the audience, the great American people, knew it and laughed at it. And nobody for an instant conceived that it ever, under any circumstances, might be otherwise.

The claim of Roscommon was among the Unfinished Business. The claimant himself, haggard, pathetic, importunate and obstinate, was among the Unfinished Business.

Various Congressmen, more or less interested in the success of the claim, were among the Unfinished Business. The member from Fresno, who had changed his derringer for a speech against the claimant, was among the Unfinished Business. The gifted Gashwiler, uneasy in his soul over certain other unfinished business in the shape of his missing letters, but dropping oil and honey as he mingled with his brothers, was King of Misrule and Lord of the Unfinished Business. Pretty Mrs Hopkinson, prudently escorted by her husband, but imprudently ogled by admiring Congressmen, lent the charm of her presence to the finishing of Unfinished Business. One or two editors, who had dreams of a finished financial business, arising out of unfinished business, were there also, like ancient bards, to record with pæan or threnody the completion of Unfinished Business. Various unclean birds, scenting carrion in Unfinished Business, hovered in the halls or roosted in the Lobby.

The lower house, under the tutelage of the gifted Gashwiler, drank deeply of Roscommon and his intoxicating claim, and passed the half empty bottle to the Senate as Unfinished Business. But alas! in the very rush and storm and tempest of the finishing business, an unlooked-for interruption arose in the person of a great Senator whose power none could oppose, whose right to free and extended utterance at all times none could gainsay. A claim for poultry, violently seized by the army of Sherman during his march through Georgia, from the hen-coop of an alleged loyal Irishman, opened a constitutional question, and with it the lips of the great Senator.

For seven hours he spoke eloquently, earnestly, convincingly. For seven hours the old issues of party and policy were severally taken up and dismissed in the old forcible rhetoric that had early made him famous. Interruption from other Senators, now forgetful of Unfinished

Business and wild with reanimated party zeal; interruptions from certain Senators mindful of Unfinished Business, and unable to pass the Roscommon bottle, only spurred him to fresh exertion. The tocsin sounded in the Senate was heard in the lower house. Highly excited members congregated at the doors of the Senate, and left Unfinished Business to take care of itself.

Left to itself for seven hours, Unfinished Business gnashed its false teeth and tore its wig in impotent fury in corridor and hall. For seven hours the gifted Gashwiler had continued the manufacture of oil and honey, whose sweetness, however, was slowly palling upon the Congressional lip; for seven hours Roscommon and friends beat with impatient feet the lobby and shook fists, more or less discoloured, at the distinguished senator. For seven hours the one or two editors were obliged to sit and calmly compliment the great speech which that night flashed over the wires of a continent with the old electric thrill. And, worse than all, they were obliged to record with it the closing of the LXIX Congress, with more than the usual amount of Unfinished Business.

A little group of friends surrounded the great Senator with hymns of praise and congratulations. Old adversaries saluted him courteously as they passed by, with the respect of strong men. A little woman with a shawl drawn over her shoulders, and held with one small brown hand, approached him timidly—

"I speak not the English well," she said gently, "but I have read much. I have read in the plays of your Shakspeare. I would like to say to you the words of Rosalind to Orlando, when he did fight: 'Sir, you have wrestled well, and have overthrown more than your enemies.'" And with these words she was gone.

Yet not so quickly but that pretty Mrs. Hopkinson, coming—as Victrix always comes to Victor—to thank the

great Senator, albeit the faces of her escorts were shrouded
in gloom, saw the shawled figure disappear.

"There," she said, pinching Wiles mischievously, "there!
that's the woman you were afraid of. Look at her. Look
at that dress. Ah, Heavens; look at that shawl. Didn't
I tell you she had no style?"

"Who is she?" said Wiles sullenly.

"Carmen de Haro, of course," said the lady vivaciously.
"What are you hurrying away so for? You're absolutely
pulling me along."

Mr. Wiles had just caught sight of the travel-worn face of
Royal Thatcher among the crowd that thronged the staircase. Thatcher appeared pale and *distrait;* Mr Harlowe,
his counsel, at his side, rallied him.

"No one would think you had just got a new lease of
your property, and escaped a great swindle. What's the
matter with you? Miss De Haro passed us just now. It
was she who spoke to the Senator. Why did you not
recognise her?"

"I was thinking," said Thatcher gloomily.

"Well, you take things coolly! And certainly you are
not very demonstrative towards the woman who saved you
to-day. For as sure as you live it was she who drew that
speech out of the Senator."

Thatcher did not reply, but moved away. He *had*
noticed Carmen De Haro, and was about to greet her with
mingled pleasure and embarrassment. But he had heard
her compliment to the Senator, and this strong, preoccupied,
automatic man, who only ten days before had no thought
beyond his property, was now thinking more of that compliment to another than of his success—and was beginning to
hate the Senator who had saved him, the lawyer who stood
beside him, and even the little figure that had tripped down
the steps unconscious of him.

## CHAPTER XVI.

### AND WHO FORGOT IT.

It was somewhat inconsistent with Royal Thatcher's embar-rassment and sensitiveness that he should, on leaving the Capitol, order a carriage and drive directly to the lodgings of Miss De Haro. That on finding she was not at home he should become again sulky and suspicious, and even be ashamed of the honest impulse that led him there, was, I suppose, man-like and natural. He felt that he had done all that courtesy required ; he had promptly answered her despatch with his presence. If she chose to be absent at such a moment, *he* had at least done *his* duty. In short, there was scarcely any absurdity of the imagination which this once practical man did not permit himself to indulge in, yet always with a certain consciousness that he was al-lowing his feelings to run away with him—a fact that did not tend to make him better humoured, and rather inclined him to place the responsibility of the elopement on some-body else. If Miss De Haro had been home, &c., &c., and not going into ecstacies over speeches, &c., &c., and had attended to her business—*i. e.,* being exactly what he had supposed her to be—all this would not have happened.

I am aware that this will not heighten the reader's respect for my hero. But I fancy that the imperceptible progress of a sincere passion in the matured strong man is apt to be marked with even more than the usual haste and absurdity of callous youth. The fever that runs riot in the veins of the robust is apt to pass your ailing weakling by. Possibly there may be some immunity in inoculation. It is Lothario who is always self-possessed and does and says the right thing, while poor honest Cælebs becomes ridiculous with genuine emotion.

He rejoined his lawyer in no very gracious mood. The chambers occupied by Mr. Harlowe were in the basement of a private dwelling once occupied and made historic by an Honourable Somebody, who, however, was remembered only by the landlord and the last tenant. There were various shelves in the walls divided into compartments, sarcastically known as "pigeon-holes," in which the dove of peace had never rested, but which still perpetuated, in their legends, the feuds and animosities of suitors now but common dust together. There was a portrait, apparently of a cherub, which on nearer inspection turned out to be a famous English Lord Chancellor in his flowing wig. There were books with dreary, unenlivening titles—egotistic always, as recording Smith's opinions on this, and Jones' commentaries on that. There was a handbill tacked on the wall, which at first offered hilarious suggestions of a circus or a steamboat excursion, but which turned out only to be a sheriff's sale. There were several oddly-shaped packages in newspaper wrappings, mysterious and awful in dark corners, that might have contained forgotten law papers or the previous week's washing of the eminent counsel. There were one or two newspapers, which at first offered entertaining prospects to the waiting client, but always proved to be a law record or a Supreme Court decision. There was the bust of a late distinguished jurist, which apparently had never been dusted since he himself became dust, and had already grown a perceptibly dusty moustache on his severely-judicial upper lip. It was a cheerless place in the sunshine of day; at night, when it ought, by every suggestion of its dusty past, to have been left to the vengeful ghosts, the greater part of whose hopes and passions were recorded and gathered there—when in the dark the dead hands of forgotten men were stretched from their dusty graves to fumble once more for their old title deeds—at night, when it was lit up by flaring gaslight, the hollow mockery of this dissipation was so apparent that people in the streets, looking through the illuminated windows, felt as if the privacy of a family vault had been intruded upon by body-snatchers.

Royal Thatcher glanced around the room, took in all its dreary suggestions in a half-weary, half-indifferent sort of way, and dropped into the lawyer's own revolving chair as that gentleman entered from the adjacent room.

"Well, you got back soon, I see," said Harlowe briskly.

"Yes," said his client without looking up, and with this notable distinction between himself and all other previous clients, that he seemed absolutely less interested than the lawyer. "Yes, I'm here, and upon my soul I don't exactly know why."

"You told me of certain papers you had discovered," said the lawyer suggestively.

"Oh yes," returned Thatcher with a slight yawn. "I've got here some papers somewhere "—he began to feel in his coat-pocket languidly—" but, by the way, this is a rather dreary and God-forsaken sort of place! Let's go up to Welcker's, and you can look at them over a bottle of champagne."

"After I've looked at them, I've something to show you myself," said Harlowe, "and as for the champagne, we'll have that in the other room, by and by. At present I want to have my head clear, and yours too—if you'll oblige me by becoming sufficiently interested in your own affairs to talk to me about them."

Thatcher was gazing abstractedly at the fire. He started. "I dare say," he began, "I'm not very interesting ; yet it's possible that my affairs have taken up a little too much of my time. However—" he stopped, took from his pocket an envelope and threw it on the desk—"there are some papers. I don't know what value they may be ; that is for you to determine. I don't know that I've any legal right to their possession—that's for you to say, too. They came to me in a queer way. On the overland journey here I lost my bag, containing my few traps and some letters and papers 'of no value,' as the advertisements always say, 'to any but the owner.' Well, the bag was lost, but the stage-driver declares that it was stolen by a fellow passenger, a—man by the name of Giles, or Stiles, or Biles "——

"Wiles," said Harlowe earnestly.

"Yes," continued Thatcher, suppressing a yawn; "yes, I guess you're right—Wiles. Well, the stage-driver, firmly believing this, goes to work and quietly and unostentatiously steals—I say, have you got a cigar?"

"I'll get you one."

Harlowe disappeared in the adjoining room. Thatcher dragged Harlowe's heavy revolving desk chair, which never before had been removed from his sacred position, to the fire, and began to poke the coals abstractedly.

Harlowe reappeared with cigars and matches. Thatcher lit one mechanically, and said, between the puffs—

"Do you—ever—talk—to yourself?"

"No!—why?"

"I thought I heard your voice just now in the other room. Anyhow, this is an awful spooky place. If I stayed here alone half an hour I'd fancy that the Lord Chancellor up there would step down in his robes, out of his frame, to keep me company."

"Nonsense! When I'm busy I often sit here and write until after midnight. It's so quiet!"

"D——mnably so!"

"Well, to go back to the papers. Somebody stole your bag, or you lost it. *You* stole "——

"The driver stole," suggested Thatcher, so languidly that it could hardly be called an interruption.

"Well, we'll say the driver stole, and passed over to you as his accomplice, confederate, or receiver, certain papers belonging"——

"See here, Harlowe, I don't feel like joking in a ghostly law office after midnight. Here are your facts. Yuba Bill, the driver, stole a bag from this passenger, Wiles, or Smiles, and handed it to me to insure the return of my own. I found in it some papers concerning my case. There they are. Do with them what you like."

Thatcher turned his eyes again abstractedly to the fire.

Harlowe took out the first paper—

"A-w, this seems to be a telegram. Yes, eh? 'Come to Washington at once. Carmen de Haro.'"

Thatcher started, blushed like a girl, and hurriedly reached for the paper.

"Nonsense. That's a mistake. A despatch I mislaid in the envelope."

"I see," said the lawyer drily.

"I thought I had torn it up," continued Thatcher, after an awkward pause. I regret to say that here that usually truthful man elaborated a fiction. He had consulted it a dozen times a day on the journey, and it was quite worn in its enfoldings. Harlowe's quick eye had noticed this, but he speedily became interested and absorbed in the other papers. Thatcher lapsed into contemplation of the fire.

"Well," said Harlowe, finally turning to his client, "here's enough to unseat Gashwiler, or close his mouth. As to the rest, it's good reading—but I needn't tell you— no *legal* evidence. But it's proof enough to stop them from ever trying it again—when the existence of this record is made known. Bribery is a hard thing to fix on a man; the only witness is naturally *particeps criminis*—but it would not be easy for them to explain away this rascal's record. One or two things I don't understand: What's this opposite the Hon. X.'s name, 'Took the medicine nicely, and feels better?' and here—just in the margin, after Y.'s, 'Must be laboured with?'"

"I suppose our California slang borrows largely from the medical and spiritual professions," returned Thatcher. "But isn't it odd that a man should keep a conscientious record of his own villany?"

Harlowe, a little abashed at his want of knowledge of American metaphor, now felt himself at home. "Well, no. It's not unusual. In one of those books yonder there is the record of a case where a man, who had committed a series of nameless atrocities, extending over a period of years, absolutely kept a memorandum of them in his pocket diary. It was produced in Court. Why, my dear fellow, one half our business arises from the fact that men and women are in the habit of keeping letters and documents that they might—I don't say, you know, that they *ought*, that's a question of sentiment or ethics—but that they *might* destroy."

Thatcher, half-mechanically, took the telegram of poor Carmen and threw it in the fire. Harlowe noticed the act and smiled.

"I'll venture to say, however, that there's nothing in the bag that *you* lost that need give you a moment's uneasiness. It's only your rascal or fool who carries with him that which makes him his own detective.

"I had a friend," continued Harlowe, "a clever fellow enough, but who was so foolish as to seriously complicate himself with a woman. He was himself the soul of honour, and at the beginning of their correspondence he proposed that they should each return the other's letters with their answer. They did so for years, but it cost him ten thousand dollars and no end of trouble, after all."

"Why?" asked Thatcher simply.

"Because he was such an egotistical ass as *to keep the letter proposing it*, which she had duly returned, among his papers as a sentimental record. Of course somebody eventually found it."

"Good-night," said Thatcher, rising abruptly. "If I stayed here much longer I should begin to disbelieve my own mother."

"I have known of such hereditary traits," returned Harlowe, with a laugh. "But come, you must not go without the champagne." He led the way to the adjacent room, which proved to be only the antechamber of another, on the threshold of which Thatcher stopped with genuine surprise. It was an elegantly furnished library.

"Sybarite! Why was I never here before?"

"Because you came as a client; to-night you are my guest. All who enter here leave their business, with their hats, in the hall. Look; there isn't a law-book on those shelves; that table never was defaced by a title-deed or parchment. You look puzzled? Well, it was a whim of mine to put my residence and my workshop under the same roof, yet so distinct that they would never interfere with each other. You know the house above is let out to lodgers. I occupy the first floor with my mother and sister, and this is my parlour. I do my work in that severe room that fronts the street; here is where I play. A man must have something else in life than mere business. I find it less harmful and expensive to have my pleasure here."

Thatcher had sunk moodily in the embracing arms of an easy chair. He was thinking deeply; he was fond of books too, and like all men who have fared hard and led wandering lives, he knew the value of cultivated repose. Like all men who have been obliged to sleep under blankets and in the open air, he appreciated the luxuries of linen sheets and a frescoed roof. It is, by the way, only your sick city clerk or your dyspeptic clergyman, who fancy that they have found in the bad bread, fried steaks and frowzy flannels of mountain picnicing the true art of living. And it is a somewhat notable fact that your true mountaineer or your gentleman who has been obliged to honestly "rough it," do not, as a general thing, write books about its advantages or implore their fellow mortals to come and share their solitude and their discomforts.

Thoroughly appreciating the taste and comfort of Harlowe's library, yet half envious of its owner, and half suspicious that his own earnest life for the past few years might have been different, Thatcher suddenly started from his seat and walked towards a parlour easel, whereon stood a picture. It was Carmen de Haro's first sketch of the furnace and the Mine.

"I see you are taken with that picture," said Harlowe, pausing with the champagne bottle in his hand. "You show your good taste. It's been much admired. Observe how splendidly that firelight plays over the sleeping face of that figure, yet brings out by very contrast its almost death-like repose. Those rocks are powerfully handled; what a suggestion of mystery in those shadows? You know the painter?"

Thatcher murmured "Miss de Haro," with a new and rather odd self-consciousness in speaking her name.

"Yes. And you know the story of the picture, of course?"

Thatcher thought he didn't—well no, in fact, he did not remember.

"Why, this recumbent figure was an old Spanish lover of hers, whom she believed to have been murdered there. It's a ghastly fancy, ain't it?"

Two things annoyed Thatcher; first, the epithet "lover," as applied to Concho by another man; second, that the

picture belonged to him ; and what the d—l did she mean
by "——

"Yes," he broke out finally, "but how did *you* get it?"

"Oh, I bought it of her. I've been a sort of patron of
hers ever since I found out how she stood towards us.
As she was quite alone here in Washington, my mother
and sister have taken her up, and have been doing the
social thing."

"How long since?" asked Thatcher.

"Oh, not long. The day she telegraphed you she came
here to know what she could do for us, and when I said
nothing could be done except to keep Congress off—why,
she went and *did it*. For *she*, and she alone, got that
speech out of the Senator. But," he added, a little mischievously, "you seem to know very little about her?"

"No !—I—that is—I've been very busy lately," returned
Thatcher, staring at the picture, "does she come here
often?"

"Yes, lately, quite often—she was here this evening with
mother; was here, I think, when you came."

Thatcher looked intently at Harlowe. But that gentleman's face betrayed no confusion. Thatcher refilled his
glass a little awkwardly, tossed off the liquor at a draught,
and rose to his feet.

"Come, old fellow, you're not going now, I shan't permit
it," said Harlowe, laying his hand kindly on his client's
shoulder. "You're out of sorts ! Stay here with me to-
night. Our accommodations are not large, but are elastic.
I can bestow you comfortably until morning. Wait here
a moment while I give the necessary orders."

Thatcher was not sorry to be left alone. In the last
half-hour he had become convinced that his love for
Carmen de Haro had been in some way most dreadfully
abused. While *he* was hard at work in California, she was

being introduced in Washington society by parties with eligible brothers who bought her paintings. It is a relief to the truly jealous mind to indulge in plurals. Thatcher liked to think that she was already beset by hundreds of brothers.

He still kept staring at the picture. By and by it faded away in part, and a very vivid recollection of the misty, midnight, moonlit walk he had once taken with her came back and refilled the canvas with its magic. He saw the ruined furnace; the dark, overhanging masses of rock, the trembling intricacies of foliage, and, above all, the flash of dark eyes under a *mantilla* at his shoulder. What a fool he had been! Had he not really been as senseless and stupid as this very Concho, lying here like a log. And she had loved that man. What a fool she must have thought him that evening? What a snob she must think him now?

He was startled by a slight rustling in the passage, that ceased almost as he turned. Thatcher looked towards the door of the outer office, as if half expecting that the Lord Chancellor, like the commander in Don Juan, might have accepted his thoughtless invitation. He listened again; everything was still. He was conscious of feeling ill at ease and a trifle nervous. What a long time Harlowe took to make his preparations. He would look out in the hall. To do this it was necessary to turn up the gas. He did so, and in his confusion turned it out!

Where were the matches? He remembered that there was a bronze Something on the table that, in the irony of modern decorative taste, might hold ashes or matches, or anything of an unpicturesque character. He knocked something over, evidently the ink, something else—this time a champagne glass. Becoming reckless and now groping at random in the ruins, he overturned the bronze

Mercury on the centre table, and then sat down hopelessly in his chair. And then a pair of velvet fingers slid into his with the matches, and this audible, musical statement—

"It is a match you are seeking? Here is of tnem."

Thatcher flushed, embarrassed, nervous—feeling the ridiculousness of saying "Thank you" to a dark Somebody—struck the match, beheld by its brief, uncertain glimmer, Carmen de Haro beside him, burned his fingers, coughed, dropped the match, and was cast again into outer darkness.

"Let me try!"

Carmen struck a match, jumped briskly on the chair, lit the gas, jumped lightly down again and said—"You do like to sit in the dark—eh? So am I—sometimes, alone."

"Miss de Haro," said Thatcher, with sudden, honest earnestness, advancing with outstretched hands, "believe me, I am sincerely delighted, overjoyed again to meet"——

She had, however, quickly retreated as he approached, esconcing herself behind the high back of a large antique chair, on the cushion of which she knelt. I regret to add also that she slapped his outstretched fingers a little sharply with her inevitable black fan as he still advanced.

"We are not in California. It is Washington. It is after midnight. I am a poor girl, and I have to lose—what you call—'a character.' You shall sit over there,' she pointed to the sofa, "and I shall sit here," she rested her boyish head on the top of the chair, "and we shall talk, for I have to speak to you—Don Royal."

Thatcher took the seat indicated, contritely, humbly, submissively. Carmen's little heart was touched. But she still went on over the back of the chair.

"Don Royal," she said, emphasising each word with her an at him, "before I saw you—ever knew of you—I was a child. Yes, I was but a child! I was a bold, bad child —and I was what you call a—a—'forgaire!'"

"A what?" asked Thatcher, hesitating between a smile and a sigh.

"A forgaire!" continued Carmen demurely. "I did of myself write the names of ozzer peoples," when Carmen was excited she lost the control of the English tongue, "I did write just to please myself—it was my onkle that did make of it money—you understand, eh? Shall you not speak? Must I again hit you?"

"Go on," said Thatcher, laughing.

"I did find out, when I came to you at the Mine, that I had forged against you the name of Micheltorena. I to the lawyer went, and found that it was so—of a verity— so! so! all the time. Look at me not now, Don Royal— it is a 'forgaire' you stare at!"

"Carmen!"

"Hoosh! Shall I have to hit you again? I did over-look all the papers. I found the application; it was written by me. There."

She tossed over the back of her chair an envelope to Thatcher. He opened it.

"I see," he said gently, "you repossessed yourself of it!"

"What is that—'r-r-r-e—possess?'"

"Why!" Thatcher hesitated—"You got possession of this paper—this innocent forgery—again."

"Oh! You think me a thief as well as a 'forgaire.' Go away! Get up. Get out."

"My dear girl"——

"Look at the paper! Will you? Oh, you Silly!"

Thatcher looked at the paper. In paper, handwriting, age and stamp it was identical with the formal, clerical application of Garcia for the grant. The indorsement of

Micheltorena was unquestionably genuine. *But the appli-cation was made for Royal Thatcher.* And his own signa-ture was imitated to the life.

"I had but one letter of yours wiz your name," said Carmen apologetically—"and it was the best poor me could do."

"Why, you blessed little goose and angel," said Thatcher, with the bold, mixed metaphor of amatory genius, "don't you see "——

"Ah, you don't like it—it is not good?"

"My darling!"

"Hoosh! There is also an old cat upstairs. And now I have, here, a character. *Will* you sit down? Is it of a necessity that up and down you should walk and awaken the whole house. There!" she had given him a vicious dab with her fan as he passed. He sat down.

"And you have not seen me nor written to me for a year?"

"Carmen!"

"Sit down, you bold, bad boy. Don't you see it is of business that you and I talk down here, and it is of business that ozzer people upstairs are thinking. Eh?"

"D—n business! See here, Carmen, my darling, tell me "—I regret to say he had by this time got hold of the back of Carmen's chair—"tell me, my own little girl—about—about that Senator. You remember what you said to him?"

"Oh, the old man? Oh, *that* was business. And you say of business d—n."

"Carmen!"

"Don Royal!"

. . . . . .

Although Miss Carmen had recourse to her fan fre-quently during this interview, the air must have been chilly

For, a moment later, on his way downstairs, poor Harlowe, a sufferer from bronchitis, was attacked with a violent fit of coughing, which troubled him all the way down.

"Well," he said, as he entered the room, " I see you have found Mr. Thatcher and shown those papers. I trust you have, for you've certainly had time enough. I am sent by mother to dismiss you all to bed."

Carmen, still in the arm-chair, covered with her *mantilla*, did not speak.

"I suppose you are by this time lawyer enough to know," continued Harlowe, "that Miss De Haro's papers, though ingenious, are not legally available, unless "——

"I chose to make her a witness. Harlowe! you're a good fellow! I don't mind saying to you that these are papers I prefer that my *wife* should not use. We'll leave it for the present—Unfinished Business."

They did. But one evening our hero brought Mrs. Royal Thatcher a paper containing a touching and beautiful tribute to the dead Senator.

"There, Carmen, love, read that. Don't you feel a little ashamed of your—your—your lobbying "——

"No," said Carmen promptly. "It was business—and, if all lobbying business was as honest—well ? "——

# Thankful Blossom:

A ROMANCE OF THE JERSEYS.

(1779.)

## PART I.

THE time was the year of grace 1779; the locality, Morristown, New Jersey.

It was bitterly cold. A north-easterly wind had been
stiffening the mud of the morning's thaw into a rigid record
of that day's wayfaring on the Baskingridge road. The
hoof prints of cavalry, the deep ruts left by baggage waggons,
and the deeper channels worn by artillery lay stark and
cold in the waning light of an April day. There were
icicles on the fences, a rime of silver on the windward bark
of maples, and occasional bare spots on the rocky protuber-
ances of the road, as if nature had worn herself out at the
knees and elbows through long waiting for the tardy spring.
A few leaves, disinterred by the thaw, became crisp again,
and rustled in the wind, making the summer a thing so
remote that all human hope and conjecture fled before
them.

Here and there the wayside fences and walls were broken
down or dismantled, and beyond them fields of snow, down-
trodden and discoloured and strewn with fragments of
leather, camp equipage, harness, and cast-off clothing,
showed traces of the recent encampment and congregation
of men. On some there were still standing the ruins of

rudely-constructed cabins, or the semblance of fortifications equally rude and incomplete. A fox stealing along a half-filled ditch, a wolf slinking behind an earthwork, typified the human abandonment and desolation.

One by one the faint sunset tints faded from the sky, the far-off crests of the Orange hills grew darker, the nearer files of pines on the Whatnong mountain became a mere black background, and with the coming on of night, came, too, an icy silence that seemed to stiffen and arrest the very wind itself; the crisp leaves no longer rustled, the waving whips of alder and willow snapped no longer, the icicles no longer dropped a cold fruitage from barren branch and spray, and the roadside trees relapsed into stony quiet. So that the sound of horse's hoofs breaking through the thin, dull, lustreless films of ice that patched the furrowed road might have been heard by the nearest Continental picket a mile away.

Either a knowledge of this or the difficulties of the road evidently irritated the viewless horseman. Long before he became visible his voice was heard in half-suppressed objurgation of the road, of his beast, of the country folk, and the country generally. "Steady, you jade!" "Jump, you devil, jump!" "Curse the road and the beggarly farmers that durst not mend it." And then the moving bulk of horse and rider suddenly arose above the hill, floundered and splashed, and then as suddenly disappeared, and the rattling hoof beats ceased.

The stranger had turned into a deserted lane, still cushioned with untrodden snow. A stone wall on one hand —in better keeping and condition than the boundary monuments of the outlying fields—bespoke protection and exclusiveness. Half-way up the lane the rider checked his speed, and dismounting, tied his horse to a wayside sapling. This done he went cautiously forward toward the end of the lane, and a farmhouse from whose gable window a light twinkled through the deepening night. Suddenly he stopped, hesitated, and uttered an impatient ejaculation. The light had disappeared. He turned sharply on his heel, and retraced his steps until opposite a farm-shed that stood a few paces from the wall. Hard by a large elm cast the gaunt shadow of its leafless limbs on the wall and surrounding snow. The stranger stepped into this shadow, and at once seemed to become a part of its trembling intricacies.

At the present moment it was certainly a bleak place for a tryst. There was snow yet clinging to the trunk of the tree, and a film of ice on its bark ; the adjacent wall was slippery with frost and fringed with icicles. Yet in all there was a ludicrous suggestion of some sentiment past and unseasonable—several dislodged stones of the wall were so disposed as to form a bench and seats, and under the elm tree's film of ice could still be seen carved on its bark the effigy of a heart, divers initials, and the legend, " Thine for ever."

The stranger, however, kept his eyes fixed only on the farm-shed, and the open field beside it. Five minutes passed in fruitless expectancy. Ten minutes ! And then the rising moon slowly lifted herself over the black range of the Orange hills, and looked at him, blushing a little, as if the appointment were her own.

The face and figure thus illuminated was that of a strongly-built, handsome man of thirty, so soldierly in bearing that it needed not the buff epaulets and facings to show his captain's rank in the Continental army. Yet there was something in his facial expression that contradicted the manliness of his presence—an irritation and querulousness, that were inconsistent with his size and strength. This fretfulness increased as the moments went by without sign or motion in the faintly lit field beyond.

until, in peevish exasperation, he began to kick the nearer stones against the wall.

" Moo-oo-w ! "

The soldier started. Not that he was frightened, nor that he had failed to recognise in these prolonged syllables the deep-chested, half-drowsy low of a cow, but that it was so near him—evidently just beside the wall. If an object so bulky could have approached him so near without his knowledge, might not she——

" Moo-oo ! "

He drew near the wall cautiously. " So, Cushy ! Mooly ! " " Come up, Bossy ! " he said persuasively. " Moo—" but here the low unexpectedly broke down, and ended in a very human and rather musical little laugh.

" Thankful ! " exclaimed the soldier, echoing the laugh a trifle uneasily and affectedly as a hooded little head arose above the wall.

" Well," replied the figure supporting a prettily-rounded chin on her hands, as she laid her elbows complacently on the wall. " Well, what did you expect ? Did you want me to stand here all night while you skulked moonstruck under a tree ? or did you look for me to call you by name ; did you expect me to shout out Captain Allan Brewster ? "

" Thankful, hush ! "

" Captain Allan Brewster of the Connecticut Contingent," continued the girl with an affected raising of a low pathetic voice that was, however, inaudible beyond the tree. " Captain Brewster, behold me—your obleeged and humble servant, and sweetheart to command."

Captain Brewster succeeded, after a slight skirmish at the wall, in possessing himself of the girl's hand. At which, although still struggling, she relented slightly.

" It isn't every lad that I'd low for," she said, with an affected pout, " and there may be others that would not take it amiss. Though there be fine ladies enough at the Assembly balls at Morristown as might think it hoydenish."

"Nonsense, love," said the Captain, who had by this time mounted the wall and encircled the girl's waist with his arm. "Nonsense! you startled me only. But," he added, suddenly taking her round chin in his hand and turning her face toward the moon, with an uneasy half suspicion, "why did you take that light from the window! What has happened?"

"We had unexpected guests, sweetheart," said Thankful; "the Count just arrived."

"That infernal Hessian!" He stopped and gazed questioningly into her face. The moon looked upon her at the same time—the face was as sweet, as placid, as truthful as her own. Possibly these two inconstants understood each other.

"Nay, Allan, he is not a Hessian; but an exiled gentleman from abroad. A nobleman"——

"There are no noblemen, now," sniffed the trooper contemptuously. "Congress has so decreed it. All men are born free and equal."

"But they are not, Allan," said Thankful, with a pretty trouble in her brows. "Even cows are not born equal. Is yon calf that was dropped last night by Brindle the equal of my red heifer whose mother came by herself in a ship from Surrey? Do they look equal?"

"Titles are but breath," said Captain Brewster doggedly. There was an ominous pause.

"Nay, there is one nobleman left," said Thankful, "and he is my own—my nature's nobleman."

Captain Brewster did not reply. From certain arched gestures and wreathed smiles with which this forward young woman accompanied her statement, it would seem to be implied that the gentleman who stood before her was the nobleman alluded to. At least he so accepted it, and embraced her closely, her arms and part of her mantle clinging around his neck. In this attitude they remained quiet for some moments, slightly rocking from side to side, like a metronome—a movement, I fancy, peculiarly bucolic, pastoral, and idyllic, and as such, I wot, observed by Theocritus and Virgil.

At these supreme moments weak woman usually keeps her wits about her much better than your superior reasoning masculine animal, and while the gallant Captain was losing himself upon her perfect lips, Miss Thankful distinctly heard the farm gate click, and otherwise noticed that the moon was getting high and obtrusive. She half-released herself from the Captain's arms, thoughtfully and tenderly, but firmly. "Tell me all about yourself, Allan dear," she said quietly, making room for him on the wall, "all, everything."

She turned upon him her beautiful eyes ; eyes habitually earnest and even grave in expression, yet holding in their brave brown depths a sweet, child-like reliance and dependency ; eyes with a certain tender deprecating droop in the brown fringed lid, and yet eyes that seemed to say to every man that looked upon them, "I am truthful, be frank with me." Indeed, I am convinced there is not one of my impressible sex, who, looking in those pleading eyes, would not have perjured himself on the spot rather than have disappointed their fair owner.

Captain Brewster's mouth resumed its old expression of discontent.

"Everything is growing worse, Thankful, and the cause is lost. Congress does nothing, and Washington is not the man for the crisis. Instead of marching to Philadelphia and forcing that wretched rabble of Hancock and Adams at the point of the bayonet, he writes letters."

"A dignified, formal old fool," interrupted Mistress Thankful indignantly; "and look at his wife! Didn't Mistress Ford and Mistress Baily—ay, and the best blood of Morris county—go down to his Excellency's in their finest bibs and tuckers; and didn't they find my lady in a pinafore doing chores? Vastly polite treatment, indeed. As if the whole world didn't know that the General was taken by surprise when my Lady came riding up from Virginia with all those fine cavaliers, just to see what his Excellency was doing at these Assembly balls. And fine doings, I dare say."

"This is but idle gossip, Thankful," said Captain Brewster, with the faintest appearance of self-consciousness; "the Assembly balls are conceived by the General to strengthen the confidence of the townsfolk, and mitigate the rigours of the winter encampment. I go there myself rarely. I have but little taste for junketting and gaviotting with my country in such need. No, Thankful! what we want is a leader! And the men of Connecticut feel it keenly. If I have been spoken of in that regard," added the Captain, with a slight inflation of his manly breast, "it is because they know of my sacrifices—because as New England yeomen they know my devotion to the cause. They know of my suffering"——

The bright face that looked into his was suddenly afire with womanly sympathy, the pretty brow was knit, the sweet eyes overflowed with tenderness. "Forgive me, Allan. I forgot—perhaps, love—perhaps, dearest, you are hungry now."

"No, not now," replied Captain Brewster, with gloomy stoicism; "yet," he added, "it is nearly a week since I have tasted meat."

"I—I—brought a few things with me," continued the girl, with a certain hesitating timidity. She reached down and produced a basket from the shadow of the wall. "These chickens,"—she held up a pair of pullets—"the Commander-in-Chief himself could not buy. I kept them for *my* Commander! And this pot of marmalade, which I know my Allan loves, is the same I put up last summer. I thought (very tenderly) you might like a piece of that bacon you liked so once, dear. Ah, sweetheart, shall we ever sit down to our little board? Shall we ever see the end of this awful war? Don't you think, dear (very pleadingly), it would be best to give it up? King George is not such a very bad man, is he? I've thought, sweetheart (very confidently), that mayhap, you and he might make it all up without the aid of those Washingtons, who do nothing but starve one to death. And if the King only knew you, Allan—should see you as I do, sweetheart—he'd do just as you say."

During this speech she handed him the several articles alluded to, and he received them, storing them away in such receptacles of his clothing as were convenient. With this notable difference; that with *her* the act was graceful and picturesque ; with him there was a ludicrousness of suggestion that his broad shoulders and uniform only heightened.

"I think not of myself, lass," he said, putting the eggs in his pocket, and buttoning the chickens within his martial breast. "I think not of myself, and perhaps I often spare that counsel which is but little heeded. But I have a duty to my men—to Connecticut. (He here tied the marmalade up in his handkerchief.) I confess I have sometimes thought I might, under provocation, be driven to extreme measures for the good of the cause. I make no pretence to leadership, but "——

"With you at the head of the army," broke in Thankful enthusiastically, "peace would be declared within a fortnight! "

There is no flattery, however outrageous, that a man will not accept from the woman whom he believes loves him. He will, perhaps, doubt its influence in the colder judgment of mankind, but he will consider that this poor creature, at least, understands him, and in some vague way represents the eternal but unrecognised verities. And when this is voiced by lips that are young, and warm, and red, it is somehow quite as convincing as the bloodless, remoter utterance of posterity.

Wherefore the trooper complacently buttoned the compliment over his chest with the pullets.

"I think you must go now, Allan," she said, looking at him with that pseudo-maternal air which the youngest of women sometimes assume to their lovers, as if the doll had suddenly changed sex and grown to man's estate. "You must go now, dear—for it may so chance that father is considering my absence over much. You will come again a' Wednesday, sweetheart, and you will not go to the assemblies, nor visit Mistress Judith, nor take any girl pick-a-back again on your black horse, and you will let me know when you are hungry?"

She turned her brown eyes lovingly, yet with a certain pretty trouble in the brow, and such a searching, pleading inquiry in her glance that the Captain kissed her at once. Then came the final embrace, performed by the Captain in a half-perfunctory quiet manner, with a due regard for the friable nature of part of his provisions. Satisfying himself of the integrity of the eggs by feeling for them in his pocket, he waved a military salute with the other hand to Miss Thankful, and was gone. A few minutes later the sound of his horse's hoofs rang sharply from the icy hill-side.

But as he reached the summit, two horsemen wheeled suddenly from the shadow of the roadside, and bade him halt.

" Captain Brewster—if this moon does not deceive me ? " queried the foremost stranger with grave civility.

" The same. Major Van Zandt, I calculate ? " returned Brewster querulously.

"Your calculation is quite right. I regret, Captain Brewster, that it is my duty to inform you that you are under arrest."

" By whose orders ? "

" The Commander-in-Chief's."

" For what ? "

" Mutinous conduct, and disrespect of your superior officers."

The sword that Captain Brewster had drawn at the sudden appearance of the strangers quivered for a moment in his strong hand. Then, sharply striking it across the pommel of his saddle, he snapped it in twain, and cast the pieces at the feet of the speaker.

" Go on," he said doggedly.

" Captain Brewster," said Major Van Zandt, with infinite gravity, " it is not for me to point out the danger to you of this outspoken emotion, except, practically, in its effect upon the rations you have in your pocket. If I mistake not, they have suffered equally with your steel. Forward, march ! "

Captain Brewster looked down and then dropped to the rear, as the discased yolks of Mistress Thankful's most precious gift slid slowly and pensively over his horse's flanks to the ground.

## PART II.

MISTRESS THANKFUL remained at the wall until her lover had disappeared. Then she turned, a mere lissom shadow in that uncertain light, and glided under the eaves of the shed, and thence from tree to tree of the orchard, lingering a moment under each as a trout lingers in the shadow of the bank in passing a shallow, and so reached the farm-house and the kitchen door, where she entered. Thence by a back staircase she slipped to her own bower, from whose window half an hour before she had taken the signalling light. This she lit again and placed upon a chest of drawers, and taking off her hood and a shapeless, sleeveless mantle she had worn, went to the mirror and proceeded to readjust a high horn comb that had been somewhat displaced by the Captain's arm, and otherwise, after the fashion of her sex, to remove all traces of a pre-vious lover. It may be here observed that a man is very apt to come from the smallest encounter with his Dulcinea, *distrait*, bored, or shamefaced—to forget that his cravat is awry, or that a long blonde hair is adhering to his button. But as to *Mademoiselle*—well, looking at Miss Pussy's sleek paws and spotless face, would you ever know that she had been at the cream jug?

Thankful was, I think, satisfied with her appearance. Small doubt but she had reason for it. And yet her gown was a mere slip of flowered chintz, gathered at the neck, and falling at an angle of fifteen degrees to within an inch of a short petticoat of grey flannel. But so surely is the complete mould of symmetry indicated in the poise or line of any single member, that, looking at the erect carriage of her graceful brown head, or below to the curves that were lost in her shapely ankles, or the little feet that hid themselves in the broad-buckled shoes, you knew that the rest was as genuine and beautiful.

Mistress Thankful, after a pause, opened the door and listened. Then she softly slipped down the back staircase to the front hall. It was dark, but the door of the "company room" or parlour was faintly indicated by the light that streamed beneath it. She stood still for a moment, hesitatingly, when suddenly a hand grasped her own, and half led, half dragged her into the sitting-room opposite. It was dark. There was a momentary fumbling for the tinder-box and flint, a muttered oath over one or two impeding articles of furniture, and Thankful laughed. And then the light was lit, and her father, a grey, wrinkled man of sixty, still holding her hand, stood before her.

"You have been out, Mistress?"

"I have," said Thankful.

"And not alone," growled the old man angrily.

"No," said Mistress Thankful, with a smile that began in the corners of her brown eyes, ran down into the dimpled curves of her mouth, and finally ended in the sudden revelation of her white teeth ; "no, not alone."

"With whom?" asked the old man, gradually weakening under her strong, saucy presence.

"Well, father," said Thankful, taking a seat on a table, and swinging her little feet somewhat ostentatiously toward him, "I was with Captain Allan Brewster of the Connecticut Contingent."

"That man?"

"That man!"

"I forbid you seeing him again."

Thankful gripped the table with a hand on each side of her, to emphasise the statement, and swinging her feet, replied—

"I shall see him as often as I like, father!"

"Thankful Blossom!"

"Abner Blossom!"

"I see you know not," said Mr. Blossom, abandoning the severely paternal mandatory air for one of confidential disclosure, "I see you know not his reputation. He is accused of inciting his regiment to revolt—of being a traitor to the cause."

"And since when, Abner Blossom, have *you* felt such concern for the cause? Since you refused to sell supplies to the Continental commissary, except at double profits? Since you told me you were glad I had not politics like Mistress Ford"——

"Hush!" said the father, motioning to the parlour.

"Hush!" echoed Thankful indignantly, "I won't be hushed! Everybody says 'hush' to me. The Count says 'hush!' Allan says 'hush!' You say 'hush!' I'm aweary of this hushing. Ah, if there was a man who didn't say it to me!" and Mistress Thankful lifted her fine eyes to the ceiling.

"You are unwise, Thankful; foolish, indiscreet. That is why you require much monition."

Thankful swung her feet in silence for a few moments, then suddenly leaped from the table, and seizing the old man by the lappels of his coat, fixed her eyes upon him, and said, suspiciously—

"Why did you keep me from going into the company room? Why did you bring me in here?"

Blossom senior was staggered for a moment. "Because, you know, the Count"——

"And you were afraid the Count should know I had a sweetheart? Well—I'll go in and tell him now," she said, marching toward the door.

"Then why did you not tell him when you slipped out an hour ago? Eh, lass?" queried the old man, grasping her hand. "But 'tis all one, Thankful—'twas not for him I stopped you. There is a young spark with him—ay, came even as you left, lass—a likely young gallant, and he and the Count are jabbering away in their own lingo—a kind of Italian, belike—eh, Thankful?"

"I know not," she said thoughtfully. "Which way came the other?" In fact, a fear that this young stranger might have witnessed the Captain's embrace, began to creep over her.

"From town, my lass."

Thankful turned to her father as if she had been waiting a reply to a long-asked question. "Well?"

"Were it not well to put on a few furbelows and a tucker?" queried the old man. "'Tis a gallant young spark; none of your country folk."

"No," said Thankful, with the promptness of a woman who was looking her best, and knew it. And the old man, looking at her, accepted her judgment, and without another word led her to the parlour door, and opening it, said briefly, "My daughter, Mistress Thankful Blossom."

With the opening of the door came the sound of earnest voices that instantly ceased upon the appearance of Mistress Thankful. Two gentlemen lolling before the fire arose instantly, and one came forward with an air of familiar yet respectful recognition.

"Nay, this is far too great happiness, Mistress Thankful," he said, with a strongly-marked foreign accent and a still more strongly-marked foreign manner. "I have been in despair, and my friend here, the Baron Pomposo, likewise."

The slightest trace of a smile and the swiftest of reproachful glances lit up the dark face of the Baron as he bowed low in the introduction. Thankful dropped the courtesy of the period—*i.e.*, a duck, with semi-circular sweep of the right foot forward. But the right foot was so pretty and the grace of the little figure so perfect, that the Baron raised his eyes from the foot to the face in serious admiration. In the one rapid feminine glance she had given him she had seen that he was handsome; in the second, which she could not help from his protracted silence, she saw that his beauty centred in his girlish, half fawn-like, dark eyes.

"The Baron," explained Mr. Blossom, rubbing his hands together, as if, through mere friction, he was trying to impart a warmth to the reception which his hard face discountenanced, "the Baron visits us under discouragement. He comes from far countries. It is the custom of gentle folk of—of—foreign extraction to wander through strange lands, commenting upon the habits and doings of the peoples. He will find in Jersey," continued Mr. Blossom, appealing to Thankful, yet really evading her contemptuous glance, "a hard-working yeomanry, ever ready to welcome the stranger, and account to him penny for penny, for all his necessary expenditure. For which purpose, in these troublous times, he will provide for himself gold or other moneys not affected by these local disturbances."

"He will find, good friend Blossom," said the Baron, in a rapid, voluble way, utterly at variance with the soft, quiet gravity of his eyes, "Beauty, Grace, Accom—plishment, and—eh—Santa Maria! what shall I say?" He turned appealingly to the Count.

"Virtue," nodded the Count.

"Truly, Birtoo! all in the fair lady of thees countries. Ah, believe me, honest friend Blossom, there is mooch more in thees than in thoss!"

So much of this speech was addressed to Mistress Thankful that she had to show at least one dimple in reply, albeit her brows were slightly knit, and she had turned upon the speaker her honest questioning eyes.

"And then the General Washington has been kind enough to offer his protection," added the Count.

"Any fool—any one," supplemented Thankful hastily, with a slight blush, "may have the General's pass—ay, and his good word. But what of Mistress Prudence Bookstaver? She that has a sweetheart in Knyphausen's Brigade —ay, I warrant a Hessian, but of gentle blood, as Mistress Prudence has often told me ; and look you, all her letters stopped by the General—ay, I warrant read by my Lady Washington, too—as if 'twere *her* fault that her lad was in arms against Congress. Riddle me that, now?"

" 'Tis but prudence, lass," said Blossom, frowning on the girl. "'Tis that she might disclose some movement of the army tending to defeat the enemy."

"And why should she not try to save her lad from capture or ambuscade, such as befell the Hessian commissary with the provisions that you "——

Mr. Blossom, in an ostensible fatherly embrace, managed to pinch Mistress Thankful sharply. "Hush, lass," he said, with simulated playfulness; "your tongue clacks like the Whippany mill. My daughter has small concern—'tis the manner of women folk—in politics," he explained to his guests. "These dangersome days have given her sore affliction, by way of parting comrades of her childhood and others whom she has much affected. It has in some sort soured her."

Mr. Blossom would have recalled this speech as soon as it escaped him, lest it should lead to a revelation from the truthful Mistress Thankful of her relations with the Continental Captain. But to his astonishment, and I may add, to my own, she showed nothing of that disposition she had exhibited a few moments before. On the contrary, she blushed slightly, and said nothing.

And then the conversation changed—upon the, weather,

the hard winter, the prospects of the cause, a criticism upon the Commander-in-Chief's management of affairs, the attitude of Congress, &c., &c., between Mr. Blossom and the Count, characterised, I hardly need say, by that positiveness of opinion that distinguishes the unprofessional. In another part of the room it so chanced that Mistress Thankful and the Baron were talking about themselves, the Assembly balls, who was the prettiest woman in Morristown, and whether General Washington's attentions to Mistress Pyne were only perfunctory gallantry or what, and if Lady Washington's hair was really gray, and if that young aide-de-camp Major Van Zandt were really in love with Lady W., or whether his attentions were only the zeal of a subaltern. In the midst of which a sudden gust of wind shook the house, and Mr. Blossom, going to the front door, came back with the announcement that it was snowing heavily.

And indeed, within that past hour, to their astonished eyes the whole face of nature had changed. The moon was gone, the sky hidden in a blinding, whirling swarm of stinging flakes. The wind, bitter and strong, had already fashioned white, feathery drifts upon the threshold, over the painted benches on the porch, and against the door posts.

Mistress Thankful and the Baron had walked to the rear door—the Baron with a slight, tropical shudder—to view this meteorological change. As Mistress Thankful looked over the snowy landscape, it seemed to her that all record of her past experience had been effaced—her very footprints of an hour before were lost—the gray wall on which she leaned was white and spotless now; even the familiar farm-shed looked dim and strange and ghostly. Had she been there—had she seen the Captain—was it all a fancy? She scarcely knew.

A sudden gust of wind closed the door behind them with

a crash, and sent Mistress Thankful, with a slight feminine scream, forward into the outer darkness. But the Baron caught her by the waist, and saved her from Heaven knows what imaginable disaster, and the scene ended in a half hysterical laugh. But the wind then set upon them both with a malevolent fury, and the Baron was, I presume, obliged to draw her closer to his side.

They were alone—save for the presence of those mischievous confederates, Nature and Opportunity. In the half obscurity of the storm she could not help turning her mischievous eyes on his ; but she was perhaps surprised to find them luminous, soft, and as it seemed to her at that moment, grave beyond the occasion. An embarrassment utterly new and singular seized upon her, and when, as she half feared yet half expected, he bent down and pressed his lips to hers, she was for a moment powerless ; but in the next instant she boxed his ears sharply and vanished in the darkness. When Mr. Blossom opened the door to the Baron he was surprised to find that gentleman alone, and still more surprised to find, when they re-entered the house, to see Mistress Thankful enter at the same moment, demurely, from the front door.

When Mr. Blossom knocked at his daughter's door the next morning it opened upon her completely dressed, but withal somewhat pale, and if the truth must be told, a little surly.

"And you were stirring so early, Thankful," he said ; "'twould have been but decent to have bidden Godspeed to the guests—especially the Baron, who seemed much concerned at your absence."

Miss Thankful blushed slightly, but answered with savage celerity, "And since when is it necessary that I should dance attendance upon every foreign jack-in-the-box that may lie at the house ? "

" He has shown great courtesy to you, mistress—and is a gentleman."

" Courtesy, indeed ! " said Mistress Thankful.

" He has not presumed ? " said Mr. Blossom suddenly, bringing his cold, gray eyes to bear upon his daughter's.

" No, no," said Thankful hurriedly, flaming a bright scarlet; "but—nothing.  But what have you there—a letter ? "

" Ay—from the Captain, I warrant ! " said Mr. Blossom, handing her a three-cornered bit of paper ; " 'twas left here by a camp-follower.  Thankful," he continued, with a meaning glance, " you will heed my counsel in season. The Captain is not meet for such as you."

Thankful suddenly grew pale and contemptuous again as she snatched the letter from his hand.  When his retiring footsteps were lost on the stairs, she regained her colour and opened the letter.  It was slovenly written, grievously misspelled, and read as follows :—

" SWEETHEART,—A tyranous Act, begotten in Envy and Jealousie, keeps me here a prisoner.  Last night I was Basely arrested by Servile Hands for that Freedom of Thought and Expression for which I have already Sacrifized so much—aye all that Man hath but Love and Honour. But the End is Near.  When for the Maintenance of Power, the Liberties of the Peoples are subdued by Martial Supremacy and the Dictates of Ambition the State is Lost. I lie in vile Bondage here in Morristown under charge of Disrespeck—me that a twelvemonth past left a home and Respectable Connexions to serve my Country.   Believe me still your own Love, albeit in the Power of Tyrants and condemned it may be to the scaffold.

" The Messenger is Trustworthy and will speed safely to me such as you may deliver unto him.   The Provender sanktified by your Hands and made precious by yr. Love was wrested from me by Servil Hands and the Eggs, Sweetheart, were somewhat Addled. The Bacon is, me-thinks, by this time on the Table of the Com$^r$-in-chief. Such is Tyranny and Ambition. Sweetheart, farewell for the present.                     ALLAN."

Mistress Thankful read this composition once, twice, and then tore it up. Then, reflecting that it was the first letter of her lover's that she had not kept, she tried to put together again the torn fragments, but vainly—and then in a pet, new to her, cast them from the window. During the rest of the day she was considerably *distraite,* and even manifested more temper than she was wont to do, and later, when her father rode away on his daily visit to Morristown, she felt strangely relieved. By noon the snow ceased, or rather turned into a driving sleet that again in turn gave way to rain. By this time she became absorbed in her household duties—in which she was usually skilful—and in her own thoughts that to-day had a novelty in their meaning. In the midst of this, at about dark, her room being in rear of the house, she was perhaps unmindful of the trampling of horse without, or the sound of voices in the hall below. Neither were uncommon at that time. Although protected by the Continental army, from forage or the rudeness of soldiery, the Blossom farm had always been a halting place for passing troopers, commissary team-sters, and reconnoitring officers. General Sullivan and Colonel Hamilton had watered their horses at its broad substantial wayside trough, and sat in the shade of its porch. Mistress Thankful was only awakened from her day dream by the entrance of the negro farm hand, Cæsar.

"Fo' God, Missy Thankful, them sogers is g'wine into camp in the road, I reckon, for they's jest makin' they seves free afo' the house, and they's an officer in the company room with his spurs cocked on the table, readin' a book."

A quick flame leaped into Thankful's cheek, and her pretty brows knit themselves over darkening eyes. She arose from her work—no longer the moody girl, but an indignant goddess, and pushing the servant aside, swept down the stairs and threw open the door.

An officer, sitting by the fire in an easy, lounging attitude that justified the servant's criticism, arose instantly, with an air of evident embarrassment and surprise that was, however, as quickly dominated and controlled by a gentleman's breeding.

" I beg your pardon," he said, with a deep inclination of his handsome head, " but I had no idea that there was any member of this household at home—at least a lady." He hesitated a moment, catching in the raising of her brown-fringed lids a sudden revelation of her beauty, and partly losing his composure. " I am Major Van Zandt ; I have the honour of addressing "——

" Thankful Blossom," said Thankful, a little proudly, divining with a woman's swift instinct the cause of the Major's hesitation. But her triumph was checked by a new embarrassment, visible in the face of the officer at the mention of her name.

" Thankful Blossom," repeated the officer quickly. "You are then the daughter of Abner Blossom ? "

" Certainly," said Thankful, turning her inquiring eyes upon him ; " he will be here betimes. He has gone only to Morristown." In a new fear that had taken possession of her, her questioning eyes asked, " Has he not ? "

The officer answering her eyes rather than her lips, came toward her gravely. " He will not return to-day, Mistress Thankful, nor perhaps even to-morrow. He is—a prisoner.'

Thankful opened her brown eyes aggressively on the Major. "A prisoner—for what?"

"For aiding and giving comfort to the enemy, and for harbouring spies," replied the Major, with military curtness.

Mistress Thankful's cheek flushed slightly at the last sentence; a recollection of the scene on the porch and the Baron's stolen kiss flashed across her, and for a moment she looked as guilty as if the man before her had been a witness to the deed. He saw it, and misinterpreted her confusion.

"Belike, then," said Mistress Thankful, slightly raising her voice, and standing squarely before the Major, "Belike, then, *I* should be a prisoner, too, for the guests of this house, if they be spies, were *my* guests, and as my father's daughter, I was their hostess. Ay, man, and right glad to be the hostess of such gallant gentlemen. Gentlemen, I warrant, too fine to insult a defenceless girl—gentlemen spies that did not cock their boots on the table or turn an honest farmer's house into a tap-room."

An expression of half pain, half amusement covered the face of the Major, but he made no other reply than by a profound and graceful bow. Courteous and deprecatory as it was, it apparently exasperated Mistress Thankful only the more.

"And pray who are these spies, and who is the informer?" said Mistress Thankful, facing the soldier, with one hand truculently placed on her flexible hip, and the other slipped behind her. "Methinks 'tis only honest we should know when and how we have entertained both."

"Your father, Mistress Thankful," said Major Van Zandt gravely, "has long been suspected of favouring the enemy; but it has been the policy of the Commander-in-Chief to overlook the political preferences of non-com-batants, and to strive to win their allegiance to the good

cause by liberal privileges. But when it was lately discovered that two strangers, although bearing a pass from
him, have been frequenters of this house under fictitious
names "——

"You mean Count Ferdinand and the Baron Pomposo,"
said Thankful quickly; "two honest gentlefolk, and if
they choose to pay their devoirs to a lass—although,
perhaps, not a quality lady, yet an honest girl "——

"Dear Mistress Thankful," said the Major, with a profound bow and smile that, spite of its courtesy, drove
Thankful to the verge of wrathful hysterics, "if you
establish that fact—and from this slight acquaintance with
your charms, I doubt not you will—your father is safe from
further inquiry or detention. The Commander-in-Chief is
a gentleman who has never underrated the influence of
your sex, nor held himself averse to its fascinations."

"What is the name of this informer?" broke in Mistress
Thankful angrily. "Who is it that has dared "——

"It is but King's evidence, mayhap, Mistress Thankful,
for the informer is himself under arrest. It is on the
information of Captain Allan Brewster, of the Connecticut
Contingent."

Mistress Thankful whitened, then flushed, and then
whitened again. Then she stood up to the Major.

"It's a lie—a cowardly lie!"

Major Van Zandt bowed. Mistress Thankful flew upstairs, and in another moment swept back again into the
room in riding hat and habit.

"I suppose I can go and see—my father," she said,
without lifting her eyes to the officer.

"You are free as air, Mistress Thankful. My orders
and instructions, far from implicating you in your father's
offences, do not even suggest your existence. Let me help
you to your horse."

The girl did not reply. During that brief interval, how-ever, Cæsar had saddled her white mare and brought it to the door. Mistress Thankful, disdaining the offered hand of the Major, sprang to the saddle.

The Major still held the reins, "One moment, Mistress Thankful."

"Let me go," she said, with suppressed passion.

"One moment, I beg."

His hand still held the bridle-rein. The mare reared, nearly upsetting her. Crimson with rage and mortification, she raised her riding-whip and laid it smartly over the face of the man before her.

He dropped the rein instantly. Then he raised to her a face, calm and colourless but for a red line extending from his eyebrow to his chin, and said quietly—

"I had no desire to detain you. I only wished to say that when you see General Washington I know you will be just enough to tell him that Major Van Zandt knew nothing of your wrongs, or even your presence here, until you pre-sented them, and that since then he has treated you as became an officer and gentleman."

Yet even as he spoke she was gone. At the moment that her fluttering skirt swept in a furious gallop down the hill-side, the Major turned and re-entered the house. The few lounging troopers who were witnesses of the scene prudently turned their eyes from the white face and blazing eyes of their officer as he strode by them. Nevertheless, when the door closed behind him, contemporary criticism broke out—

"'Tis a Tory jade, vexed that she cannot befool the Major as she has the Captain," muttered Sergeant Tibbitts.

"And going to try her tricks on the General," added Private Hicks.

Howbeit, both these critics may have been wrong. For

as Mistress Thankful thundered down the Morristown road she thought of many things. She thought of her sweetheart, Allan, a prisoner, and pining for *her* help and *her* solicitude, and yet—how dared he—if he *had* really betrayed or misjudged her! And then she thought bitterly of the Count and the Baron—and burned to face the latter, and in some vague way charge the stolen kiss upon him as the cause of all her shame and mortification. And, lastly she thought of her father, and began to hate everybody. But, above all, and through all, in her vague fears for her father, in her passionate indignation against the Baron, in her fretful impatience of Allan, one thing was ever dominant and obtrusive—one thing she tried to put away, but could not—the handsome, colourless face of Major Van Zandt with the red welt of her riding-whip overlying its cold outlines.

## PART III.

THE rising wind, which had ridden much faster than Mistress Thankful, had increased to a gale by the time it reached Morristown. It swept through the leafless maples, and rattled the dry bones of the elms. It whistled through the quiet Presbyterian churchyard, as if trying to arouse the sleepers it had known in days gone by. It shook the blank, lustreless windows of the Assembly Rooms over the Freemasons' Tavern, and wrought in their gusty curtains moving shadows of those amply-petticoated dames and tightly-hosed cavaliers who had swung in "Sir Roger," or jigged in "Money Musk" the night before.

But, I fancy, it was around the isolated "Ford Mansion," better known as the "Head-quarters," that the wind wreaked its grotesque rage. It howled under its scant eaves, it sang under its bleak porch, it tweaked the peak

**of** its front gable, it whistled through every chink and
cranny of its square, solid, unpicturesque structure. Situ-
ated on a hill-side that descended rapidly to the Whippany
river, every summer zephyr that whispered through the
porches of the Morristown farmhouses, charged as a stiff
breeze upon the swinging half-doors and windows of the
"Ford Mansion," every wintry wind became a gale that
threatened its security. The sentry who paced before its
front porch knew from experience when to linger under its
lee and adjust his threadbare outer coat to the bitter north
wind.

Within the house something of this cheerlessness prevailed. It had an ascetic gloom, which the scant firelight
of the reception-room, and the dying embers on the dining-
room hearth failed to dissipate. The central hall was
broad, and furnished plainly with a few rush-bottomed
chairs, on one of which half dozed a black body servant of
the Commander-in-Chief. Two officers in the dining-room,
drawn close by the chimney corner, chatted in undertones,
as if mindful that the door of the drawing-room was open,
and their voices might break in upon its sacred privacy.
The swinging light in the hall partly illuminated, or rather
glanced gloomily from the black, polished furniture, the
lustreless chairs, the quaint cabinet, the silent spinnet, the
skeleton-legged centre table, and finally, upon the motionless figure of a man seated by the fire.

It was a figure, since so well-known to the civilised
world, since so celebrated in print and painting as to need
no description here. Its rare combination of gentle dignity
with profound force—of a set resoluteness of purpose with
a philosophical patience have been so frequently delivered
to a people not particularly remarkable for these qualities,
that I fear it has too often provoked a spirit of playful
aggression, in which the deeper underlying meaning was

forgotten. So let me add that in manner, physical equi-
poise, and even in the mere details of dress, this figure
indicated a certain aristocratic exclusiveness. It was the
presentment of a King—a King who, by the irony of circumstances was just then waging war against all kingship:
a ruler of men who just then was fighting for the right
of these men to govern themselves, but whom, by his
own inherent right, he dominated. From the crown of his
powdered head to the silver buckle of his shoe, he was so
royal that it was not strange that his brother, George of
England and Hanover—ruling by accident, otherwise
impiously known as the "Grace of God"—could find no
better way of resisting his power than by calling him "Mr.
Washington."

The sound of horses' hoofs, the formal challenge of
sentry, the grave questioning of the officer of the guard,
followed by footsteps upon the porch, did not apparently
disturb his meditation. Nor did the opening of the outer
door and a charge of cold air into the hall that invaded
even the privacy of the reception-room and brightened the
dying embers on the hearth, stir his calm pre-occupation.
But an instant later there was the distinct rustle of a feminine skirt in the hall, a hurried whispering of men's voices,
and then the sudden apparition of a smooth, fresh-faced
young officer over the shoulder of the unconscious figure.

"I beg your pardon, General," said the officer doubtingly, "but "——

"You are not intruding, Colonel Hamilton," said the
General quietly.

"There is a young lady without who wishes an audience
of your Excellency; 'tis Mistress Thankful Blossom, the
daughter of Abner Blossom—charged with treasonous practice and favouring the enemy—now in the guard-house at
Morristown."

"Thankful Blossom?" repeated the General interrogatively.

"Your Excellency, doubtless, remembers a little provincial beauty and a famous toast of the country side—the Cressida of our Morristown epic, who led our gallant Connecticut Captain astray"——

"You have the advantages, besides the better memory of a younger man, Colonel," said Washington, with a playful smile that slightly reddened the cheek of his aide-de-camp. "Yet I think I *have* heard of this phenomenon. By all means admit her—and her escort."

"She is alone, General," responded the subordinate.

"Then the more reason why we should be polite," returned Washington, for the first time altering his easy posture, rising to his feet, and lightly grasping his ruffled hands before him. "We must not keep her waiting. Give her access, my dear Colonel, at once. And—even as she came—*alone.*"

The aide-de-camp bowed and withdrew. In another moment the half-opened door swung wide to Mistress Thankful Blossom.

She was so beautiful in her simple riding dress, so quaint and original in that very beauty, and, above all, so teeming with a certain vital earnestness of purpose, just positive and audacious enough to set off that beauty, that the grave gentleman before her did not content himself with the usual formal inclination of courtesy, but actually advanced, and taking her cold little hand in his, graciously led her to the chair he had just vacated.

"Even if your name were not known to me, Mistress Thankful," said the Commander-in-Chief, looking down upon her with grave politeness, "nature has, methinks, spared you the necessity of any introduction to the courtesy of a gentleman. But how can I especially serve you?"

Alack! the blaze of Mistress Thankful's brown eyes had become somewhat dimmed in the grave half-lights of the room, in the graver, deeper dignity of the erect, soldier-like figure before her. The bright colour, born of the tempest within and without, had somehow faded from her cheek; the sauciness begotten from bullying her horse in the last half hour's rapid ride, was so subdued by the actual presence of the man she had come to bully, that I fear she had to use all her self-control to keep down her inclination to whimper and to keep back the tears that, oddly enough, rose to her sweet eyes as she lifted them to the quietly-critical yet placid glance of her interlocutor.

"I can readily conceive the motive of this visit, Miss Thankful," continued Washington, with a certain dignified kindliness that was more reassuring than the formal gallantry of the period, "and it is, I protest, to your credit. A father's welfare—however erring and weak that father may be—is most seemly in a maiden."

Thankful's eyes flashed again as she rose to her feet. Her upper lip, that had a moment before trembled in a pretty infantine distress, now stiffened and curled as she confronted the dignified figure before her. "It is not of my father I would speak," she said saucily, "I did not ride here alone to-night, in the weather, to talk of *him;* I warrant *he* can speak for himself. I came here to speak of myself—of lies—ay, *lies*, told of me, a poor girl—ay, of cowardly gossip about me and my sweetheart, Captain Brewster, now confined in prison, because he hath loved me, a lass without politics or adherence to the cause—as if 'twere necessary every lad should ask the confidence or permission of yourself or, belike, my Lady Washington in his preferences."

She paused a moment, out of breath. With a woman's quickness of intuition she saw the change in Washington's face—saw a certain cold severity overshadowing it. With a woman's fateful persistency—a persistency which I humbly suggest might on occasion be honourably copied by our more politic sex—she went on to say what was in her, even if she were obliged, with a woman's honourable inconsistency, to unsay it an hour or two later—an inconsistency which I also humbly protest might be as honourably imitated by us—on occasion.

"It has been said," said Thankful Blossom quickly, "that my father has given entertainment knowingly to two spies—two spies that, begging your Excellency's pardon, and the pardon of Congress, I know only as two honourable gentlemen, who have as honourably tendered me their affections. It is said, and basely and most falsely too, that my sweetheart, Captain Allan Brewster, has lodged this information. I have ridden here to deny it. I have ridden here to demand of you that an honest woman's reputation shall not be sacrificed to the interests of politics. That a prying mob of ragamuffins shall not be sent to an honest farmer's house to spy and spy—and turn a poor girl out of doors that they might do it. 'Tis shameful—so it is—there! 'Tis most scandalous—so it is—there now. Spies indeed—what are *they*, pray?"

In the indignation which the recollection of her wrongs had slowly gathered in her, from the beginning of this speech, she had advanced her face, rosy with courage, and beautiful in its impertinence, within a few inches of the dignified features and quiet grey eyes of the great commander. To her utter stupefaction, he bent his head and kissed her, with a grave benignity, full on the centre of her audacious forehead.

"Be seated, I beg, Mistress Blossom," he said, taking her cold hand in his, and quietly replacing her in the unoccupied chair. "Be seated, I beg, and give me, if you

can, your attention for a moment. The officer entrusted
with the ungracious task of occupying your father's house
is a member of my military family and a gentleman. If he
has so far forgotten himself—if he has so far disgraced himself and me as "——

"No! no!" uttered Thankful, with feverish alacrity,
"the gentleman was most considerate! On the contrary—
mayhap—I,"—— she hesitated, and then came to a full
stop, with a heightened colour, as a vivid recollection of
that gentleman's face, with the mark of her riding whip
lying across it, rose before her.

"I was about to say that Major Van Zandt, as a gentleman, has known how to fully excuse the natural impulses
of a daughter," continued Washington, with a look of perfect understanding, " but let me now satisfy you on another
point, where, it would seem, we greatly differ."

He walked to the door and summoned his servant, to
whom he gave an order. In another moment the fresh-
faced young officer, who had at first admitted her, reappeared with a file of official papers. He glanced slyly
at Thankful Blossom's face with an amused look, as if he
had already heard the colloquy between her and his
superior officer, and had appreciated that which neither of
the earnest actors in the scene had themselves felt—a certain sense of humour in the situation.

Howbeit, standing before them, Colonel Hamilton gravely
turned over the file of papers. Thankful bit her lips in
embarrassment. A slight feeling of awe and a presentiment of some fast-coming shame ; a new and strange consciousness of herself, her surroundings, of the dignity of
the two men before her, an uneasy feeling of the presence
of two ladies who had in some mysterious way entered the
room from another door, and who seemed to be intently
regarding her from afar with a curiosity as if she were some

strange animal, and a wild premonition that her whole future life and happiness depended upon the events of the next few moments, so took possession of her that the brave girl trembled for a moment in her isolation and loneliness. In another instant, Colonel Hamilton speaking to his superior, but looking obviously at one of the ladies who had entered, handed a paper to Washington, and said, " Here are the charges."

" Read them," said the General coldly.

Colonel Hamilton with a manifest consciousness of another hearer than Mistress Blossom and his General, read the paper. It was couched in phrases of military and legal precision, and related briefly that upon the certain and personal knowledge of the writer, Abner Blossom of the "Blossom Farm," was in the habit of entertaining two gentlemen, namely, the "Count Ferdinand" and the "Baron Pomposo," suspected enemies of the cause, and possible traitors to the Continental Army. It was signed by Allan Brewster, late Captain in the Connecticut Contingent. As Colonel Hamilton exhibited the sig- nature, Thankful Blossom had no difficulty in recognising the familiar bad hand, and equally familiar misspelling of her lover.

She rose to her feet. With eyes that showed her present trouble and perplexity as frankly as they had a moment before blazed with her indignation, she met, one by one, the glances of the group who now seemed to be closing round her. Yet with a woman's instinct she felt, I am constrained to say, more unfriendliness in the silent presence of the two women than in the possible outspoken criticism of our much abused sex.

" Of course," said a voice, which Thankful at once, by a woman's unerring instinct, recognised as the elder of the two ladies, and the legitimate keeper of the conscience of some one of the men who were present, "of course Mistress Thankful will be able to elect which of her lovers among her country's enemies she will be able to cling to for support in her present emergency. She does not seem to have been so special in her favours as to have positively excluded any one."

"At least, dear Lady Washington, she will not give it to the man who has proven a traitor to *her,*" said the younger woman impulsively. That is—I beg your lady-ship's pardon"—she hesitated, observing in the dead silence that ensued that the two superior male beings present looked at each other in lofty astonishment.

"He that is trait'rous to his country," said Lady Washington coldly, "is apt to be trait'rous elsewhere."

"'Twere as honest to say that he that was trait'rous to his King, was trait'rous to his country," said Mistress Thankful, with sudden audacity, bending her knit brows on Lady Washington. But that lady turned dignifiedly away, and Mistress Thankful again faced the General.

"I ask your pardon," she said proudly, "for troubling you with my wrongs. But it seems to me that even if another and a greater wrong were done me by my sweetheart, through jealousy, it would not justify this accusation against me, even though," she added, darting a wicked glance at the placid brocaded back of Lady Washington, "even though that accusation came from one who knows that jealousy may belong to the wife of a patriot as well as a traitor." She was herself again, after this speech, although her face was white with the blow she had taken and returned.

Colonel Hamilton passed his hand across his mouth and coughed slightly. General Washington standing by the fire with an impassive face turned to Thankful gravely—

"You are forgetting, Mistress Thankful, that you have

not told me how I can serve you. It cannot be that you are still concerned in Captain Brewster, who has given evidence against your other——*friends,* and tacitly against *you.* Nor can it be on their account, for I regret to say they are still free and unknown. If you come with any information exculpating them, and showing they are not spies or hostile to the cause, your father's release shall be certain and speedy. Let me ask you a single question. Why do you believe them honest ? "

" Because," said Mistress Thankful, " they were—were— gentlemen."

" Many spies have been of excellent family, good address, and fair talents," said Washington gravely ; " but you have, mayhap, some other reason."

" Because they talked only to ME," said Mistress Thankful, blushing mightily ; " because they preferred my company to father's—because "—— she hesitated a moment—" because they spoke not of politics, but—of—that which lads mainly talk of—and—and,"—— here she broke down a little ; " and the Baron I only saw once, but he "—— here she broke down utterly—" I know they weren't spies—there now ! "

" I must ask you something more," said Washington, with grave kindness ; " whether you give me the information or not, you will consider that if what you believe is true, it cannot in any way injure the gentlemen you speak of, while, on the other hand, it may relieve your father of suspicion. Will you give to Colonel Hamilton, my secretary, a full description of them ? That fuller description which Captain Brewster, for reasons best known to yourself, was unable to give."

Mistress Thankful hesitated for a moment, and then, with one of her truthful glances at the Commander-in-Chief, began a detailed account of the outward semblance of the

Count. Why she began with him I am unable to say, but possibly, it was because it was easier, for when she came to describe the Baron, she was, I regret to say, somewhat vague and figurative. Not so vague, however, but that Colonel Hamilton suddenly started up with a look at his chief, who instantly checked it with a gesture of his ruffled hand.

" I thank you, Mistress Thankful," he said, quite impassively, " but did this other gentleman, this Baron "——

"Pomposo," said Thankful proudly. A titter originated in the group of ladies by the window, and became visible on the fresh face of Colonel Hamilton, but the dignified colour of Washington's countenance was unmoved.

" May I ask if the Baron made an honourable tender of his affections to you," he continued, with respectful gravity —" if his attentions were known to your father, and were such as honest Mistress Blossom could receive ? "

" Father introduced him to me, and wanted me to be kind to him. He—he kissed me, and I slapped his face," said Thankful quickly, with cheeks as red, I warrant, as the Baron's might have been.

The moment the words had escaped her truthful lips she would have given her life to recall them. To her astonishment, however, Colonel Hamilton laughed outright, and the ladies turned and approached her, but were checked by a slight gesture from the otherwise impassive figure of the General.

"It is possible, Mistress Thankful," he resumed, with undisturbed composure, "that one, at least, of these gentlemen may be known to us, and that your instincts may be correct. At least rest assured that we shall fully inquire into it, and that your father shall have the benefit of that inquiry."

" I thank your Excellency," said Thankful, still reddening under the contemplation of her own late frankness and retreating towards the door, "I—think—I—must—go—now. It is late, and I have far to ride."

To her surprise, however, Washington stepped forward, and again taking her hands in his, said with a grave smile, "For that very reason, if for none other, you must be our guest to-night, Mistress Thankful Blossom. We still retain our Virginian ideas of hospitality, and are tyrannous enough to make strangers conform to them, even though we have but perchance the poorest of entertainment to offer them. Lady Washington will not permit Mistress Thankful Blossom to leave her roof to-night until she has partaken of her courtesy as well as her counsel."

"Mistress Thankful Blossom will make us believe that she has, at least, in so far trusted our desire to serve her justly by accepting our poor hospitality for a single night," said Lady Washington, with a stately courtesy.

Thankful Blossom still stood irresolutely at the door. But the next moment a pair of youthful arms encircled her, and the younger gentlewoman, looking into her brown eyes, with an honest frankness equal to her own, said, caressingly, "Dear Mistress Thankful, though I am but a guest in her ladyship's house, let me, I pray you, add my voice to hers. I am Mistress Schuyler of Albany, at your service, Mistress Thankful, as Colonel Hamilton here will bear me witness, did I need any interpreter to your honest heart. Believe me, dear Mistress Thankful, I sympathise with you, and only beg you to give me an opportunity to-night to serve you. You will stay, I know, and you will stay with me, and we shall talk over the faithlessness of that over-jealous Yankee Captain who has proved himself, I doubt not, as unworthy of *you* as he is of his country."

Hateful to Thankful as was the idea of being commiserated, she nevertheless could not resist the gentle courtesy and gracious sympathy of Miss Schuyler. Besides, it must be confessed that for the first time in her life she felt a doubt of the power of her own independence, and a strange fascination for this young gentlewoman whose arms were around her, who could so thoroughly sympathise with her, and yet allow herself to be snubbed by Lady Washington !

"You have a mother, I doubt not?" said Thankful, raising her questioning eyes to Miss Schuyler.

Irrelevant as this question seemed to the two young gentlemen, Miss Schuyler answered it with feminine intuition. "And you, dear Mistress Thankful "——

"Have none," said Thankful ; and here, I regret to say, she whimpered slightly, at which Miss Schuyler, with tears in her own fine eyes, bent her head suddenly to Thankful's ear, put her arm about the waist of the pretty stranger, and then, to the astonishment of Colonel Hamilton, quietly swept her out of the august presence.

When the door had closed upon them, Colonel Hamilton turned half-smilingly, half-inquiringly to his chief. Washington returned his glance kindly, but gravely, and then said quietly—

"If your suspicions jump with mine, Colonel, I need not remind you that it is a matter so delicate that it would be as well if you locked it in your own breast for the present. At least that you should not intimate to the gentleman whom you may have suspected aught that has passed this evening."

"As you will, General," said the subaltern respectfully ; "but may I ask," he hesitated, "if you believe that anything more than a passing fancy for a pretty girl "——

"When I asked your silence, Colonel," interrupted Washington kindly, laying his hand upon the shoulders of the younger man, "it was because I thought the matter sufficiently momentous to claim my own private and especial attention."

"I ask your Excellency's pardon," said the young man, reddening through his fresh complexion like a girl; "I only meant "——

"That you would ask to be relieved to-night," interrupted Washington, with a benign smile, "forasmuch as you wished the more to show entertainment to our dear friend, Miss Schuyler, and her guest. A wayward girl, Colonel, but, methinks, an honest one. Treat her of your own quality, Colonel, but discreetly, and not too kindly; lest we have Mistress Schuyler, another injured damsel, on our hands," and with a half playful gesture, peculiar to the man, and yet not inconsistent with his dignity, he half led, half pushed his youthful secretary from the room.

When the door had closed upon the Colonel, Lady Washington rustled toward her husband, who stood still, quiet, and passive on the hearth-stone.

"You surely see in this escapade nothing of political intrigue—no treachery?" she said hastily.

"No," said Washington quietly.

"Nothing more than idle, wanton intrigue with a foolish, vain country girl?"

"Pardon me, my lady," said Washington gravely. "I doubt not we may misjudge her. 'Tis no common rustic lass that can thus stir the country side. 'Twere an insult to your sex to believe it. It is not yet sure that she has not captured even so high game as she has named. If she has, it would add another interest to a treaty of comity and alliance."

"That creature!" said Lady Washington—"that light o' love with her Connecticut Captain lover? Pardon me, but this is preposterous," and with a stiff courtesy, she swept from the room, leaving the central figure of history—as such central figures usually are apt to be left—alone.

Later in the evening, Mistress Schuyler so far subdued the tears and emotions of Thankful that she was enabled to dry her eyes and rearrange her brown hair in the quaint little mirror in Mistress Schuyler's chamber, Mistress Schuyler herself lending a touch and suggestion here and there after the secret freemasonry of her sex.    " You are well rid of this forsworn Captain, dear Mistress Thankful, and methinks that with hair as beautiful as yours, the new style of wearing it—though a modish frivolity—is most becoming.    I assure you, ' tis much affected in New York and Philadelphia— drawn straight back from the forehead, after this manner, as you see."

The result was that in an hour later Mistress Schuyler and Mistress Blossom presented themselves to Colonel Hamilton in the reception-room with a certain freshness and elabor- ation of toilet that not only quite shamed the young officer's *affairé* negligence, but caused him to open his eyes in as- tonishment.    " Perhaps she would rather be alone, that she might indulge her grief," he said doubtingly, in an aside to Miss Schuyler, " rather than appear in company."

" Nonsense," quoth Mistress Schuyler.    " Is a young woman to mope and sigh because her lover proves false ? "

" But her father is a prisoner," said Hamilton in amaze- ment.

" Can you look me in the face," said Mistress Schuyler mischievously, " and tell me that you don't know that in twenty-four hours her father will be cleared of these charges ? Nonsense !  Do you think I have no eyes in my head ? Do you think I misread the General's face and your own ? "

" But, my dear girl," said the officer in alarm.

" Oh, I told her so—but not *why*," responded Miss Schuyler, with a wicked look in her dark eyes, " though I had warrant enough to do so to serve you for keeping a secret from *me !* "

And with this Parthian shot she returned to Mistress Thankful, who, with her face pressed against the window, was looking out on the moonlight slope beside the Whippany river.

For by one of those freaks peculiar to the American springtide the weather had again marvellously changed. The rain had ceased, and the ground was covered with an icing of sleet and snow, that now glittered under a clear sky and a brilliant moon. The north-east wind that shook the loose sashes of the windows had transformed each dripping tree and shrub to icy stalactites that silvered under the moon's cold touch.

"'Tis a beautiful sight, ladies," said a bluff, hearty, middle-aged man, joining the group by the window; "but God send the spring to us quickly, and spare us any more such cruel changes. My lady moon looks fine enough, glittering in yonder tree tops, but I doubt not she looks down upon many a poor fellow shivering under his tattered blankets in the camp beyond. Had ye seen the Connecticut tattarde-malions file by last night, with arms reversed, showing their teeth at his Excellency and yet not daring to bite—had ye watched these fainthearts, these doubting Thomases, ripe for rebellion against his Excellency, against the cause, but chiefly against the weather, ye would pray for a thaw that would melt the hearts of these men as it would these stubborn fields around us. Two weeks more of such weather would raise up not one Allan Brewster, but a dozen such malcontent puppies ripe for a drum-head court-martial."

"Yet 'tis a fine night, General Sullivan," said Colonel Hamilton, sharply nudging the ribs of his superior officer with his elbow, "there would be little trouble on such a night, I fancy, to track our ghostly visitant." Both of the ladies becoming interested, and Colonel Hamilton having thus adroitly turned the flank of his superior officer, he went on : " You should know that the camp, and indeed the whole locality here, is said to be haunted by the apparition of a gray-coated figure, whose face is muffled and hidden in his collar, but who has the password pat to his lips, and whose identity hath baffled the sentries.  This figure, it is said, forasmuch as it has been seen just before an assault, an attack, or some tribulation of the army, is believed by many to be the genius or guardian spirit of the cause, and, as such, has incited sentries and guards to greater vigilance, and has to some seemed a premonition of disaster.  Before the last outbreak of the Connecticut Militia, Master Graycoat haunted the outskirts of the weather-beaten and bedraggled camp, and, I doubt not, saw much of that preparation that sent that regiment of faint-hearted onion-gatherers to flaunt their woes and their wrongs in the face of the General himself."  Here Colonel Hamilton, in turn, received a slight nudge from Mistress Schuyler, and ended his speech somewhat abruptly.

Mistress Thankful was not unmindful of both these allusions to her faithless lover, but only a consciousness of mortification and wounded pride was awakened by them. In fact, during the first tempest of her indignation at his arrest, still later at the arrest of her father, and finally at the discovery of his perfidy to her, she had forgotten that he was her lover ; she had forgotten her previous tenderness toward him ; and now that her fire and indignation were spent, only a sense of numbness and vacancy remained. All that had gone before seemed not something to be regretted as her own act, but rather as the act of another Thankful Blossom, who had been lost that night in the snow-storm ; she felt she had become within the last twenty-four hours not perhaps *another* woman, but for the first time a *woman*.

Yet it was singular that she felt more confused when a

few moments later, the conversation turned upon Major
Van Zandt ; it was still more singular that she even felt
considerably frightened at that confusion.   Finally she
found herself listening with alternate irritability, shame, and
curiosity to praises of that gentleman, of his courage, his
devotion, and his personal graces.   For one wild moment
Thankful felt like throwing herself on the breast of Mistress
Schuyler and confessing her rudeness to the Major, but a
conviction that Mistress Schuyler would share that secret
with Colonel Hamilton, that Major Van Zandt might not
like that revelation, and oddly enough associated with this,
a feeling of unconquerable irritability toward that handsome
and gentle young officer, kept her mouth closed.   "Besides,"
she said to herself, "he ought to know, if he is such a fine
gentleman as they say, just how I was feeling, and that I
didn't mean any rudeness to him," and with this unanswerable feminine logic, poor Thankful, to some extent, stilled
her own honest little heart.

But not, I fear, entirely ; the night was a restless one to
her ; like all impulsive natures the season of reflection and
perhaps distrust came to her upon acts that were already
committed, and when reason seemed to light the way only
to despair.   She saw the folly of her intrusion at the head-
quarters, as she thought, only when it was too late to
remedy it ; she saw the gracelessness and discourtesy of
her conduct to Major Van Zandt only when distance and
time rendered an apology weak and ineffectual.   I think
she cried a little to herself, lying in the strange gloomy
chamber of the healthfully sleeping Mistress Schuyler, the
sweet security of whose manifest goodness and kindness
she alternately hated and envied, and at last, unable to
stand it longer, slipped noiselessly from her bed and stood
very wretched and disconsolate before the window that
looked out upon the slope towards the Whippany river.

The moon on the new-fallen, frigid, and untrodden snow shone brightly. Far to the left it glittered on the bayonet of a sentry pacing beside the river bank, and gave a sense of security to the girl that perhaps strengthened another idea that had grown up in her mind. Since she could not sleep why should she not ramble about until she could? She had been accustomed to roam about the farm in all weathers and at all times and seasons. She recalled to herself the night—a tempestuous one—when she had risen in serious concern as to the lying-in of her favourite Alderney heifer, and how she had saved the life of the calf, a weakling, dropped apparently from the clouds in the tempest, as it lay beside the barn. With this in her mind she donned her dress again, and with Mistress Schuyler's mantle over her shoulders noiselessly crept down the narrow staircase, passed the sleeping servant on the settee, and opening the rear door, in another moment was inhaling the crisp air and tripping down the crisp snow of the hill-side.

But Mistress Thankful had overlooked one difference between her own farm and a military encampment. She had not proceeded a dozen yards before a figure apparently started out of the ground beneath her, and levelling a bayonetted musket across her path called, "Halt!"

The hot blood mounted to the girl's cheek at the first imperative command she had ever received in her life; nevertheless she halted unconsciously, and without a word confronted the challenger with her old audacity.

"Who goes there?" reiterated the sentry, still keeping his bayonet level with her breast.

"Thankful Blossom," she responded promptly.

The sentry brought his musket to a "present." "Pass, Thankful Blossom, and God send it soon, and the spring with it, and good-night," he said, with a strong Milesian accent. And before the still amazed girl could comprehend the meaning of his abrupt challenge, or his equally abrupt departure, he had resumed his monotonous pace in the moonlight. Indeed, as she stood looking after him, the whole episode, the odd unreality of the moonlit landscape, the novelty of her position, the morbid play of her thoughts seemed to make it part of a dream which the morning light might dissipate but could never fully explain.

With something of this feeling still upon her, she kept her way to the river. Its banks were still fringed with ice, through which its dark current flowed noiselessly. She knew it flowed through the camp where lay her faithless lover, and for an instant indulged the thought of following it and facing him with the proof of his guilt; but even at the thought she recoiled with a new and sudden doubt in herself, and stood dreamily watching the shimmer of the moon on the icy banks, until another and it seemed to her equally unreal vision suddenly stayed her feet, and drove the blood from her feverish cheeks.

A figure was slowly approaching from the direction of the sleeping encampment. Tall, erect, and habited in a gray surtout, with a hood partially concealing its face, it was the counterfeit presentment of the ghostly visitant she had heard described. Thankful scarcely breathed. The brave little heart that had not quailed before the sentry's levelled musket a moment before, now faltered and stood still as the phantom, with a slow and majestic tread, moved toward her. She had only time to gain the shelter of a tree before the figure, majestically unconscious of her presence, passed slowly by. Through all her terror Thankful was still true to a certain rustic habit of practical perception to observe that the tread of the phantom was quite audible over the crust of snow, and was visible and palpable as the imprint of a military boot!

The blood came back to Thankful's cheek, and with it

her old audacity. In another instant she was out from the tree, and tracking with a light feline tread the appari-tion that now loomed up the hill before her. Slipping from tree to tree, she followed until it paused before the door of a low hut or farm-shed that stood midway up the hill. Here it entered, and the door closed behind it. With every sense feverishly alert, Thankful, from the secure advantage of a large maple, watched the door of the hut. In a few moments it re-opened to the same figure free of its gray enwrappings. Forgetful of everything now but detecting the face of the impostor, the fearless girl left the tree and placed herself directly in the path of the figure. At the same moment it turned toward her inquiringly, and the moonlight fell full upon the calm, composed features of General Washington.

In her consternation Thankful could only drop an embarrassed courtesy and hang out two lovely signals of distress on her cheeks. The face of the pseudo ghost alone remained unmoved.

"You are wandering late, Mistress Thankful," he said, at last, with a paternal gravity, "and I fear that the formal restraint of a military household has already given you some embarrassment. Yonder sentry, for instance, might have stopped you."

'Oh, he did!" said Thankful quickly; "but it's all right, please your Excellency. He asked me 'who went there,' and I told him, and he was vastly polite, I assure you."

The grave features of the Commander-in-Chief relaxed in a smile. "You are more happy than most of your sex in turning a verbal compliment to practical account. For know then, dear young lady, that in honour of your visit to the head-quarters, the pass-word to-night through this encampment was none other than your own pretty pat-ronymic—'Thankful Blossom.'"

The tears glittered in the girl's eyes, and her lip trembled. But with all her readiness of speech, she could only say, "Oh, your Excellency."

"Then you *did* pass the sentry?" continued Washington, looking at her intently with a certain grave watchfulness in his gray eyes. "And doubtless you wandered at the river bank. Although I myself, tempted by the night, sometimes extend my walk as far as yonder shed, it were a hazardous act for a young lady to pass beyond the protection of the line."

"Oh, I met no one, your Excellency," said the usually truthful Thankful hastily, rushing to her first lie with grateful impetuosity.

"And saw no one?" asked Washington quietly.

"No one," said Thankful, raising her brown eyes to the General's.

They both looked at each other—the naturally most veracious young woman in the colonies and the subsequent allegorical impersonation of Truth in America—and knew each other lied, and, I imagine, respected each other for it.

"I am glad to hear you say so, Mistress Thankful," said Washington quietly, "for 'twould have been natural for you to have sought an interview with your recreant lover in yonder camp, though the attempt would have been unwise and impossible."

"I had no such thought, your Excellency," said Thankful, who had really quite forgotten her late intention, "yet if with your permission I could hold a few moments' converse with Captain Brewster, it would greatly ease my mind."

"'Twould not be well for the present," said Washington thoughtfully. "But in a day or two Captain Brewster will be tried by court-martial at Morristown. It shall be so ordered that when he is conveyed thither his guard shall halt at the Blossom Farm. I will see that the officer in command gives you an opportunity to see him. And I think I can promise also, Mistress Thankful, that your father shall also be present under his own roof—a free man."

They had reached the entrance to the mansion and entered the hall. Thankful turned impulsively and kissed the extended hand of the Commander. "You are so good. I have been so foolish—so very, very wrong," she said, with a slight trembling of her lip. "And your Excellency believes my story, and those gentlemen were not spies, but even as they gave themselves to be."

"I said not that much," replied Washington, with a kindly smile, "but no matter. Tell me rather, Mistress Thankful, how far your acquaintance with these gentlemen has gone, or did it end with the box on the ear that you gave the Baron?"

"He had asked me to ride with him to the Baskingridge, and I—had said—yes," faltered Mistress Thankful.

"Unless I misjudge you, Mistress Thankful, you can, without such sacrifice, promise me that you will not see him until I give you my permission," said Washington, with grave playfulness.

The swinging light shone full in Thankful's truthful eyes as she lifted them to his.

"I do," she said quietly.

"Good-night," said the Commander, with a formal bow.

"Good-night, your Excellency."

## PART IV.

The sun was high over the Short Hills when Mistress Thankful, the next day, drew up her sweating mare beside the Blossom Farm gate. She had never looked prettier, she had never felt more embarrassed as she entered her own house. During her rapid ride she had already framed a speech of apology to Major Van Zandt, which, however, utterly fled from her lips as that officer showed himself respectfully on the threshold. Yet she permitted him to usurp the functions of the grinning Cæsar, and help her from her horse, albeit she was conscious of exhibiting the awkward timidity of a bashful rustic, until at last, with a stammering "Thank ye," she actually ran upstairs to hide her glowing face and far too conscious eyelids.

During the rest of that day Major Van Zandt quietly kept out of her way, without obtrusively seeming to avoid her. Yet when they met casually in the performance of her household duties, the innocent Mistress Thankful noticed, under her downcast, penitential eyelids, that the eyes of the officer followed her intently. And thereat she fell unconsciously to imitating him, and so they eyed each other furtively like cats, and rubbed themselves along the walls of rooms and passages when they met, lest they should seem designedly to come near each other, and enacted the gravest and most formal of genuflections, courtesies, and bows, when they accidentally *did* meet. And just at the close of the second day, as the elegant Major Van Zandt was feeling himself fast becoming a drivelling idiot and an awkward country booby, the arrival of a courier from head-quarters saved that gentleman his self-respect for ever.

Mistress Thankful was in her sitting-room when he

knocked at the door. She opened it in sudden, conscious trepidation.

"I ask pardon for intruding, Mistress Thankful Blossom," he said gravely, "but I have here"—he held out a pretentious document—"a letter for you from head-quarters. May I hope that it contains good news—the release of your father—and that it relieves you from my presence, and an *espionage* which I assure you cannot be more unpleasant to you than it has been to myself."

As he entered the room, Thankful had risen to her feet with the full intention of delivering to him her little set apology, but as he ended his speech she looked at him blandly—and burst out crying.

Of course he was in an instant at her side and holding her cold little hand. Then she managed to say, between her tears, that she had been wanting to make an apology to him; that she had wanted to say ever since she arrived that she had been rude, very rude, and that she knew he never could forgive her; that she had been trying to say hat she never could forget his gentle forbearance, "only," she added, suddenly raising her tear-fringed brown lids to the astonished man, "*you wouldn't ever let me !*"

"Dear Mistress Thankful," said the Major, in conscience-stricken horror, "if I have made myself distant to you, believe me it was only because I feared to intrude upon your sorrow. I really—dear Mistress Thankful—I "——

"When you took all the pains to go round the hall instead of through the dining-room lest I should ask you to forgive me," sobbed Mistress Thankful, "I thought— you—must—hate me, and preferred to "——

"Perhaps this letter may mitigate your sorrow, Mistress Thankful," said the officer, pointing to the letter she still held unconsciously in her hand.

With a blush at her pre-occupation, Thankful opened

the letter. It was a half-official document, and ran as
follows :—

"The Commander-in-Chief is glad to inform Mistress
Thankful Blossom that the charges preferred against her
father have, upon fair examination, been found groundless
and trivial. The Commander-in-Chief further begs to
inform Mistress Blossom that the gentleman known to her
under the name of the 'Baron Pomposo,' was his Excellency
Don Juan Morales, Ambassador and Envoy Extraordinary
of the Court of Spain, and that the gentleman known to
her as the 'Count Ferdinand,' was Señor Godoy, Secretary
to the Embassy. The Commander-in-Chief wishes to add,
that Mistress Thankful Blossom is relieved of any further
obligation of hospitality toward these honourable gentlemen, as the Commander-in-Chief regrets to record the
sudden and deeply-to-be-deplored death of his Excellency
this morning by typhoid fever, and the possible speedy
return of the Embassy.

"In conclusion, the Commander-in-Chief wishes to bear
testimony to the Truthfulness, Intuition, and Discretion of
Mistress Thankful Blossom.

"By order of his Excellency,

"General GEORGE WASHINGTON

"ALEX. HAMILTON, Secretary.

"To Mistress THANKFUL BLOSSOM, of Blossom Farm."

Thankful Blossom was silent for a few moments, and
then raised her abashed eyes to Major Van Zandt. A
single glance satisfied her that he knew nothing of the
imposture that had been practised upon her—knew nothing of the trap into which her vanity and self-will had led
her.

"Dear Mistress Thankful," said the Major, seeing the distress in her face. "I trust the news is not ill. Surely I gathered from the Sergeant that"——

"What?" said Thankful, looking at him intently.

"That in twenty-fours hours at furthest your father would be free, and that I should be relieved"——

"I know that you are aweary of your task, Major," said Thankful bitterly; "rejoice, then, to know your information is correct, and that my father is exonerated—unless—unless this is a forgery, and General Washington should turn out to be somebody else, and *you* should turn out to be somebody else"—and she stopped short and hid her wet eyes in the window curtains.

"Poor girl!" said Major Van Zandt to himself, "this trouble has undoubtedly frenzied her. Fool that I was, to lay up the insult of one that sorrow and excitement had bereft of reason and responsibility. 'Twere better I should retire at once and leave her to herself," and the young man slowly retreated toward the door.

But at this moment there were alarming symptoms of distress in the window curtain, and the Major paused as a voice from its dimity depths said plaintively, "And *you* are going without forgiving me!"

"Forgive *you*, Mistress Thankful," said the Major, striding to the curtain, and seizing a little hand that was obtruded from its folds, "forgive you; rather can you forgive me—for the folly—the cruelty of mistaking—of—of"——and here the Major, hitherto famous for facile compliments, utterly broke down. But the hand he held was no longer cold, but warm and intelligent, and in default of coherent speech he held fast by that as the thread of his discourse, until Mistress Thankful quietly withdrew it, thanked him for his forgiveness, and retired deeper behind the curtain.

When he had gone, she threw herself in a chair and again

gave way to a passionate flood of tears. In the last twenty-four hours her pride had been utterly humbled; the independent spirit of this self-willed little beauty had met for the first time with defeat. When she had got over her womanly shock at the news of the sham Baron's death, she had, I fear, only a selfish regret at his taking off—believing that if living he would in some way show the world, which just then consisted of the head-quarters and Major Van Zandt, that he had really made love to her, and possibly did honourably love her still, and might yet give her an opportunity to reject him. And now he was dead, and she was held up to the world as the conceited plaything of a fine gentleman's masquerading sport. That her father's cupidity and ambition made him sanction the imposture in her bitterness she never doubted. No! Lover, friend, father—all had been false to her, and the only kindness she had received was from the men she had wantonly insulted. Poor little Blossom! Indeed, a most premature Blossom; I fear a most unthankful Blossom, sitting there, shivering in the first chill wind of adversity, rocking backward and forward with the skirt of her dimity short gown over her shoulders, and her little buckled shoes and clocked stockings pathetically crossed before her.

But healthy youth is reactive, and in an hour or two Thankful was down at the cow-shed with her arms around the neck of her favourite heifer, to whom she poured out much of her woes, and from whom she won an intelligent sort of slobbering sympathy. And then she sharply scolded Cæsar for nothing at all, and a moment after returned to the house with the air and face of a deeply-injured angel, who had been disappointed in some celestial idea of setting this world right, but was still not above forgiveness. A spectacle that sunk Major Van Zandt into the dark depths of remorse, and eventually sent him to smoke a pipe of

Virginia with his men in the roadside camp.   Seeing which,
Thankful went early to bed and cried herself to sleep.
And Nature, possibly, followed her example, for at sunset a
great thaw set in, and by midnight the freed rivers and
brooks were gurgling melodiously, and tree, and shrub, and
fence were moist and dripping.

The red dawn at last struggled through the vaporous veil
that hid the landscape.   Then occurred one of those magi-
cal changes peculiar to the climate, yet perhaps pre-
eminently notable during that historic winter and spring.
By ten o'clock on that 3rd of May, 1780, a fervent June-like
sun had rent that vaporous veil, and poured its direct rays
upon the gaunt and haggard profile of the Jersey hills.
The chilled soil responded but feebly to that kiss ; perhaps
a few of the willows that yellowed the river banks took on
a deeper colour.   But the country folk were certain that
spring had come at last, and even the correct and self-
sustained Major Van Zandt came running in to announce
to Mistress Thankful that one of his men had seen a violet
in the meadow.   In another moment Mistress Thankful had
donned her cloak and pattens to view this firstling of the
laggard summer.   It was quite natural that Major Van
Zandt should accompany her as she tripped on, and so without a thought of their past differences, they ran like very
children down the moist and rocky slope that led to the
quaggy meadow.   Such was the influence of the vernal
season.

But the violets were hidden.   Mistress Thankful, regardless of the wet leaves and her new gown, groped with her
fingers among the withered grasses.   Major Van Zandt
leaned against a boulder and watched her with admiring
eyes.

"You'll never find flowers that way," she said at last,
looking up to him impatiently.   "Go down on your knees

like an honest man. There are some things in this world worth stooping for."

The Major instantly dropped on his knees beside her. But at that moment Mistress Thankful found her posies and rose to her feet. "Stay where you are," she said mischievously, as she stooped down and placed a flower in the lappel of his coat. "That is to make amends for my rudeness. Now, get up."

But the Major did not rise. He caught the two little hands that had seemed to flutter like birds against his breast, and, looking up into the laughing face above him, said, "Dear Mistress Thankful; dare I remind you of your own words that 'there be some things worth stooping for.' Think of my love, Mistress Thankful, as a flower—mayhap, not as gracious to you as your violets, but as honest and—and—and—as "——

"Ready to spring up in a single night," laughed Thankful. "But, no; get up, Major! What would the fine ladies of Morristown say of your kneeling at the feet of a country girl, the play and sport of every fine gentleman? What if Mistress Bolton should see her own cavalier, the modish Major Van Zandt, proffering his affections to the disgraced sweetheart of a perjured traitor? Leave go my hand, I pray you, Major—if you respect "——

She was free, yet she faltered a moment beside him, with tears quivering on her long brown lashes. Then she said, tremulously, "Rise up, Major. Let us think no more of this. I pray you forgive me, if I have again been rude."

The Major struggled to rise to his feet. But he could not. And then I regret to have to record that the fact became obvious that one of his shapely legs was in a bog-hole, and that he was perceptibly sinking out of sight. Whereat Mistress Thankful trilled out a three-syllabled laugh, looked demure and painfully concerned at his con-

dition, and then laughed again.   The Major joined in her
mirth, albeit his face was crimson.   And then, with a little cry
of alarm, she flew to his side, and put her arms around him.

"Keep away, keep away, for heaven's sake, Mistress
Blossom," he said quickly, "or I shall plunge you into
my mishap, and make you as ridiculous as myself."

But the quick-witted girl had already leaped to an
adjacent boulder.  "Take off your sash," she said quickly,
"fasten it to your belt, and throw it to me."  He did so.
She straightened herself back on the rock.  "Now, altogether," she cried, with a preliminary strain on the sash,
and then the cords of her well-trained muscles stood out
on her rounded arms, and with a long pull, and a strong
pull, and a pull all together, she landed the Major upon the
rock.   And then she laughed.   And then, inconsistent as
it may appear, she became grave, and at once proceeded to
scrape him off, and rub him down with dried leaves, with
fern twigs, with her handkerchief, with the border of her
mantle, as if he were a child, until he blushed with alternate shame and secret satisfaction.

They spoke but little on their return to the farmhouse,
for Mistress Thankful had again become grave.   And yet
the sun shone cheerily above them ; the landscape was filled
with the joy of resurrection and new and awakened life ;
the breeze whispered gentle promises of hope and the frui-
tion of their hopes in the summer to come.   And these two
fared on until they reached the porch with a half-pleased,
half-frightened consciousness that they were not the same
beings who had left it a half hour before.

Nevertheless, at the porch Mistress Thankful regained
something of her old audacity.   As they stood together in
the hall, she handed him back the sash she had kept with
her.   As she did so she could not help saying, "There are
some things worth stooping for, Major Van Zandt."

But she had not calculated upon the audacity of the man, and as she turned to fly she was caught by his strong arm and pinioned to his side. She struggled, honestly, I think, and perhaps more frightened at her own feelings than at his strength, but it is to be recorded that he kissed her in a moment of comparative yielding, and then, frightened himself, released her quickly, whereat she fled to her room, and threw herself, panting and troubled, upon her bed. For an hour or two she lay there, with flushed cheeks and conflicting thoughts. " He must never kiss me again," she said, softly to herself, "unless——" but the interrupting thought said, "I shall die if he kiss me not again; and I never can kiss another." And then she was roused by a footstep upon the stair—which, in that brief time, she had learned to know and look for—and a knock at the door. She opened it to Major Van Zandt, white and so colourless as to bring out once more the faint red line made by her riding whip two days before, as if it had risen again in accusation. The blood dropped out of her cheeks as she gazed at him in silence.

"An escort of dragoons," said Major Van Zandt, slowly and with military precision, "has just arrived, bringing with them one Captain Allan Brewster, of the Connecticut Contingent, on his way to Morristown to be tried for mutiny and treason. A private note from Colonel Hamilton instructs me to allow him to have a private audience with you—if *you* so wish it."

With a woman's swift and too often hopeless intuition, Thankful knew that this was not the sole contents of the letter, and that her relations with Captain Brewster were known to the man before her. But she drew herself up a little proudly, and turning her truthful eyes upon the Major, said, " I *do* so wish it."

" It shall be done as you desire, Mistress Blossom," returned the officer, with cold politeness, as he turned upon his heel.

"One moment, Major Van Zandt," said Thankful swiftly.

The Major turned quickly. But Thankful's eyes were gazing thoughtfully forward, and scarcely glanced at him. "I would prefer," she said timidly and hesitatingly, "that this interview should not take place under the roof where— where—where my father lives. Half way down the meadow there is a barn, and before it a broken part of the wall, fronting on a sycamore tree. *He* will know where it is. Tell him I will see him there in half an hour."

A smile, which the Major had tried to make a careless one, curled his lip satirically as he bowed in reply. "It is the first time," he said drily, "that I believe I have been honoured with arranging a tryst for two lovers, but believe me, Mistress Thankful, I will do my best. In half an hour I will turn my prisoner over to you."

In half an hour the punctual Mistress Thankful, with a hood hiding her pale face, passed the officer in the hall on the way to her rendezvous. An hour later, Cæsar came with a message that Mistress Thankful would like to see him. When the Major entered the sitting-room he was shocked to find her lying pale and motionless on the sofa, but as the door closed she rose to her feet and confronted him.

"I do not know," she said slowly, "whether you are aware that the man I just now parted from was, for a twelvemonth past, my sweetheart, and that I believed I loved him, and *knew* I was true to him. If you have not heard it I tell you now, for the time will come when you will hear part of it from the lips of others, and I would rather you should take the whole truth from mine. This man was false to me. He betrayed two friends of mine as spies. I could have forgiven it had it been only foolish jealousy, but it was, I have since learned from his own lips, only that he might gratify his spite against the Commander-in-Chief by procuring their arrest and making a serious difficulty in the American camp, by means of which he hoped to serve his own ends. He told me this, believing that I sympathised with him in his hatred of the Commander-in-Chief, and in his own wrongs and sufferings. I confess, to my shame, Major Van Zandt, that two days ago I did believe him, and that I looked upon you as a mere catch-poll or bailiff of the tyrant. That I found out how I was deceived when I saw the Commander-in-Chief, you, Major, who know him so well, need not be told. Nor was it necessary for me to tell this man that he had deceived me —for I felt—that—that—was—not—the—only reason— why I could no longer return—his love."

She paused, as the Major approached her earnestly, and waved him back with her hand. "He reproached me bitterly with my want of feeling for his misfortunes," she went on again; "he recalled my past protestations! he showed me my love letters—and he told me that if I were still his true sweetheart I ought to help him. I told him if he would never call me by that name again ; if he would give up all claim to me; if he would never speak, write to me, or see me again ; if he would hand me back my letters, I would help him." She stopped—the blood rushed into her pale face. "You will remember, Major, that I accepted this man's love as a young, foolish, trustful girl; but when I made him this offer—he—he—accepted it."

"The dog !" said Major Van Zandt. "But in what way could you help this double traitor?"

"I *have* helped him," said Thankful quietly.

"But how?" said Major Van Zandt.

"By becoming a traitor myself," she said, turning upon him almost fiercely. "Hear me ! While you were quietly pacing these halls, while your men were laughing and talking in the road, Cæsar was saddling my white mare, the fleetest in the country. He led her to the lane below. That mare is now two miles away, with Captain Brewster on her back. Why do you not start, Major? Look at me. *I* am a traitor, and this is my bribe," and she drew a package of letters from her bosom, and flung them on the table.

She had been prepared for an outbreak or exclamation from the man before her, but not for his cold silence. "Speak," she cried, at last, passionately, "speak. Open your lips if only to curse me! Order in your men to arrest me. I will proclaim myself guilty, and save your honour. But only speak!"

"May I ask," said Major Van Zandt coldly, "why you have twice honoured me with a blow?"

"Because I loved you! Because when I first saw you I saw the only man that was my master, and I rebelled. Because when I found I could not help but love you, I knew I never had loved before, and I would wipe out with one stroke all the past that rose in judgment against me. Because I would not have you ever confronted with one endearing word of mine that was not meant for you?"

Major Van Zandt turned from the window where he had stood, and faced the girl with sad resignation. "If I have, in my foolishness, Mistress Thankful, shown you how great was your power over me, when you descended to this artifice to spare my feelings by confessing your own love for me, you should have remembered that you were doing that which for ever kept me from wooing or winning you. If you had really loved me, your heart, as a woman's, would have warned you against that which my heart, as a gentleman's, has made a law of honour. When I tell you, as much for the sake of relieving your own conscience as for the sake of justifying mine, that if this man, a traitor, my prisoner, and your recognised lover, had escaped from my custody without your assistance, connivance or even knowledge, I should have deemed it my duty to forsake you until I caught him, even if we had been standing before the altar."

Thankful heard him, but only as a strange voice in the distance, as she stood with fixed eyes and breathless, parted lips before him. Yet even then I fear that, woman-like, she did not comprehend his rhetoric of honour, but only caught here and there a dull, benumbing idea that he despised her, and that in her effort to win his love she had killed it, and ruined him for ever.

"If you think it strange," continued the Major, "that, believing as I do, I stand here only to utter moral axioms when my duty calls me to pursue your lover, I beg you to believe that it is only for your sake. I wish to allow a reasonable time between your interview with him and his escape, that shall save you from any suspicion of compli-city. Do not think," he added, with a sad smile, as the girl made an impatient step towards him, "do not think I am running any risk. The man cannot escape. A cordon of pickets surrounds the camp for many miles. He has not the countersign, and his face and crime are known."

"Yes," said Thankful eagerly, "but a part of his own regiment guards the Baskingridge road."

"How know you this?" said the Major, seizing her hand.

"He told me."

Before she could fall on her knees and beg his forgive-ness, he had darted from the room, given an order, and returned with cheeks and eyes blazing.

"Hear me," he said rapidly, taking the girl's two hands, "you know not what you've done. I forgive you. But this is no longer a matter of duty, but of my personal honour. I shall pursue this man alone. I shall return with him, or not at all. Farewell; God bless you!"

But before he reached the door she caught him again. "Only say you have forgiven me once more."

"I do."

"Guert!"

There was something in the girl's voice more than this first utterance of his Christian name that made him pause.

"I told—a—lie—just—now. There is a fleeter horse in the stable than my mare; 'tis the roan filly in the second stall."

"God bless you."

He was gone. She waited to hear the clatter of his horse's hoofs in the roadway. When Cæsar came in a few moments later to tell the news of Captain Brewster's escape, the room was empty. But it was soon filled again by a dozen turbulent troopers.

"Of course she's gone," said Sergeant Tibbitts; "the jade flew with the Captain."

"Ay, 'tis plain enough. Two horses are gone from the stable besides the Major's," said Private Hicks.

Nor was this military criticism entirely a private one. When the courier arrived at head-quarters the next morning, it was to bring the report that Mistress Thankful Blossom, after assisting her lover to escape, had fled with him. "The renegade is well off our hands," said General Sullivan gruffly. "He has saved us the public disgrace of a trial, but this is bad news of Major Van Zandt."

"What news of the Major?" asked Washington quickly.

"He pursued the vagabond as far as Springfield, killing his horse, and falling himself insensible before Major Merton's quarters. Here he became speedily delirious

fever supervened, and the regimental surgeon, after a careful examination, pronounced his case one of small-pox."

A whisper of horror and pity went round the room. " Another gallant soldier who should have died leading a charge,
laid by the heels by a beggar's filthy distemper," growled
Sullivan ; "where will it end ? "

"God knows," said Hamilton. " Poor Van Zandt. But
whither was he sent ; to the hospital ? "

" No. A special permit was granted in his case, and 'tis
said he was removed to the Blossom Farm—it being remote
from neighbours, and the house was placed under quaran-
tine. Abner Blossom has prudently absented himself from
the chances of infection, and the daughter has fled. The
sick man is attended only by a black servant and an ancient
crone, so that if the poor Major escapes with his life or
without disfigurement, pretty Mistress Bolton of Morristown
need not be scandalised or jealous."

## PART V.

THE ancient crone alluded to in the last chapter had been
standing behind the window-curtains of that bedroom
which had been Thankful Blossom's in the weeks gone by.
She did not move her head, but stood looking demurely,
after the manner of ancient crones, over the summer landscape. For the summer had come before the tardy spring
was scarce gone, and the elms before the window no longer
lisped, but were eloquent in the softest zephyrs. There
was the flash of birds in among the bushes, the occasional
droning of bees in and out the open window, and a perpetually swinging censer of flower incense rising from
below. The farm had put on its gayest bridal raiment,
and, looking at the old farmhouse shadowed with foliage,
and green with creeping vines, it was difficult to conceive

that snow had ever lain on its porches or icicles swung from its mossy eaves.

"Thankful!" said a voice still tremulous with weakness.

The ancient crone turned, drew aside the curtains, and showed the sweet face of Thankful Blossom, more beautiful even in its paleness.

"Come here, darling," repeated the voice.

Thankful stepped to the sofa whereon lay the convalescent Major Van Zandt.

"Tell me, sweetheart," said the Major, taking her hand in his, "when you married me, as you told the chaplain, that you might have the right to nurse me, did you never think that if death had spared me, I might have been so disfigured that even you, dear love, would have turned from me with loathing?"

"That was why I did it, dear," said Thankful mischievously. "I know that the pride, and the sense of honour, and self-devotion of some people would have kept them from keeping their promises to a poor girl."

"But, darling," continued the Major, raising her hand to his lips, "suppose the case had been reversed; suppose you had taken the disease; that I had recovered without disfigurement, but that this sweet face "——

"I thought of that too," interrupted Thankful.

"Well, what would you have done, dear," said the Major, with his old mischievous smile.

"I should have died," said Thankful gravely.

"But how?"

"Somehow. But you are to go to sleep, and not ask impertinent and frivolous questions, for father is coming to-morrow."

"Thankful, dear, do you know what the trees and the birds said to me as I lay there tossing with the fever?"

"No, dear."

"Thankful Blossom! Thankful Blossom! Thankful Blossom is coming!"

"Do you know what I said, sweetheart, as I lifted your dear head from the ground when you reeled from your horse just as I overtook you at Springfield?"

"No, dear."

"There are some things in life worth stooping for."

And she winged this Parthian arrow home with a kiss.

They lived to a good old age, but she survived him. My mother met her in 1833, when she remembered much more of her interview with General Washington than I have dared to transcribe here. At that time the Spanish Ambassador had presented her with a *trousseau* of incalculable richness. The marriage was to have taken place at the head-quarters, but his Excellency died on that very day. At other times she even hinted at a secret marriage. But it was observable that Major Van Zandt receded into the background with advancing years, and for that reason I have given him a prominent place in these pages. The worthy Allan Brewster reached Hartford, Connecticut, in safety, and after the peace, was elected a member of Congress from that district, where his troubles with the Commander-in-Chief were deemed by a patriotic community as simply an honest, though somewhat premature opposition to Federalism.

# The Twins of Table Mountain.

## PART I.

### A CLOUD ON THE MOUNTAIN.

THEY lived on the verge of a vast stony level, upheaved so far above the surrounding country that its vague outlines, viewed from the nearest valley, seemed a mere cloud-streak resting upon the lesser hills. The rush and roar of the turbulent river that washed its eastern base were lost at that height; the winds that strove with the giant pines that half-way climbed its flanks spent their fury below the summit. For, at variance with most meteorological specu-lation, an eternal calm seemed to invest this serene altitude. The few Alpine flowers seldom thrilled their petals to a passing breeze; rain and snow fell alike perpendicularly, heavily, and monotonously over the granite boulders scat-tered along its brown expanse. Although by actual measurement an inconsiderable elevation of the Sierran range, and a mere shoulder of the nearest white-faced peak that glimmered in the west, it seemed to lie so near the quiet, passionless stars that at night it caught something of their calm remoteness. The articulate utterance of such a locality should have been a whisper; a laugh or exclama-tion was discordant, and the ordinary tones of the human voice on the night of the 15th of May 1868, had a gro-tesque incongruity.

In the thick darkness that clothed the mountain that night, the human figure would have been lost or confounded with the outlines of outlying boulders, which at such times took upon themselves the vague semblance of men and animals. Hence the voices in the following colloquy seemed the more grotesque and incongruous from being the apparent expression of an upright monolith, ten feet high, on the right, and another mass of granite that, reclining, peeped over the verge.

" Hello ! "

" Hello yourself ! "

" You're late."

" I lost the trail, and climbed up the slide."

Here followed a stumble, the clatter of stones down the mountain side, and an oath, so very human and undignified that it at once relieved the boulders of any complicity of expression. The voices, too, were close together now, and unexpectedly in quite another locality.

" Anything up ? "

" Looey Napoleon's declared war agin Germany ! "

" Sho-o-o ! "

Notwithstanding this exclamation, the interest of the latter speaker was evidently only polite and perfunctory. What, indeed, were the political convulsions of the Old World to the dwellers in this serene, isolated eminence of the New?

" I reckon it's so," continued the first voice ; " French Pete and that thar feller that keeps the Dutch grocery hev hed a row over it. Emptied their six-shooters into each other. The Dutchman's got two balls in his leg, and the Frenchman's got an onnessary button-hole in his shirt buzzum, and hez caved in."

This concise, local corroboration of the conflict of remote nations, however confirmatory, did not appear to excite

any further interest. Even the last speaker, now that he
was in this calm, dispassionate atmosphere, seemed to lose
his own concern in his tidings, and to have abandoned
everything of a sensational and lower-worldly character in
the pines below. There was a few moments of absolute
silence, and then another stumble. But now the voices of
both speakers were quite patient and philosophical.

"Hold on, and I'll strike a light," said the second
speaker. "I brought a lantern along, but I didn't light
up. I kem out afore sundown, and you know how it allers
is up yer. *I* didn't want it, and didn't keer to light up.
I forgot you're always a little dazed and strange-like when
you first come up."

There was a crackle, a flash, and presently a steady glow
which the surrounding darkness seemed to resent. The
faces of the two men thus revealed were singularly alike.
The same thin, narrow outline of jaw and temple; the
same dark, grave eyes; the same brown growth of curly
beard and moustache, which concealed the mouth, and
hid what might have been any individual idiosyncrasy of
thought or expression, showed them to be brothers, or
better known as the "Twins of Table Mountain." A
certain animation in the face of the second speaker—the
first comer—a certain light in his eye, might have at first
distinguished him; but even this faded out in the steady
glow of the lantern, and had no value as a permanent
distinction, for by the time they had reached the western
verge of the mountain, the two faces had settled into a
homogeneous calmness and melancholy. The vague horizon of darkness that, a few feet from the lantern, still
encompassed them, gave no indication of their progress
until their feet actually trod the rude planks and thatch
that formed the roof of their habitation. For their cabin
half burrowed in the mountain, and half clung, like a

swallow's nest, to the side of the deep declivity that terminated the northern limit of the summit. Had it not been for the windlass of a shaft, a coil of rope, and a few heaps of stone and gravel, which were the only indications of human labour in that stony field, there was nothing to interrupt its monotonous dead level. And when they descended a dozen well-worn steps to the door of their cabin, they left the summit as before, lonely, silent, motionless, uninterrupted, basking in the cold light of the stars.

The simile of a "nest," as applied to the cabin of the brothers, was no mere figure of speech, as the light of the lantern first flashed upon it. The narrow ledge before the door was strewn with feathers. A suggestion that it might be the home and haunt of predatory birds was promptly checked by the spectacle of the nailed-up carcases of a dozen hawks against the walls, and the outspread wings of an extended eagle emblazoning the gable above the door, like an armorial bearing. Within the cabin the walls and chimney-piece were dazzlingly bedecked with the parti-coloured wings of jays, yellow-birds, woodpeckers, kingfishers, and the poly-tinted wood-duck. Yet in that dry, highly rarefied atmosphere there was not the slightest suggestion of odour or decay.

The first speaker hung the lantern upon a hook that dangled from the rafters, and going to the broad chimney, kicked the half-dead embers into a sudden resentful blaze. He then opened a rude cupboard, and without looking around, called "Ruth!"

The second speaker turned his head from the open doorway where he was leaning, as if listening to something in the darkness, and answered abstractedly—

"Rand!"

"I don't believe you have touched grub to-day!"

Ruth grunted out some indifferent reply.

"Thar hezent been a slice cut off that bacon since I left," continued Rand, bringing a side of bacon and some biscuits from the cupboard and applying himself to the discussion of them at the table. "You're gettin' off yer feed, Ruth. What's up?"

Ruth replied by taking an uninvited seat beside him, and resting his chin on the palms of his hands. He did not eat, but simply transferred his inattention from the door to the table.

"You're workin' too many hours in the shaft," continued Rand. "You're always up to some such d—n fool business when I'm not yer."

"I dipped a little west to-day," Ruth went on, without heeding the brotherly remonstrance, "and struck quartz and pyrites."

"Thet's you!—allers dippin' west or east for quartz and the colour, instead of keeping on plumb down to the ' cement ! ' " *

"We've been three years digging for cement," said Ruth, more in abstraction than reproach; "three years!"

"And we may be three years more—may be only three days. Why, you couldn't be more impatient if—if—if you lived in a valley."

Delivering this tremendous comparison as an unanswerable climax, Rand applied himself once more to his repast. Ruth, after a moment's pause, without speaking or looking up, disengaged his hand from under his chin and slid it along, palm uppermost, on the table beside his brother. Thereupon Rand slowly reached forward his left hand, the right being engaged in conveying victual to his mouth, and laid it on his brother's palm. The act was evidently an habitual, half-mechanical one, for in a few moments the

* The local name for gold-bearing alluvial drift—the bed of a pre-historic river.

hands were as gently disengaged, without comment or expression. At last Rand leaned back in his chair, laid down his knife and fork, and complacently loosening the belt that held his revolver, threw it and the weapon on his bed. Taking out his pipe, and chipping some tobacco on the table, he said carelessly, " I came a piece through the woods with Mornie just now." The face that Ruth turned upon his brother was very distinct in expression at that moment, and quite belied the popular theory that the twins could not be told apart. "Thet gal," continued Rand, without looking up, "is either flighty, or—or suthin'," he added, in vague disgust, pushing the table from him as if it were the lady in question. " Don't tell me ! "

Ruth's eyes quickly sought his brother's, and were as quickly averted, as he asked hurriedly, " How ? "

" What gets me," continued Rand in a petulant *non sequitur*, "is that *you*, my own twin brother, never lets on about her comin' yer, permiskus like, when I ain't yer, and you and her gallivantin' and promanadin', and swoppin' sentiments and mottoes."

Ruth tried to contradict his blushing face with a laugh of worldly indifference.

" She came up yer on a sort of *pasear*"——

" Oh yes !—a short cut to the creek," interpolated Rand satirically.

" Last Tuesday or Wednesday," continued Ruth, with affected forgetfulness.

" Oh, in course, Tuesday or Wednesday, or Thursday ! You've so many folks climbing up this yer mountain to call on ye," continued the ironical Rand, "that you disre- member ; only you remembered enough not to tell me. *She* did ! She took me for you, or pretended to."

The colour dropped from Ruth's cheek.

" Took you for me ? " he asked, with an awkward laugh.

"Yes," sneered Rand; "chirped and chattered away about *our* picnic, *our* nosegays, and lord knows what! Said she'd keep them blue jay's wings, and wear 'em in her hat. Spouted poetry, too; the same sort o' rot you get off now and then."

Ruth laughed again, but rather ostentatiously and nervously.

"Ruth, look yer!"

Ruth faced his brother.

"What's your little game? Do you mean to say you don't know what thet gal is? Do you mean to say you don't know that she's the laughing-stock of the Ferry; thet her father's a d—d old fool, and her mother's a drunkard, and worse—thet she's got any right to be hanging round yer? You can't mean to marry her, even if you kalkilate to turn me out to do it, for she wouldn't live alone with ye up here. 'Tain't her kind. And if I thought you was thinking of"——

"What?" said Ruth, turning upon his brother quickly.

"Oh, thet's right! Holler! Swear and yell, and break things, do! Tear round," continued Rand, kicking his boots off in a corner, "just because I ask you a civil question. That's brotherly," he added, jerking his chair away against the side of the cabin, "ain't it?"

"She's not to blame because her mother drinks, and her father's a shyster," said Ruth, earnestly and strongly. "The men who make her the laughing-stock of the Ferry tried to make her something worse, and failed, and take this sneak's revenge on her. 'Laughing-stock!' Yes, they knew she could turn the tables on them."

"Of course; go on! She's better than me; I know I'm a fratricide, that's what I am," said Rand, throwing himself on the upper of the two berths that formed the bedstead of the cabin.

" I've seen her three times," continued Ruth.

" And you've known me twenty years," interrupted his brother.

Ruth turned on his heel, and walked towards the door.

" That's right ; go on ! Why don't you get the chalk ? "

Ruth made no reply. Rand descended from the bed, and taking a piece of chalk from the shelf, drew a line on the floor, dividing the cabin in two equal parts.

" You can have the east half," he said, as he climbed slowly back into bed.

This mysterious rite was the usual termination of a quarrel between the twins. Each man kept his half of the cabin until the feud was forgotten. It was the mark of silence and separation, over which no words of recrimination, argument, or even explanation were delivered until it was effaced by one or the other. This was considered equivalent to apology or reconciliation, which each were equally bound in honour to accept.

It may be remarked that the floor was much whiter at this line of demarcation, and under the fresh chalk line appeared the faint evidences of one recently effaced.

Without apparently heeding this potential ceremony, Ruth remained leaning against the doorway, looking upon the night, the bulk of whose profundity and blackness seemed to be gathered below him. The vault above was serene and tranquil, with a few large far-spread stars ; the abyss beneath, untroubled by sight or sound. Stepping out upon the ledge, he leaned far over the shelf that sustained their cabin, and listened. A faint rhythmical roll, rising and falling in long undulations against the invisible horizon, to his accustomed ears told him the wind was blowing among the pines in the valley. Yet, mingling with this familiar sound, his ear, now morbidly acute, seemed to detect a stranger inarticulate murmur, as of confused and excited voices, swelling up from the mysterious depths to the stars above, and again swallowed up in the gulfs of silence below.   He was roused from a consideration of this phenomena by a faint glow towards the east, which at last brightened, until the dark outline of the distant walls of the valley stood out against the sky.   Were his other senses participating in the delusion of his ears?   For with the brightening light came the faint odour of burning timber.

His face grew anxious as he gazed.   At last he rose and re-entered the cabin.   His eyes fell upon the faint chalk mark, and taking his soft felt hat from his head, with a few practical sweeps of the brim, he brushed away the ominous record of their late estrangement.   Going to the bed, whereon Rand lay stretched, open-eyed, he would have laid his hand upon his arm lightly, but the brother's fingers sought and clasped his own.   "Get up," he said quietly; " there's a strange fire in the Cañon head that I can't make out."

Rand slowly clambered from his shelf, and, hand in hand, the brothers stood upon the ledge.   "It's a right smart chance beyond the Ferry, and a piece beyond the Mill too," said Rand, shading his eyes with his hand from force of habit.   " It's in the woods where "—— He would have added where he met Mornie, but it was a point of honour with the twins, after reconciliation, not to allude to any topic of their recent disagreement.

Ruth dropped his brother's hand.   " It doesn't smell like the woods," he said slowly.

"Smell!" repeated Rand incredulously.   "Why, it's twenty miles in a bee-line yonder.   Smell, indeed!"

Ruth was silent, but presently fell to listening again with his former abstraction.   "You don't hear anything—do you?" he asked, after a pause.

"It's blowin' in the pines on the river," said Rand shortly.

"You don't hear anything else?"

"No."

"Nothing like—like—like"——

Rand, who had been listening with an intensity that distorted the left side of his face, interrupted him impatiently.

"Like what?"

"Like a woman sobbin'?"

"Ruth," said Rand, suddenly looking up in his brother's face, "what's gone of you?"

Ruth laughed. "The fire's out," he said, abruptly re-entering the cabin. "I'm goin' to turn in."

Rand, following his brother half reproachfully, saw him divest himself of his clothing and roll himself in the blankets of his bed.

"Good-night, Randy."

Rand hesitated. He would have liked to ask his brother another question ; but there was clearly nothing to be done but follow his example.

"Good-night, Ruthy," he said, and put out the light. As he did so the glow in the eastern horizon faded too, and darkness seemed to well up from the depths below, and, flowing in the open door, wrapped them in deeper slumber.


## PART II.

### THE CLOUDS GATHER.

TWELVE months had elapsed since the quarrel and reconciliation, during which interval no reference was made by either of the brothers to the cause which had provoked it. Rand was at work in the shaft, Ruth having that morning undertaken the replenishment of the larder with game from

the wooded skirt of the mountain.    Rand had taken
advantage of his brother's absence to "prospect" in the
"drift"—a proceeding utterly at variance with his previous
condemnation of all such speculative essay; but Rand,
despite his assumption of a superior practical nature, was
not above certain local superstitions.    Having that morning
put on his grey flannel shirt wrong side out, an abstraction
recognised among the miners as the sure forerunner of
divination and treasure discovery, he could not forego that
opportunity of trying his luck without hazarding a dangerous
example.    He was also conscious of feeling "chipper,"
another local expression for buoyancy of spirit, not common
to men who work fifty feet below the surface, without the
stimulus of air and sunshine, and not to be overlooked as
an important factor in fortunate adventure.    Nevertheless,
noon came without the discovery of any treasure; he had
attacked the walls on either side of the lateral "drift," skilfully, so as to expose their quality, without destroying their
cohesive integrity, but had found nothing.    Once or twice,
returning to the shaft for rest and air, its grim silence had
seemed to him pervaded with some vague echo of cheerful
holiday voices above.    This set him to thinking of his
brother's equally extravagant fancy of the wailing voices
in the air on the night of the fire, and of his attributing it
to a lover's abstraction.

"I laid it to his being struck after that gal, and yet,"
Rand continued to himself, "here's me, who haven't been
foolin' round no gal, and dog my skin if I didn't think I
heard one singin' up thar!"    He put his foot on the lower
round of the ladder, paused, and slowly ascended a dozen
steps.    Here he paused again.    All at once the whole shaft
was filled with the musical vibrations of a woman's song.
Seizing the rope that hung idly from the windlass, he half
climbed, half swung himself to the surface.

The voice was there, but the sudden transition to the dazzling level before him at first blinded his eyes; so that he took in, only by degrees, the unwonted spectacle of the singer—a pretty girl standing on tiptoe on a boulder, not a dozen yards from him, utterly absorbed in tying a gaily striped neckerchief, evidently taken from her own plump throat, to the halliards of a freshly cut hickory pole, newly reared as a flag-staff beside her. The hickory pole, the halliards, the fluttering scarf, the young lady herself, were all glaring innovations on the familiar landscape ; but Rand, with his hand still on the rope, silently and demurely enjoyed it.

For the better understanding of the general reader, who does not live on an isolated mountain, it may be observed that the young lady's position on the rock exhibited some study of *pose*, and a certain exaggeration of attitude that betrayed the habit of an audience; also that her voice had an artificial accent that was not wholly unconscious even in this lofty solitude. Yet the very next moment, when she turned and caught Rand's eye fixed upon her, she started naturally, coloured slightly, uttered that feminine adjuration, " Good Lord I gracious I goodness me I" which is seldom used in reference to its effect upon the hearer, and skipped instantly from the boulder to the ground. Here, however, she alighted in a *pose*—brought the right heel of her neatly fitting left boot closely into the hollowed side of her right instep; at the same moment deftly caught her flying skirt, whipped it around her ankles, and slightly raising it behind, permitted the chaste display of an inch or two of frilled white petticoat. The most irreverent critic of the sex will, I think, admit that it has some movements that are automatic.

" Hope I didn't disturb ye," said Rand, pointing to the flag-staff.

The young lady slightly turned her head.   " No," she said;
"but I didn't know anybody was here, of course.  Our
*party*"—she emphasised the word, and accompanied it
with a look toward the farther extremity of the plateau, to
show she was not alone—" our party climbed this ridge,
and put up this pole as a sign that they did it."  The ridiculous self-complacency of this record in the face of a man
who was evidently a dweller on the mountain, apparently
struck her for the first time.   " We didn't know," she stammered, looking at the shaft from which Rand had emerged,
"that—that"——  She stopped, and glancing again towards the distant range where her friends had disappeared,
began to edge away.

" They can't be far off," interposed Rand quietly, as if
it were the most natural thing in the world for the lady
to be there ;  " Table Mountain ain't as big as all that.
Don't you be scared !  So you thought nobody lived up
here ? "

She turned upon him a pair of honest hazel eyes, which
not only contradicted the somewhat meretricious smartness
of her dress, but was utterly inconsistent with the palpable
artificial colour of her hair—an obvious imitation of a certain
popular fashion then known in artistic circles as the " British
Blonde,"—and began to ostentatiously resume a pair of
lemon-coloured kid gloves.   Having, as it were, thus indicated her standing and respectability, and put an immeasu-
rable distance between herself and her bold interlocutor,
she said impressively, " We evidently made a mistake ; I
will rejoin our party, who will, of course, apologise."

" What's your hurry ? " said the imperturbable Rand,
disengaging himself from the rope and walking towards her.
" As long as you're up here, you might stop a spell."

" I have no wish to intrude—that is, our party certainly
has not," continued the young lady, pulling the tight gloves,

and smoothing the plump, almost bursting fingers, with an affectation of fashionable ease.

"Oh, I haven't anything to do just now," said Rand, "and it's about grub time, I reckon. Yes, I live here, Ruth and me ; right here."

The young woman glanced at the shaft.

"No, not down there," said Rand, following her eye, with a laugh. "Come here, and I'll show you."

A strong desire to keep up an appearance of genteel reserve, and an equally strong inclination to enjoy the adventurous company of this good-looking, hearty young fellow, made her hesitate. Perhaps she regretted having undertaken a *rôle* of such dignity at the beginning ; she could have been so perfectly natural with this perfectly natural man, whereas, any relaxation now might increase his familiarity. And yet she was not without a vague sus-picion that her dignity and her gloves were alike thrown away on him—a fact made the more evident when Rand stepped to her side, and without any apparent conscious-ness of disrespect or gallantry, laid his large hand, half persuasively, half fraternally upon her shoulder, and said, "Oh, come along, do."

The simple act either exceeded the limits of her forbear-ance or decided the course of her subsequent behaviour. She instantly stepped back a single pace, and drew her left foot slowly and deliberately after her. Then she fixed her eyes and uplifted eyebrows upon the daring hand, and taking it by the ends of her thumb and forefinger, lifted it and dropped it in mid-air. She then folded her arms. It was the indignant gesture with which "Alice," the Pride of Dum-ballin Village, received the loathsome advances of the bloated aristocrat, Sir Parkyns Parkyn, and had at Marysville, a few nights before, brought down the house.

This effect was, I think, however, lost upon Rand. The

slight colour that rose to his cheek as he looked down upon
his clay-soiled hands, was due to the belief that he had
really contaminated her outward superfine person.    But his
colour quickly passed, his frank, boyish smile returned, as
he said, "It'll rub off.    Lord, don't mind that.    Thar,
now—come on!"

The young woman bit her lip.    Then nature triumphed,
and she laughed, although a little scornfully.    And then
Providence assisted her with the sudden presentation of
two figures—a man and woman, slowly climbing up over the
mountain verge, not far from them.    With a cry of, "There's
Sol, now," she forgot her dignity and her confusion, and ran
towards them.

Rand stood looking after her neat figure, less concerned
in the advent of the strangers than in her sudden caprice.
He was not so young and inexperienced but that he noted
certain ambiguities in her dress and manner ; he was by no
means impressed by her dignity.    But he could not help
watching her as she appeared to be volubly recounting her
late interview to her companions; and still unconscious of
any impropriety or obtrusiveness, he lounged down lazily
towards her.    Her humour had evidently changed, for she
turned an honest pleased face upon him, as she girlishly
attempted to drag the strangers forward.

The man was plump and short ; unlike the natives of the
locality, he was closely cropped and shaven, as if to keep
down the strong blue-blackness of his beard and hair,
which nevertheless asserted itself over his round cheeks
and upper lip like a tattooing of Indian ink.    The woman
at his side was reserved and indistinctive, with that appearance of being an unenthusiastic family servant peculiar to
some men's wives.    When Rand was within a few feet of
him, he started, struck a theatrical attitude, and shading
his eyes with his hand, cried, "What, do me eyes deceive

me !" burst into a hearty laugh, darted forward, seized Rand's hand and shook it briskly.

"Pinkney! Pinkney, my boy, how are you? And this is your little 'prop?' your quarter-section, your country seat, that we've been trespassing on—eh? A nice little spot—cool, sequestered, remote! A trifle unimproved : carriage road as yet unfinished—ha! ha! But to think of our making a discovery of this inaccessible mountain ; climbing it, sir, for two mortal hours; christening it 'Sol's Peak ;' getting up a flag-pole, unfurling our standard to the breeze, sir, and then, by Jingo, winding up by finding Pinkney—the festive Pinkney—living on it at home! "

Completely surprised, but still perfectly good-humoured, Rand shook one of the stranger's hands warmly, and received on his broad shoulders a welcoming thwack from the other, without question. "She don't mind her friends making free with *me*, evidently," said Rand to himself, as he tried to suggest that fact to the young lady in a meaning glance.

The stranger noted his glance, and suddenly passed his hand thoughtfully over his shaven cheeks. "No!" he said. "Yes, surely, I forget! Yes, I see ; of course you don't. Rosy," turning to his wife, "of course, Pinkney doesn't know Phemie—eh?"

"No, nor *me* either, Sol," said that lady warningly.

"Certainly," continued Sol. "It's his misfortune! You weren't with me at Gold Hill. Allow me," he said, turning to Rand, "to present Mrs. Sol Saunders, wife of the under-signed, and Miss Euphemia Neville, otherwise known as the 'Marysville Pet,' the best variety-actress known on the p ovincial boards. Played Ophelia at Marysville, Friday ; domestic drama at Gold Hill, Saturday; Sunday night, four songs in character, different dress each time, and a clog-dance. The best clog-dance on the Pacific Slope," he added, in a stage aside, "The minstrels are crazy to get her in 'Frisco. But money can't buy her—prefers the legitimate drama to this sort of thing." Here he took a few steps of a jig, to which the Marysville Pet beat time with her feet, and concluded with a laugh and a wink—the combined expression of an artist's admiration for her ability, and a man of the world's scepticism of feminine ambition.

Miss Euphemia responded to the formal introduction by extending her hand frankly with a reassuring smile to Rand, and an utter obliviousness of her former *hauteur*. Rand shook it warmly, and then dropped carelessly on a rock beside them.

"And you never told me you lived up here in the attic, you rascal," continued Sol with a laugh.

"No," replied Rand simply. "How could I? I never saw you before, that I remember."

Miss Euphemia stared at Sol. Mrs. Sol looked up in her lord's face, and folded her arms in a resigned expression. Sol rose to his feet again, and shaded his eyes with his hand, but this time quite seriously, and gazed at Rand's smiling face.

"Good Lord! Do you mean to say your name isn't Pinkney?" he asked, with a half-embarrassed laugh.

"It *is* Pinkney," said Rand, "but I never met you before."

"Didn't you come to see a young lady that joined my troupe at Gold Hill, last month, and say you'd meet me at Keeler's Ferry in a day or two?"

"No-o-o," said Rand, with a good-humoured laugh. "I haven't left this mountain for two months."

He might have added more, but his attention was directed to Miss Euphemia, who during this short dialogue, having stuffed alternately her handkerchief, the corner of her mantle, and her gloves into her mouth, restrained herself no longer, but gave way to an uncontrollable fit of laughter. "O Sol," she gasped explanatorily, as she threw herself alternately against him, Mrs. Sol, and a boulder, "you'll kill me yet! O Lord! first we take possession of this man's property, then we claim *him*." The contemplation of this humorous climax affected her so that she was fain at last to walk away and confide the rest of her speech to space.

Sol joined in the laugh until his wife plucked his sleeve, and whispered something in his ear. In an instant his face became at once mysterious and demure. "I owe you an apology," he said, turning to Rand, but in a voice ostentatiously pitched high enough for Miss Euphemia to overhear; "I see I have made a mistake. A resemblance —only a mere resemblance, as I look at you now—led me astray. Of course you don't know any young lady in the profession?"

"Of course he doesn't, Sol," said Miss Euphemia. "*I* could have told you that. He didn't even know *me*!"

The voice and mock-heroic attitude of the speaker was enough to relieve the general embarrassment with a laugh. Rand, now pleasantly conscious of only Miss Euphemia's presence, again offered the hospitality of his cabin—with the polite recognition of her friends in the sentence, "and you might as well come along too!"

"But won't we incommode the lady of the house?" said Mrs. Sol politely.

"What lady of the house?" said Rand, almost angrily.

"Why—Ruth, you know!"

It was Rand's turn to become hilarious. "Ruth," he said, "is short for Rutherford, my brother." His laugh, however, was echoed only by Euphemia.

"Then you have a brother?" said Mrs. Sol benignly.

o

"Yes," said Rand; "he will be here soon." A sudden thought dropped the colour from his cheek. "Look here," he said, turning impulsively upon Sol. "I have a brother, a twin brother. It couldn't be *him*"——

Sol was conscious of a significant feminine pressure on his right arm. He was equal to the emergency. "I think not," he said dubiously, "unless your brother's hair is much darker than yours. Yes! now I look at you, yours is brown. He has a mole on his right cheek—hasn't he?"

The red came quickly back to Rand's boyish face. He laughed. "No, sir; my brother's hair is, if anything, a shade lighter than mine; and nary mole! Come along!"

And leading the way, Rand disclosed the narrow steps winding down to the shelf on which the cabin hung. "Be careful," said Rand, taking the now unresisting hand of the Marysville Pet as they descended: "a step that way, and down you go, two thousand feet on the top of a pine-tree."

But the girl's slight cry of alarm was presently changed to one of unaffected pleasure, as they stood on the rocky platform. "It isn't a house; it's a *nest*, and the loveliest!" said Euphemia breathlessly.

"It's a scene! a perfect scene, sir!" said Sol enraptured. "I shall take the liberty of bringing my scene-painter to sketch it, some day. It would do for 'The Mountaineer's Bride' superbly, or," continued the little man, warming through the blue-black border of his face with professional enthusiasm, "it's enough to make a play itself! 'The Cot on the Crags.' Last scene—moonlight—the struggle on the ledge!—The Lady of the Crags—throws herself from the beetling heights!—A shriek from the depths—a woman's wail!"

"Dry up!" sharply interrupted Rand, to whom this speech recalled his brother's half-forgotten strangeness "Look at the prospect."

In the full noon of a cloudless day, beneath them a tumultuous sea of pines surged, heaved, rode in giant crests, stretched and spent itself in the ghostly, snow-peaked horizon. The thronging woods choked every defile, swept every crest, filled every valley with its dark-green tilting spears, and left only Table Mountain sunlit and bare. Here and there were profound olive depths, over which the grey hawk hung lazily, and into which blue jays dipped. A faint, dull, yellowish streak marked an occasional water-course; a deeper reddish riband, the mountain road and its overhanging murky cloud of dust.

"Is it quite safe here?" asked Mrs. Sol, eyeing the little cabin. "I mean from storms?"

"It never blows up here," replied Rand, "and nothing happens."

"It must be lovely!" said Euphemia, clasping her hands.

"It *is* that," said Rand proudly. "It's four years since Ruth and I took up this yer claim, and raised this shanty. In that four years we haven't left it alone a night, or cared to. It's only big enough for two, and them two must be brothers. It wouldn't do for mere pardners to live here alone—they couldn't do it. It wouldn't be exactly the thing for man and wife to shut themselves up here alone. But Ruth and me know each other's ways, and here we'll stay until we've made a pile. We sometimes—one of us—takes a *pasear* to the Ferry, to buy provisions, but we're glad to crawl up to the back of old 'Table' at night."

"You're quite out of the world here, then?" suggested Mrs. Sol.

"That's it—just it! We're out of the world, out of rows, out of liquor, out of cards, out of bad company, out of temptation. Cussedness and foolishness hez got to follow us up here to find us, and there's too many ready to climb down to them things to tempt 'em to come up to us."

There was a little boyish conceit in his tone, as he stood there, not altogether unbecoming his fresh colour and sim- plicity. Yet when his eyes met those of Miss Euphemia, he coloured, he hardly knew why, and the young lady herself blushed rosily.

When the neat cabin, with its decorated walls, and squirrel and wild-cat skins, were duly admired, the luncheon- basket of the Saunders party was reinforced by provisions from Rand's larder, and spread upon the ledge; the dimen- sions of the cabin not admitting four. Under the potent influence of a bottle, Sol became hilarious and professional. The "Pet" was induced to favour the company with a recitation, and, under the plea of teaching Rand, to perform the clog-dance with both gentlemen. Then there was an interval, in which Rand and Euphemia wandered a little way down the mountain side to gather laurel, leaving Mr. Sol to his *siesta* on a rock, and Mrs. Sol to take some knitting from the basket, and sit beside him.

When Rand and his companion had disappeared, Mrs. Sol nudged her sleeping partner. "Do you think that *was* the brother?"

Sol yawned. "Sure of it. They're as like as two peas, in looks."

"Why didn't you tell him so, then?"

"Will you tell me, my dear, why you stopped me when I began?"

"Because something was said about Ruth being here and I supposed Ruth was a woman, and perhaps Pinkney's wife, and knew you'd be putting your foot in it by talking of that other woman. I supposed it was for fear of that he denied knowing you."

"Well, when *he*,—this Rand,—told me he had a twin brother, he looked so frightened that I knew he knew nothing of his brother's doings with that woman, and I threw him off the scent. He's a good fellow, but awfully green, and I didn't want to worry him with tales. I like him, and I think Phemie does too."

"Nonsense! He's a conceited prig! Did you hear his sermon on the world and its temptations? I wonder if he thought temptation had come up to him in the person of us professionals, out on a picnic. I think it was positively rude."

" My dear woman, you're always seeing slights and insults. I tell you, he's taken a shine to Phemie, and he's as good as four seats and a bouquet to that child next Wednesday evening. To say nothing of the *éclat* of getting this St. Simeon—what do you call him—Stalactites?"

"Stylites," suggested Mrs. Sol.

"Stylites, off from his pillar here. I'll have a paragraph in the paper, that the hermit crabs of Table Mountain "——

"Don't be a fool, Sol!"

"The hermit twins of Table Mountain bespoke the chaste performance."

"One of them being the protector of the well-known Mornie Nixon," responded Mrs. Sol, viciously accenting the name with her knitting-needles.

"Rosy, you're unjust. You're prejudiced by the reports of the town. Mr. Pinkney's interest in her may be a purely artistic one—although mistaken. She'll never make a good variety-actress—she's too heavy. And the boys don't give her a fair show. No woman can make a *début* in my version of ' Somnambula,' and have the front row in the pit say to her, in the sleep-walking scene, ' You're out rather late, Mornie. Kinder forgot to put on your things, didn't you? Mother sick, I suppose, and you're goin' for more gin? Hurry along, or you'll ketch it when ye get home.' Why, you couldn't do it yourself, Rosy!"

To which Mrs. Sol's illogical climax was that, "bad as

Rutherford might be—this Sunday-school superintendent, Rand, was worse."

Rand and his companion returned late, but in high spirits. There was an unnecessary effusiveness in the way in which Euphemia kissed Mrs. Sol—the one woman present, who *understood*, and was to be propitiated—which did not tend to increase her good humour. She had her basket packed already for departure, and even the earnest solicitation of Rand, that they would defer their going until sunset, produced no effect.

" Mr. Rand—Mr. Pinkney, I mean, says the sunsets here are so lovely," pleaded Euphemia.

"There is a rehearsal at seven o'clock, and we have no time to lose," said Mrs. Sol significantly.

" I forgot to say," said the Marysville Pet timidly, glancing at Mrs. Sol, " that Mr. Rand says he will bring his brother on Wednesday night, and wants four seats in front, so as not to be crowded."

Sol shook the young man's hand warmly. " You'll not regret it, sir ; it's a surprising, a remarkable performance."

" I'd like to go a piece down the mountain with you," said Rand with evident sincerity, looking at Miss Euphemia; " but Ruth isn't here yet, and we make a rule never to leave the place alone. I'll show you the slide : it's the quickest way to go down. If you meet any one who looks like me, and talks like me, call him ' Ruth,' and tell him I'm waitin' for him yer."

Miss Phemia, the last to go, standing on the verge of the declivity, here remarked, with a dangerous smile, that if she met any one who bore that resemblance, she might be tempted to keep him with her—a playfulness that brought the ready colour to Rand's cheek. When she added to this the greater audacity of kissing her hand to him, the young hermit actually turned away in sheer embarrassment. When he looked around again, she was gone, and for the first time in his experience, the mountain seemed barren and lonely.

The too sympathetic reader who would rashly deduce from this any newly awakened sentiment in the virgin heart of Rand, would quite misapprehend that peculiar young man. That singular mixture of boyish inexperience and mature doubt and disbelief, which was partly the result of his temperament, and partly of his cloistered life on the mountain, made him regard his late companions, now that they were gone, and his intimacy with them, with remorseful distrust. The mountain was barren and lonely, because it was no longer *his*. It had become a part of the great world which, four years ago, he and his brother had put aside ; and in which, as two self-devoted men, they walked alone. More than that, he believed he had acquired some understanding of the temptations that assailed his brother, and the poor little vanities of the " Marysville Pet" were transformed into the blandishments of a Circe. Rand, who would have succumbed to a wicked, superior woman, believed he was a saint in withstanding the foolish weakness of a simple one.

He did not resume his work that day. He paced the mountain, anxiously awaiting his brother's return, and eager to relate his experiences. He would go with him to the dramatic entertainment; from his example and wisdom Ruth should learn how easily temptation might be overcome. But, first of all, there should be the fullest exchange of confidences and explanations. The old rule should be rescinded for once—the old discussion in regard to Mornie re-opened ; and Rand, having convinced his brother of error, would generously extend his forgiveness.

The sun sank redly. Lingering long upon the ledge before their cabin, it at last slipped away almost imperceptibly, leaving Rand still wrapped in reverie. Darkness, the smoke of distant fires in the woods, and the faint evening incense of the pines crept slowly up, but Ruth came not. The moon rose—a silver gleam on the farther ridge ; and Rand becoming uneasy at his brother's prolonged absence, resolved to break another custom and leave the summit, to seek him on the trail. He buckled on his revolver, seized his gun, when a cry from the depths arrested him. He leaned over the ledge and listened. Again the cry arose, and this time more distinctly. He held his breath ; the blood settled around his heart in superstitious terror. It was the wailing voice of a woman !

"Ruth ! Ruth ! for God's sake come and help me !"

The blood flew back hotly to Rand's cheek. It was Mornie's voice ! By leaning over the ledge he could distinguish something moving along the almost precipitous face of the cliff, where an abandoned trail, long since broken off and disrupted by the fall of a portion of the ledge, stopped abruptly a hundred feet below him. Rand knew the trail, a dangerous one always ; in its present condition a single mis-step would be fatal. Would she make that mis-step ? He shook off a horrible temptation that seemed to be sealing his lips and paralysing his limbs, and almost screamed to her, "Drop on your face, hang on to the *chapparal*, and don't move !" In another instant, with a coil of rope around his arm, he was dashing down the almost perpendicular " slide." When he had nearly reached the level of the abandoned trail, he fastened one end of the rope to a jutting splinter of granite, and began to "lay out," and work his way laterally along the face of the mountain. Presently he struck the regular trail at the point from which the woman must have diverged.

"It is Rand ! " she said, without lifting her head.

"It is," replied Rand coldly. "Pass the rope under your arms, and I'll get you back to the trail."

"Where is Ruth?" she demanded again, without moving. She was trembling, but with excitement rather than fear.

"I don't know," returned Rand impatiently. "Come! the ledge is already crumbling beneath our feet."

"Let it crumble!" said the woman passionately.

Rand surveyed her with profound disgust, then passed the rope around her waist, and half lifted, half swung her from her feet. In a few moments she began to mechanically help herself, and permitted him to guide her to a place of safety. That reached, she sank down again.

The rising moon shone full upon her face and figure. Through his growing indignation Rand was still impressed and even startled with the change the last few months had wrought upon her. In place of the silly, fanciful, half-hysterical hoyden whom he had known, a matured woman, strong in passionate self-will, fascinating in a kind of wild savage beauty, looked up at him as if to read his very soul.

"What are you staring at?" she said finally. "Why don't you help me on?"

"Where do you want to go?" said Rand quietly.

"Where!—up there!"—she pointed savagely to the top of the mountain,—"to *him!* Where else should I go?" she said, with a bitter laugh.

"I've told you he wasn't there," said Rand roughly. "He hasn't returned."

"I'll wait for him!—do you hear?—wait for him! Stay there till he comes! If you won't help me, I'll go alone!"

She made a step forward, but faltered, staggered, and was obliged to lean against the mountain for support. Stains of travel were on her dress; lines of fatigue and pain, and traces of burning, passionate tears, were on her face; her black hair flowed from beneath her gaudy bonnet; and shamed out of his brutality, Rand placed his strong arm round her waist, and, half carrying, half supporting her,

began the ascent.   Her head dropped wearily on his
shoulder ; her arm encircled his neck ; her hair as if caressingly lay across his breast and hands ; her grateful eyes
were close to his, her breath was upon his cheek ; and yet
his only consciousness was of the possibly ludicrous figure
he might present to his brother should he meet him with
Mornie Nixon in his arms.   Not a word was spoken by
either till they reached the summit.   Relieved at finding
his brother still absent, he turned not unkindly toward
the helpless figure on his arm.   " I don't see what makes
Ruth so late," he said.   " He's always here by sundown.
Perhaps "——

" Perhaps he knows I'm here," said Mornie, with a bitter
laugh.

" I didn't say that," said Rand, " and I don't think it.
What I meant was, he might have met a party that was
picnicing here to-day.   Sol Saunders and wife, and Miss
Euphemia "——

Mornie flung his arm away from her with a passionate gesture.   " *They* here ! picnicing *here !*—those people
*here ?* "

" Yes," said Rand, unconsciously a little ashamed.
" They came here accidently."

Mornie's quick passion had subsided ; she had sunk
again wearily and helplessly on a rock beside him.   " I
suppose," she said, with a weak laugh—" I suppose they
talked of *me*.   I suppose they told you how—with their lies
and fair promises—they tricked me out, and set me before
an audience of brutes and laughing hyenas to make merry
over !   Did they tell you of the insults that I received ?—
how the sins of my parents were flung at me instead of
bouquets ?   Did they tell you they could have spared me
this, but they wanted the few extra dollars taken in at the
door ?   No ! "

"They said nothing of the kind," replied Rand surlily.

"Then you must have stopped them! You were horrified enough to know that I had dared to take the only honest way left me to make a living. I know you, Randolph Pinkney. You'd rather see Joaquin Muriatta, the Mexican bandit, standing before you to-night with a revolver, than the helpless, shamed, miserable Mornie Nixon! And you can't help yourself, unless you throw me over the cliff. Perhaps you'd better," she said, with a bitter laugh that faded from her lips as she leaned, pale and breathless, against the boulder.

"Ruth will tell you "—— began Rand.

"D—n Ruth!"

Rand turned away.

"Stop!" she said suddenly, staggering to her feet. "I'm sick—for all I know, dying. God grant that it may be so! But, if you are a man, you will help me to your cabin—to some place where I can lie down *now* and be at rest. I'm very, very tired."

She paused; she would have fallen again, but Rand, seeing more in her face than her voice interpreted to his sullen ears, took her sullenly in his arms and carried her to the cabin. Her eyes glanced around the bright parti-coloured walls, and a faint smile came to her lips as she put aside her bonnet, adorned with a companion pinion of the bright wings that covered it.

"Which is Ruth's bed?" she asked.

Rand pointed to it.

"Lay me there!"

Rand would have hesitated, but with another look at her face complied.

She lay quite still a moment. Presently she said, "Give me some brandy or whisky!"

Rand was silent and confused.

"I forgot," she added, half bitterly; "I know **you have** not that commonest and cheapest of vices."

She lay quite still again. Suddenly she raised herself partly on her elbow, and in a strong, firm voice, said— "Rand!"

"Yes, Mornie."

"If you are wise and practical, as you assume to be, you will do what I ask you without a question. If you do it *at once* you may save yourself and Ruth some trouble, some mortification, and perhaps some remorse and sorrow. Do you hear me?"

"Yes!"

"Go to the nearest doctor and bring him here with you."

"But *you!*"

Her voice was strong, confident, steady and patient. "You can safely leave me until then."

In another moment, Rand was plunging down the "slide." But it was past midnight when he struggled over the last boulder up the ascent, dragging the half-exhausted medical wisdom of Brown's Ferry on his arm.

"I've been gone long, doctor," said Rand feverishly, "and she looked *so* death-like when I left. If we should be too late?"

The doctor stopped suddenly, lifted his head, and pricked his ears like a hound on a peculiar scent. "We *are* too late," he said, with a slight professional laugh.

Indignant and horrified, Rand turned upon him.

"Listen," said the doctor, lifting his hand.

Rand listened; so intently that he heard the familiar moan of the river below, but the great stony field lay silent before him. And then, borne across its bare barren bosom, like its own articulation, came faintly the feeble wail of a new-born babe.

## PART III.

### STORM.

THE doctor hurried ahead in the darkness. Rand, who had stopped paralysed at the ominous sound, started forward again mechanically; but as the cry arose again more distinctly, and the full significance of the doctor's words came to him, he faltered, stopped, and with cheeks burning with shame and helpless indignation, sank upon a stone beside the shaft, and, burying his face in his hands, fairly gave way to a burst of boyish tears. Yet even then, the recollection that he had not cried since, years ago, his mother's dying hands had joined his and Ruth's childish fingers together, stung him fiercely and dried his tears in angry heat upon his cheeks.

How long he sat there he remembered not; what he thought he recalled not. But the wildest and most extravagant plans and resolves availed him nothing in the face of this for ever desecrated home, and this shameful culmination of his ambitious life on the mountain. Once he thought of flight, but the reflection that he would still abandon his brother to shame, perhaps a self-contented shame, checked him hopelessly. Could he avert the future? He *must*—but how? Yet he could only sit and stare into the darkness in dumb abstraction.

Sitting there, his eyes fell upon a peculiar object in a crevice of the ledge beside the shaft. It was the tin pail containing his dinner, which, according to their custom, it was the duty of the brother who stayed above ground to prepare and place for the brother who worked below. Ruth must, consequently, have put it there before he left that morning, and Rand had overlooked it while sharing the repast of the strangers at noon. At the sight of this dumb witness of their mutual cares and labours Rand sighed—half in brotherly sorrow, half in a selfish sense of injury done him. He took up the pail mechanically, removed its cover and—started! For on top of the carefully bestowed provisions lay a little note, addressed to him in Ruth's peculiar scrawl.

He opened it with feverish hands, held it in the light of the peaceful moon, and read as follows :—

"DEAR, DEAR BROTHER,—When you read this I shall be far away. I go because I shall not stay to disgrace you, and because the girl that I brought trouble upon has gone away too, to hide her disgrace and mine; and where she goes, Rand, I ought to follow her, and, please God, I will! I am not as wise or as good as you are, but it seems the best I can do; and God bless you, dear old Randy, boy! Times and times again I've wanted to tell you all, and reckoned to do so; but whether you was sitting before me in the cabin, or working beside me in the drift, I couldn't get to look upon your honest face, dear brother, and say what things I'd been keeping from you so long. I'll stay away until I've done what I ought to do, and if you can say, 'Come, Ruth,' I will come; but until you can say it, the mountain is yours, Randy boy, the mine is yours, the cabin is yours, *all* is yours! Rub out the old chalk marks, Rand, as I rub them out here in my " (a few words here were blurred and indistinct, as if the moon had suddenly become dim-eyed too). "God bless you, brother.

"P.S.—You know I mean Mornie all the time. It's she I'm going to seek; but don't you think so bad of her as you do; I am so much worse than she. I wanted to tell you that all along, but I didn't dare. She's run away from the Ferry, half crazy; said she was going to Sacramento, and I am going there to find her alive or dead. Forgive me, brother! Don't throw this down, right away; hold it in your hand a moment, Randy, boy, and try hard to think it's my hand in yours. And so good-bye, and God bless you, old Randy.—From your loving brother,

"RUTH."

A deep sense of relief overpowered every other feeling in Rand's breast. It was clear that Ruth had not yet discovered the truth of Mornie's flight; he was on his way to Sacramento, and before he could return, Mornie could be removed. Once despatched in some other direction, with Ruth once more returned and under his brother's guidance, the separation could be made easy and final. There was evidently no marriage as yet, and now, the fear of an immediate meeting over, there should be none. For Rand had already feared this; had recalled the few infelicitous relations, legal and illegal, which were common to the adjoining camp; the flagrantly miserable life of the husband of a San Francisco anonyma, who lived in style at the Ferry; the shameful carousals and more shameful quarrels of the Frenchman and Mexican woman, who "kept house" at "the Crossing;" the awful spectacle of the three half-bred Indian children who played before the cabin of a fellow miner and townsman. Thank heaven, the Eagle's Nest on Table Mountain should never be pointed at from the valley as another.

A heavy hand upon his arm brought him trembling to his feet. He turned and met the half-anxious, half-contemptuous glance of the doctor.

"I'm sorry to disturb you," he said drily, "but it's about time you or somebody else put in an appearance at that cabin. Luckily for *her*, she's one woman in a thousand—has had her wits about her better than some folks I know, and has left me little to do but make her comfortable.

But she's gone through too much—fought her little fight too gallantly—is altogether too much of a trump to be played off upon now. So rise up out of that, young man; pick up your scattered faculties, and fetch a woman—some sensible creature of her own sex—to look after her; for, without wishing to be personal, I'm d——d if I trust her to the likes of you."

There was no mistaking Doctor Duchesne's voice and manner, and Rand was affected by it, as most people were, throughout the valley of the Stanislaus. But he turned upon him his frank and boyish face, and said simply, " But I don't know any woman, or where to get one."

The doctor looked at him again. " Well, I'll find you some one," he said, softening.

"Thank you," said Rand.

The doctor was disappearing. With an effort Rand recalled him. " One moment, doctor." He hesitated, and his cheeks were glowing. " You'll please say nothing about this down there"—he pointed to the valley—" for a time. And you'll say to the woman you send "——

Dr. Duchesne, whose resolute lips were sealed upon the secrets of half Tuolumne county, interrupted him scornfully. "I cannot answer for the woman—you must talk to her yourself. As for me, generally I keep my professional visits to myself, but "—he laid his hand on Rand's arm—"if I find out you're putting on any airs to that poor creature,—if on my next visit her lips or her pulse tell me you haven't been acting on the square to her, I'll drop a hint to drunken old Nixon where his daughter is hidden. I reckon she could stand his brutality better than yours. Good-night !"

In another moment he was gone. Rand, who had held back his quick tongue, feeling himself in the power of this man, once more alone, sank on a rock, and buried his face in his hands. Recalling himself in a moment, he rose, wiped his hot eyelids, and staggered toward the cabin. It was quite still now ; he paused on the topmost step and listened ; there was no sound from the ledge or the Eagle's Nest that clung to it. Half timidly he descended the winding steps, and paused before the door of the cabin. "Mornie," he said, in a dry, metallic voice, whose only indication of the presence of sickness was in the lowness of its pitch— "Mornie." There was no reply. "Mornie," he repeated impatiently, "it's me—Rand ! If you want anything you're to call me. I am just outside." Still no answer came from the silent cabin. He pushed open the door gently, hesitated, and stepped over the threshold.

A change in the interior of the cabin within the last few hours, showed a new presence. The guns, shovels, picks, and blankets had disappeared, the two chairs were drawn against the wall, the table placed by the bedside. The swinging lantern was shaded towards the bed—the object of Rand's attention. On that bed, his brother's bed, lay a helpless woman, pale from the long black hair that matted her damp forehead, and clung to her hollow cheeks. Her face was turned to the wall, so that the softened light fell upon her profile, which to Rand, at that moment, seemed even noble and strong. But the next moment his eye fell upon the shoulder and arm that lay nearest to him, and the little bundle swathed in flannel that it clasped to her breast. His brow grew dark as he gazed. The sleeping woman moved : perhaps it was an instinctive consciousness of his presence—perhaps it was only the current of cold air from the opened door,—but she shuddered slightly, and, still unconscious, drew the child as if away from *him*, and nearer to her breast. The shamed blood rushed to Rand's face, and saying half aloud, "I'm not going to take your precious babe away from you," turned in half-boyish pettishness away. Nevertheless, he came back again, shortly, to the bedside, and gazed upon them both. She certainly did look altogether more ladylike and less aggressive lying there so still; sickness, that cheap refining power of some natures, was not unbecoming to her. But this bundle ! A boyish curiosity, stronger than even his strong objection to the whole episode, was steadily impelling him to lift the blanket from it. "I suppose she'd waken if I did," said Rand, "but I'd like to know what right the doctor had to wrap it up in my best flannel shirt." This fresh grievance, the fruit of his curiosity, sent him away again to meditate on the ledge. After a few moments he returned again, opened the cupboard at the foot of the bed softly, took thence a piece of chalk, and scrawled in large letters upon the door of the cupboard, "If you want anything, sing out : I'm just outside—RAND." This done, he took a blanket and bear-skin from the corner, and walked to the door. But here he paused, looked back at the inscription ; evidently not satisfied with it, returned, took up the chalk, added a line, but rubbed it out again, repeated this operation a few times until he produced 'the polite postcript— "Hope you'll be better soon." Then he retreated to the ledge, spread the bear-skin beside the door, and rolling himself in a blanket, lit his pipe for his night-long vigil. But Rand, although a martyr, a philosopher, and a moralist, was young. In less than ten minutes the pipe dropped from his lips, and he was asleep.

He awoke with a strange sense of heat and suffocation, and with difficulty shook off his covering. Rubbing his eyes, he discovered that an extra blanket had in some mysterious way been added in the night, and beneath his head was a pillow he had no recollection of placing there when he went to sleep. By degrees the events of the past night forced themselves upon his benumbed faculties, and he sat up. The sun was riding high, the door of the cabin was open. Stretching himself, he staggered to his feet, and looked in through the yawning crack at the hinges. He rubbed his eyes again. Was he still asleep, and followed by a dream of yesterday? For there, even in the very attitude he remembered to have seen her sitting at her luncheon on the previous day, with her knitting on her lap, sat Mrs. Sol Saunders! What did it mean? or had she really been sitting there ever since, and all the events that followed only a dream?

A hand was laid upon his arm, and turning he saw the murky black eyes and Indian-inked beard of Sol beside him. That gentleman put his finger on his lips with a theatrical gesture, and then slowly retreating in the well-known manner of the buried Majesty of Denmark waved him, like another Hamlet, to a remoter part of the ledge. This reached, he grasped Rand warmly by the hand, shook it heartily, and said, "It's all right, my boy; all right!"

"But "—— began Rand. The hot blood flowed to his cheeks, he stammered and stopped short.

"It's all right, I say! Don't you mind! We'll pull you through"

"But, Mrs. Sol! what does she "——

"Rosey has taken the matter in hand, sir, and when that woman takes a matter in hand, whether it's a baby or a rehearsal, sir, she makes it buzz."

"But how did she know?" stammered Rand.

"How? Well, sir, the scene opened something like this," said Sol professionally. "Curtain rises on me and Mrs. Sol. Domestic interior—practicable chairs, table, books, newspapers. Enter Doctor Duchesne—eccentric character part, very popular with the boys; tells off-hand affecting story of strange woman—one 'more unfortunate,' having baby in Fogie's Nest—lonely place on 'peaks of

Snowdon,' midnight; eagles screaming, you know, and far down unfathomable depths; only attendant, cold-blooded ruffian, evidently father of child, with sinister designs on child and mother."

"He didn't say *that!*" said Rand, with an agonised smile.

"Order! Sit down in front!" continued Sol, easily. "Mrs. Sol highly interested—a mother herself—demands name of place? 'Table Mountain!' No, it cannot be— it is! Excitement. Mystery! Rosey rises to occasion— comes to front: 'Some one must go; I—I—will go my-self!' Myself, coming to centre: 'Not alone, dearest; I—I will accompany you!' A shriek at right upper en-trance. Enter the Marysville Pet. 'I have heard all. 'Tis a base calumny. It cannot be *he!* Randolph! Never!' 'Dare you accompany us?' 'I will!' Tableau!"

"Is Miss Euphemia—here?" gasped Rand, practical, even in his embarrassment.

"Or-r-rder! Scene second. Summit of mountain— moonlight. Peaks of Snowdon in distance. Right—lonely cabin. Enter slowly up defile, Sol, Mrs. Sol, the Pet. Advance slowly to cabin. Suppressed shriek from the Pet, who rushes to recumbent figure—Left—discovered lying beside cabin door. ''Tis he! Hist!—he sleeps!' Throws blanket over him and retires up stage—so." Here Sol achieved a vile imitation of the Pet's most enchanting stage manner. "Mrs. Sol advances — Centre — throws open door! Shriek! ''Tis Mornie—the lost found!' The Pet advances—'And the father is——?' 'Not Rand!' The Pet kneeling, 'Just Heaven, I thank thee!' 'No, it is'"——

"Hush!" said Rand appealingly, looking toward the cabin.

"Hush it is!" said the actor good-naturedly; "But it's all right, Mr. Rand—we'll pull you through."

Later in the morning, Rand learned that Mornie's ill-fated connection with the "Star Variety Troup" had been a source of anxiety to Mrs. Sol, and she had reproached herself for the girl's infelicitous *début.*

"But Lord bless you, Mr. Rand," said Sol, "it was all in the way of business. She came to us—was fresh and new—her chance, looking at it professionally, was as good as any amateur's; but, what with her relations here, and her bein' known, she didn't take! We lost money on her! It's natural she should feel a little ugly. We all do when we get sorter kicked back onto ourselves, and find we can't stand alone. Why, you wouldn't believe it," he continued, with a moist twinkle of his black eyes, "but the night I lost my little Rosey of diphtheria in Gold Hill, the child was down on the bills for a comic song, and I had to drag Mrs. Sol on, cut up as she was, and filled up with that much of old Bourbon to keep her nerves stiff, so she could do an old gag with me to gain time and make up the 'variety.' Why, sir, when I came to the front *I* was ugly! And when one of the boys in the front row sang out, 'Don't expose that poor child to the night air, Sol'—meaning Mrs. Sol, I acted ugly. No, sir, it's human nature; and it was quite natural that Mornie, when she caught sight o' Mrs. Sol's face last night, should rise up and cuss us both. Lord, if she'd only acted like that! But the old lady got her quiet at last, and, as I said before, it's all right, and we'll pull her through! But don't *you* thank us; it's a little matter betwixt us and Mornie. We've got everything fixed, so that Mrs. Sol can stay right along. We'll pull Mornie through, and get her away from this and her baby too, as soon as we can. You won't get mad if I tell you something?" said Sol, with a half-apologetic laugh. "Mrs. Sol was rather down on you the other day—hated you on sight, and preferred your brother to you; but when she found he'd run off and left *you*—you don't mind my sayin' it—a 'mere boy,' to take what oughter be *his* place, why she just wheeled round agin' him. I suppose he got flustered and couldn't face the music. Never left a word of explanation? Well, it wasn't exactly square—though I tell the old woman it's human nature. He might have dropped a hint where he was goin'. Well, there, I won't say a word more agin' him. I know how you feel! Hush it is!"

It was the firm conviction of the simple-minded Sol that no one knew the various natural indications of human passion better than himself; perhaps it was one of the fallacies of his profession that the expression of all human passion was limited to certain conventional signs and sounds. Consequently, when Rand coloured violently, became confused, stammered, and at last turned hastily away, the good-hearted fellow instantly recognised the unfailing evidence of modesty and innocence embarrassed by recognition. As for Rand, I fear his shame was only momentary; confirmed in the belief of his ulterior wisdom and virtue, his first embarrassment over, he was not displeased with this half-way tribute, and really believed that the time would come when Mr. Sol should eventually praise his sagacity and reservation, and acknowledge that he was something more than a mere boy. He, nevertheless, shrank from meeting Mornie that morning, and was glad that the presence of Mrs. Sol relieved him from that duty.

The day passed uneventfully. Rand busied himself in his usual avocations, and constructed a temporary shelter for himself and Sol beside the shaft, besides rudely shaping a few necessary articles of furniture for Mrs. Sol.

"It will be a little spell yet afore Mornie's able to be moved," suggested Sol, "and you might as well be comfortable."

Rand sighed at this prospect, yet presently forgot him

self in the good humour of his companion, whose admiration for himself he began to patronisingly admit. There was no sense of degradation in accepting the friendship of this man who had travelled so far, seen so much, and yet, as a practical man of the world, Rand felt was so inferior to himself. The absence of Miss Euphemia, who had early left the mountain, was a source of odd, half-definite relief. Indeed, when he closed his eyes to rest that night, it was with a sense that the reality of his situation was not as bad as he had feared. Once only, the figure of his brother, haggard, weary and footsore, on his hopeless quest, wandering in lonely trails and lonelier settlements, came across his fancy; but with it came the greater fear of his return, and the pathetic figure was banished. "And besides, he's in Sacramento by this time, and like as not forgotten us all," he muttered; and twining this poppy and mandragora around his pillow, he fell asleep.

His spirits had quite returned the next morning, and once or twice he found himself singing while at work in the shaft. The fear that Ruth might return to the mountain before he could get rid of Mornie, and the slight anxiety that had grown upon him to know something of his brother's movements, and to be able to govern them as he wished, caused him to hit upon the plan of constructing an ingenious advertisement to be published in the San Francisco journals, wherein the missing Ruth should be advised that news of his quest should be communicated to him by "a friend," through the same medium, after an interval of two weeks. Full of this amiable intention, he returned to the surface to dinner. Here, to his momentary confusion, he met Miss Euphemia, who, in absence of Sol, was assisting Mrs. Sol in the details of the household.

If the honest frankness with which that young lady greeted him was not enough to relieve his embarrassment, he would have forgotten it in the utterly new and changed aspect she presented. Her extravagant walking costume of the previous day was replaced by some bright calico, a little white apron, and a broad-brimmed straw hat, which seemed to Rand, in some odd fashion, to restore her original girlish simplicity. The change was certainly not unbecoming to her : if her waist was not as tightly pinched, *à la mode*, there still was an honest, youthful plumpness about it ; her step was freer for the absence of her high-heel boots ; and even the hand she extended to Rand, if not quite so small as in her tight gloves, and a little brown from exposure, was magnetic in its strong, kindly grasp. There was perhaps a slight suggestion of the practical Mr. Sol in her wholesome presence, and Rand could not help wondering if Mrs. Sol had ever been a Gold Hill " pet " before her marriage with Mr. Sol. The young girl noticed his curious glance.

" You never saw me in my rehearsal dress before," she said, with a laugh ; " but I'm not 'company' to-day, and didn't put on my best harness to knock round in. I suppose I look dreadful."

" I don't think you look bad," said Rand simply.

" Thank you," said Euphemia, with a laugh and a curtsey. " But this isn't getting the dinner."

As part of that operation evidently was the taking off of her hat, the putting up of some thick blonde locks that had escaped, and the rolling up of her sleeves over a pair of strong rounded arms, Rand lingered near her. All trace of the Pet's previous professional coquetry was gone—perhaps it was only replaced by a more natural one—but as she looked up and caught sight of Rand's interested face, she laughed again and coloured a little. Slight as was the blush, it was sufficient to kindle a sympathetic fire in Rand's own cheeks, which was so utterly unexpected to him that he

turned on his heel in confusion. " I reckon she thinks I'm
soft and silly, like Ruth," he soliloquised, and determining
not to look at her again, betook himself to a distant and
contemplative pipe. In vain did Miss Euphemia address
herself to the ostentatious getting of the dinner in full view
of him ; in vain did she bring the coffee-pot away from the
fire, and nearer Rand, with the apparent intention of examining its contents in a better light ; in vain, while wiping a
plate, did she, absorbed in the distant prospect, walk to the
verge of the mountain, and become statuesque and forgetful. The sulky young gentleman took no outward notice
of her.

Mrs. Sol's attendance upon Mornie prevented her leaving
the cabin, and Rand and Miss Euphemia dined in the open
air alone. The ridiculousness of keeping up a formal
attitude to his solitary companion caused Rand to relax ;
but, to his astonishment, the Pet seemed to have become
correspondingly distant and formal. After a few moments
of discomfort, Rand, who had eaten little, arose, and " believed he would go back to work."

" Ah yes," said the Pet, with an indifferent air, " I suppose you must. Well, good-bye, Mr. Pinkney."

Rand turned. " *You* are not going ? " he asked, in some
uneasiness.

" *I've* got some work to do, too," returned Miss Euphemia,
a little curtly.

" But," said the practical Rand, " I thought you allowed
that you were fixed to stay until to-morrow ? "

But here Miss Euphemia, with rising colour and slight
acerbity of voice, was not aware that she was " fixed to stay "
anywhere, least of all when she was in the way. More than
that, she *must* say, although perhaps it made no difference,
and she ought not to say it—that she was not in the habit
of intruding upon gentlemen, who plainly gave her to under-

stand that her company was not desirable. She did not know why she said this—of course it could make no difference to anybody who didn't, of course, care ; but she only wanted to say that she only came here because her dear friend, her adopted mother—and a better woman never breathed—had come and had asked her to stay. Of course, Mrs. Sol was an intruder herself—Mr. Sol was an intruder —they were all intruders : she only wondered that Mr. Pinkney had borne with them so long. She knew it was an awful thing to be here, taking care of a poor—poor, helpless woman ; but perhaps Mr. Rand's *brother* might forgive them if he couldn't. But no matter, she would go—Mr. Sol would go—*all* would go, and then, perhaps, Mr. Rand——

She stopped breathless ; she stopped with the corner of her apron against her tearful hazel eyes ; she stopped with, what was more remarkable than all—Rand's arm actually around her waist, and his astonished, alarmed face within a few inches of her own.

"Why, Miss Euphemia, Phemie, my dear girl ! I never meant anything like *that*," said Rand earnestly. "I really didn't, now ! Come now !"

"You never once spoke to me when I sat down," said Miss Euphemia, feebly endeavouring to withdraw from Rand's grasp.

"I really didn't ! Oh, come now, look here ! I didn't ! Don't! There's a dear—*there !*"

This last conclusive exposition was a kiss. Miss Euphemia was not quick enough to release herself from his arms. He anticipated that act a full half-second, and had dropped his own, pale and breathless.

The girl recovered herself first. "There, I declare, I'm forgetting Mrs. Sol's coffee !" she exclaimed hastily, and snatching up the coffee-pot, disappeared. When she returned, Rand was gone. Miss Euphemia busied herself, demurely, in clearing up the dishes, with the tail of her eye sweeping the horizon of the summit level around her. But no Rand appeared. Presently she began to laugh quietly to herself. This occurred several times during her occupation, which was somewhat prolonged. The result of this meditative hilarity was summed up in a somewhat grave and thoughtful deduction, as she walked slowly back to the cabin, "I do believe I'm the first woman that that boy ever kissed."

Miss Euphemia stayed that day and the next, and Rand forgot his embarrassment. By what means, I know not, Miss Euphemia managed to restore Rand's confidence in himself and in her, and in a little ramble on the mountain side, got him to relate, albeit somewhat reluctantly, the particulars of his rescue of Mornie from her dangerous position on the broken trail.

"And if you hadn't got there as soon as you did, she'd have fallen?" asked the Pet.

"I reckon," returned Rand gloomily, "she was sorter dazed and crazed like."

"And you saved her life?"

"I suppose so, if you put it that way," said Rand sulkily.

"But how did you get her up the mountain again?"

"Oh, I got her up," returned Rand moodily.

"But how? Really, Mr. Rand, you don't know how interesting this is. It's as good as a play," said the Pet, with a little excited laugh.

"Oh, I carried her up!"

"In your arms?"

"Y-e-e-s."

Miss Euphemia paused, and bit off the stalk of a flower, made a wry face, and threw it away from her in disgust.

Then she dug a few tiny holes in the earth with her parasol, and buried bits of the flower-stalk in them, as if they had been tender memories. " I suppose you knew Mornie very well ? " she asked.

" I used to run across her in the woods," responded Rand shortly, " a year ago. I didn't know her so well then as "—— He stopped.

" As what ? as *now ?* " asked the Pet abruptly. Rand, who was colouring over his narrow escape from a topic which a delicate kindness of Sol had excluded from their intercourse on the mountain, stammered " as *you* do—I meant."

The Pet tossed her head a little, " Oh, I don't know her at all—except through Sol ! "

Rand stared hard at this. The Pet, who was looking at him intently, said, " Show me the place where you saw Mornie clinging that night."

" It's dangerous," suggested Rand.

" You mean I'd be afraid ! Try me ! I don't believe she was *so* dreadfully frightened ! "

" Why ? " asked Rand, in astonishment.

" Oh,—because "——

Rand sat down in vague wonderment.

" Show it to me," continued the Pet, " or—I'll find it a*lone !* "

Thus challenged, he rose, and after a few moments' climbing stood with her upon the trail. " You see that thorn-bush where the rock has fallen away. It was just there ! It is not safe to go farther. No, really ! Miss Euphemia ! Please don't ! It's almost certain death ! "

But the giddy girl had darted past him, and, face to the wall of the cliff, was creeping along the dangerous path. Rand followed mechanically. Once or twice the trail crumbled beneath her feet, but she clung to a projecting root of *chapparal*, and laughed. She had almost reached her elected goal when, slipping, the treacherous *chapparal* she clung to yielded in her grasp, and Rand, with a cry, sprung forward. But the next instant she quickly transferred her hold to a cleft in the cliff and was safe. Not so her companion. The soil beneath him, loosened by the impulse of his spring, slipped away; he was falling with it, when she caught him sharply with her disengaged hand, and together they scrambled to a more secure footing.

"I could have reached it alone," said the Pet, "if you'd left me alone."

"Thank Heaven, we're saved," said Rand gravely.

"*And without a rope*," said Miss Euphemia significantly.

Rand did not understand her. But as they slowly returned to the summit he stammered out the always difficult thanks of a man who has been physically helped by one of the weaker sex. Miss Euphemia was quick to see her error.

"I might have made you lose your footing by catching at you," she said meekly. "But I was so frightened for you, and could not help it."

The superior animal, thoroughly bamboozled, thereupon complimented her on her dexterity.

"Oh, that's nothing," she said, with a sigh. "I used to do the flying-trapeze business with papa when I was a child, and I've not forgotten it." With this and other confidences of her early life, in which Rand betrayed considerable interest, they beguiled the tedious ascent. "I ought to have made you carry me up," said the lady, with a little laugh, when they reached the summit; "but you haven't known me as long as you have Mornie—have you?" With this mysterious speech she bade Rand "Good-night," and hurried off to the cabin.

And so a week passed by—the week so dreaded by Rand,

yet passed so pleasantly, that at times it seemed as if that dread were only a trick of his fancy, or as if the circumstances that surrounded him were different from what he believed them to be.   On the seventh day the doctor had stayed longer than usual, and Rand, who had been sitting with Euphemia on the ledge by the shaft, watching the sunset, had barely time to withdraw his hand from hers as Mrs. Sol, a trifle pale and wearied-looking, approached him.

"I don't like to trouble you," she said—indeed they had seldom troubled him with the details of Mornie's convalescence, or even her needs and requirements,—" but the doctor is alarmed about Mornie, and she has asked to see you.   I think you'd better go in and speak to her.   You know," continued Mrs. Sol delicately, "you haven't been in there since the night she was taken sick, and maybe a new face might do her good."

The guilty blood flew to Rand's face as he stammered, "I thought I'd be in the way.   I didn't believe she cared much to see me.   Is she worse?"

"The doctor is looking very anxious," said Mrs. Sol simply.

The blood returned from Rand's face, and settled around his heart.   He turned very pale.   He had consoled himself always for his complicity in Ruth's absence, that he was taking good care of Mornie, or—what is considered by most selfish natures an equivalent—permitting or encouraging some one else to "take good care of her," but here was a contingency utterly unforeseen.   It did not occur to him that this "taking good care" of her could result in anything but a perfect solution of her troubles, or that there could be any future to her condition but one of recovery.   But what if she should die?   A sudden and helpless sense of his responsibility to Ruth—to *her*—brought him trembling to his feet.

He hurried to the cabin, where Mrs. Sol left him with a word of caution. "You'll find her changed and quiet— very quiet. If I was you I wouldn't say anything to bring back her old self."

The change which Rand saw was so great, the face that was turned to him so quiet, that, with a new fear upon him, he would have preferred the savage eyes and reckless mien of the old Mornie whom he hated. With his habitual impulsiveness he tried to say something that should express that fact not unkindly,—but faltered, and awkwardly sank into the chair by her bedside.

" I don't wonder you stare at me now," she said, in a far-off voice ; " it seems to you strange to see me lying here so quiet. You are thinking how wild I was when I came here that night. I must have been crazy, I think. I dreamed that I said dreadful things to you ; but you must forgive me, and not mind it. I was crazy then." She stopped and folded the blanket between her thin fingers. "I didn't ask you to come here to tell you that, or to remind you of it, but—but when I was crazy, I said so many worse, dreadful things of *him ;* and you—*you* will be left behind to tell him of it."

Rand was vaguely murmuring something to the effect that "he knew she didn't mean anything," that "she mustn't think of it again," that "he'd forgotten all about it," when she stopped him with a tired gesture.

"Perhaps I was wrong to think that, after I am gone, you would care to tell him anything. Perhaps I'm wrong to think of it at all, or to care what he will think of me— except for the sake of the child—*his* child, Rand !—that I must leave behind me. He will know that *it* never abused him. No, God bless its sweet heart ! *it* never was wild and wicked and hateful, like its cruel, crazy mother. And he will love it ; and you, perhaps, will love it too—just a little,

Rand! Look at it!" She tried to raise the helpless
bundle beside her in her arms, but failed. "You must
lean over," she said, faintly, to Rand. "It looks like him,
doesn't it?"

Rand, with wondering, embarrassed eyes, tried to see
some resemblance in the little blue red oval, to the sad,
wistful face of his brother, which even then was haunting
him from some mysterious distance. He kissed the child's
forehead, but even then so vaguely and perfunctorily, that
the mother sighed, and drew it closer to her breast.

"The doctor says," she continued, in a calmer voice,
"that I'm not doing as well as I ought to. I don't think,"
she faltered, with something of her old bitter laugh, "that
I'm ever doing as well as I ought to, and perhaps it's not
strange now that I don't. And he says, that in case anything happens to me, I ought to look ahead! I have
looked ahead! It's a dark look ahead, Rand—a horror of
blackness, without kind faces, without the baby, without—
without *him!*"

She turned her face away, and laid it on the bundle by
her side. It was so quiet in the cabin, that through the
open door, beyond, the faint rhythmical moan of the pines
below was distinctly heard.

"I know it's foolish—but that is what 'looking ahead'
always meant to me," she said, with a sigh. "But, since
the doctor has been gone, I've talked to Mrs. Sol, and find
it's for the best. And I look ahead, and see more clearly.
I look ahead, and see my disgrace removed far away from
*him* and you. I look ahead, and see you and *he* living together, happily, as you did before I came between you. I
look ahead, and see my past life forgotten, my faults forgiven,
and I think I see you both loving my baby, and perhaps
loving me a little for its sake. Thank you, Rand, thank
you!"

For Rand's hand had caught hers beside the pillow, and he was standing over her, whiter than she. Something in the pressure of his hand emboldened her to go on, and even lent a certain strength to her voice.

"When it comes to *that*, Rand, you'll not let these people take the baby away. You'll keep it *here* with you until *he* comes. And something tells me that he will come when I am gone. You'll keep it here in the pure air and sunlight of the mountain, and out of those wicked depths below ; and when I am gone, and they are gone, and only you and Ruth and baby are here, maybe you'll think that it came to you in a cloud on the mountain—a cloud that lingered only long enough to drop its burden, and faded, leaving the sunlight and dew behind. What is it—Rand ? What are you looking at ? "

" I was thinking," said Rand, in a strange altered voice, " that I must trouble you to let me take down those duds and furbelows that hang on the wall, so that I can get at some traps of mine behind them." He took some articles from the wall, replaced the dresses of Mrs. Sol, and answered Mornie's look of inquiry. " I was only getting at my purse and my revolver," he said, showing them. " I've got to get some stores at the Ferry, by daylight."

Mornie sighed. " I'm giving you great trouble, Rand, I know ; but it won't be for long."

He muttered something, took her hand again, and bade her " good-night." When he reached the door he looked back. The light was shining full upon her face as she lay there with her babe on her breast, bravely "looking ahead."

## PART IV.

### THE CLOUDS PASS.

IT was early morning at the Ferry. The " up coach " had passed with lights unextinguished, and the " outsides " still asleep. The ferryman had gone up to the Ferry Mansion House, swinging his lantern, and had found the sleepy-looking " all-night " bar-keeper on the point of withdrawing for the day on a mattress under the bar. An Indian half-breed, porter of the Mansion House, was washing out the stains of recent nocturnal dissipation from the bar-room and verandah, a few birds were twittering on the cotton woods beside the river, a bolder few had alighted upon the verandah and were trying to reconcile the existence of so much lemon-peel and cigar stumps with their ideas of a beneficent Creator. A faint earthy freshness and perfume rose along the river banks. Deep shadows still lay upon the opposite shore, but in the distance, four miles away, morning along the level crest of Table Mountain walked with rosy tread.

The sleepy bar-keeper was that morning doomed to disappointment. For scarcely had the coach passed, when steps were heard upon the verandah, and a weary dusty traveller threw his blanket and knapsack to the porter, and then dropped into a vacant arm-chair, with his eyes fixed on the distant crest of Table Mountain. He remained motionless for some time, until the bar-keeper, who had already concocted the conventional welcome of the Mansion House, appeared with it in a glass, put it upon the table, glanced at the stranger, and then, thoroughly awake, cried out—

" Ruth Pinkney—or I'm a Chinaman ! "

The stranger lifted his eyes wearily. Hollow circles

were around their orbits, haggard lines were in his cheeks.
But it was Ruth.

He took the glass and drained it at a single draught.
"Yes," he said absently, "Ruth Pinkney," and fixed his
eyes again on the distant rosy crest.

"On your way up home?" suggested the bar-keeper,
following the direction of Ruth's eyes.

"Perhaps."

"Been upon a *pasear*—hain't yer? Been havin' a little
tear round Sacramento—seein' the sights."

Ruth smiled bitterly. "Yes."

The bar-keeper lingered—ostentatiously wiping a glass.
But Ruth again became abstracted in the mountain, and
the bar-keeper turned away.

How pure and clear that summit looked to him! how
restful and steadfast with serenity and calm! how unlike
his own feverish, dusty, travel-worn self! A week had
elapsed since he had last looked upon it—a week of disappointment, of anxious fears, of doubts, of wild imagin-
ings, of utter helplessness. In his hopeless quest of the
missing Mornie, he had, in fancy, seen this serene eminence
haunting his remorseful passion-stricken soul. And now,
without a clue to guide him to her unknown hiding-place,
he was back again to face the brother whom he had
deceived, with only the confession of his own weakness.
Hard as it was to lose for ever the fierce reproachful
glances of the woman he loved, it was still harder to a man
of Ruth's temperament to look again upon the face of the
brother he feared. A hand laid upon his shoulder startled
him. It was the bar-keeper.

"If it's a fair question, Ruth Pinkney, I'd like to ask ye
how long ye kalkilate to hang around the Ferry to-day?"

"Why?" demanded Ruth haughtily.

"Because, whatever you've been and done, I want ye to

have a square show.   Ole Nixon has been cavoortin' round
yer the last two days, swearin' to kill you on sight for
runnin' off with his darter.   Sabe ?   Now let me ax ye two
questions.   *First*—are you heeled ? "

Ruth responded to this dialectical inquiry affirmatively,
by putting his hand on his revolver.

" Good !   Now, *Second*—have you got the gal along here
with you ? "

"No," responded Ruth, in a hollow voice.

" That's better yet," said the man, without heeding the
tone of the reply.   " A woman—and especially *the* woman,
in a row of this kind—handicaps a man awful."   He paused
and took up the empty glass.   " Look yer, Ruth Pinkney,
I'm a square man, and I'll be square with you.   So I'll just
tell you, you've got the demdest odds agin' ye.   Pr'aps ye
know it, and don't keer.   Well, the boys around yer are all
sidin' with the old man Nixon.   It's the first time the old
rip ever had a hand in his favour ; so the boys will see fair
play for Nixon and agin' *you*.   But I reckon you don't
mind him ? "

" So little, I shall never pull trigger on him ! " said Ruth
gravely.

The bar-keeper stared, and rubbed his chin thoughtfully.
" Well, thar's that Kanaka Joe, who used to be sorter sweet
on Mornie—he's an ugly devil—he's helpin' the old man ! "

The sad look faded from Ruth's eyes suddenly.   A certain wild Berserker rage—a taint of the blood, inherited
from heaven knows what Old-World ancestry, which had
made the twin brothers' South-western eccentricities respected in the settlement—glowed in its place.   The bar-
keeper noted it, and augured a lively future for the day's
festivities.   But it faded again; and Ruth, as he rose,
turned hesitatingly towards him.

" Have you seen my brother Rand lately ? "

" Nary."

" He hasn't been here, or about the Ferry?"

" Nary time."

" You haven't heard," said Ruth, with a faint attempt at a smile, "if he's been around here asking after me—sorter looking me up, you know?"

" Not much," returned the bar-keeper deliberately. "Ez far ez I know Rand—that ar brother o' yours—he's one of yer high-toned chaps ez doesn't drink, thinks bar-rooms is pizen, and ain't the sort to come round yer and sling yarns with me."

Ruth rose ; but the hand that he placed upon the table, albeit a powerful one, trembled so that it was with difficulty he resumed his knapsack. When he did so, his bent figure, stooping shoulders, and haggard face made him appear another man from the one who had sat down. There was a slight touch of apologetic deference and humility in his manner as he paid his reckoning, and slowly and hesitatingly began to descend the steps.

The bar-keeper looked after him thoughtfully. " Well, dog my skin !" he ejaculated to himself, " ef I hadn't seen that man—that same Ruth Pinkney—straddle a friend's body in this yer very room, and dare a whole crowd to come on, I'd swar that he hadn't any grit in him ! Thar's something up !"

But here Ruth reached the last step, and turned again.

" If you see old man Nixon, say I'm in town ; if you see that —— —— ——" (I regret to say that I cannot repeat his exact and brief characterisation of the present condition and natal antecedents of Kanaka Joe), " say I'm looking out for him," and was gone.

He wandered down the road towards the one long strag-gling street of the settlement. The few people who met him at that early hour greeted him with a kind of constrained civility ; certain cautious souls hurried by without seeing him ; all turned and looked after him, and a few followed him at a respectful distance.  A somewhat notorious practical joker, and recognised wag at the Ferry, apparently awaited his coming with something of invitation and expectation, but catching sight of Ruth's haggard face and blazing eyes, became instantly practical and by no means jocular in his greeting.  At the top of the hill, Ruth turned to look once more upon the distant mountain, now again a mere cloud-line on the horizon.  In the firm belief that he would never again see the sun rise upon it, he turned aside into a hazel thicket, and tearing out a few leaves from his pocket-book, wrote two letters—one to Rand and one to Mornie ; but which, as they were never delivered, shall not burden this brief chronicle of that eventful day.  For while transcribing them, he was startled by the sounds of a dozen pistol-shots, in the direction of the hotel he had recently quitted.  Something in the mere sound provoked the old hereditary fighting instinct, and sent him to his feet with a bound, and a slight distension of the nostrils and sniffing of the air not unknown to certain men who become half intoxicated by the smell of powder.  He quickly folded his letters and addressed them carefully, and taking off his knapsack and blanket, methodically arranged them under a tree, with the letters on top.  Then he examined the lock of his revolver, and then, with the step of a man ten years younger, leaped into the road.  He had scarcely done so when he was seized, and by sheer force dragged into a blacksmith's shop at the roadside.  He turned his savage face and drawn weapon upon his assailant, but was surprised to meet the anxious eyes of the bar-keeper of the Mansion House.

'Don't be a d—d fool," said the man quickly.  " Thar's fifty agin' you down thar.  But why, in h—ll, didn't you wipe out old Nixon when you had such a good chance ? "

"Wipe out old Nixon?" repeated Ruth.

"Yes, just now, when you had him covered!"

"What!"

The bar-keeper turned quickly upon Ruth, stared at him, and then suddenly burst into a fit of laughter. "Well! I've knowed you two were twins, but damn me if I ever thought I'd be sold like this." And he again burst into a roar of laughter.

"What do you mean?" demanded Ruth savagely.

"What do I mean?" returned the bar-keeper, "why, I mean this. I mean that your brother, Rand, as you call him, he'z bin—for a young feller, and a pious feller—doin' about the tallest kind o' fightin' to-day that's been done at the Ferry. He's laid out that ar Kanaka Joe and two of his chums! He was pitched into on your quarrel, and he took it up for you like a little man! I managed to drag him off, up yer, in the hazel bush for safety, and out you pops, and I thought you was him! He can't be far away. Hallo! There they're comin'; and thar's the doctor trying to keep them back!"

A crowd of angry excited faces filled the road suddenly, but before them Dr. Duchesne, mounted, and with a pistol in his hand, opposed their further progress.

"Back, in the bush!" whispered the bar-keeper. "Now's your time!"

But Ruth stirred not. "Go you back," he said, in a low voice; "find Rand, and take him away. I will fill his place here." He drew his revolver, and stepped into the road.

A shout, a report, and the spatter of red dust from a bullet near his feet, told him he was recognised. He stirred not; but another shout, and a cry, "There they are—*both* of 'em!" made him turn.

His brother Rand, with a smile on his lip and fire in his

eye, stood by his side! Neither spoke. Then Rand, quietly, as of old, slipped his hand into his brother's strong palm. Two or three bullets sang by them, a splinter flew from the blacksmith's shed, but the brothers, hard gripping each other's hands, and looking into each other's faces, with a quiet joy, stood there, calm and imperturbable.

There was a momentary pause. The voice of Dr. Duchesne rose above the crowd.

"Keep back, I say! Keep back! Or hear me!—for five years I've worked among you, and mended and patched the holes you've drilled through each other's carcasses— Keep back, I say!—Or the next man that pulls trigger, or steps forward, will get a hole from me that no surgeon can stop! I'm sick of your bungling ball practice! Keep back!—or, by the living Jingo, I'll show you where a man's vitals are!"

There was a burst of laughter from the crowd, and for a moment the twins were forgotten in this audacious speech and coolly impertinent presence.

"That's right! Now let that infernal old hypocritical drunkard, Mat Nixon, step to the front."

The crowd parted right and left, and half pushed, half dragged Nixon before him.

"Gentlemen," said the doctor, "this is the man who has just shot at Rand Pinkney for hiding his daughter. Now, I tell you, gentlemen, and I tell him, that for the last week his daughter, Mornie Nixon, has been under my care as a patient, and my protection as a friend. If there's anybody to be shot, the job must begin with me!"

There was another laugh, and a cry of "Bully for old Sawbones!" Ruth started convulsively, and Rand answered his look with a confirming pressure of his hand.

"That isn't all, gentlemen, this drunken brute has just shot at a gentleman, whose only offence, to my knowledge, is that he has, for the last week, treated her with a brother's kindness, has taken her into his own home, and cared for her wants as if she were his own sister."

Ruth's hand again grasped his brother's. Rand coloured, and hung his head.

"There's more yet, gentlemen. I tell you that that girl, Mornie Nixon, has, to my knowledge, been treated like a lady, has been cared for as she never was cared for in her father's house, and while that father has been proclaiming her shame in every bar-room at the Ferry, has had the sympathy and care, night and day, of two of the most accomplished ladies of the Ferry—Mrs. Sol Saunders, gentlemen, and Miss Euphemia!"

There was a shout of approbation from the crowd. Nixon would have slipped away, but the doctor stopped him.

"Not yet! I've one thing more to say. I've to tell you, gentlemen, on my professional word of honour, that besides being an old hypocrite, this same old Mat Nixon is the ungrateful, unnatural *grandfather* of the first boy born in the district!"

A wild huzza greeted the doctor's climax. By a common consent the crowd turned toward the Twins, who, grasping each other's hands, stood apart. The doctor nodded his head. The next moment the Twins were surrounded and lifted in the arms of the laughing throng, and borne in triumph to the bar-room of the Mansion House.

"Gentlemen," said the bar-keeper, "call for what you like : the Mansion House treats to-day in honour of its being the first time that Rand Pinkney has been admitted to the Bar."

. . . . . .

It was agreed that, as her condition was still precarious, the news should be broken to her gradually and indirectly. The indefatigable Sol had a professional idea, which was not displeasing to the Twins. It being a lovely summer afternoon, the couch of Mornie was lifted out on the ledge, and she lay there basking in the sunlight, drinking in the pure air, and looking bravely ahead in the daylight as she had in the darkness—for her couch commanded a view of the mountain flank. And lying there she dreamed a pleasant dream, and in her dream saw Rand returning up the mountain trail. She was·half conscious that he had good news for her, and when he at last reached her bed-side, he began gently and kindly to tell his news. But she heard him not, or rather in her dream was most occupied with his ways and manners, which seemed unlike him, yet inexpressibly sweet and tender. The tears were fast coming in her eyes, when he suddenly dropped on his knees beside her, threw away Rand's disguising hat and coat, and clasped her in his arms. And by that she *knew* it was Ruth !

But what they said ; what hurried words of mutual explanation and forgiveness passed between them ; what bitter yet tender recollections of hidden fears and doubts, now for ever chased away in the rain of tears and joyous sunshine of that mountain top, were then whispered ; what-ever of this little chronicle, that to the reader seems strange and inconsistent,—as all human records must ever be strange and imperfect except to the actors—was then made clear, was never divulged by them, and must remain with them for ever. The rest of the party had withdrawn and they were alone. But when Mornie turned and placed the baby in its father's arms, they were so isolated in their happiness, that the lower world beneath them might have swung and drifted away, and left that mountain top the beginning and creation of a better planet.

   .    .    .    .    .    .

"You know all about it now," said Sol, the next day

explaining the previous episodes of this history to Ruth, "you've got the whole plot before you. It dragged a little in the second act, for the actors weren't up in their parts. But, for an amateur performance, on the whole, it wasn't bad."

"I don't know, I'm sure," said Rand impulsively, "how we'd have got on without Euphemia. It's too bad she couldn't be here to-day."

"She wanted to come," said Sol, "but the gentleman she's engaged to came up from Marysville last night."

"Gentleman—engaged!" repeated Rand, white and red by turns.

"Well, yes! I say 'gentleman,' although he's in the Variety profession. She always said," said Sol quietly, looking at Rand, "that she'd never marry *out* of it."

# Jeff Briggs's Love Story.

## CHAPTER I.

It was raining and blowing at Eldridge's Crossing. From the stately pine trees on the hill-tops, which were dignifiedly protesting through their rigid spines upward, to the hysterical willows in the hollow, that had whipped themselves into a maudlin fury, there was a general tumult. When the wind lulled the rain kept up the distraction, firing long volleys across the road, letting loose miniature cataracts from the hill-sides to brawl in the ditches, and beating down the heavy heads of wild oats on the levels ; when the rain ceased for a moment the wind charged over the already defeated field, ruffled the gulleys, scattered the spray from the roadside pines, and added insult to injury. But both wind and rain concentrated their energies in a malevolent attempt to utterly disperse and scatter the "Halfway House," which seemed to have wholly lost its way, and strayed into the open, where, dazed and bewildered, unprepared and unprotected, it was exposed to the taunting fury of the blast. A loose, shambling, disjointed, hastily-built structure—representing the worst features of Pioneer *renaissance*—it rattled its loose window-sashes like chattering teeth, banged its ill-hung shutters, and admitted so much of the invading storm, that it might have blown up or blown down with equal facility.

Jefferson Briggs, proprietor and landlord of the "Half-

way House," had just gone through the formality of closing
his house for the night, hanging dangerously out of the
window in the vain attempt to subdue a rebellious shutter
that had evidently entered into conspiracy with the invaders,
and shutting a door as against a sheriff's *posse*, was going to
bed—*i.e.*, to read himself asleep, as was his custom. As he
entered his little bedroom in the attic with a highly exciting
novel in his pocket and a kerosene lamp in his hand, the
wind, lying in wait for him, instantly extinguished his lamp
and slammed the door behind him. Jefferson Briggs
relighted the lamp, as if confidentially, in a corner, and
shielding it in the bosom of his red flannel shirt, which gave
him the appearance of an illuminated shrine, hung a heavy
bear-skin across the window, and then carefully deposited
his lamp upon a chair at his bedside. This done, he kicked
off his boots, flung them into a corner, and rolling himself
in a blanket, lay down upon the bed. A habit of early
rising, bringing with it, presumably, the proverbial accompaniment of health, wisdom, and pecuniary emoluments,
had also brought with it certain ideas of the effeminacy of
separate toilettes and the virtue of readiness.

In a few moments he was deep in a chapter.

A vague pecking at his door—as of an unseasonable
woodpecker, finally asserted itself to his consciousness.
"Come in," he said, with his eye still on the page.

The door opened to a gaunt figure, partly composed of
bed-quilt and partly of plaid shawl. A predominance of the
latter and a long wisp of iron-gray hair determined her sex.
She leaned against the post with an air of fatigue, half moral
and half physical.

"How ye kin lie thar, abed, Jeff, and read and smoke on
sich a night! The sperrit o' the Lord abroad over the yearth
—and up stage not gone by yet. Well, well! it's well thar
ez *some* ez *can't* sleep."

"The up coach, like as not, is stopped by high water on the North Fork, ten miles away, aunty," responded Jeff, keeping to the facts.    Possibly not recognising the hand of a beneficent Creator in the rebellious window shutter, he avoided theology.

"Well," responded the figure, with an air of delivering an unheeded and thankless warning, "it is not for *me* to say. P'raps it's all His wisdom that some will keep to their own mind.    It's well ez some hezn't narves, and kin luxuriate in terbacker in the night watches.    But He says, 'I'll come like a thief in the night!'—like a thief in the night, Jeff."

Totally unable to reconcile this illustration with the delayed "Pioneer" coach and Yuba Bill, its driver, Jeff lay silent.    In his own way, perhaps, he was uneasy—not to say shocked—at his aunt's habitual freedom of scriptural quotation, as that good lady herself was with an occasional oath from his lips.    A fact, by the way, not generally understood by purveyors of Scripture, licensed and unlicensed.

"I'd take a pull at them bitters, aunty," said Jeff feebly, with his wandering eye still recurring to his page.    "They'll do ye a power of good in the way o' calmin' yer narves."

"Ef I was like some folks I wouldn't want bitters—tho' made outer the simplest yarbs of the yearth, with jest enough sperrit to bring out the vartoos—ez Deacon Stoer's Balm 'er Gilead is—what yer meaning?    Ef I was like some folks I could lie thar and smoke in the lap o' idleness—with fourteen beds in the house empty, and nary lodger for one of 'em.    Ef I was that indifferent to havin' invested my fortin in the good will o' this house, and not ez much ez a single transient lookin' in, I could lie down and take comfort in profane literatoor.    But it ain't in me to do it.    And it wasn't your father's way, Jeff, neither!"

As the elder Briggs' way had been to seek surcease from such trouble at the gambling table, and eventually, in suicide, Jeff could not deny it. But he did not say that a full realisation of his unhappy venture overcame him as he closed the blinds of the hotel that night; and that the half desperate idea of abandoning it then and there to the warring elements that had resented his trespass on Nature, seemed to him an act of simple reason and justice. He did not say this, for easy-going natures are not apt to explain the processes by which their content or resignation is reached, and are therefore supposed to have none. Keeping to the facts, he simply suggested the weather was unfavourable to travellers, and again found his place on the page before him. Fixing it with his thumb, he looked up resignedly. The figure wearily detached itself from the door-post, and Jeff's eyes fell on his book. "You won't stop, aunty?" he asked mechanically, as if reading aloud from the page; but she was gone.

A little ashamed, although much relieved, Jeff fell back again to literature, interrupted only by the charging of the wind and the heavy volleys of rain. Presently he found himself wondering if a certain banging were really a shutter, and then, having settled in his mind that it *was*, he was startled by a shout. Another, and in the road before the house!

Jeff put down his book, and marked the place by turning down the leaf, being one of that large class of readers whose mental faculties are butter-fingered, and easily slip their hold. Then he resumed his boots and was duly caparisoned. He extinguished the kerosene lamp, and braved the outer air and strong currents of the hall and stairway in the darkness. Lighting two candles in the bar-room, he proceeded to unlock the hall door. At the same instant a furious blast shook the house, the door yielded slightly and impelled a thin, meek-looking stranger violently against Jeff, who still struggled with it.

"An accident has occurred," began the stranger, "and
——" But here the wind charged again, blew open the
door, pinned Jeff behind it back against the wall, overturned the dripping stranger, and dashing up the staircase,
slammed every door in the house, ending triumphantly with
No. 14, and a crash of glass in the window.

"Come, rouse up !" said Jeff, still struggling with the
door, " rouse up and lend a hand yer !"

Thus abjured, the stranger crept along the wall towards
Jeff and began again, "We have met with an accident."
But here another and mightier gust left him speechless,
covered him with spray of a wildly disorganised water-spout
that, dangling from the roof, seemed to be playing on the
front door, drove him into black obscurity and again sand-
wiched his host between the door and the wall. Then
there was a lull, and in the midst of it, Yuba Bill, driver of
the "Pioneer" coach, quietly and coolly, impervious in
waterproof, walked into the hall, entered the bar-room,
took a candle, and going behind the bar, selected a bottle,
critically examined it, and returning, poured out a quantity
of whisky in a glass and gulped it in a single draught. All
this while Jeff was closing the door, and the meek-looking
man was coming into the light again.

Yuba Bill squared his elbows behind him and rested
them on the bar, crossed his legs easily and awaited them.
In reply to Jeff's inquiring but respectful look, he said
shortly—

"Oh, you're thar, are ye ?"

"Yes, Bill."

"Well, this yer new-fangled road o' yours is ten feet deep
in the hollow with back water from the North Fork ! I've
taken that yar coach inter fower feet of it, and then I reckoned I couldn't hev any more. 'I'll stand on this yer
hand,' sez I ; I brought the horses up yer and landed 'em

in your barn to eat their blessed heads off till the water goes down. That's wot's the matter, old man, and jist about wot I kalkilated on from those durned old improvements o' yours."

Colouring a little at this new count in the general indictment against the uselessness of the "Half-way House," Jeff asked if there were "any passengers?"

Yuba Bill indicated the meek stranger with a jerk of his thumb. "And his wife and darter in the coach. They're all right and tight, ez if they was in the Fifth Avenue Hotel. But I reckon he allows to fetch 'em up yer," added Bill, as if he strongly doubted the wisdom of the transfer.

The meek man, much meeker for the presence of Bill, here suggested that such indeed was his wish, and further prayed that Jeff would accompany him to the coach to assist in bringing them up. "It's rather wet and dark," said the man apologetically; "my daughter is not strong. Have you such a thing as a waterproof?"

Jeff had not; but would a bear-skin do?

It would.

Jeff ran, tore down his extempore window curtain, and returned with it. Yuba Bill, who had quietly and disapprovingly surveyed the proceeding, here disengaged himself from the bar with evident reluctance.

"You'll want another man," he said to Jeff, "onless ye can carry double. Ez *he*," indicating the stranger, "ez no sort o' use, he'd better stay here and 'tend bar,' while you and me fetch the wimmen off. 'Specially ez I reckon we've got to do some tall wadin' by this time to reach 'em."

The meek man sat down helplessly in a chair indicated by Bill, who at once strode after Jeff. In another moment they were both fighting their way, step by step, against the storm, in that peculiar, drunken, spasmodic way so amusing to the spectator and so exasperating to the performer. It was no time for conversation, even interjectional profanity was dangerously exhaustive.

The coach was scarcely a thousand yards away, but its bright lights were reflected in a sheet of dark silent water that stretched between it and the two men. Wading and splashing they soon reached it, and a gulley where the surplus water was pouring into the valley below. "Fower feet o' water round her, but can't get any higher. So ye see she's all right for a month o' sich weather." Inwardly admiring the perspicacity of his companion, Jeff was about to open the coach door when Bill interrupted.

"I'll pack the old woman, if you'll look arter the darter and enny little traps."

A female face, anxious and elderly, here appeared at the window.

"Thet's my little game," said Bill, *sotto voce.*

"Is there any danger? where is my husband?" asked the woman impatiently.

"Ez to the danger, ma'am,—thar ain't any. Yer ez safe *here* ez ye'd be in a Sacramento steamer; ez to your husband, he allowed I was to come yer and fetch yer up to the hotel. That's his look-out!" With this cheering speech, Bill proceeded to make two or three ineffectual scoops into the dark interior, manifestly with the idea of scooping out the lady in question. In another instant he had caught her, lifted her gently but firmly in his arms, and was turning away.

"But my child!—my daughter! she's asleep"—expostulated the woman; but Bill was already swiftly splashing through the darkness. Jeff, left to himself, hastily examined the coach: on the back seat a slight small figure, enveloped in a shawl, lay motionless. Jeff threw the bear-skin over it gently, lifted it on one arm, and gathering a few travelling bags and baskets with the other, prepared to follow his quickly disappearing leader. A few feet from the coach the water appeared to deepen, and the bear-skin to draggle. Jeff drew the figure up higher, but in vain.

"Sis," he said softly.

No reply.

"Sis," shaking her gently.

There was a slight movement within the wrappings.

"Couldn't ye climb up on my shoulder, honey? that's a good child!"

There were one or two spasmodic jerks of the bear-skin, and, aided by Jeff, the bundle was presently seated on his shoulder.

"Are you all right now, Sis?"

Something like a laugh came from the bear-skin. Then a childish voice said, "Thank you, I think I am!"

"Ain't afraid you'll fall off?"

"A little."

Jeff hesitated. It was beginning to blow again.

"You couldn't reach down and put your arm round my neck, could ye, honey?"

."I am afraid not!"—although there *was* a slight attempt to do so.

"No?"

"No!"

"Well, then, take a good holt, a firm strong holt, o' my hair! Don't be afraid!"

A small hand timidly began to rummage in Jeff's thick curls.

"Take a firm holt; thar, just back o' my neck! That's right."

The little hand closed over half a dozen curls. The little figure shook, and giggled.

"Now don't you see, honey, if I'm keerles with you, and don't keep you plumb level up thar, you jist give me a pull and fetch me up all standing!"

"I see!"

"Of course you do! That's because you're a little lady!"

Jeff strode on. It was pleasant to feel the soft warm fingers in his hair, pleasant to hear the faint childish voice, pleasant to draw the feet of the enwrapped figure against his broad breast. Altogether he was sorry when they reached the dry land and the lee of the "Half-way House," where a slight movement of the figure expressed a wish to dismount.

"Not yet, missy," said Jeff; "not yet! You'll get blown away, sure! And then what'll they say? No, honey! I'll take you right into your papa, just as ye are!"

A few steps more and Jeff strode into the hall, made his way to the sitting-room, walked to the sofa, and deposited his burden. The bear-skin fell back, the shawl fell back, and Jeff—fell back too! For before him lay a small, slight, but beautiful and perfectly formed woman.

He had time to see that the meek man, no longer meek, but apparently a stern uncompromising parent, was standing at the head of the sofa; that the elderly and nervous female was hovering at the foot, that his aunt, with every symptom of religious and moral disapproval of his conduct, sat rigidly in one of the rigid chairs—he had time to see all this before the quick, hot blood, flying to his face, sent the water into his eyes, and he could see nothing!

The cause of all this smiled—a dazzling smile though a faint one—that momentarily lit up the austere gloom of the room and its occupants. "You must thank this gentleman, papa," said she, languidly turning to her father, "for his kindness and his trouble. He has carried me here as gently and as carefully as if I were a child." Seeing symptoms of a return of Jeff's distress in his colouring face, she added softly, as if to herself, "It's a great thing to be strong—a greater thing to be strong *and* gentle."

The voice thrilled through Jeff. But into this dangerous

human music twanged the accents of special spiritual revelation, and called him to himself again. "Be ye wise as sarpints, but harmless as duvs," said Jeff's aunt, generally, "and let 'em be thankful ez doesn't aboos the stren'th the Lord gives 'em, but be allers ready to answer for it at the bar o' their Maker." Possibly some suggestion in her figure of speech reminded her of Jeff's forgotten duties, so she added in the same breath and tone, "especially when transient customers is waiting for their licker, and Yuba Bill hammerin' on the counter with his glass; and yer ye stand, Jeff, never even takin' up that wet bar-skin—enuff to give that young woman her deth."

Stammering out an incoherent apology, addressed vaguely to the occupants of the room, but looking toward the languid goddess on the sofa, Jeff seized the bear-skin and backed out of the door. Then he flew to his room with it, and then returned to the bar-room; but the impatient William of Yuba had characteristically helped himself and gone off to the stable. Then Jeff stole into the hall and halted before the closed door of the sitting-room. A bold idea of going in again, as became the landlord of the "Half-way House," with an inquiry if they wished anything further, had seized him, but the remembrance that he had always meekly allowed that duty to devolve upon his aunt, and that she would probably resent it with Scriptural authority and bring him to shame again, stayed his timid knuckles at the door. In this hesitation he stumbled upon his aunt coming down the stairs with an armful of blankets and pillows, attended by their small Indian servant, staggering under a mattress.

"Is everything all right, aunty?"

"Ye kin be thankful to the Lord, Jeff Briggs, that this didn't happen last week when I was down on my back with rheumatiz. But ye'r never grateful."

"The young lady—is *she* comfortable?" said Jeff, accepting his aunt's previous remark as confirmatory.

"Ez well ez enny critter marked by the finger of the Lord with gallopin' consumption kin be, I reckon. And she, ez oughter be putting off airthly vanities, askin' for a lookin'-glass! And you! trapsin' through the hall with her on yer shoulder, and dancin' and jouncin' her up and down ez if it was a ball-room!" A guilty recollection that he had skipped with her through the passage struck him with remorse as his aunt went on: "It's a mercy that betwixt you and the wet bar-skin she ain't got her deth!"

"Don't ye think, aunty," stammered Jeff, "that—that— my bein' the landlord, yer know, it would be the square thing—just out o' respect, ye know—for me to drop in thar and ask 'em if thar's anythin' they wanted?"

His aunt stopped, and resignedly put down the pillows. "Sarah," she said meekly to the handmaiden, "ye kin leave go that mattress. Yer's Mr. Jefferson thinks we ain't good enough to make the beds for them two city women folks, and he allows he'll do it himself!"

"No, no! aunty!" began the horrified Jeff; but failing to placate his injured relative, took safety in flight.

Once safe in his own room his eye fell on the bear-skin. It certainly *was* wet. Perhaps he had been careless— perhaps he had imperilled her life! His cheeks flushed as he threw it hastily in the corner. Something fell from it to the floor. Jeff picked it up and held it to the light. It was a small, a very small, lady's slipper. Holding it within the palm of his hand as if it had been some delicate flower which the pressure of a finger might crush, he strode to the door, but stopped. Should he give it to his aunt? Even if she overlooked this evident proof of *his* carelessness, what would she think of the young lady's? Ought he—seductive thought!—go downstairs again, knock at the door, and give it to its fair owner, with the apology he was longing to make? Then he remembered that he had but a few moments before been dismissed the room very much as if he were the original proprietor of the skin he had taken. Perhaps they were right; perhaps he *was* only a foolish clumsy animal! Yet *she* had thanked him—she had said in her sweet childlike voice, "It is a great thing to be strong; a greater thing to be strong and gentle." He *was* strong; strong men had said so. He did not know if he was gentle too. Had she meant *that*, when she turned her strangely soft dark eyes upon him? For some moments he held the slipper hesitatingly in his hand, then he opened his trunk, and disposing various articles around it as if it were some fragile, perishable object, laid it carefully therein.

This done, he drew off his boots, and rolling himself in his blanket, lay down upon the bed. He did not open his novel—he did not follow up the exciting love episode of his favourite hero—so ungrateful is humanity to us poor romancers, in the first stages of their real passion. Ah, me! 'tis the jongleurs and troubadours they want then, not us! When Master Slender, sick for sweet Anne Page, would "rather than forty shillings" he had his "book of songs and sonnets" there, what availed it that the Italian Boccacio had contemporaneously discoursed wisely and sweetly of love in prose? I doubt not that Master Jeff would have mumbled some verse to himself had he known any: knowing none, he lay there and listened to the wind.

Did she hear it; did it keep her awake? He had an uneasy suspicion that the shutter that was banging so outrageously was the shutter of her room. Filled with this miserable thought, he arose softly, stole down the staircase, and listened. The sound was repeated. It was truly the refractory shutter of No. 7—the best bedroom adjoining the sitting-room. The next room, No. 8, was vacant. Jeff entered it softly, as softly opened the window, and leaning far out in the tempest, essayed to secure the nocturnal disturber. But in vain. Cord or rope he had none, nor could he procure either without alarming his aunt— an extremity not to be considered. Jeff was a man o clumsy but forceful expedients. He hung far out of the window, and with one powerful hand, lifted the shutter off its hinges and dragged it softly into No. 8. Then as softly he crept upstairs to bed. The wind howled and tore round the house; the crazy water-pipe below Jeff's window creaked, the chimneys whistled, but the shutter banged no more. Jeff began to doze. " It's a great thing to be strong," the wind seemed to say as it charged upon the defenceless house, and then another voice seemed to reply, " A greater thing to be strong and gentle; " and hearing this he fell asleep.

## CHAPTER II.

IT was not yet daylight when he awoke with an idea that brought him hurriedly to his feet. Quickly dressing himself, he began to count the money in his pocket. Apparently the total was not satisfactory, as he endeavoured to augment it by loose coins fished from the pockets of his other garments, and from the corner of his washstand drawer. Then he cautiously crept downstairs, seized his gun, and stole out of the still sleeping house. The wind had gone down, the rain had ceased, a few stars shone steadily in the north, and the shapeless bulk of the coach, its lamps extinguished, loomed high and dry above the lessening water, in the twilight. With a swinging tread Jeff strode up the hill and was soon upon the highway and stage road. A half-hour's brisk walk brought him to the summit, and the first rosy flashes of morning light. This enabled him to knock over half-a-dozen early quail, lured by the proverb, who were seeking their breakfast in the chapparal, and gave him courage to continue on his mission, which his perplexed face and irresolute manner had for the last few moments shown to be an embarrassing one. At last the white fences and imposing outbuildings of the "Summit Hotel" rose before him, and he uttered a deep sigh. There, basking in the first rays of the morning sun, stood his successful rival! Jeff looked at the well-built, comfortable structure, the commanding site, and the air of serene independence that seemed to possess it, and no longer wondered that the great world passed him by to linger and refresh itself there.

He was relieved to find the landlord was not present in person, and so confided his business to the bar-keeper. At first it appeared that that functionary declined interference, and with many head-shakings and audible misgivings, was inclined to await the coming of his principal, but a nearer view of Jeff's perplexed face, and an examination of Jeff's gun, and the few coins spread before him, finally induced him to produce certain articles, which he packed in a basket and handed to Jeff, taking the gun and coins in exchange. Thus relieved, Jeff set his face homewards, and ran a race with the morning into the valley, reaching the "Half-way House" as the sun laid waste its bare, bleak outlines, and relentlessly pointed out its defects one by one.

It was cruel to Jeff at that moment, but he hugged his basket close and slipped to the back door. and the kitchen, where his aunt was already at work.

"I didn't know ye were up yet, aunty," said Jeff submissively. "It isn't more than six o'clock."

"Thar's four more to feed at breakfast," said his aunt

severely, "and yer's the top blown off the kitchen chimbly, and the fire only just got to go."

Jeff saw that he was in time. The ordinary breakfast of the "Half-way House," not yet prepared, consisted of codfish, ham, yellow-ochre biscuit, made after a peculiar receipt of his aunt's, and potatoes.

"I got a few fancy fixins up at the Summit this morning, aunty," he began apologetically, " seein' we had sick folks, you know—you and the young lady—and thinkin' it might save you trouble. I've got 'em here," and he shyly produced the basket.

"If ye kin afford it, Jeff," responded his aunt resignedly, " I'm thankful."

The reply was so unexpectedly mild for Aunt Sally, that Jeff put his arms around her and kissed her hard cheek. "And I've got some quail, aunty, knowin' you liked 'em."

"I reckoned you was up to some such foolishness," said Aunt Sally, wiping her cheek with her apron, "when I missed yer gun from the hall." But the allusion was a dangerous one, and Jeff slipped away.

He breakfasted early with Yuba Bill that morning; the latter gentleman's taciturnity being intensified at such moments through a long habit of confining himself strictly to eating in the limited time allowed his daily repasts, and it was not until they had taken the horses from the stable and were harnessing them to the coach that Jeff extracted from his companion some facts about his guests. They were Mr. and Mrs. Mayfield, eastern tourists, who had been to the Sandwich Islands for the benefit of their daughter's health, and before returning to New York, intended, under the advice of their physician, to further try the effects of mountain air at the "Summit Hotel," on the invalid. They were apparently rich people, the coach had been engaged for them solely—even the mail and express had been sent on by a separate conveyance, so that they might be more independent. It is hardly necessary to say that this fact was by no means palatable to Bill—debarring him not only the social contact and attentions of the "Express Agent," but the selection of a box-seated passenger who always "acted like a man."

"Ye kin kalkilate what kind of a pardner that 'ar yaller-livered Mayfield would make up on that box, partik'ly ez I heard before we started that he'd requested the kimpany's agent in Sacramento to select a driver ez didn't cuss, smoke, or drink. He did, sir, by gum !"

"I reckon you were very careful, then, Bill," said Jeff.

"In course," returned Bill, with a perfectly diabolical wink. "In course ! You know that 'Blue Grass,'" pointing out a spirited leader; "she's a fair horse ez horses go, but she's apt to feel her oats on a down grade, and takes a pow'ful deal o' soothin' and explanation afore she buckles down to her reg'lar work. Well, sir, I exhorted and laboured in a Christian-like way with that mare to that extent that I'm cussed if that chap didn't want to get down afore we got to the level !"

"And the ladies?" asked Jeff, whose laugh—possibly from his morning's experience—was not as ready as formerly.

"The ladies ! Ef you mean that 'ar livin' skellington I packed up to yer house," said Bill promptly, "it's a pair of them in size and colour, and ready for any first-class under-taker's team in the kintry. Why, you remember that curve on Break Neck hill, where the leaders allus look as if they was alongside o' the coach and faced the other way ? Well, that woman sticks her skull outer the window, and sez she, confidential-like to old yaller-belly, sez she, 'William Henry,' sez she, 'tell that man his horses are running away !'"

"You didn't get to see the—the—daughter, Bill, did you?" asked Jeff, whose laugh had become quite uneasy.

"No, I didn't," said Bill, with sudden and inexplicable vehemence, "and the less *you* see of her, Jefferson Briggs, the better for you."

Too confounded and confused by Bill's manner to question further, Jeff remained silent until they drew up at the door of the " Half-way House." But here another surprise awaited him. Mr. Mayfield, erect and dignified, stood upon the front porch as the coach drove up.

"Driver!" began Mr. Mayfield.

There was no reply.

"Driver," said Mr. Mayfield, slightly weakening under Bill's eye, " I shall want you no longer. I have"——

"Is he speaking to me?" said Bill audibly to Jeff, "'cause they call me ' Yuba Bill ' yer abouts."

"He is," said Jeff hastily.

"Mebbee he's drunk," said Bill audibly; "a drop or two afore breakfast sometimes upsets his kind."

"I was saying, Bill," said Mr. Mayfield, becoming utterly limp and weak again under Bill's cold grey eyes, " that I've changed my mind, and shall stop here awhile. My daughter seems already benefited by the change. You can take my traps from the boot and leave them here."

Bill laid down his lines resignedly, coolly surveyed Mr. Mayfield, the house, and the half-pleased, half-frightened Jeff, and then proceeded to remove the luggage from the boot, all the while whistling loud and offensive incredulity. Then he climbed back to his box. Mr. Mayfield, completely demoralised under this treatment, as a last resort essayed patronage.

"You can say to the Sacramento agents, Bill, that I am entirely satisfied, and "——

"**Ye** needn't fear but I'll give ye a good character," interrupted Bill coolly, gathering up his lines. The whip snapped, the six horses dashed forward as one, the coach plunged down the road and was gone.

With its disappearance, Mr. Mayfield stiffened slightly again. "I have just told your aunt, Mr. Briggs," he said, turning upon Jeff, "that my daughter has expressed a desire to remain here a few days; she has slept well, seems to be invigorated by the air, and although we expected to go on to the 'Summit,' Mrs. Mayfield and myself are willing to accede to her wishes. Your house seems to be new and clean. Your table—judging from the breakfast this morning—is quite satisfactory."

Jeff, in the first flush of delight at this news, forgot what that breakfast had cost him—forgot all his morning's experience, and, I fear, when he did remember it, was too full of a vague, hopeful courage to appreciate it. Conscious of showing too much pleasure, he affected the necessity of an immediate interview with his aunt, in the kitchen. But his short cut round the house was arrested by a voice and figure. It was Miss Mayfield, wrapped in a shawl and seated in a chair, basking in the sunlight at one of the bleakest and barest angles of the house. Jeff stopped in a delicious tremor.

As we are dealing with facts, however, it would be well to look at the cause of this tremor with our own eyes and not Jeff's. To be plain, my dear madam, as she basked in that remorseless, matter-of-fact California sunshine, she looked her full age—twenty-five, if a day! There were wrinkles in the corners of her dark eyes, contracted and frowning in that strong, merciless light; there was a nervous pallor in her complexion; but being one of those "fast-coloured" brunettes, whose dyes are a part of their temperament, no sickness nor wear could bleach it out. The red of her small mouth was darker than yours, I wot, and there were certain faint lines from the corners of her delicate nostrils indicating alternate repression and excitement under certain experiences, which are not found in the classic ideals. Now Jeff knew nothing of the classic ideal—did not know that a thousand years ago certain sensual idiots had, with brush and chisel, inflicted upon the world the personification of the strongest and most delicate, most controlling and most subtle passion that humanity is capable of, in the likeness of a thick-waisted, idealess, expressionless, perfectly contented female animal; and that thousands of idiots had since then insisted upon perpetuating this model for the benefit of a world that had gone on sighing for, pining for, fighting for, and occasionally blowing its brains out over types far removed from that idiotic standard. Consequently Jeff saw only a face full of possibilities and probabilities, framed in a small delicate oval, saw a slight woman's form—more than usually small—and heard a low voice, to him full of gentle pride, passion, pathos, and human weakness, and was helpless.

"I only said 'good morning,'" said Miss Mayfield, with that slight, arch satisfaction in the observation of masculine bashfulness, which the best of her sex cannot forego.

"Thank you, miss; good morning. I've been wanting to say to you that I hope you wasn't mad, you know," stammered Jeff, desperately intent upon getting off his apology.

"It is *so* lovely this morning—such a change!" continued Miss Mayfield.

"Yes, miss! You know I reckoned—at least what your father said, made me kalkilate that you "——

Miss Mayfield, still smiling, knitted her brows and went on: "I slept so well last night," she said gratefully, "and feel so much better this morning, that I ventured out. I seem to be drinking in health in this clear sunlight."

"Certainly, miss. As I was sayin', your father says his daughter is in the coach; and Bill says, says he to me, 'I'll pack—I'll carry the old—I'll bring up Mrs. Mayfield, if you'll bring up the daughter;' and when we come to the coach I saw you asleep-like in the corner, and bein' small, why, miss, you know how nat'ral it is, I"——

"Oh, Mr. Jeff! Mr. Briggs!" said Miss Mayfield plaintively, "don't, please—don't spoil the best compliment I've had in many a year. You thought I was a child, I know, and—well, you find," she said audaciously, suddenly bringing her black eyes to bear on him like a rifle, "you find—well?"

What Jeff thought was inaudible but not invisible. Miss Mayfield saw enough of it in his eye to protest with a faint colour in her cheek. Thus does Nature betray itself to Nature the world over.

The colour faded. "It's a dreadful thing to be so weak and helpless, and to put everybody to such trouble, isn't it, Mr. Jeff? I beg your pardon—your aunt calls you Jeff."

"Please call me Jeff," said Jeff, to his own surprise rapidly gaining courage. "Everybody calls me that."

Miss Mayfield smiled. "I suppose I must do what *everybody* does. So it seems that we are to give you the trouble of keeping us here until I get better or worse?"

"Yes, miss."

"Therefore I won't detain you now. I only wanted to thank you for your gentleness last night, and to assure you that the bear-skin did *not* give me my death."

She smiled and nodded her small head, and wrapped her shawl again closely around her shoulders, and turned her eyes upon the mountains, gestures which the now quick-minded Jeff interpreted as a gentle dismissal, and flew to seek his aunt.

Here he grew practical. Ready money was needed;

for the " Half-way House " was such a public monument
of ill-luck, that Jeff had no credit.   He must keep up the
table to the level of that fortunate breakfast—to do which
he had $1·50 in the till, left by Bill, and $2·50 produced
by his Aunt Sally from her work-basket.

"Why not ask Mr. Mayfield to advance ye suthin?"
said Aunt Sally.

The blood flew to Jeff's face.   "Never!  Don't say
that again, aunty."

The tone and manner were so unlike Jeff that the old
lady sat down half frightened, and taking the corners of
her apron in her hands began to whimper.

"Thar now, aunty!  I didn't mean nothin',—only if you
care to have me about the place any longer, and I reckon
it's little good I am any way," he added, with a new-found
bitterness in his tone, "ye'll not ask me to do that."

"What's gone o' ye, Jeff?" said his aunt lugubriously;
"ye ain't nat'ral like."

Jeff laughed.   "See here, aunty; I'm goin' to take your
advice.   You know Rabbit?"

"The mare?"

"Yes; I'm going to sell her.   The blacksmith offered
me a hundred dollars for her last week."

"Ef ye'd done that a month ago, Jeff, ez I wanted ye to,
instead o' keeping the brute to eat ye out o' house and
home, ye'd be better off."   Aunt Sally never let slip an
opportunity to "improve the occasion," but preferred to
exhort over the prostrate body of the "improved."   "Well,
I hope he mayn't change his mind."

Jeff smiled at such a suggestion regarding the best horse
within fifty miles of the " Half-way House."   Nevertheless
he went briskly to the stable, led out and saddled a handsome grey mare, petting her the while, and keeping up a
running commentary of caressing epithets to which Rabbit

responded with a whinny and playful reaches after Jeff's red flannel sleeve. Whereat Jeff, having loved the horse until it was displaced by another mistress, grew grave and suddenly threw his arms around Rabbit's neck, and then taking Rabbit's nose, thrust it in the bosom of his shirt and held it there silently for a moment. Rabbit becoming uneasy, Jeff's mood changed too, and having caparisoned himself and charger in true *vaquero* style, not without a little Mexican dandyism as to the set of his doeskin trousers, and the tie of his red sash, put a *sombrero* rakishly on his curls and leaped into the saddle.

Jeff was a fair rider in a country where riding was understood as a natural instinct, and not as a purely artificial habit of horse and rider, consequently he was not perched up, jockey fashion, with a knee-grip for his body, and a rein-rest for his arms on the beast's mouth, but rode with long, loose stirrups, his legs clasping the barrel of his horse, his single rein lying loose upon her neck, leaving her head free as the wind. After this fashion he had often emerged from a cloud of dust on the red mountain road, striking admiration into the hearts of the wayfarers and coach-passengers, and leaving a trail of pleasant incense in the dust behind him. It was therefore with considerable confidence in himself, and a little human vanity, that he dashed round the house, and threw his mare skilfully on her haunches exactly a foot before Miss Mayfield—himself a resplendent vision of flying riata, crimson scarf, fawn-coloured trousers, and jingling silver spurs.

"Kin I do anythin' for ye, miss, at the Forks?"

Miss Mayfield looked up quietly. "I think not," she said indifferently, as if the flaming Jeff was a very common occurrence.

Jeff here permitted the mare to bolt fifty yards, caught her up sharply, swung her round on her off hind heel, permitted her to paw the air once or twice with her white-stockinged fore-feet, and then, with another dash forward, pulled her up again just before she apparently took Miss Mayfield and her chair in a running leap.

"Are you sure, miss?" asked Jeff, with a flushed face and a rather lugubrious voice.

"Quite so, thank you," she said coldly, looking past this centaur to the wooded mountain beyond.

Jeff, thoroughly crushed, was pacing meekly away when a childlike voice stopped him.

"If you are going near a carpenter's shop you might get a new shutter for my window; it blew away last night."

"It did, miss?"

"Yes," said the shrill voice of Aunt Sally, from the doorway, "in course it did! Ye must be crazy, Jeff, for thar it stands in No. 8, whar ye must have put it after ye picked it up outside."

Jeff, conscious that Miss Mayfield's eyes were on his suffused face, stammered "that he would attend to it," and put spurs to the mare, eager only to escape.

It was not his only discomfiture; for the blacksmith, seeing Jeff's nervousness and anxiety, was suspicious of something wrong, as the world is apt to be, and appeased his conscience after the worldly fashion, by driving a hard bargain with the doubtful brother in affliction—the morality of a horse trade residing always with the seller. Whereby Master Jeff received only eighty dollars for horse and outfit —worth at least two hundred—and was also mulcted of forty dollars, principal and interest for past service of the blacksmith. Jeff walked home with forty dollars in his pocket—capital to prosecute his honest calling of inn-keeper; the blacksmith retired to an adjoining tavern to discuss Jeff's affairs, and further reduce his credit. Yet I doubt which was the happier—the blacksmith estimating his possible gains, and doubtful of some uncertain sequence in his luck, or Jeff, temporarily relieved, boundlessly hopeful, and filled with the vague delights of a first passion. The only discontented brute in the whole transaction was poor Rabbit, who, missing certain attentions, became indignant, after the manner of her sex, bit a piece out of her crib, kicked a hole in her box, and receiving a bad character from the blacksmith, gave a worse one to her late master.

Jeff's purchases were of a temporary and ornamental quality, but not always judicious as a permanent investment. Overhearing some remark from Miss Mayfield concerning the dangerous character of the two-tined steel fork, which was part of the table equipage of the " Halfway House," he purchased half a dozen of what his aunt was pleased to specify as "split spoons," and thereby lost his late good standing with her. He not only repaired the window-shutter, but tempered the glaring window itself with a bit of curtain ; he half carpeted Miss Mayfield's bedroom with wild-cat skins and the now historical bear-skin, and felt himself overpaid when that young lady, passing the soft tabby-skins across her cheek, declared they were "lovely." For Miss Mayfield, deprecating slaughter in the abstract, accepted its results gratefully, like the rest of her sex, and while willing to "let the hart ungalled play," nevertheless was able to console herself with its venison. The woods, besides yielding aid and comfort of this kind to the distressed damsel, were *flamboyant* with vivid spring blossoms, and Jeff lit up the cold, white walls of her virgin cell with demonstrative colour, and made—what his aunt, a cleanly soul, whose ideas of that quality were based upon the absence of any colour whatever—called " a litter."

The result of which was to make Miss Mayfield, otherwise languid and *ennuyé*, welcome Jeff's presence with a smile; to make Jeff, otherwise anxious, eager, and keenly attentive, mute and silent in her presence. Two symptoms bad for Jeff.

Meantime Mr. Mayfield's small conventional spirit pined for fellowship, only to be found in larger civilisations, and sought, under plea of business, a visit to Sacramento, where a few of the Mayfield type, still surviving, were to be found.

This was a relief to Jeff, who only through his regard for the daughter, was kept from open quarrel with the father. He fancied Miss Mayfield felt relieved too, although Jeff had noticed that Mayfield had deferred to his daughter more often than to his wife—over whom your conventional small autocrat is always victorious. It takes the legal matrimonial contract to properly develop the first-class tyrant, male or female.

On one of these days Jeff was returning through the woods from marketing at the Forks, which, since the sale of Rabbit, had become a foot-sore and tedious business. He had reached the edge of the forest, and through the wider-spaced trees, the bleak sunlit plateau of his house was beginning to open out, when he stopped instantly. I know not what Jeff had been thinking of, as he trudged along, but here, all at once, he was thrilled and possessed with the odour of some faint, foreign perfume. He flushed a little at first, and then turned pale. Now the woods were as full of as delicate, as subtle, as grateful, and, I wot, far healthier and purer odours than this; but this represented to Jeff the physical contiguity of Miss Mayfield, who had the knack—peculiar to some of her sex—of selecting a perfume that ideally identified her. Jeff looked around cautiously; at the foot of a tree hard by lay one of her wraps, still redolent of her. Jeff put down the bag which, in lieu of a market basket, he was carrying on his shoulder, and with a blushing face hid it behind a tree. It contained her dinner !

He took a few steps forwards with an assumption of ease and unconsciousness. Then he stopped, for not a hundred yards distant sat Miss Mayfield on a mossy boulder, her cloak hanging from her shoulders, her hands clasped round her crossed knees, and one little foot out—an exasperating combination of Evangeline and little Red Riding Hood in everything, 1 fear, but credulousness and self-devotion. She looked up as he walked towards her (*non constat* that the little witch had not already seen him half a mile away !) and smiled sweetly as she looked at him. So sweetly, indeed, that poor Jeff felt like the hulking wolf of the old world fable, and hesitated—as that wolf did *not*. The California *faunæ* have possibly depreciated.

"Come here !" she cried, in a small head voice, not unlike a bird's twitter.

Jeff lumbered on clumsily. His high boots had become suddenly very heavy.

"I'm so glad to see you. I've just tired poor mother out—I'm always tiring people out—and she's gone back to the house to write letters. Sit down, Mr. Jeff, do, *please !*"

Jeff, feeling uncomfortablely large in Miss Mayfield's presence, painfully seated himself on the edge of a very low stone, which had the effect of bringing his knees up on a level with his chin, and affected an ease glaringly simu·lated.

"Or lie down, *there*, Mr. Jeff—it is *so* comfortable."

Jeff, with a dreadful conviction that he was crashing down like a falling pine tree, managed at last to acquire a recumbent position at a respectful distance from the little figure.

"There, isn't it nice ?"

"Yes, Miss Mayfield."

"But, perhaps," said Miss Mayfield, now that she had him down, "perhaps you *too* have got something to do. Dear me! I'm like that naughty boy in the story-book, who went round to all the animals, in turn, asking them to play with him. He could only find the butterfly who had nothing to do. I don't wonder he was disgusted. I hate butterflies."

Love clarifies the intellect! Jeff, astonished at himself, burst out, "Why, look yer, Miss Mayfield, the butterfly on'y hez a day or two to—to—to live and—be happy!"

Miss Mayfield crossed her knees again, and instantly, after the sublime fashion of her sex, scattered his intellect by a swift transition from the abstract to the concrete. "But *you're* not a butterfly, Mr. Jeff. You're always doing something. You've been hunting."

"No-o!" said Jeff, scarlet, as he thought of his gun in pawn at the "Summit."

"But you *do* hunt; I know it."

"How?"

"You shot those quail for me the morning after I came. I heard you go out—early—very early."

"Why, you allowed you slept so well that night, Miss Mayfield."

"Yes; but there's a kind of delicious half-sleep that sick people have sometimes, when they know and are gratefully conscious that other people are doing things for them, and it makes them rest all the sweeter."

There was a dead silence. Jeff, thrilling all over, dared not say anything to dispel his delicious dream. Miss Mayfield, alarmed at his readiness with the butterfly illustration, stopped short. They both looked at the prospect, at the distant "Summit Hotel"—a mere snow-drift on the mountain—at the clear sunlight on the barren plateau, at the bleak, uncompromising "Half-way House," and—said nothing.

"I ought to be very grateful," at last began Miss Mayfield, in quite another voice, and a suggestion that she was now approaching real and profitable conversation, "that I'm so much better. This mountain air has been like balm to me. I feel I am growing stronger day by day. I do not wonder that you are so healthy and so strong as you are, Mr. Jeff."

Jeff, who really did not know before that he was so healthy, apologetically admitted the fact. At the same time, he was miserably conscious that Miss Mayfield's condition, despite her ill health, was very superior to his own.

"A month ago," she continued reflectively, "my mother would never have thought it possible to leave me here alone. Perhaps she may be getting worried now."

Miss Mayfield had calculated over much on Jeff's recumbent position. To her surprise and slight mortification, he rose instantly to his feet, and said anxiously—

"Ef you think so, miss, p'raps I'm keeping you here."

"Not at all, Mr. Jeff. Your being here is a sufficient excuse for my staying," she replied, with the large dignity of a small body.

Jeff, mentally and physically crushed again, came down a little heavier than before, and reclined humbly at her feet. Second knock-down blow for Miss Mayfield.

"Come, Mr. Jeff," said the triumphant goddess, in her first voice, "tell me something about yourself. How do you live here—I mean, what do you do? You ride, of course—and very well too, I can tell you! But you know *that*. And of course that scarf and the silver spurs and the whole dashing equipage are not intended entirely for yourself. No! Some young woman is made happy by that exhibition, of course. Well, then, there's the riding

down to see her, and perhaps the riding out *with* her, and
—what else ? "

"Miss Mayfield," said Jeff, suddenly rising above his
elbow and his grammar, "thar isn't *no* young woman !
Thar isn't another soul except yourself that I've laid eyes
on, or cared to see since I've been yer. Ef my aunt hez
been telling ye that—she's—she—she—she—she—lies."

Absolute, undiluted truth, even of a complimentary
nature, is confounding to most women. Miss Mayfield
was no exception to her sex. She first laughed, as she felt
she ought to, and properly might with any other man than
Jeff ; then she got frightened, and said hurriedly, "No,
no ! you misunderstand me. Your aunt has said nothing."
And then she stopped with a pink spot on her cheek-bones.
First blood for Jeff !

Now this would never do ; it was worse than the butterflies ! She rose to her full height—four feet eleven and a
half—and drew her cloak over her shoulders. "I think I
will return to the house," she said quietly ; "I suppose I
ought not to overtask my strength."

"You'd better let me go with you, miss," said Jeff
submissively.

"I will, on one condition," she said, recovering her
archness, with a little venom in it, I fear. "You were
going home, too, when I called to you. Now, I do not
intend to let you leave that bag behind that tree, and then
have to come back for it, just because you feel obliged to go
with me. Bring it with you on one arm, and I'll take the
other, or else—I'll go alone. Don't be alarmed," she added
softly ; "I'm stronger than I was the first night I came, when
you carried me and all my worldly goods besides."

She turned upon him her subtle magnetic eyes, and
looked at him as she had the first night they met. Jeff
turned away bewildered, but presently appeared again with

the bag on his shoulder, and her wrap on his arm. As she slipped her little hand over his sleeve, he began, apologetically and nervously—

"When I said that about Aunt Sally, miss, I "——

The hand immediately became limp, the grasp conventional.

" I was mad, miss," Jeff blundered on, "and I don't see how *you* believed it—knowing everything ez you do."

"How knowing everything as I do?" asked Miss Mayfield coldly.

" Why, about the quail, and about the bag !"

" Oh," said Miss Mayfield.

Five minutes later, Yuba Bill nearly ditched his coach in his utter amazement at an apparently simple spectacle— a tall, good-looking young fellow, in a red shirt and high boots, carrying a bag on his back, and beside him, hanging confidentially on his arm, a small, slight, pretty girl in a red cloak. " Nothing *mean* about *her*, eh, Bill?" said an admiring box-passenger. " Young couple, I reckon, just out from the States."

" No ! " roared Bill.

" Oh, well, his sweetheart, I reckon?" suggested the box-passenger.

"Nary time !" growled Bill. " Look yer ! I know 'em both, and they knows *me*. Did ye notiss she never drops his arm when she sees the stage comin', but kinder trapes along jist the same? Had they been courtin', she'd hev dropped his arm like pizen, and walked on t'other side the road."

Nevertheless, for some occult reason, Bill was evidently out of humour ; and for the next few miles exhorted the impenitent Blue Grass horse with considerable fervour.

Meanwhile this pair, outwardly the picture of pastoral conjugality, slowly descended the hill. In that brief time,

failing to get at any further facts regarding Jeff's life, or
perhaps reading the story quite plainly, Miss Mayfield had
twittered prettily about herself. She painted her tropic
life in the Sandwich Islands—her delicious "laziness," as
she called it; "for, you know," she added, "although I
had the excuse of being an invalid, and of living in the
laziest climate in the world, and of having money, I think,
Mr. Jeff, that I'm naturally lazy. Perhaps if I lived here
long enough, and got well again, I might do something,
but I don't think I could ever be like your aunt. And
there she is now, Mr. Jeff, making signs for you to hasten.
No, don't mind me, but run on ahead; else I shall have
*her* blaming me for demoralising *you* too. Go; I insist
upon it! I can walk the rest of the way alone. Will you
go? You won't? Then I shall stop here and not stir
another step forward until you do."

She stopped, half jestingly, half earnestly, in the middle
of the road, and emphasised her determination with a nod
of her head—an action that, however, shook her hat first
rakishly over one eye, and then on the ground. At which
Jeff laughed, picked it up, presented it to her, and then ran
off to the house.


## CHAPTER III.

His aunt met him angrily on the porch. "Thar ye are at
last, and yer's a stranger waitin' to see you. He's been
axin all sorts o' questions about the house and the business,
and kinder snoopin' round permiskiss. I don't like his
looks, Jeff, but thet's no reason why *ye* should be gallivantin'
round in business hours."

A large, thick-set man, with a mechanical smile that was
an overt act of false pretence, was lounging in the bar-room.
Jeff dimly remembered to have seen him at the last county

election, distributing tickets at the polls. This gave Jeff a slight prejudice against him, but a greater presentiment of some vague evil in the air caused him to motion the stranger to an empty room in the angle of the house behind the bar-room, which was too near the hall through which Miss Mayfield must presently pass.

It was an infelicitous act of precaution, for at that very moment Miss Mayfield slowly passed beneath its open window, and seeing her chair in the sunny angle, dropped into it for rest and possibly meditation. Consequently she overheard every word of the following colloquy.

The Stranger's voice: "Well, now, seein' ez I've been waitin' for ye over an hour, off and on, and ez my bizness with ye is two words, it strikes me yer puttin' on a little too much style in this yer interview, Mr. Jefferson Briggs."

Jeff's voice (a little husky with restraint): "What is yer business?"

The Stranger's voice (lazily): "It's an at-tachment on this yer property for principal, interest, and costs—one hundred and twelve dollars and seventy-five cents, at the suit of Cyrus Parker."

Jeff's voice (in quick surprise): "Parker? Why, I saw him only yesterday, and he agreed to wait a spell longer."

The Stranger's voice: "Mebbee he did! Mebbee he heard afterwards suthin' about the goin's on up yar. Mebbee he heard suthin' o' property bein' converted into ready cash—sich property ez horses, guns, and sich! Mebbee he heard o' gay and festive doin's—chickin every day, fresh eggs, butcher's meat, port wine, and sich! Mebbee he allowed that his chances o' gettin' his own honest grub outer his debt was lookin' mighty slim! Mebbee" (louder) "he thought he'd ask the man who bought yer horse, and the man you pawned your gun to, what was goin' on! Mebbee he thought he'd like to get a holt a suthin' himself, even if it was only some of that yar chickin and port wine!"

Jeff's voice (earnestly and hastily): "They're not for me. I have a family boarding here, with a sick daughter. You don't think"——

The Stranger's voice (lazily): "I reckon! I seed you and her pre-ambulating down the hill, lockin' arms. A good deal o' style, Jeff—fancy! expensive! How does Aunt Sally take it?"

A slight shaking of the floor and window—a dead silence.

The Stranger's voice (very faintly): "For God's sake, let me up!"

Jeff's voice (very distinctly): "Another word! raise your voice above a whisper, and by the living G——"

Silence.

The Stranger's voice (gasping): "I—I—promise!"

Jeff's voice (low and desperate): "Get up out of that! Sit down thar! Now hear me! I'm not resisting your process. If you had all h—ll as witnesses you daren't say *that*. I've shut up your foul jaw, and kept it from poisoning the air, and thar's no law in Californy agin it! Now listen. What! You will, will you?"

Everything quiet; a bird twittering on the window ledge, nothing more.

The Stranger's voice (very husky): "I cave! Gimme some whisky."

Jeff's voice: "When we're through. Now listen! You can take possession of the house; you can stand behind the bar and take every cent that comes in; you can prevent anything going out; but ez long as Mr. Mayfield and his family stay here, by the living God—law or no law—I'll be boss here, and they shall never know it!"

The Stranger's voice (weakly and submissively): "That

sounds square. Anythin' not agin the law and in reason, Jeff!"

Jeff's voice: "I mean to be square. Here is all the money I have, ten dollars. Take it for any extra trouble you may have to satisfy me."

A pause—the clinking of coin.

The Stranger's voice (deprecatingly): "Well! I reckon that *would* be about fair. Consider the *trouble*" (a weak laugh here) "just *now*. 'Tain't every man ez hez your grip. He! he! Ef ye hadn't took me so suddent like— he! he!—well!—how about that ar whisky?"

Jeff's voice (coolly): "I'll bring it."

Steps, silence, coughing, spitting, and throat-clearing from the stranger.

Steps again and the click of glass.

The Stranger's voice (submissively): "In course I must go back to the Forks and fetch up my duds. Ye know what I mean! Thar now—don't, Mr. Jeff!"

Jeff's voice (sternly): "If I find you go back on me"——

The Stranger's voice (hurriedly): "Thar's my hand on it. Ye can count on Jim Dodd."

Steps again. Silence. A bird lights on the window ledge, and peers into the room. All is at rest.

.        .        .        .        .        .

Jeff and the deputy-sheriff walked through the bar-room and out on the porch. Miss Mayfield in an arm-chair looked up from her book.

"I've written a letter to my father that I'd like to have mailed at the Forks this afternoon," she said, looking from Jeff to the stranger; "perhaps this gentleman will oblige me by taking it, if he's going that way."

"I'll take it, miss," said Jeff hurriedly.

"No," said Miss Mayfield archly, "I've taken up too much of your time already."

"I'm at your service, miss," said the stranger, considerably affected by the spectacle of this pretty girl, who certainly at that moment, in her bright eyes and slightly pink cheeks, belied the suggestion of ill health.

"Thank you. Dear me!" She was rummaging in a reticule and in her pockets. "Oh, Mr. Jeff!"

"Yes, miss?"

"I'm so frightened!"

"How, miss?"

"I have—yes!—I have left that letter on the stump in the woods, where I was sitting when you came. Would you"——

Jeff darted into the house, seized his hat, and stopped. He was thinking of the stranger.

"Could you be so kind?"

Jeff looked in her agitated face, cast a meaning glance at the stranger, and was off like a shot.

The fire dropped out of Miss Mayfield's eyes and cheeks. She turned towards the stranger.

"Please step this way."

She always hated her own childish treble. But just at that moment she thought she had put force and dignity into it, and was correspondingly satisfied. The deputy-sheriff was equally pleased, and came towards the upright little figure with open admiration.

"Your name is Dodd—James Dodd."

"Yes, miss."

"You are the deputy-sheriff of the county! Don't look round—there is no one here!"

"Well, miss—if you say so—yes!"

"My father—Mr. Mayfield—understood so. I regret

he is not here. I regret still more I could not have seen you before you saw Mr. Briggs, as he wished me to."

"Yes, miss."

"My father is a friend of Mr. Briggs, and knows something of his affairs. There was a debt to a Mr. Parker" (here Miss Mayfield apparently consulted an entry in her tablets) "of one hundred and twelve dollars and seventy-five cents—am I right?"

The deputy, with great respect, "That is the figgers."

"Which he wished to pay without the knowledge of Mr. Briggs, who would not have consented to it."

The official opened his eyes. "Yes, miss."

"Well, as Mr. Mayfield is *not* here, I am here to pay it for him. You can take a cheque on Wells, Fargo & Co., I suppose?"

"Certainly, miss."

She took a cheque-book and pen and ink from her reticule, and filled up a cheque. She handed it to him, and the pen and ink. "You are to give me a receipt."

The deputy looked at the matter-of-fact little figure, and signed and handed over the receipted bill.

"My father said Mr. Briggs was not to know this."

"Certainly not, miss."

"It was Mr. Briggs' intention to let the judgment take its course, and give up the house. You are a man of business, Mr. Dodd, and know that this is ridiculous!"

The deputy laughed. "In course, miss."

"And whatever Mr. Briggs may have proposed to you to do, when you go back to the Forks, you are to write him a letter, and say that you will simply hold the judgment without levy."

"All right, miss," said the deputy, not ill-pleased to hold himself in this superior attitude to Jeff.

"And"——

"Yes, miss?"

She looked steadily at him. "Mr. Briggs told my father that he would pay you ten dollars for the privilege of staying here."

"Yes, miss."

"And of course *that's* not necessary now."

"No-o, miss."

A very small white hand—a mere child's hand—was here extended, palm uppermost.

The official, demoralised completely, looked at it a moment, then went into his pockets and counted out into the palm the coins given by Jeff; they completely filled the tiny receptacle.

Miss Mayfield counted the money gravely, and placed it in her *porte-monnaie* with a snap.

Certain qualities affect certain natures. This practical business act of the diminutive beauty before him—albeit he was just ten dollars out of pocket by it—struck the official into helpless admiration. He hesitated.

"That's all," said Miss Mayfield coolly; "you need not wait. The letter was only an excuse to get Mr. Briggs out of the way."

"I understand ye, miss." He hesitated still. "Do you reckon to stop in these parts long?"

"I don't know."

"'Cause ye ought to come down some day to the Forks."

"Yes."

"Good morning, miss."

"Good morning."

Yet at the corner of the house the rascal turned and looked back at the little figure in the sunlight. He had just been physically overcome by a younger man—he had lost ten dollars—he had a wife and three children. He forgot all this. He had been captivated by Miss Mayfield!

That practical heroine sat there five minutes. At the end of that time Jeff came bounding down the hill, his curls damp with perspiration; his fresh, honest face the picture of woe, *her* woe, for the letter could not be found !

"Never mind, Mr. Jeff. I wrote another and gave it to him."

Two tears were standing on her cheeks. Jeff turned white.

"Good God, miss !"

"It's nothing. You were right, Mr. Jeff! I ought not to have walked down here alone. I'm very, very tired, and—so—so miserable."

What woman could withstand the anguish of that honest boyish face? I fear Miss Mayfield could, for she looked at him over her handkerchief, and said, " Perhaps you had something to say to your friend, and I've sent him off."

"Nothing," said Jeff hurriedly; and she saw that all his other troubles had vanished at the sight of her weakness. She rose tremblingly from her seat. "I think I will go in now, but I think—I think—I must ask you to—to—carry me !"

Oh, lame and impotent conclusion !

The next moment Jeff, pale, strong, passionate, but tender as a mother, lifted her in his arms and brought her into the sitting-room. A simultaneous ejaculation broke from Aunt Sally and Mrs. Mayfield—the possible comment of posterity on the whole episode.

"Well, Jeff, I reckoned you'd be up to suthin' like that ! "

"Well, Jessie ! I knew you couldn't be trusted."


Mr. James Dodd did not return from the Forks that afternoon, to Jeff's vague uneasiness. Towards evening a messenger brought a note from him, written on the back of a printed legal form, to this effect—

"DEAR SIR,—Seeing as you Intend to act on the Square in regard to that little Mater I have aranged Things so that I ant got to stop with you but I'll drop in onct in a wile to keep up a show for a Drink—respy yours,

"J. DODD."

In this latter suggestion our legal Cerberus exhibited all three of his heads at once. One could keep faith with Miss Mayfield, one could see her "onct in a wile," and one could drink at Jeff's expense. Innocent Jeff saw only generosity and kindness in the man he had half-choked, and a sense of remorse and shame almost outweighed the relief of his absence. "He might hev been ugly," said Jeff. He did not know how, in this selfish world, there is very little room for gratuitous, active ugliness.

Miss Mayfield did not leave her room that afternoon. The wind was getting up, and it was growing dark when Jeff, idly sitting on his porch, hoping for her appearance, was quite astounded at the apparition of Yuba Bill as a pedestrian, dusty and thirsty, making for his usual refreshment. Jeff brought out the bottle, but could not refrain from mixing his verbal astonishment with the conventional cocktail. Bill, partaking of his liquor and becoming once more a speaking animal, slowly drew off his heavy, baggy driving-gloves. No one had ever seen Bill without them— he was currently believed to sleep in them—and when he laid them on the counter they still retained the grip of his hand, which gave them an entertaining likeness to two plethoric and over-fed spiders.

"Ef I concluded to pass over my lines to a friend and take a *pasear* up yer this evening," said Bill, eyeing Jeff sharply, "I don't know ez thar's any law agin it! Onless yer keepin' a private branch o' the Occidental Ho-tel, and on'y take in fash'n'ble fammerlies!"

Jeff, with a rising colour, protested against such a supposition.

"Because ef ye *are*," said Bill, lifting his voice, and crushing one of the overgrown spiders with his fist, "I've got a word or two to say to the son of Joe Briggs of Tuolumne. Yes, sir! Joe Briggs—yer father—ez blew his brains out for want of a man ez could stand up and say a word to him at the right time."

"Bill," said Jeff, in a low, resolute tone—that tone yielded up only from the smitten chords of despair and desperation—"thar's a sick woman in the house. I'll listen to anything you've got to say if you'll say it quietly. But you must and *shall* speak low."

Real men quickly recognise real men the world over ; it is only your shams who fence and spar. Bill, taking in the voice of the speaker more than his words, dropped his own.

"I said I had a kepple of words to say to ye. Thar isn't any time in the last fower months—ever since ye took stock in this old shanty, for the matter o' that—that I couldn't hev said them to ye. I've knowed all your doin's. I've knowed all your debts, 'spesh'ly that ye owe that sneakin' hound Parker ; and thar isn't a time that I couldn't and wouldn't hev chipped in and paid 'em for ye—for your father's sake—ef I'd allowed it to be the square thing for ye. But I know ye, Jeff. I know what's in your *blood*. I knew your father—allus dreamin', hopin', waitin' ; I know *you*, Jeff, dreamin', hopin', waitin' till the end. And I stood by, givin' you a free rein, and let it come !"

Jeff buried his face in his hands.

"It ain't your blame—it's blood ! It ain't a week ago ez the kimpany passes me over a hoss. 'Three quarters Morgan,' sez they. Sez I, 'Wot's the other quarter?' Sez they, 'A Mexican half-breed.' Well, she was a fair sort of hoss. Comin' down Heavytree Hill last trip, we meets a drove o' Spanish steers. In course she goes wild directly. Blood!"

Bill raised his glass, softly swirled its contents round and round, tasted it, and set it down.

"The kepple o' words I had to say to ye was this: Git up and git!"

Something like this had passed through Jeff's mind the day before the Mayfields came. Something like it had haunted him once or twice since. He turned quickly upon the speaker.

"Ez how? you sez," said Bill, catching at the look. "I drives up yer some night, and you sez to me, 'Bill, hev you got two seats over to the Divide for me and aunty—out on a *pasear*.' And I sez, 'I happen to hev one inside and one on the box with me.' And you hands out yer traps and any vallybles ye don't want ter leave, and you puts your aunt inside, and gets up on the box with me. And you sez to me, ez man to man, 'Bill,' sez you, 'might you hev a kepple o' hundred dollars about ye that ye could lend a man ez was leaving the county, dead broke?' and I sez, 'I've got it, and I know of an op'nin' for such a man in the next county.' And you steps into *that* op'nin', and your creditors—'spesh'ly Parker—slips into *this*, and in a week they offers to settle with ye ten cents on the dollar."

Jeff started, flushed, trembled, recovered himself, and after a moment said, doggedly, "I can't do it, Bill; I couldn't."

"In course," said Bill, putting his hands slowly into his pockets, and stretching his legs out—"in course ye can't because of a woman!"

Jeff turned upon him like a hunted bear. Both men rose, but Bill already had his hand on Jeff's shoulder.

"I reckoned a minute ago there was a sick gal in the

house! Who's going to make a row now! Who's going
to stamp and tear round, eh?"

Jeff sank back on his chair.

"I said thar was a woman," continued Bill; "thar allus
is one! Let a man be hell-bent or heaven-bent, somewhere
in his tracks is a woman's feet. I don't say anythin' agin
this gal, ez a gal. The best on 'em, Jeff, is only guide-
posts to p'int a fellow on his right road, and only a fool or
a drunken man holds on to 'em or leans agin 'em. Allowin'
this gal is all you think she is, how far is your guide-post
goin' with ye, eh? Is she goin' to leave her father and
mother for ye? Is she goin' to give up herself and her
easy ways and her sicknesses for ye? Is she willin' to take
ye for a perpetooal landlord the rest of her life? And if
she is, Jeff, are ye the man to let her? Are ye willin' to
run on her errands, to fetch her dinners ez ye do? Thar
ez men ez does it; not yer in Californy, but over in the
States thar's fellows is willin' to take that situation. I've
heard," continued Bill, in a low, mysterious voice, as of
one describing the habits of the Anthropophagi—"I've
heard o' fellows ez call themselves men, sellin' of themselves to rich women in that way. I've heard o' rich gals
buyin' of men for their shape; sometimes—but thet's in
furrin' kintries—for their pedigree! I've heard o' fellows
bein' in that business, and callin' themselves men instead
o' hosses! Ye ain't that kind o' man, Jeff. 'Tain't in yer
blood. Yer father was a fool about women, and in course
they ruined him, ez they allus do the best men. It's on'y
the fools and sneaks ez a woman ever makes anythin' out
of. When ye hear of a man a woman hez made, ye hears
of a nincompoop! And when they does produce 'em in
the way o' nater, they ain't responsible for 'em, and sez
they're the image o' their fathers! Ye ain't a man ez is
goin' to trust yer fate to a woman!"

"No," said Jeff darkly.

"I reckoned not," said Bill, putting his hands in his pockets again. "Ye might if ye was one o' them kind o' fellows as kem up from 'Frisco with her to Sacramento. One o' them kind o' fellows ez could sling poetry and French and Latin to her—one of *her* kind—but ye ain't! No, sir!"

Unwise William of Yuba! In any other breast but Jeff's, that random shot would have awakened the irregular auxiliary of love—jealousy! But Jeff, being at once proud and humble, had neither vanity nor conceit, without which jealousy is impossible. Yet he winced a little, for he had feeling, and then said earnestly—

"Do you think that opening you spoke of would hold for a day or two longer?"

"I reckon."

"Well then, I think I can settle up matters here my own way, and go with you, Bill."

He had risen and yet hesitatingly kept his hand on the back of his chair. "Bill!"

"Jeff!"

"I want to ask you a question; speak up, and don't mind me, but say the truth."

Our crafty Ulysses, believing that he was about to be entrapped, ensconced himself in his pockets, cocked one eye, and said, "Go on, Jeff."

"Was my father *very* bad?"

Bill took his hands from his pockets. "Thar isn't a man ez crawls above his grave ez is worthy to lie in the same ground with him!"

"Thank you, Bill. Good-night; I'm going to turn in!"

"Look yar, boy! G—d d—n it all, Jeff! what do ye mean?"

There were two tears—twin sisters of those in his sweet heart's eyes that afternoon—now standing in Jeff's!

Bill caught both his hands in his own. Had they been of the Latin race they would have, right honestly, taken each other in their arms, and perhaps kissed! Being Anglo-Saxons, they gripped each other's hands hard, and one, as above stated, swore!

When Jeff ascended to his room that night, he went directly to his trunk and took out Miss Mayfield's slipper. Alack! during the day Aunt Sally had "put things to rights" in his room, and the trunk had been moved. This had somewhat disordered its contents, and Miss Mayfield's slipper contained a dozen shot from a broken Eley's cartridge, a few quinine pills, four postage stamps, part of a coral earring which Jeff—on the most apocryphal authority—fondly believed belonged to his mother, whom he had never seen, and a small silver school medal which Jeff had once received for "good conduct," much to his own surprise, but which he still religiously kept as evidence of former conventional character. He coloured a little, rubbed the medal and earring ruefully on his sleeve, replaced them in his trunk, and then hastily emptied the rest of the slipper's contents on the floor. This done, he drew off his boots, and gliding noiselessly down the stair, hung the slipper on the knob of Miss Mayfield's door, and glided back again without detection.

Rolling himself in his blankets, he lay down on his bed. But not to sleep! Staringly wide awake, he at last felt the lulling of the wind that nightly shook his casement, and listened while the great, rambling, creaking, disjointed "Half-way House" slowly settled itself to repose. He thought of many things; of himself, of his past, of his future, but chiefly, I fear, of the pale proud face now sleeping contentedly in the chamber below him. He tossed with many plans and projects, more or less impracticable, and then began to doze. Whereat the moon, creeping in the window, laid a cold white arm across him, and eventually dried a few foolish tears upon his sleeping lashes.

## CHAPTER IV.

AUNT SALLY was making pies in the kitchen the next morning when Jeff hesitatingly stole upon her. The moment was not a felicitous one. Pie-making was usually an agressive pursuit with Aunt Sally, entered into severely, and prosecuted unto the bitter end. After watching her a few moments Jeff came up and placed his arms tenderly around her. People very much in love find relief, I am told, in this vicarious expression.

"Aunty."

"Well, Jeff! Thar, now—yer gittin' all dough!" Nevertheless, the hard face relaxed a little. Something of a smile stole round her mouth, showing what she might have been before theology and bitters had supplied the natural feminine longings.

"Aunty dear!"

"You —— boy!"

It *was* a boy's face—albeit bearded like the pard, with an extra fierceness in the mustachios—that looked upon hers. She could not help bestowing a grim floury kiss upon it.

"Well, what is it now?"

"I'm thinking, aunty, it's high time you and me packed up our traps and 'shook' this yar shanty, and located somewhere else." Jeff's voice was ostentatiously cheerful, but his eyes were a little anxious.

"What for *now?*"

Jeff hastily recounted his ill luck, and the various reasons
—excepting of course the dominant one—for his resolution.

"And when do you kalkilate to go?"

"If you'll look arter things here," hesitated Jeff, "I
reckon I'd go up along with Bill to-morrow, and look round
a bit."

"And how long do you reckon that gal would stay here
after yar gone?"

This was a new and startling idea to Jeff. But in his
humility he saw nothing in it to flatter his conceit. Rather
the reverse. He coloured, and then said apologetically—

"I thought that you and Jinny could get along without
me. The butcher will pack the provisions over from the
Fork."

Laying down her rolling-pin, Aunt Sally turned upon Jeff
with ostentatious deliberation. "Ye ain't," she began slowly,
"ez taking a man with wimmin ez your father was—that's a
fact, Jeff Briggs! They used to say that no woman as he
went for could get away from him. But ye don't mean to
say yer think yer not good enough—such as ye are—for this
snip of an old maid, ez big as a gold dollar, and as yaller?"

"Aunty," said Jeff, dropping his boyish manner, and his
colour as suddenly, "I'd rather ye wouldn't talk that way
of Miss Mayfield. Ye don't know her; and there's times,"
he added, with a sigh, "ez I reckon ye don't quite know
*me* either. That young lady, bein' sick, likes to be looked
after. Any one can do that for her. She don't mind who
it is. She don't care for me except for that, and," added
Jeff humbly, "it's quite natural."

"I didn't say she did," returned Aunt Sally viciously;
"but seeing ez you've got an empty house yer on yer hands,
and me a-slavin' here on jist nothin', if this gal, for the sake
o' gallivantin' with ye for a spell, chooses to stay here and
keep her family here, and pay high for it, I don't see why

it ain't yer duty to Providence and me to take advantage of it."

Jeff raised his eyes to his aunt's face. For the first time it struck him that she might be his father's sister and yet have no blood in her veins that answered to his. There are few shocks more startling and overpowering to original natures than this sudden sense of loneliness. Jeff could not speak, but remained looking fiercely at her.

Aunt Sally misinterpreted his silence, and returned to her work on the pies. "The gal ain't no fool," she continued, rolling out the crust as if she were laying down broad propositions. "*She* reckons on it too, ez if it was charged in the bill with the board and lodging. Why, didn't she say to me, last night, that she kalkilated afore she went away to bring up some friends from 'Frisco for a few days' visit? and didn't she say, in that pipin', affected v'ice o' hers, ' I oughter make some return for yer kindness and yer nephew's kindness, Aunt Sally, by showing people that can help you, and keep your house full, how pleasant it is up here.' She ain't no fool, with all her faintin's and dyin's away! No, Jeff Briggs. And if she wants to show ye off agin them city fellows ez she knows, and ye ain't got spunk enough to stand up and show off with her—why"—— she turned her head impatiently, but he was gone.

If Jeff had ever wavered in his resolution he would have been steady enough *now*. But he had never wavered ; the convictions and resolutions of suddenly awakened character are seldom moved by expediency. He was eager to taste the bitter dregs of his cup at once. He began to pack his trunk, and made his preparations for departure. Without avoiding Miss Mayfield in this new excitement, he no longer felt the need of her presence. He had satisfied his feverish anxieties by placing his trunk in the hall beside his open door, and was sitting on his bed, wrestling with a faded and overtasked carpet-bag that would not close and accept his hard conditions, when a small voice from the staircase thrilled him. He walked to the corridor, and, looking down, beheld Miss Mayfield midway on the steps of the staircase.

She had never looked so beautiful before! Jeff had only seen her in those soft enwrappings and half *deshabille* that belong to invalid femininity. Always refined and modest thus, in her present walking costume there was added a slight touch of coquettish adornment. There was a brightness of colour in her cheek and eye, partly the result of climbing the staircase, partly the result of that audacious impulse that had led her—a modest virgin—to seek a gentleman in this personal fashion. Modesty in a young girl has a comfortable satisfying charm, recognised easily by all humanity; but he must be a sorry knave or a worse prig who is not deliciously thrilled when Modesty puts her charming little foot just òver the threshold of Propriety.

"The mountain would not come to Mohammed, so Mohammed must come to the mountain," said Miss Mayfield. "Mother is asleep, Aunt Sally is at work in the kitchen, and here am I, already dressed for a ramble in this bright afternoon sunshine, and no one to go with me. But, perhaps, you too are busy?"

"No, miss. I will be with you in a moment."

I wish I could say that he went back to calm his pulses, which the dangerous music of Miss Mayfield's voice had set to throbbing, by a few moments' calm and dispassionate reflection. But he only returned to brush his curls out of his eyes and ears, and to button over his blue flannel shirt a white linen collar, which he thought might better harmonise with Miss Mayfield's attire.

She was sitting on the staircase, poking her parasol through the balusters. "You need not have taken that

trouble, Mr. Jeff," she said pleasantly.   " *You* are a part of
this mountain picture at all times; but *I* am obliged to
think of dress."

"It was no trouble, miss."

Something in the tone of his voice made her look in his
face as she rose.   It was a trifle paler, and a little older.
The result, doubtless, thought Miss Mayfield, of his yesterday's experience with the deputy-sheriff.   Such was her
rapid deduction.   Nevertheless, after the fashion of her
sex, she immediately began to argue from quite another
hypothesis.

"You are angry with me, Mr. Jeff."

"What, I—Miss Mayfield?"

"Yes, you!"

"Miss Mayfield!"

"Oh yes, you are.   Don't deny it!"

"Upon my soul"——

"Yes!   You give me punishments and—penances!"

Jeff opened his blue eyes on his tormentor.   Could Aunt
Sally have been saying anything?

"If anybody, Miss Mayfield"—— he began.

"Nobody but you.   Look here!"

She extended her little hand with a smile.   In the centre
of her palm lay four shining double B *shot.*

"There!   I found those in my slipper this morning!"

Jeff was speechless.

"Of course *you* did it!   Of course it was *you* who found
my slipper!" said Miss Mayfield, laughing.   "But why did
you put shot in it, Mr. Jeff?   In some Catholic countries,
when people have done wrong, the priests make them do
penance by walking with peas in their shoes!   What have
I ever done to you?   And why *shot?*   They're ever so
much harder than peas."

Seeing only the mischievous laughing face before him,

and the open palm containing the damning evidence of the broken Eley's cartridge, Jeff stammered out the truth.

"I found the slipper in the bear-skin, Miss Mayfield. I put it in my trunk to keep, thinking yer wouldn't miss it, and it's being a kind of remembrance after you're gone away —of—of the night you came here. Somebody moved the trunk in my room," and he hung his head here. "The things inside all got mixed up."

"And that made you change your mind about keeping it?" said Miss Mayfield, still smiling.

"No, miss."

"What was it, then?"

"I gave it back to you, Miss Mayfield, because *I* was going away."

"Indeed! Where?"

"I'm going to find another location. Maybe you've noticed," he continued, falling back into his old apologetic manner in spite of his pride of resolution—" maybe you've noticed that this place here has no advantages for a hotel."

"I had not, indeed. I have been very comfortable."

"Thank you, miss."

"When do you go?"

"To-night."

For all his pride and fixed purpose he could not help looking eagerly in her face. Miss Mayfield's eyes met his pleasantly and quietly.

"I'm sorry to part with you so soon," she said, as she stepped back a pace or two with folded hands. "Of course every moment of your time now is occupied. You must not think of wasting it on me."

But Jeff had recovered his sad composure. "I'd like to go with you, Miss Mayfield. It's the last time, you know," he added simply.

Miss Mayfield did not reply. It was a tacit assent, however, although she moved somewhat stiffly at his side as they walked towards the door. Quite convinced that Jeff's resolution came from his pecuniary troubles, Miss Mayfield was wondering if she had not better assure him of his security from further annoyance from Dodd. Wonderful complexity of female intellect! she was a little hurt at his ingratitude to her for a kindness he could not possibly have known. Miss Mayfield felt that in some way she was un-justly treated. How many of our miserable sex, incapable of divination, have been crushed under that unreasonable feminine reproof—" You ought to have known!"

The afternoon sun was indeed shining brightly as they stepped out before the bleak angle of the " Half-way House;" but it failed to mitigate the habitually practical austerity of the mountain breeze—a fact which Miss May-field had never before noticed. The house was certainly bleak and exposed; the site by no means a poetical one. She wondered if she had not put a romance into it, and perhaps even into the man beside her, which did not belong to either. It was a moment of dangerous doubt.

" I don't know but that you're right, Mr. Jeff," she said finally, as they faced the hill, and began the ascent together. " This place is a little queer, and bleak, and—unattractive."

" Yes, miss," said Jeff, with direct simplicity, " I've always wondered what you saw in it to make you content to stay, when it would be so much prettier, and more suit-able for you at the 'Summit.'"

Miss Mayfield bit her lip, and was silent. After a few moments' climbing she said, almost pettishly, " Where is this famous 'Summit'?"

Jeff stopped. They had reached the top of the hill. He pointed across an olive-green chasm to a higher level, where, basking in the declining sun, clustered the long rambling outbuildings around the white blinking façade of the "Summit House." Framed in pines and hemlocks, tender with soft grey shadows, and nestling beyond a fore ground of cultivated slope, it was a charming rustic picture.

Miss Mayfield's quick eye took in its details. Her quick intellect took in something else. She had seated herself on the road-bank, and clasping her knees between her locked fingers, she suddenly looked up at Jeff. "What possessed you to come half-way up a mountain, instead of going on to the top?"

"Poverty, miss!"

Miss Mayfield flushed a little at this practical direct answer to her half-figurative question. However, she began to think that moral Alpine-climbing youth might have pecuniary restrictions in their high ambitions, and that the hero of "Excelsior" might have succumbed to more power-ful opposition than the wisdom of Age or the blandishments of Beauty.

"You mean that property up there is more expensive?"

"Yes, miss."

"But you would like to live there?"

"Yes."

They were both silent. Miss Mayfield glanced at Jeff under the corners of her lashes. He was leaning against a tree, absorbed in thought. Accustomed to look upon him as a pleasing picturesque object, quite fresh, original, and characteristic, she was somewhat disturbed to find that to-day he presented certain other qualities which clearly did not agree with her preconceived ideas of his condition. He had abandoned his usual large top-boots for low shoes, and she could not help noticing that his feet were small and slender, as were his hands, albeit browned by ex-posure. His ruddy colour was gone too, and his face, pale with sorrow and experience, had a new expression. His buttoned-up coat and white collar, so unlike his usual self, also had its suggestions—which Miss Mayfield was at first inclined to resent. Women are quick to notice and augur more or less wisely from these small details. Nevertheless, she began in quite another tone.

"Do you remember your mother—*Mr.—Mr.—Briggs?*"

Jeff noticed the new epithet. "No, miss; she died when I was quite young."

"Your father, then?"

Jeff's eye kindled a little, aggressively. "I remember *him.*"

"What was he?"

"Miss Mayfield!"

"What was his business or profession?"

"He—hadn't—any!"

"Oh, I see—a gentleman of property."

Jeff hesitated, looked at Miss Mayfield hurriedly, coloured, and did not reply.

"And lost his property, Mr. Briggs?"

With one of those rare impulses of an overtasked gentle nature, Jeff turned upon her almost savagely. "My father was a gambler, and shot himself at a gambling table."

Miss Mayfield rose hurriedly. "I—I—beg your pardon, Mr. Jeff."

Jeff was silent.

"You know—you *must* know—that I did not mean"——
No reply.

"Mr. Jeff!"

Her little hand fluttered towards him, and lit upon his sleeve, where it was suddenly captured and pressed passionately to his lips.

"I did not mean to be thoughtless or unkind," said Miss Mayfield, discreetly keeping to the point, and trying weakly to disengage her hand. "You know I wouldn't hurt your feelings."

" I know, Miss Mayfield."   (Another kiss.)

"I was ignorant of your history."

" Yes, miss."   (A kiss.)

"And if I could do anything for you, Mr. Jeff"——
She stopped.

It was a very trying position.   Being small, she was
drawn after her hand quite up to Jeff's shoulder, while he,
assenting in monosyllables, was parting the fingers, and
kissing them separately.   Reasonable discourse in this
attitude was out of the question.   She had recourse to
strategy.

" Oh ! "

" Miss Mayfield ! "

" You hurt my hand."

Jeff dropped it instantly.   Miss Mayfield put it in the
pocket of her sacque for security.   Besides, it had been so
bekissed that it seemed unpleasantly conscious.

"I wish you would tell me all about yourself," she went
on, with a certain charming feminine submission of manner
quite unlike her ordinary speech; "I should like to help
you.   Perhaps I can.   You know I am quite independent;
I mean "——

She paused, for Jeff's face betrayed no signs of sympathetic following.

"I mean I am what people call rich in my own right.
I can do as I please with my own.   If any of your trouble,
Mr. Jeff, arises from want of money, or capital; if any
consideration of that kind takes you away from your home ;
if I could save you *that trouble,* and find for you—perhaps
a little nearer—that which you are seeking, I would be *so*
glad to do it.   You will find the world very wide, and very
cold, Mr. Jeff," she continued, with a certain air of practical
superiority quite natural to her, but explicable to her friends
and acquaintances only as the consciousness of pecuniary

independence; "and I wish you would be frank with me. Although I am a woman, I know something of business."

"I will be frank with you, miss," said Jeff, turning a colourless face upon her. "If you was ez rich as the Bank of California, and could throw your money on any fancy or whim that struck you at the moment; if you felt you could buy up any man and woman in California that was willing to be bought up; and if me and my aunt were starving in the road, we wouldn't touch the money that we hadn't earned fairly, and didn't belong to us. No, miss, I ain't that sort o' man!"

How much of this speech, in its brusqueness and slang, was an echo of Yuba Bill's teaching, how much of it was a part of Jeff's inward weakness, I cannot say. He saw Miss Mayfield recoil from him. It added to his bitterness that his thought, for the first time voiced, appeared to him by no means as effective or powerful as he had imagined it would be, but he could not recede from it; and there was the relief that the worst had come, and was over now.

Miss Mayfield took her hand out of her pocket. "I don't think you quite understand me, Mr. Jeff," she said quietly; "and I *hope* I don't understand you." She walked stiffly at his side for a few moments, but finally took the other side of the road. They had both turned, half unconsciously, back again to the " Half-way House."

Jeff felt, like all quarrel-seekers, righteous or unrighteous, the full burden of the fight. If he could have relieved his mind, and at the next moment leaped upon Yuba Bill's coach, and so passed away—without a further word of explanation—all would have been well. But to walk back with this girl, whom he had just shaken off, and who must now thoroughly hate him, was something he had not preconceived, in that delightful forecast of the imagination, when we determine what *we* shall say and do without the least consideration of what may be said or done to us in return. No quarrel proceeds exactly as we expect; people have such a way of behaving illogically! And here was Miss Mayfield, who was clearly derelict, and who should have acted under that conviction, walking along on the other side of the road, trailing the splendour of her parasol in the dust like an offended goddess.

They had almost reached the house. "At what time do you go, Mr. Briggs?" asked the young lady quietly.

"At eleven to-night, by the up stage."

"I expect some friends by that stage—coming with my father."

"My aunt will take good care of them," said Jeff, a little bitterly.

"I have no doubt," responded Miss Mayfield gravely; "but I was not thinking of that. I had hoped to introduce them to you to-morrow. But I shall not be up so late to-night. And I had better say good-bye to you now."

She extended the unkissed hand. Jeff took it, but presently let the limp fingers fall through his own.

"I wish you good fortune, Mr. Briggs."

She made a grave little bow, and vanished into the house. But here, I regret to say, her lady-like calm also vanished. She upbraided her mother peevishly for obliging her to seek the escort of Mr. Briggs in her necessary exercise, and flung herself with an injured air upon the sofa.

"But I thought you liked this Mr. Briggs. He seems an accommodating sort of person."

"Very accommodating. Going away just as we are expecting company!"

"Going away?" said Mrs. Mayfield in alarm. "Surely he must be told that we expect some preparation for our friends?"

"Oh," said Miss Mayfield quickly, "his aunt will arrange *that*."

Mrs. Mayfield, habitually mystified at her daughter's moods, said no more. She, however, fulfilled her duty conscientiously by rising, throwing a wrap over the young girl, tucking it in at her feet, and having, as it were, drawn a charitable veil over her peculiarities, left her alone.

At half-past ten the coach dashed up to the "Half-way House," with a flash of lights and a burst of cheery voices. Jeff, coming upon the porch, was met by Mr. Mayfield, accompanying a lady and two gentlemen; evidently the guests alluded to by his daughter. Accustomed as Jeff had become to Mr. Mayfield's patronising superiority, it seemed unbearable now, and the easy indifference of the guests to his own presence touched him with a new bitterness. Here were *her* friends, who were to take his place! It was a relief to grasp Yuba Bill's large hand and stand with him alone beside the bar.

"I'm ready to go with you to-night, Bill," said Jeff, after a pause.

Bill put down his glass—a sign of absorbing interest.

"And these yar strangers I fetched?"

"Aunty will take care of them. I've fixed everything."

Bill laid both his powerful hands on Jeff's shoulders, backed him against the wall, and surveyed him with great gravity.

"Briggs's son clar through! A little off colour, but the grit all thar! Bully for you, Jeff." He wrung Jeff's hand between his own.

"Bill!" said Jeff hesitatingly.

"Jeff!"

"You wouldn't mind my getting up on the box *now* before all the folks get round?"

"I reckon not. Thar's the box-seat all ready for ye."

Climbing to his high perch, Jeff, indistinguishable in the darkness, looked out upon the porch and the moving figures of the passengers, on Bill growling out his orders to his active hostler, and on the twinkling lights of the hotel windows. In the mystery of the night and the bitterness of his heart, everything looked strange. There was a light in Miss Mayfield's room, but the curtains were drawn. Once he thought they moved, but then, fearful of the fascination of watching them, he turned his face resolutely away.

Then, to his relief, the hour came ; the passengers re-entered the coach ; Bill had mounted the box, and was slowly gathering his reins, when a shrill voice rose from the porch.

"Oh, Jeff ! "

Jeff leaned an anxious face out over the coach lamps.

It was Aunt Sally, breathless and on tiptoe, reaching with a letter. "Suthin' you forgot ! " Then, in a hoarse stage whisper, perfectly audible to every one: "From *her !* "

Jeff seized the letter with a burning face. The whip snapped, and the stage plunged forward into the darkness. Presently Yuba Bill reached down, coolly detached one of the coach lamps, and handed it to Jeff without a word.

Jeff tore open the envelope. It contained Cyrus Parker's bill receipted, and the writ. Another small enclosure contained ten dollars, and a few lines written in pencil in a large masculine business hand. By the light of the lamp Jeff read as follows :—

"I hope you will forgive me for having tried to help you even in this accidental way, before I knew how strong were your objections to help from me. Nobody knows this but myself. Even Mr. Dodd thinks my father advanced the

money.    The ten dollars the rascal would have kept, but I
made him disgorge it.    I did it all while you were looking
for the letter in the woods.    Pray forget all about it, and
any pain you may have had from

"J. M."

Frank and practical as this letter appeared to be, and,
doubtless, as it was intended to be by its writer, the reader
will not fail to notice that Miss Mayfield said nothing of
having overheard Jeff's quarrel with the deputy, and left him
to infer that that functionary had betrayed him.    It was
simply one of those unpleasant details not affecting the
result, usually overlooked in feminine ethics.

For a moment Jeff sat pale and dumb, crushed under the
ruins of his pride and self-love.    For a moment he hated
Miss Mayfield, small and triumphant!    How she must
have inwardly laughed at his speech that morning!    With
what refined cruelty she had saved this evidence of his
humiliation, to work her vengeance on him now.    He
could not stand it!    He could not live under it!    He
would go back and sell the house—his clothes—everything
—to pay this wicked, heartless, cruel girl, that was killing
—yes, killing——

A strong hand took the swinging lantern from his un-
steady fingers, a strong hand possessed itself of the papers
and Miss Mayfield's note, a strong arm was drawn around
him—for his figure was swaying to and fro, his head was
giddy, and his hat had fallen off—and a strong voice, albeit
a little husky, whispered in his ear—

"Easy, boy! easy on the down grade.    It'll be all one
in a minit."

Jeff tried to comprehend him, but his brain was whirling.

"Pull yourself together, Jeff!" said Bill, after a pause

"Thar! Look yar!" he said suddenly. "*Do you think you can drive* six?"

The words recalled Jeff to his senses. Bill laid the six reins in his hands. A sense of life, of activity, of *power*, came back to the young man, as his fingers closed deliciously on the far-reaching, thrilling, living leathern sinews that controlled the six horses, and seemed to be instinct and magnetic with their bounding life. Jeff, leaning back against them, felt the strong youthful tide rush back to his heart, and was himself again. Bill meantime took the lamp, examined the papers, and read Miss Mayfield's note. A grim smile stole over his face. After a pause, he said again, "Give Blue Grass her head, Jeff. D—n it, she ain't Miss Mayfield!"

Jeff relaxed the muscles of his wrists, so as to throw the thumb and forefingers a trifle forward. This simple action relieved Blue Grass, *alias* Miss Mayfield, and made the coach steadier and less jerky. Wonderful co-relation of forces.

"Thar!" said Yuba Bill, quietly putting the coach lamp back in its place; "you're better already. Thar's nothing like six horses to draw a woman out of a man. I've knowed a case where it took eight mustangs, but it was a mulatter from New Orleans, and they are pizen! Ye might hit up a little on the Pinto hoss—he ain't harmin' ye. So! Now, Jeff, take your time, and take it easy, and what's all this yer about?"

To control six fiery mustangs, and at the same time give picturesque and affecting exposition of the subtle struggles of Love and Pride, was a performance beyond Jeff's powers. He had recourse to an angry staccato, which somehow seemed to him as ineffective as his previous discourse to Miss Mayfield; he was a little incoherent, and perhaps mixed his impressions with his facts, but he nevertheless managed to convey to Bill some general idea of the events of the past three days.

"And she sent ye off after that letter, that wasn't thar, while she fixed things up with Dodd?"

"Yes," said Jeff furiously.

"Ye needn't bully the Pinto colt, Jeff; he is doin' his level best. And she snaked that 'ar ten dollars outer Dodd?"

"Yes; and sent it back to *me*. To ME, Bill! At such a time as this! As if I was dead broke!—a mere tramp. As if"——

"In course! in course!" said Bill soothingly, yet turning his head aside to bestow a deceitful smile upon the trees that whirled beside him. "And ye told her ye didn't want her money?"

"Yes, Bill!—but it—it—it was *after* she had done this!"

"Surely! I'll take the lines now, Jeff."

He took them. Jeff relapsed into gloomy silence. The starlight of that dewless Sierran night was bright, and cold, and passionless. There was no moon to lead the fancy astray with its faint mysteries and suggestions; nothing but a clear, greyish blue twilight, with sharply silhouetted shadows, pointed here and there with bright large-spaced constant stars. The deep breath of the pine-woods, the faint ʼcool resinous spices of bay and laurel, at last brought surcease to his wounded spirit. The blessed weariness of exhausted youth stole tenderly on him. His head nodded, dropped. Yuba Bill, with a grim smile, drew him to his side, enveloped him in his blanket, and felt his head at last sink upon his own broad shoulder.

A few minutes later the coach drew up at the "Summit House." Yuba Bill did not dismount, an unusual and disturbing circumstance that brought the bar-keeper to the verandah.

"What's up, old man?"

"I am."

"Sworn off your reg'lar pizen?"

"My physician," said Bill gravely, "hez ordered me dry champagne every three hours."

Nevertheless, the bar-keeper lingered.

"Who's that you're dry-nussin' up there?"

I regret that I may not give Yuba Bill's literal reply. It suggested a form of inquiry at once distant, indirect, outrageous, and impossible.

The bar-keeper flashed a lantern upon Jeff's curls and his drooping eyelashes and mustachios.

"It's that son o' Briggs o' Tuolumne—pooty boy, ain't he?"

Bill disdained a reply.

"Played himself out down there, I reckon. Left his rifle here in pawn."

"Young man," said Bill gravely.

"Old man."

"Ef you're looking for a safe investment ez will pay ye better than forty-rod whisky at two bits a glass, jist you hang onter that 'ar rifle. It may make your fortin yet, or save ye from a drunkard's grave." With this ungracious pleasantry he hurried his dilatory passengers back into the coach, cracked his whip, and was again upon the road. The lights of the "Summit House" presently dropped here and there into the wasting shadows of the trees. Another stretch through the close-set ranks of pines, another dash through the opening, another whirl and rattle by overhanging rocks, and the vehicle was swiftly descending. Bill put his foot on the brake, threw his reins loosely on the necks of his cattle, and looked leisurely back. The great mountain was slowly and steadily rising between them and the valley they quitted.

And at that same moment Miss Mayfield had crept from her bed, and with a shawl around her pretty little figure, was pressing her eyes against a blank window of the "Half-way House," and wondering where *he* was now.

## CHAPTER V.

THE "opening" suggested by Bill was not a fortunate one. Possibly views of business openings in the public-house line taken from the tops of stage-coaches are not as judicious as those taken from less exalted levels. Certain it is that the "good-will" of the "Lone Star House" promised little more pecuniary value than a conventional blessing. It was in an older and more thickly settled locality than the "Half-way House;" indeed, it was but half a mile away from Campville, famous in '49—a place with a history and a disaster. But young communities are impatient of settlements that through any accident fail to fulfil the extravagant promise of their youth, and the wounded hamlet of Campville had crept into the woods and died. The "Lone Star House" was an attempt to woo the passing travellers from another point; but its road led to Campville, and it was already touched by its dry-rot. Bill, who honestly conceived that the infusion of fresh young blood like Jeff's into the stagnant current would quicken it, had to confess his disappointment. "I thought ye could put some go into the shanty, Jeff," said Bill, "and make it lively and invitin'!" But the lack of vitality was not in the landlord, but in the guests. The regular customers were disappointed, vacant, hopeless men, who gathered listlessly on the verandah, and talked vaguely of the past. Their hollow-eyed, feeble impotency affected the stranger, even as it checked all ambition among themselves. Do what Jeff might, the habits of the locality were stronger than his individuality; the dead ghosts of the past Campville held their property by invisible mortmain.

In the midst of this struggle the "Half-way House" was sold. Spite of Bill's prediction, the proceeds barely paid Jeff's debts. Aunt Sally prevented any troublesome consideration of *her* future, by applying a small surplus of profit to the expenses of a journey back to her relatives in Kentucky. She wrote Jeff a letter of cheerless instruction, reminded him of the fulfilment of her worst prophecies regarding him, but begged him, in her absence, to rely solely upon the "Word." "For the sperrit killeth," she added vaguely. Whether this referred figuratively to Jeff's business, he did not stop to consider. He was more interested in the information that the Mayfields had removed to the "Summit Hotel" two days after he had left. "She allowed it was for her health's sake," continued Aunt Sally, "but I reckon it's another name for one of them city fellers who j'ined their party and is keepin' company with her now. They talk o' property and stocks and sich worldly trifles all the time, and it's easy to see their idees is set together. It's allowed at the Forks that Mr. Mayfield paid Parker's bill for you. I said it wasn't so, fur ye'd hev told me; but if it is so, Jeff, and ye didn't tell me, it was for only one puppos, and that wos that Mayfield bribed ye to break off with his darter! That was *why* you went off so suddent, 'like a thief in the night,' and why Miss Mayfield never let on a word about you after you left—not even your name!"

Jeff crushed the letter between his fingers, and going behind the bar, poured out half a glass of stimulant and drank it. It was not the first time since he came to the "Lone Star House" that he had found this easy relief from his present thought; it was not the first time that he had found this dangerous ally of sure and swift service in bringing him up or down to that level of his dreary, sodden guests, so necessary to his trade. Jeff had not the excuse of the in-born drunkard's taste. He was impulsive and extreme. At the end of the four weeks he came out on the porch one night as Bill drew up. "You must take me from this place to-night," he said, in a broken voice scarce like his own. "When we're on the road we can arrange matters, but I must go to-night."

"But where?" asked Bill.

"Anywhere! Only I must go from here. I shall go if I have to walk."

Bill looked hard at the young man. His face was flushed, his eyes blood-shot, and his hands trembled, not with excitement, but with a vacant, purposeless impotence. Bill looked a little relieved. "You've been drinking too hard. Jeff, I thought better of ye than that!"

"I think better of *myself* than that," said Jeff, with a certain wild, half-hysterical laugh, "and that is why I want to go. Don't be alarmed, Bill," he added; "I have strength enough to save myself, and I shall! But it isn't worth the struggle *here.*"

He left the "Lone Star House" that night. He would, he said to Bill, go on to Sacramento, and try to get a situation as clerk or porter there; he was too old to learn a trade. He said little more. When, after forty-eight hours' inability to eat, drink, or sleep, Bill, looking at his haggard face and staring eyes, pressed him to partake, medicinally, from a certain black bottle, Jeff gently put it aside, and saying, with a sad smile, "I can get along without it; I've gone through more than this," left his mentor in a state of mingled admiration and perplexity.

At Sacramento he found a commercial "opening." But certain habits of personal independence, combined with a direct ʽtruthfulness and simplicity, were not conducive to business advancement. He was frank, and, in his habits, impulsive and selfishly outspoken. His employer, a good-natured man, successful in his way, anxious to serve his own interest and Jeff's equally, strove and laboured with him, but in vain. His employer's wife, a still more good-natured woman, successful in her way, and equally anxious to serve Jeff's interests and her own, also strove with him as unsuccessfully. At the end of a month he discharged his employer, after a simple, boyish, utterly unbusiness-like interview, and secretly tore up the wife's letter. "I don't know what to make of that chap," said the husband to his wife; "he's about as civilised as an Injun." "And as conceited," added the lady.

Howbeit he took his conceit, his sorrows, his curls, mustachios, broad shoulders, and fifty dollars into humble lodgings in a back street. The days succeeding this were the most restful he had passed since he left the "Half-way House." To wander through the town, half conscious of its strangeness and novel bustling life, and to dream of a higher and nobler future with Miss Mayfield—to feel no responsibility but that of waiting—was, I regret to say, a pleasure to him. He made no acquaintances except among the poorer people and the children. He was sometimes hungry, he was always poorly clad, but these facts carried no degradation with them now. He read much, and in his way—Jeff's way—tried to improve his mind; his recent commercial experience had shown him various infelicities in his speech and accent. He learned to correct certain provincialisms. He was conscious that Miss Mayfield must have noticed them, yet his odd irrational pride kept him from ever regretting them, if they had offered a possible excuse for her treatment of him.

On one of these nights his steps chanced to lead him into a gambling saloon. The place had offered no temptation to him; his dealings with the goddess Chance had been of less

active nature. Nevertheless he placed his last five dollars
on the turn of a card. He won. He won repeatedly; his
gains had reached a considerable sum, when, flushed,
excited, and absorbed, he was suddenly conscious that he
had become the centre of observation at the table. Looking up, he saw that the dealer had paused, and with the
cards in his motionless fingers, was gazing at him with fixed
eyes and a white face.

Jeff rose and passed hurriedly to his side. "What's the
matter?" he asked.

The gambler shrunk slightly as he approached. "What's
your name?"

"Briggs."

"God!—I knew it! How much have you got there?"
he continued, in a quick whisper, pointing to Jeff's winnings.

"Five hundred dollars."

"I'll give you double if you'll get up and quit the board!"

"Why?" asked Jeff haughtily.

"Why?" repeated the man fiercely; "why? Well, your
father shot himself thar, where you're sittin', at this table;"
and he added, with a half-forced, half-hysterical laugh,
"*he's playin' at me over your shoulders!*"

Jeff lifted a face as colourless as the gambler's own, went
back to his seat, and placed his entire gains on a single
card. The gambler looked at him nervously, but dealt.
There was a pause, a slight movement where Jeff stood, and
then a simultaneous cry from the players as they turned
towards him. But his seat was vacant. "Run after him!
Call him back! *He's won again!*" But he had vanished
utterly.

*How* he left, or what indeed followed, he never clearly
remembered. His movements must have been automatic,
for when, two hours later, he found himself at the
'Pioneer" coach office, with his carpet bag and blankets by

his side, he could not recall how or why he had come ! He had a dumb impression that he had barely escaped some dire calamity—rather that he had only temporarily averted it—and that he was still in the shadow of some impending catastrophe of destiny. He must go somewhere, he must do something to be saved ! He had no money, he had no friends ; even Yuba Bill had been transferred to another route, miles away. Yet, in the midst of this stupefaction, it was a part of his strange mental condition that trivial details of Miss Mayfield's face and figure, and even apparel, were constantly before him, to the exclusion of consecutive thought. A collar she used to wear, a ribbon she had once tied around her waist, a blue vein in her dropped eyelid, a curve in her soft, full, bird-like throat, the arch of her instep in her small boots—all these were plainer to him than the future, or even the present. But a voice in his ear, a figure before his abstracted eyes, at last broke upon his reverie.

"Jeff Briggs !"

Jeff mechanically took the outstretched hand of a young clerk of the Pioneer Coach Company, who had once accompanied Yuba Bill and stopped at the "Half-way House." He endeavoured to collect his thoughts ; here seemed to be an opportunity to go somewhere !

"What are you doing now?" said the young man briskly.

"Nothing," said Jeff simply.

"Oh, I see—going home !"

Home ! The word stung sharply through Jeff's benumbed consciousness.

"No," he stammered, "that is "——

"Look here, Jeff," broke in the young man, "I've got a chance for you that don't fall in a man's way every day. Wells, Fargo & Co.'s treasure messenger from Robinson's

Ferry to Mempheys has slipped out. The place is vacant. I reckon I can get it for you."

"When?"

"Now, to-night."

"I'm ready."

"Come, then."

In ten minutes they were in the Company's office, where its manager, a man famous in those days for his boldness and shrewdness, still lingered in the despatch of business.

The young clerk briefly but deferentially stated certain facts. A few questions and answers followed, of which Jeff heard only the words " Tuolumne " and " Yuba Bill."

" Sit down, Mr. Briggs. Good-night, Roberts."

The young clerk, with an encouraging smile to Jeff, bowed himself out as the manager seated himself at his desk and began to write.

"You know the country pretty well between the Fork and the Summit, Mr. Briggs?" he said, without looking up.

" I lived there," said Jeff.

" That was some months ago, wasn't it?"

" Six months," said Jeff, with a sigh.

" It's changed for the worse since your house was shut up. There's a long stretch of unsettled country infested by bad characters."

Jeff sat silent.

" Briggs."

" Sir?"

" The last man but one who precedes you was shot by road agents." *

" Yes, sir."

"We lost sixty thousand dollars up there."

" Yes?"

" Your father was Briggs of Tuolumne?"

* Highway robbers.

"Yes, sir." Jeff's head dropped, but, glancing shyly up, he saw a pleasant smile on his questioner's face. He was still writing rapidly, but was apparently enjoying at the same time some pleasant recollection.

"Your father and I lost nearly sixty thousand dollars together one night, ten years ago, when we were both younger."

"Yes, sir," said Jeff dubiously.

"But it was *our own money*, Jeff."

"Yes, sir."

"Here's your appointment," he said briefly, throwing away his pen, folding what he had written, and handing it to Jeff. It was the first time that he had looked at him since he entered. He now held out his hand, grasped Jeff's, and said, "Good-night!"

## CHAPTER VI.

IT was late the next evening when Jeff drew up at the coach office at Robinson's Ferry, where he was to await the coming of the Summit coach. His mind, lifted only temporarily out of its benumbed condition during his interview with the manager, again fell back into its dull abstraction. Fully embarked upon his dangerous journey, accepting all the meaning of the trust imposed upon him, he was yet vaguely conscious that he did not realise its full importance. He had neither the dread nor the stimulation of coming danger. He had faced death before in the boyish confidence of animal spirits; his pulse now was scarcely stirred with anticipation. Once or twice before, in the extravagance of his passion, he had imagined himself rescuing Miss Mayfield from danger, or even dying for her. During his journey his mind had dwelt fully and minutely on every detail of their brief acquaintance; she was continually before him, the tones of her voice were in his ears, the suggestive touch of her fingers, the thrill that his lips had felt when he kissed them—all were with him now, but only as a memory. In his coming fate, in his future life, he saw her not. He believed it was a premonition of coming death.

He made a few preparations. The Company's agent had told him that the treasure, letters, and despatches, which had accumulated to a considerable amount, would be handed to him on the box; and that the arms and ammunition were in the boot. A less courageous and determined man might have been affected by the cold, practical brutality of certain advice and instructions offered him by the agent, but Jeff recognised this compliment to his determination, even before the agent concluded his speech by saying, "But I reckon they knew what they were about in the lower office when they sent *you* up. I daresay you kin give me p'ints, ef ye cared to, for all ye're soft spoken. There are only four passengers booked through; we hev to be a little partikler, suspectin' spies! Two of the four ye kin depend upon to get the top o' their d—d heads blowed off the first fire," he added grimly.

At ten o'clock the Summit coach flashed, rattled, glittered, and snapped, like a disorganised firework, up to the door of the Company's office. A familiar figure, but more than usually truculent and  aggressive, slowly descended with violent oaths from the box. Without seeing Jeff, it strode into the office.

"Now then," said Yuba Bill, addressing the agent, "whar's that God-forsaken fool that Wells, Fargo & Co. hev sent up yar to take charge o' their treasure? Because I'd like to introduce him to the champion idgit of Calaveras county, that's been selected to go to h—ll with him ; and that's me Yuba Bill! P'int him out. Don't keep me waitin'!"

The agent grinned and pointed to Jeff.

Both men recoiled in astonishment. Yuba Bill was the first to recover his speech.

"It's a lie!" he roared; "or somebody has been putting up a job on ye, Jeff! Because I've been twenty years in the service, and am such a nat'ral born mule that when the Company strokes my back and sez, 'You're the on'y mule we kin trust, Bill,' I starts up and goes out as a blasted wooden figgerhead for road agents to lay fur and practise on, it don't follow that *you've* any call to go."

"It was my own seeking, Bill," said Jeff, with one of his old, sweet, boyish smiles. "I didn't know *you* were to drive. But you're not going back on me now, Bill, are you? —you're not going to send me off with another volunteer?"

"That be d—d!" growled Bill. Nevertheless, for ten minutes he reviled the Pioneer Coach Company with picturesque imprecation, tendered his resignation repeatedly to the agent, and at the end of that time, as everybody expected, mounted the box, and with a final malediction, involving the whole settlement, was off.

On the road, Jeff, in a few hurried sentences, told his story. Bill scarcely seemed to listen. "Look yar, Jeff," he said suddenly.

"Yes, Bill."

"If the worst happens, and ye go under, you'll tell your father, *if I don't happen to see him first*, it wasn't no job of mine, and I did my best to get ye out of it."

"Yes," said Jeff, in a faint voice.

"It mayn't be so bad," said Bill softening; "they *know*, d—n 'em, we've got a pile aboard, ez well ez if they seed that agent gin it ye, but they also know we've pre-pared!"

"I wasn't thinking of that, Bill; I was thinking of my father." And he told Bill of the gambling episode at Sacramento.

" D'ye mean to say ye left them hounds with a thousand dollars of yer hard-earned "——

" Gambling gains, Bill," interrupted Jeff quietly.

" Exactly ! Well !"   Bill subsided into an incoherent growl.   After a few moments' pause, he began again. " Yer ready as ye used to be with a six-shooter, Jeff, time's when ye was a boy, and I uster chuck half-dollars in the air fur ye to make warts on ? "

" I reckon," said Jeff, with a faint smile.

" Thar's two p'ints on the road to be looked to : the woods beyond the blacksmith's shop that uster be ; the fringe of alder and buckeye by the crossing below your house—p'ints where they kin fetch you without a show. Thar's two ways o' meetin' them thar.   One way ez to pull up and trust to luck and brag.   The other way is to whip up and yell, and send the whole six kiting by like h—ll ! "

" Yes," said Jeff.

" The only drawback to that plan is this : the road lies along the edge of a precipice, straight down a thousand feet into the river.   Ef these devils get a shot into any one o' the six and it *drops*, the coach turns sharp off, and down we go, the whole kerboodle of us, plump into the Stanislaus ! "

" *And they don't get the money,*" said Jeff quietly.

" Well, no !" replied Yuba Bill, staring at Jeff, whose face was set as a flint against the darkness.   " I should reckon not."   He then drew a long breath, glanced at Jeff again, and said between his teeth, " Well, I'm d—d ! "

At the next station they changed horses, Bill personally supervising, especially as regarded the welfare and proper condition of Blue Grass, who here was brought out as a leader.   Formerly there was no change of horses at this station, and this novelty excited Jeff's remark.   " These yar chaps say thar's no station at the Summit now," growled

Bill, in explanation; "the hotel is closed, and it's all private property, bought by some chap from 'Frisco. Thar ought to be a law agin such doin's!"

This suggested obliteration of the last traces of Miss Mayfield seemed to Jeff as only a corroboration of his premonition. He should never hear from her again! Yet to have stood under the roof that last sheltered her; to, perchance, have met some one who had seen her later—this was a fancy that had haunted him on his journey. It was all over now. Perhaps it was for the best.

With the sinking behind of the lights of the station, the occupants of the coach knew that the dangerous part of the journey had begun. The two guards in the coach had already made obtrusive and warlike preparations, to the ill-concealed disgust of Yuba Bill. "I'd hev been willin' to get through this yar job without the burnin' of powder, but ef any of them devils ez is waitin' for us would be content with a shot at them fancy policemen inside, I'd pull up and give 'em a show!" Having relieved his mind, Bill said no more, and the two men relapsed into silence. The moon shone brightly and peacefully, a fact pointed out by Bill as unfavourably deepening the shadows of the woods, and bringing the coach and the road into greater relief.

An hour passed. What were Yuba Bill's thoughts are not a part of this history; that they were turbulent and aggressive might be inferred from the occasional growls and interjected oaths that broke from his lips. But Jeff, strange anomaly, due perhaps to youth and moonlight, was wrapped in a sensuous dream of Miss Mayfield, of the scent of her dark hair as he had drawn her to his side, of the outlines of her sweet form, that had for a moment lightly touched his own—of anything, I fear, but the death he believed he was hastening to. But——

"Jeff," said Bill, in an unmistakable tone.

" Yes," said Jeff.

" *That ar clump o' buckeye on the ridge !*   Ready there !*"*
(Leaning over the box, to the guards within.)   A responsive
rustle in the coach, which now bounded forward as if instinct with life and intelligence.

" Jeff," said Bill, in an odd, altered voice, "take the lines
a minit." Jeff took them.   Bill stooped towards the boot.
A peaceful moment !   A peaceful outlook from the coach ;
the white moonlit road stretching to the ridge, no noise but
the steady gallop of the horses !

Then a yellow flash, breaking from the darkness of the
buckeye ; a crack like the snap of a whip ; Yuba Bill
steadying himself for a moment, and then dropping at Jeff's
feet !

"They got me, Jeff !   But—*I drawed their fire !*   Don't
drop the lines !   Don't speak !   For—they—think I'm *you*
and you *me !*"

The flash had illuminated Jeff as to the danger, as to
Bill's sacrifice, but above all, and overwhelming all, to a
thrilling sense of his own power and ability.

Yet he sat like a statue.   Six masked figures had appeared
from the very ground, clinging to the bits of the horses.
The coach stopped.   Two wild purposeless shots—the first
and last fired by the guards—were answered by the muzzle
of six rifles pointed into the windows, and the passengers
foolishly and impotently filed out into the road.

" Now, Bill," said a voice, which Jeff instantly recognised
as the blacksmith's, "we won't keep ye long.   So hand
down the treasure."

The man's foot was on the wheel ; in another instant
he would be beside Jeff, and discovery was certain.   Jeff
leaned over and unhooked the coach lamp, as if to assist
him with its light.   As if in turning, he *stumbled*, broke the
lamp, ignited the kerosene, and scattered the wick and

blazing fluid over the haunches of the wheelers! The maddened animals gave one wild plunge forwards, the coach followed twice its length, throwing the blacksmith under its wheels, and driving the other horses towards the bank. But as the lamp broke in Jeff's right hand, his practised left hand discharged its hidden Derringer at the head of the robber who had held the bit of Blue Grass, and throwing the useless weapon away, he laid the whip smartly on her back. She leaped forward madly, dragging the other leaders with her, and in the next moment they were free and wildly careering down the grade.

A dozen shots followed them. The men were protected by the coach, but Yuba Bill groaned.

"Are you hit again?" asked Jeff hastily. He had forgotten his saviour.

"No; but the horses are! I felt 'em! Look at 'em, Jeff."

Jeff had gathered up the almost useless reins. The horses were running away; but Blue Grass was limping.

"For God's sake," said Bill, desperately dragging his wounded figure above the dash-board, "keep her up! *Lift her up,* Jeff, till we pass the curve. Don't let her drop or we're "——

"Can you hold the reins?" said Jeff quickly.

"Give 'em here!"

Jeff passed them to the wounded man. Then, with his bowie-knife between his teeth, he leaped over the dash-board on the backs of the wheelers. He extinguished the blazing drops that the wind had not blown out on their smarting haunches, and with the skill and instinct of a Mexican *vaquero,* made his way over their turbulent tossing backs to Blue Grass, cut her traces and reins, and as the vehicle neared the curve, with a sharp lash, drove her to the bank, where she sank even as the coach darted by. Bill uttered a feeble "hurrah!" but at the same moment the reins dropped from his fingers, and he sank at the bottom of the boot.

Riding postilion-wise, Jeff could control the horses. The dangerous curve was passed, but not the possibility of pursuit. The single leader he was bestriding was panting— more than that, he was *sweating*, and from the evidence of Jeff's hands, sweating *blood!* Back of his shoulder was a jagged hole, from which his life-blood was welling. The off-wheel horse was limping too. That last volley was no foolish outburst of useless rage, but was deliberate and pre-meditated skill. Jeff drew the reins, and as the coach stopped, the horse he was riding fell dead. Into the silence that followed broke the measured beat of horses' hoofs on the road above. He was pursued!

To select the best horse of the remaining unscathed three, to break open the boot and place the treasure on his back, and to abandon and leave the senseless Bill lying there, was the unhesitating work of a moment. Great heroes and great lovers are invariably one-idead men, and Jeff was at that moment both.

Eighty thousand dollars in gold dust and Jeff's weight was a handicap. Nevertheless he flew forward like the wind. Presently he fell to listening. A certain hoof-beat in the rear was growing more distinct. A bitter thought flashed through his mind. He looked back. Over the hill appeared the foremost of his pursuers. It was the blacksmith, mounted on the fleetest horse in the county— Jeff's *own* horse—Rabbit!

But there are compensations in all new trials. As Jeff faced round again, he saw he had reached the open table-land, and the bleak walls and ghastly, untenanted windows of the " Half-way House " rose before him in the distance. Jeff was master of the ground here! He was entering the shadow of the woods—Miss Mayfield's woods! and there was a cut off from the road, and a bridle path, known only to himself, hard by. To find it, leap the roadside ditch, dash through the thicket, and rein up by the road again, was swiftly done.

Take a gentle woman, betray her trust, outrage her best feelings, drive her into a corner, and you have a fury! Take a gentle, trustful man, abuse him, show him the folly of this gentleness and kindness, prove to him that it is weakness, drive him into a corner, and you have a savage! And it was this savage, with an Indian's memory, and an Indian's eye and ear, that suddenly confronted the blacksmith.

What more! A single shot from a trained hand and one-idead intellect settled the blacksmith's business, and temporarily ended this Iliad! I say temporarily, for Mr. Dodd, formerly deputy-sheriff, prudently pulled up at the top of the hill, and observing his principal bend his head forwards and act like a drunken man, until he reeled, limp and sideways, from the saddle, and noticing further that Jeff took his place with a well-filled saddle-bag, concluded to follow cautiously and unobtrusively in the rear.

## CHAPTER VII.

BUT Jeff saw him not. With mind and will bent on one object—to reach the first habitation, the " Summit," and send back help and assistance to his wounded comrade—he urged Rabbit forward. The mare knew her rider, but he had no time for caresses. Through the smarting of his hands he had only just noticed that they were badly burned, and the skin was peeling from them; he had confounded the blood that was flowing from a cut on his scalp, with that from the wounded horse. It was one hour yet to the "Summit," but the road was good, the moon was bright, he knew what Rabbit could do, and it was not yet ten o'clock.

As the white outbuildings and irregular outlines of the "Summit House" began to be visible, Jeff felt a singular return of his former dreamy abstraction. The hour of peril, anger, and excitement he had just passed through seemed something of years ago, or rather to be obliterated with all else that had passed since he had looked upon that scene. Yet it was all changed—strangely changed! What Jeff had taken for the white, wooden barns and outhouses, were greenhouses and conservatories. The "Summit Hotel" was a picturesque villa, nestling in the self-same trees, but approached through cultivated fields, dwellings of labourers, parklike gates and walls, and all the bountiful appointments of wealth and security. Jeff thought of Yuba Bill's malediction, and understood it as he gazed.

The barking of dogs announced his near approach to the principal entrance. Lights were still burning in the upper windows of the house and its offices. He was at once surrounded by the strange medley of a Californian ranchero's service, peons, Chinese, and *vaqueros*. Jeff briefly stated his business. "Ah, Carrajo!" This was a matter for the major-domo, or, better, the *padrone*—Wilson! But the *padrone*, Wilson, called out by the tumult, appeared in person—a handsome, resolute, middle-aged man, who, in a twinkling, dispersed the group to barn and stable with a dozen orders of preparation, and then turned to Jeff.

"You are hurt; come in."

Jeff followed him dazedly into the house. The same sense of remote abstraction, of vague dreaminess, was overcoming him. He resented it, and fought against it, but in vain; he was only half conscious that his host had bathed his head and given him some slight restorative, had said

something to him soothingly, and had left him. Jeff
wondered if he had fainted, or was about to faint—he had
a nervous dread of that womanish weakness—or if he were
really hurt worse than he believed. He tried to master
himself and grasp the situation by minutely examining the
room. It was luxuriously furnished; Jeff had but once
before sat in such an arm-chair as the one that half embraced him, and as a boy he had dim recollections of a life
like this, of which his father was part. To poor Jeff, with
his throbbing head, his smarting hands, and his lapsing
moments of half forgetfulness, this seemed to be a return
of his old premonition. There was a vague perfume in the
room, like that which he remembered when he was in the
woods with Miss Mayfield. He believed he was growing
faint again, and was about to rise, when the door opened
behind him.

"Is there anything we can do for you? Mr. Wilson
has gone to seek your friend, and has sent Manuel for a
doctor."

*Her* voice! He rose hurriedly, turned; *she* was standing in the doorway!

She uttered a slight cry, turned very pale, advanced
towards him, stopped and leaned against the chimney-
piece.

"I didn't know it was *you.*"

With her actual presence Jeff's dream and weakness
fled. He rose up before her, his old bashful, stammering,
awkward self.

"*I* didn't know *you* lived here, Miss Mayfield."

"If you had sent word you were coming," said Miss
Mayfield, recovering her colour brightly in one cheek.

The possibility of having sent a messenger in advance
to advise Miss Mayfield of his projected visit did not strike
Jeff as ridiculous. Your true lover is far beyond such

trivialities.  He accepted the rebuke meekly.  He said he was sorry.

"You might have known it."

"What, Miss Mayfield?"

"That I was here, if you *wished* to know."

Jeff did not reply.  He bowed his head and clasped his burned hands together.  Miss Mayfield saw their raw surfaces, saw the ugly cut on his head, pitied him, but went on hastily, with both cheeks burning, to say, womanlike, what was then deepest in her heart.

"My brother-in-law told me your adventure; but I did not know until I entered this room that the gentleman I wished to help was one who had once rejected my assistance, who had misunderstood me, and cruelly insulted me! Oh, forgive me, Mr. Briggs" (Jeff had risen).  "I did not mean *that*.  But, Mr. Jeff—Jeff—oh!" (She had caught his tortured hand and had wrung a movement of pain from him.)  "Oh, dear! what did I do now?  But, Mr. Jeff, after what had passed, after what you said to me when you went away, when you were at that dreadful place, Campville, when you were two months in Sacramento, you might —*you ought to have let me know it!*"

Jeff turned.  Her face, more beautiful than he had ever seen it, alive and eloquent with every thought that her woman's speech but half-expressed, was very near his—so near, that under her honest eyes the wretched scales fell from his own, his self-wrought shackles crumbled away, and he dropped upon his knees at her feet as she sank into the chair he had quitted.  Both his hands were grasped in her own.

"*You* went away, and I *stayed*," she said reflectively.

"I had no home, Miss Mayfield."

"Nor had I.  I had to buy this," she said, with delicious simplicity, "and bring a family here too," she added, "in case *you*"—— she stopped, with a slight colour.

"Forgive me," said Jeff, burying his face in her hands.

"Jeff."

"Jessie."

"Don't you think you were a *little*—just a little—mean?"

"Yes."

Miss Mayfield uttered a faint sigh.    He looked into her anxious cheeks and eyes, his arm stole round her; their lips met for the first time in one long lingering kiss.    Then, I fear, for the second time.

"Jeff," said Miss Mayfield, suddenly becoming practical and sweetly possessory, "you must have your hands bound up in cotton."

"Yes," said Jeff cheerfully.

"And you must go instantly to bed."

Jeff stared.

"Because my sister will think it very late for me to be sitting up with a gentleman."

The idea that Miss Mayfield was responsible to anybody was something new to Jeff.    But he said hastily, "I must stay and wait for Bill.    He risked his life for me."

"Oh yes!    You must tell me all about it.    I may wait for *that.*"

Jeff possessed himself of the chair; in some way he also possessed himself of Miss Mayfield without entirely dispossessing her.    Then he told his story.    He hesitated over the episode of the blacksmith.    "I'm afraid I killed him, Jessie."

Miss Mayfield betrayed little concern at this possible extreme measure with a dangerous neighbour.    "He cut your head, Jeff," she said, passing her little hand through his curls.

"No," said Jeff hastily   "that must have been done *before.*"

"Well," said Miss Mayfield conclusively, "he would

if he'd dared. And you brought off that wretched money in spite of him. Poor dear Jeff!"

"Yes," said Jeff, kissing her.

"Where is it?" asked Jessie, looking round the room.

"Oh, just out there!"

"Out where?"

"On my horse, you know, outside the door," continued Jeff, a little uneasily, as he rose. "I'll go and "——

"You careless boy," said Miss Mayfield, jumping up, "I'll go with you."

They passed out on the porch together, holding each other's hands, like children. The forgotten Rabbit was not there. Miss Mayfield called a *vaquero.*

"Ah, yes!—the *caballero's* horse. Of a certainty the other *caballero* had taken it!"

"The *other caballero!*" gasped Jeff.

"*Si, Señor.* The one who arrived with you, or a moment, the very next moment, after you. 'Your friend,' he said."

Jeff staggered against the porch, and cast one despairing reproachful look at Miss Mayfield.

"Oh, Jeff! Jeff! don't look so! I know I ought not to have kept you! It's a mistake, Jeff, believe me."

"It's no mistake," said Jeff hoarsely. "Go!" he said, turning to the *vaquero,* "go!—bring"—— But his speech failed. He attempted to gesticulate with his hands, ran forward a few steps, staggered, and fell fainting on the ground.

"Help me with the *caballero* into the blue room," said Miss Mayfield, white as Jeff. "And hark ye, Manuel! You know every ruffian, man or woman, on this road. That horse and those saddle-bags must be here to-morrow, if you have to pay *double what they're worth!*"

"*Si, Señora.*"

Jeff went off into fever, into delirium, into helpless stupor

From time to time he moaned " Bill," and " the treasure."
On the third day, in a lucid interval, as he lay staring at
the wall, Miss Mayfield put in his hand a letter from the
Company, acknowledging the receipt of the treasure,
thanking him for his zeal, and enclosing a handsome
cheque.

Jeff sat up, and put his hands to his head.

" I told you it was taken by mistake, and was easily
found," said Miss Mayfield, "didn't I ? "

" Yes,—and Bill ? "

" You know he is so much better that he expects to
leave us next week."

" And—Jessie ! "

" There—go to sleep ! "

At the end of a week she introduced Jeff to her sister-in-
law, having previously run her fingers through his hair to
ensure that becomingness to his curls which would better
indicate his moral character; and spoke of him as one of
her oldest Californian friends.

At the end of two weeks she again presented him as her
affianced husband—a long engagement of a year being just
passed.   Mr. Wilson, who was bored by the mountain life,
undertaken to please his rich wife and richer sister, saw a
chance of escape here, and bore willing testimony to the
distant Mr. and Mrs. Mayfield of the excellence of Miss
Jessie's choice.   And Yuba Bill was Jeff's best man.

The name of Briggs remained a power in Tuolumne and
Calaveras county.   Mr. and Mrs. Briggs never had but one
word of disagreement or discussion.   One day, Jeff, looking
over some old accounts of his wife's, found an unreceipted,
unvouched-for expenditure of twenty thousand dollars.
" What is this for, Jessie ? " he asked.

" Oh, it's all right, Jeff ! "

But here the now business-like and practical Mr. Briggs,

father of a family, felt called upon to make some general remarks regarding the necessity of exactitude in accounts, &c.

" But I'd rather not tell you, Jeff."

" But you ought to, Jessie."

" Well then, dear, it was to get those saddle-bags of
yours from that rascal, Dodd," said little Mrs. Briggs
meekly.

# CONDENSED NOVELS.

# 𝔐𝔲𝔠𝔨=𝔞=𝔐𝔲𝔠𝔨.

### *A MODERN INDIAN NOVEL.*

#### AFTER COOPER.

## CHAPTER I.

IT was toward the close of a bright October day. The last rays of the setting sun were reflected from one of those sylvan lakes peculiar to the Sierras of California. On the right the curling smoke of an Indian village rose between the columns of the lofty pines, while to the left the log cottage of Judge Tompkins, embowered in buckeyes, completed the enchanting picture.

Although the exterior of the cottage was humble and unpretentious, and in keeping with the wildness of the landscape, its interior gave evidence of the cultivation and refinement of its inmates. An aquarium, containing gold-fishes, stood on a marble centre-table at one end of the apartment, while a magnificent grand piano occupied the other. The floor was covered with a yielding tapestry carpet, and the walls were adorned with paintings from the pencils of Van Dyke, Rubens, Tintoretto, Michael Angelo, and the productions of the more modern Turner, Kensett, Church, and Bierstadt. Although Judge Tompkins had chosen the frontiers of civilisation as his home, it was impossible for him to entirely forego the habits and tastes of his former life. He was seated in a luxurious arm-chair,

writing at a mahogany *éscritoire*, while his daughter, a lovely
young girl of seventeen summers, plied her crotchet-needle
on an ottoman beside him. A bright fire of pine logs
flickered and flamed on the ample hearth.

Genevra Octavia Tompkins was Judge Tompkins's only
child. Her mother had long since died on the Plains.
Reared in affluence, no pains had been spared with the
daughter's education. She was a graduate of one of the
principal seminaries, and spoke French with a perfect
Benicia accent. Peerlessly beautiful, she was dressed in a
white *moire antique* robe trimmed with *tulle.* That simple
rosebud, with which most heroines exclusively decorate
their hair, was all she wore in her raven locks.

The Judge was the first to break the silence.

"Genevra, the logs which compose yonder fire seem to
have been incautiously chosen. The sibilation produced
by the sap, which exudes copiously therefrom, is not conducive to composition."

"True, father, but I thought it would be preferable to
the constant crepitation which is apt to attend the combus-
tion of more seasoned ligneous fragments."

The Judge looked admiringly at the intellectual features
of the graceful girl, and half forgot the slight annoyances
of the green wood in the musical accents of his daughter.
He was smoothing her hair tenderly, when the shadow of
a tall figure, which suddenly darkened the doorway, caused
him to look up.

## CHAPTER II.

IT needed but a glance at the new-comer to detect at once
the form and features of the haughty aborigine,—the un-
taught and untrammelled son of the forest. Over one
shoulder a blanket, negligently but gracefully thrown, dis-

closed a bare and powerful breast, decorated with a quantity of three-cent postage-stamps which he had despoiled from an Overland Mail stage a few weeks previous. A cast-off beaver of Judge Tompkins's, adorned by a simple feather, covered his erect head, from beneath which his straight locks descended. His right hand hung lightly by his side, while his left was engaged in holding on a pair of panta-loons, which the lawless grace and freedom of his lower limbs evidently could not brook.

"Why," said the Indian, in a low sweet tone,—"why does the Pale Face still follow the track of the Red Man? Why does he pursue him, even as *O-kee chow*, the wild-cat, chases *Ka-ka*, the skunk? Why are the feet of *Sorrel-top*, the white chief, among the acorns of *Muck-a-Muck*, the mountain forest? Why," he repeated, quietly but firmly abstracting a silver spoon from the table—"why do you seek to drive him from the wigwams of his fathers? His brothers are already gone to the happy hunting-grounds. Will the Pale Face seek him there?" And, averting his face from the Judge, he hastily slipped a silver cake-basket beneath his blanket, to conceal his emotion.

"*Muck-a-Muck* has spoken," said Genevra softly. "Let him now listen. Are the acorns of the mountain sweeter than the esculent and nutritious bean of the Pale Face miner? Does my brother prize the edible qualities of the snail above that of the crisp and oleaginous bacon? Delicious are the grasshoppers that sport on the hill-side,—are they better than the dried apples of the Pale Faces? Pleasant is the gurgle of the torrent, *Kish-Kish*, but is it better than the cluck-cluck of old Bourbon from the old stone bottle?"

"Ugh!" said the Indian,—"ugh! good. The White Rabbit is wise. Her words fall as the snow on Tootoonolo, and the rocky heart of Muck-a-Muck is hidden. What says my brother the Gray Gopher of Dutch Flat?"

"She has spoken, Muck-a-Muck," said the Judge, gazing fondly on his daughter. "It is well. Our treaty is concluded. No, thank you,—you need *not* dance the Dance of Snow Shoes, or the Moccasin Dance, the Dance of Green Corn, or the Treaty Dance. I would be alone. A strange sadness overpowers me."

"I go," said the Indian. "Tell your great chief in Washington, the Sachem Andy, that the Red Man is retiring before the footsteps of the adventurous Pioneer. Inform him, if you please, that westward the star of empire takes its way, that the chiefs of the Pi-Ute nation are for Reconstruction to a man, and that Klamath will poll a heavy Republican vote in the fall."

And folding his blanket more tightly around him, Muck-a-Muck withdrew.

## CHAPTER III.

GENEVRA TOMPKINS stood at the door of the log-cabin, looking after the retreating Overland Mail stage which conveyed her father to Virginia City. "He may never return again," sighed the young girl, as she glanced at the frightfully rolling vehicle and wildly careering horses,— "at least, with unbroken bones. Should he meet with an accident! I mind me now a fearful legend, familiar to my childhood. Can it be that the drivers on this line are privately instructed to despatch all passengers maimed by accident, to prevent tedious litigation? No, no. But why this weight upon my heart?"

She seated herself at the piano and lightly passed her hand over the keys. Then, in a clear mezzo-soprano voice, she sang the first verse of one of the most popular Irish ballads—

> "O *Arrah, ma dheelish*, the distant *dudheen*
> Lies soft in the moonlight, *ma bouchal vourneen:*
> The springing *gossoons* on the heather are still,
> And the *caubeens* and *colleens* are heard on the hill."

But as the ravishing notes of her sweet voice died upon the air, her hands sank listlessly to her side. Music could not chase away the mysterious shadow from her heart. Again she rose. Putting on a white crape bonnet, and carefully drawing a pair of lemon-coloured gloves over her taper fingers, she seized her parasol and plunged into the depths of the pine forest.

## CHAPTER IV.

GENEVRA had not proceeded many miles before a weariness seized upon her fragile limbs, and she would fain seat herself upon the trunk of a prostrate pine, which she previously dusted with her handkerchief. The sun was just sinking below the horizon, and the scene was one of gorgeous and sylvan beauty. "How beautiful is Nature!" murmured the innocent girl, as, reclining gracefully against the root of the tree, she gathered up her skirts and tied a handkerchief around her throat. But a low growl interrupted her meditation. Starting to her feet, her eyes met a sight which froze her blood with terror.

The only outlet to the forest was the narrow path, barely wide enough for a single person, hemmed in by trees and rocks, which she had just traversed. Down this path, in Indian file, came a monstrous grizzly, closely followed by a California lion, a wild cat, and a buffalo, the rear being brought up by a wild Spanish bull. The mouths of the three first animals were distended with frightful significance, the horns of the last were lowered as ominously. As

Genevra was preparing to faint, she heard a low voice behind her.

"Eternally dog-gone my skin ef this ain't the puttiest chance yet."

At the same moment, a long, shining barrel dropped lightly from behind her, and rested over her shoulder.

Genevra shuddered.

"Dern ye—don't move !"

Genevra became motionless.

The crack of a rifle rang through the woods. Three frightful yells were heard, and two sullen roars. Five animals bounded into the air and five lifeless bodies lay upon the plain. The well-aimed bullet had done its work. Entering the open throat of the grizzly it had traversed his body only to enter the throat of the California lion, and in like manner the catamount, until it passed through into the respective foreheads of the bull and the buffalo, and finally fell flattened from the rocky hillside.

Genevra turned quickly. "My preserver!" she shrieked, and fell into the arms of Natty Bumpo, the celebrated Pike Ranger of Donner Lake.

## CHAPTER V.

The moon rose cheerfully above Donner Lake. On its placid bosom a dug-out canoe glided rapidly, containing Natty Bumpo and Genevra Tompkins.

Both were silent. The same thought possessed each, and perhaps there was sweet companionship even in the unbroken quiet. Genevra bit the handle of her parasol and blushed. Natty Bumpo took a fresh chew of tobacco. At length Genevra said, as if in half-spoken reverie—

"The soft shining of the moon and the peaceful ripple

of the waves seem to say to us various things of an instructive and moral tendency."

"You may bet yer pile on that, miss," said her companion gravely. "It's all the preachin' and psalm-singin' I've heern since I was a boy."

"Noble being!" said Miss Tompkins to herself, glancing at the stately Pike as he bent over his paddle to conceal his emotion. "Reared in this wild seclusion, yet he has become penetrated with visible consciousness of a Great First Cause." Then, collecting herself, she said aloud: "Methinks 'twere pleasant to glide ever thus down the stream of life, hand in hand with the one being whom the soul claims as its affinity. But what am I saying?"—and the delicate-minded girl hid her face in her hands.

A long silence ensued, which was at length broken by her companion.

"Ef you mean you're on the marry," he said thoughtfully, "I ain't in no wise partikler!"

"My husband," faltered the blushing girl; and she fell into his arms.

In ten minutes more the loving couple had landed at Judge Tompkins's.

## CHAPTER VI.

A YEAR has passed away. Natty Bumpo was returning from Gold Hill, where he had been to purchase provisions. On his way to Donner Lake, rumours of an Indian uprising met his ears. "Dern their pesky skins, ef they dare to touch my Jenny," he muttered between his clenched teeth.

It was dark when he reached the borders of the lake. Around a glittering fire he dimly discerned dusky figures dancing. They were in war paint. Conspicuous among them was the renowned Muck-a-Muck. But why did the fingers of Natty Bumpo tighten convulsively around his rifle?

The chief held in his hand long tufts of raven hair. The heart of the pioneer sickened as he recognised the clustering curls of Genevra. In a moment his rifle was at his shoulder, and with a sharp "ping," Muck-a-Muck leaped into the air a corpse. To knock out the brains of the remaining savages, tear the tresses from the stiffening hand of Muck-a-Muck, and dash rapidly forward to the cottage of Judge Tompkins, was the work of a moment.

He burst open the door. Why did he stand transfixed with open mouth and distended eyeballs? Was the sight too horrible to be borne? On the contrary, before him, in her peerless beauty, stood Genevra Tompkins, leaning on her father's arm.

"Ye'r not scalped, then!" gasped her lover.

"No. I have no hesitation in saying that I am not; but why this abruptness?" responded Genevra.

Bumpo could not speak, but frantically produced the silken tresses. Genevra turned her face aside.

"Why, that's her waterfall!" said the Judge.

Bumpo sank fainting to the floor.

The famous Pike chieftain never recovered from the deceit, and refused to marry Genevra, who died, twenty years afterwards, of a broken heart. Judge Tompkins lost his fortune in Wild Cat. The stage passes twice a week the deserted cottage at Donner Lake. Thus was the death of Muck-a-Muck avenged.

# Selina Sedilia.

BY MISS M. E. B—DD—N AND MRS. H—N—Y W—D.

## CHAPTER I.

THE sun was setting over Sloperton Grange, and reddened the window of the lonely chamber in the western tower, supposed to be haunted by Sir Edward Sedilia, the founder of the Grange. In the dreamy distance arose the gilded mausoleum of Lady Felicia Sedilia, who haunted that portion of Sedilia Manor known as "Stiff-uns Acre." A little to the left of the Grange might have been seen a mouldering ruin, known as "Guy's Keep," haunted by the spirit of Sir Guy Sedilia, who was found, one morning, crushed by one of the fallen battlements. Yet, as the setting sun gilded these objects, a beautiful and almost holy calm seemed diffused about the Grange.

The Lady Selina sat by an oriel window overlooking the park. The sun sank gently in the bosom of the German Ocean, and yet the lady did not lift her beautiful head from the finely curved arm and diminutive hand which supported it. When darkness finally shrouded the landscape she started, for the sound of horse-hoofs clattered over the stones of the avenue. She had scarcely risen before an aristocratic young man fell on his knees before her.

"My Selina!"

"Edgardo! You here?"

"Yes, dearest."

"And—you—you—have—seen nothing?" said the lady in an agitated voice and nervous manner, turning her face aside to conceal her emotion.

"Nothing—that is, nothing of any account," said Edgardo. "I passed the ghost of your aunt in the park, noticed the spectre of your uncle in the ruined keep, and observed the familiar features of the spirit of your great-grandfather at his usual post. But nothing beyond these trifles, my Selina. Nothing more, love, absolutely nothing."

The young man turned his dark, liquid orbs fondly upon the ingenuous face of his betrothed.

"My own Edgardo!—and you still love me? You still would marry me in spite of this dark mystery which surrounds me? In spite of the fatal history of my race? In spite of the ominous predictions of my aged nurse?"

"I would, Selina;" and the young man passed his arm around her yielding waist. The two lovers gazed at each other's faces in unspeakable bliss. Suddenly Selina started.

"Leave me, Edgardo! leave me! A mysterious something—a fatal misgiving—a dark ambiguity—an equivocal mistrust oppresses me. I would be alone!"

The young man arose, and cast a loving glance on the lady. "Then we will be married on the seventeenth."

"The seventeenth," repeated Selina, with a mysterious shudder.

They embraced and parted. As the clatter of hoofs in the courtyard died away, the Lady Selina sank into the chair she had just quitted.

"The seventeenth," she repeated slowly, with the same fateful shudder. "Ah!—what if he should know that I have another husband living? Dare I reveal to him that I have two legitimate and three natural children? Dare

I repeat to him the history of my youth? Dare I confess that at the age of seven I poisoned my sister, by putting verdigris in her cream-tarts,—that I threw my cousin from a swing at the age of twelve? That the lady's-maid who incurred the displeasure of my girlhood now lies at the bottom of the horse-pond? No! no! he is too pure,—too good,—too innocent,—to hear such improper conversation!" and her whole body writhed as she rocked to and fro in a paroxysm of grief.

But she was soon calm. Rising to her feet, she opened a secret panel in the wall, and revealed a slow-match ready for lighting.

"This match," said the Lady Selina, "is connected with a mine beneath the western tower, where my three children are confined; another branch of it lies under the parish church, where the record of my first marriage is kept. I have only to light this match and the whole of my past life is swept away!" She approached the match with a lighted candle.

But a hand was laid upon her arm, and with a shriek the Lady Selina fell on her knees before the spectre of Sir Guy.

## CHAPTER II.

"FORBEAR, Selina," said the phantom in a hollow voice.

"Why should I forbear?" responded Selina haughtily, as she recovered her courage. "You know the secret of our race?"

"I do. Understand me,—I do not object to the eccentricities of your youth. I know the fearful destiny which, pursuing you, led you to poison your sister and drown your lady's-maid. I know the awful doom which I have brought upon this house! But if you make away with these children "——

"Well," said the Lady Selina hastily.

"They will haunt you!"

"Well, I fear them not," said Selina, drawing her superb figure to its full height.

"Yes, but, my dear child, what place are they to haunt? The ruin is sacred to your uncle's spirit. Your aunt monopolises the park, and, I must be allowed to state, not unfrequently trespasses upon the grounds of others. The horsepond is frequented by the spirit of your maid, and your murdered sister walks these corridors. To be plain, there is no room at Sloperton Grange for another ghost. I cannot have them in my room,—for you know I don't like children. Think of this, rash girl, and forbear! Would you, Selina," said the phantom mournfully,—"would you force your great-grandfather's spirit to take lodgings elsewhere?"

Lady Selina's hand trembled; the lighted candle fell from her nerveless fingers.

"No," she cried passionately; "never!" and fell fainting to the floor.

## CHAPTER III.

EDGARDO galloped rapidly towards Sloperton. When the outline of the Grange had faded away in the darkness, he reined his magnificent steed beside the ruins of Guy's Keep.

"It wants but a few minutes of the hour," he said, consulting his watch by the light of the moon. "He dare not break his word. He will come." He paused, and peered anxiously into the darkness. "But come what may, she is mine," he continued, as his thoughts reverted fondly to the fair lady he had quitted. "Yet if she knew all. If she knew that I were a disgraced and ruined man,—a felon and an outcast. If she knew that at the age of fourteen I murdered my Latin tutor and forged my uncle's will. If she knew that I had three wives already, and that the fourth victim of misplaced confidence and my unfortunate peculiarity is expected to be at Sloperton by to-night's train with her baby. But no ; she must not know it. Constance must not arrive ; Burke the Slogger must attend to that.

"Ha ! here he is ! Well?"

These words were addressed to a ruffian in a slouched hat, who suddenly appeared from Guy's Keep.

"I be's here, measter," said the villain, with a disgracefully low accent and complete disregard of grammatical rules.

"It is well. Listen: I'm in possession of facts that will send you to the gallows. I know of the murder of Bill Smithers, the robbery of the toll-gate-keeper, and the making away of the youngest daughter of Sir Reginald de Walton. A word from me, and the officers of justice are on your track."

Burke the Slogger trembled.

"Hark ye ! serve my purpose, and I may yet save you. The 5.30 train from Clapham will be due at Sloperton at 9.25. *It must not arrive !* "

The villain's eyes sparkled as he nodded at Edgardo.

"Enough,—you understand ; leave me ! "

## CHAPTER IV.

ABOUT half a mile from Sloperton Station the South Clapham and Medway line crossed a bridge over Sloperton-on-Trent. As the shades of evening were closing, a man in a slouched hat might have been seen carrying a saw and axe under his arm, hanging about the bridge. From time to time he disappeared in the shadow of its abutments, but the sound of a saw and axe still betrayed his vicinity. At exactly nine o'clock he reappeared, and crossing to the

Sloperton side, rested his shoulder against the abutment and gave a shove. The bridge swayed a moment, and then fell with a splash into the water, leaving a space of one hundred feet between the two banks. This done, Burke the Slogger,—for it was he,—with a fiendish chuckle seated himself on the divided railway track and awaited the coming of the train.

A shriek from the woods announced its approach. For an instant Burke the Slogger saw the glaring of a red lamp. The ground trembled. The train was going with fearful rapidity. Another second and it had reached the bank. Burke the Slogger uttered a fiendish laugh. But the next moment the train leaped across the chasm, striking the rails exactly even, and dashing out the life of Burke the Slogger, sped away to Sloperton.

The first object that greeted Edgardo, as he rode up to the station on the arrival of the train, was the body of Burke the Slogger hanging on the cow-catcher; the second was the face of his deserted wife looking from the window of a second-class carriage.

## CHAPTER V.

A NAMELESS terror seemed to have taken possession of Clarissa, Lady Selina's maid, as she rushed into the presence of her mistress.

"Oh, my lady, such news!"

"Explain yourself," said her mistress, rising.

"An accident has happened on the railway, and a man has been killed."

"What—not Edgardo!" almost screamed Selina.

"No, Burke the Slogger, your ladyship!"

"My first husband!" said Lady Selina, sinking on her knees. "Just Heaven, I thank thee!"

## CHAPTER VI.

THE morning of the seventeenth dawned brightly over Sloperton. "A fine day for the wedding," said the sexton to Swipes, the butler of Sloperton Grange. The aged retainer shook his head sadly. "Alas! there's no trusting in signs!" he continued. "Seventy-five years ago, on a day like this, my young mistress "—— but he was cut short by the appearance of a stranger.

"I would see Sir Edgardo," said the new-comer impatiently.

The bridegroom, who, with the rest of the wedding-train, was about stepping into the carriage to proceed to the parish church, drew the stranger aside.

"It's done!" said the stranger, in a hoarse whisper.

"Ah! and you buried her?"

"With the others!"

"Enough. No more at present. Meet me after the ceremony, and you shall have your reward."

The stranger shuffled away, and Edgardo returned to his bride. "A trifling matter of business I had forgotten, my dear Selina; let us proceed." And the young man pressed the timid hand of his blushing bride as he handed her into the carriage. The cavalcade rode out of the courtyard. At the same moment, the deep bell on Guy's Keep tolled ominously.

## CHAPTER VII.

SCARCELY had the wedding-train left the Grange, than Alice Sedilia, youngest daughter of Lady Selina, made her escape from the western tower, owing to a lack of watchfulness on the part of Clarissa. The innocent child, freed from restraint, rambled through the lonely corridors, and finally, opening a door, found herself in her mother's boudoir. For some time she amused herself by examining the various ornaments and elegant trifles with which it was filled. Then, in pursuance of a childish freak, she dressed herself in her mother's laces and ribbons. In this occupation she chanced to touch a peg which proved to be a spring that opened a secret panel in the wall. Alice uttered a cry of delight as she noticed what, to her childish fancy, appeared to be the slow-match of a firework. Taking a lucifer match in her hand she approached the fuse. She hesitated a moment. What would her mother and her nurse say?

Suddenly the ringing of the chimes of Sloperton parish church met her ear. Alice knew that the sound signified that the marriage-party had entered the church, and that she was secure from interruption. With a childish smile upon her lips, Alice Sedilia touched off the slow-match.

## CHAPTER VIII.

At exactly two o'clock on the seventeenth, Rupert Sedilia, who had just returned from India, was thoughtfully descending the hill toward Sloperton manor. "If I can prove that my aunt, Lady Selina, was married before my father died, I can establish my claim to Sloperton Grange," he uttered, half aloud. He paused, for a sudden trembling of the earth beneath his feet, and a terrific explosion, as of a park of artillery, arrested his progress. At the same moment he beheld a dense cloud of smoke envelope the churchyard of Sloperton, and the western tower of the Grange seemed to be lifted bodily from its foundation. The air seemed filled with falling fragments, and two dark objects struck the earth close at his feet. Rupert picked them up. One seemed to be a heavy volume bound in brass.

A cry burst from his lips.

"The Parish Records." He opened the volume hastily. It contained the marriage of Lady Selina to "Burke the Slogger."

The second object proved to be a piece of parchment. He tore it open with trembling fingers. It was the missing will of Sir James Sedilia !

## CHAPTER IX.

WHEN the bells again rang on the new parish church of Sloperton it was for the marriage of Sir Rupert Sedilia and his cousin, the only remaining members of the family.

Five more ghosts were added to the supernatural population of Sloperton Grange. Perhaps this was the reason why Sir Rupert sold the property shortly afterward, and that for many years a dark shadow seemed to hang over the ruins of Sloperton Grange.

# The Ninety-Nine Guardsmen.

BY AL—X—D—R D—M—S.

## CHAPTER I.

### SHOWING THE QUALITY OF THE CUSTOMERS OF THE INNKEEPER OF PROVINS.

TWENTY years after, the gigantic innkeeper of Provins stood looking at a cloud of dust on the highway.

This cloud of dust betokened the approach of a traveller. Travellers had been rare that season on the highway between Paris and Provins.

The heart of the innkeeper rejoiced. Turning to Dame Perigord, his wife, he said, stroking his white apron—

"St. Denis! make haste and spread the cloth. Add a bottle of Charlevoix to the table. This traveller, who rides so fast, by his pace must be a Monseigneur."

Truly the traveller, clad in the uniform of a musketeer, as he drew up to the door of the hostelry, did not seem to have spared his horse. Throwing his reins to the landlord, he leaped lightly to the ground. He was a young man of four-and-twenty, and spoke with a slight Gascon accent.

"I am hungry, *Morbleu!* I wish to dine!"

The gigantic innkeeper bowed and led the way to a neat apartment, where a table stood covered with tempting viands. The musketeer at once set to work. Fowls, fish, and *pâtés* disappeared before him. Perigord sighed as he witnessed the devastations.   Only once the stranger paused.

"Wine !" Perigord brought wine.   The stranger drank a dozen bottles.   Finally he rose to depart   Turning to the expectant landlord, he said—

" Charge it."

"To whom, your highness ? " said Perigord anxiously.

" To his Eminence ! "

" Mazarin ! " ejaculated the innkeeper.

" The same.   Bring me my horse," and the musketeer, remounting his favourite animal, rode away.

The innkeeper slowly turned back into the inn.   Scarcely had he reached the courtyard before the clatter of hoofs again called him to the doorway.   A young musketeer of a light and graceful figure rode up.

" *Parbleu,* my dear Perigord, I am famishing.   What have you got for dinner ? "

" Venison, capons, larks, and pigeons, your excellency," replied the obsequious landlord, bowing to the ground.

" Enough ! "   The young musketeer dismounted and entered the inn.   Seating himself at the table replenished by the careful Perigord, he speedily swept it as clean as the first comer.

" Some wine, my brave Perigord," said the graceful young musketeer, as soon as he could find utterance.

Perigord brought three dozen of Charlevoix.   The young man emptied them almost at a draught.

" By-by, Perigord," he said lightly, waving his hand, as, preceding the astonished landlord, he slowly withdrew.

" But, your highness,—the bill," said the astounded Perigord.

" Ah, the bill.   Charge it ! "

" To whom ? "

" The Queen ! "

"What, Madame?"

"The same. Adieu, my good Perigord." And the graceful stranger rode away. An interval of quiet succeeded, in which the innkeeper gazed wofully at his wife. Suddenly he was startled by a clatter of hoofs, and an aristocratic figure stood in the doorway.

"Ah," said the courtier good-naturedly. "What, do my eyes deceive me? No, it is the festive and luxurious Perigord. Perigord, listen. I famish. I languish. I would dine."

The innkeeper again covered the table with viands. Again it was swept clean as the fields of Egypt before the miraculous swarm of locusts. The stranger looked up.

"Bring me another fowl, my Perigord."

"Impossible, your excellency; the larder is stripped clean."

"Another flitch of bacon, then."

"Impossible, your highness; there is no more."

"Well, then, wine!"

The landlord brought one hundred and forty-four bottles. The courtier drank them all.

"One may drink if one cannot eat," said the aristocratic stranger good-humouredly.

The innkeeper shuddered.

The guest rose to depart. The innkeeper came slowly forward with his bill, to which he had covertly added the losses which he had suffered from the previous strangers.

"Ah, the bill. Charge it."

"Charge it! to whom?"

"To the King," said the guest.

"What! his Majesty?"

"Certainly. Farewell, Perigord."

The innkeeper groaned. Then he went out and took down his sign. Then remarked to his wife—

"I am a plain man, and don't understand politics. It seems, however, that the country is in a troubled state. Between his Eminence the Cardinal, his Majesty the King, and her Majesty the Queen, I am a ruined man."

"Stay," said Dame Perigord, "I have an idea."

"And that is "——

"Become yourself a musketeer."

## CHAPTER II.

### THE COMBAT.

ON leaving Provins the first musketeer proceeded to Nangis, where he was reinforced by thirty-three followers. The second musketeer, arriving at Nangis at the same moment, placed himself at the head of thirty-three more. The third guest of the landlord of Provins arrived at Nangis in time to assemble together thirty-three other musketeers.

The first stranger led the troops of his Eminence.

The second led the troops of the Queen.

The third led the troops of the King.

The fight commenced. It raged terribly for seven hours. The first musketeer killed thirty of the Queen's troops. The second musketeer killed thirty of the King's troops. The third musketeer killed thirty of his Eminence's troops.

By this time it will be perceived the number of musketeers had been narrowed down to four on each side.

Naturally the three principal warriors approached each other.

They simultaneously uttered a cry.

"Aramis!"

"Athos!"

"D'Artagnan!"

They fell into each other's arms.

"And it seems that we are fighting against each other, my children," said the Count de la Fere, mournfully.

"How singular!" exclaimed Aramis and D'Artagnan.

"Let us stop this fratricidal warfare," said Athos.

"We will!" they exclaimed together.

"But how to disband our followers?" queried D'Artagnan.

Aramis winked. They understood each other. "Let us cut 'em down!"

They cut 'em down. Aramis killed three. D'Artagnan three. Athos three.

The friends again embraced. "How like old times," said Aramis. "How touching!" exclaimed the serious and philosophic Count de la Fere.

The galloping of hoofs caused them to withdraw from each other's embraces. A gigantic figure rapidly approached.

"The innkeeper of Provins!" they cried, drawing their swords.

"Perigord, down with him!" shouted D'Artagnan.

"Stay," said Athos.

The gigantic figure was beside them. He uttered a cry.

"Athos, Aramis, D'Artagnan!"

"Porthos!" exclaimed the astonished trio.

"The same." They all fell in each other's arms.

The Count de la Fere slowly raised his hands to Heaven. "Bless you! Bless us, my children! However different our opinion may be in regard to politics, we have but one opinion in regard to our own merits. Where can you find a better man than Aramis?"

"Than Porthos?" said Aramis.

"Than D'Artagnan?" said Porthos.

"Than Athos?" said D'Artagnan.

## CHAPTER III.

### SHOWING HOW THE KING OF FRANCE WENT UP A LADDER.

THE King descended into the garden. Proceeding cautiously along the terraced walk, he came to the wall immediately below the windows of Madame. To the left were two windows, concealed by vines. They opened into the apartments of La Valliere.

The King sighed.

"It is about nineteen feet to that window," said the King. "If I had a ladder about nineteen feet long, it would reach to that window. This is logic."

Suddenly the King stumbled over something. "St. Denis!" he exclaimed, looking down. It was a ladder, just nineteen feet long.

The King placed it against the wall. In so doing, he fixed the lower end upon the abdomen of a man who lay concealed by the wall. The man did not utter a cry or wince. The King suspected nothing. He ascended the ladder.

The ladder was too short. Louis the Grand was not a tall man. He was still two feet below the window.

"Dear me!" said the King.

Suddenly the ladder was lifted two feet from below. This enabled the King to leap in the window. At the farther end of the apartment stood a young girl, with red hair and a lame leg. She was trembling with emotion.

"Louise!"

"The King!"

"Ah, my God, mademoiselle."

"Ah, my God, sire."

But a low knock at the door interrupted the lovers. The King uttered a cry of rage ; Louise one of despair.

The door opened and D'Artagnan entered.

"Good evening, sire," said the musketeer.

The King touched a bell. Porthos appeared in the doorway.

"Good evening, sire."

"Arrest M. D'Artagnan."

Porthos looked at D'Artagnan, and did not move.

The King almost turned purple with rage. He again touched the bell. Athos entered.

"Count, arrest Porthos and D'Artagnan."

The Count de la Fere glanced at Porthos and D'Artagnan, and smiled sweetly.

"*Sacre!* Where is Aramis?" said the King violently.

"Here, sire," and Aramis entered.

"Arrest Athos, Porthos, and D'Artagnan."

Aramis bowed and folded his arms.

"Arrest yourself!"

Aramis did not move.

The King shuddered and turned pale. "Am I not King of France?"

"Assuredly, sire, but we are also severally, Porthos, Aramis, D'Artagnan, and Athos."

"Ah!" said the King.

"Yes, sire."

"What does this mean?"

"It means, your Majesty," said Aramis, stepping forward, "that your conduct as a married man is highly improper. I am an Abbé, and I object to these improprieties. My friends here, D'Artagnan, Athos, and Porthos, pure-minded young men, are also terribly shocked. Observe, sire, how they blush!"

Athos, Porthos, and D'Artagnan blushed.

"Ah," said the King thoughtfully. "You teach me a lesson. You are devoted and noble young gentlemen, but your only weakness is your excessive modesty. From this moment I make you all Marshals and Dukes, with the exception of Aramis.

" And me, sire ? " said Aramis.

" You shall be an Archbishop ! "

The four friends looked up and then rushed into each other's arms. The King embraced Louise de la Valliere, by way of keeping them company. A pause ensued. At last Athos spoke—

" Swear, my children, that, next to yourselves, you will respect—the King of France ; and remember that ' Forty years after ' we will meet again."

## 𝔐𝔦𝔰𝔰 𝔐𝔦𝔵.

**BY** CH—L—TTE BR—NTE.

## CHAPTER I.

My earliest impressions are of a huge, misshapen rock, against which the hoarse waves beat unceasingly. On this rock three pelicans are standing in a defiant attitude. A dark sky lowers in the background, while two sea-gulls and a gigantic cormorant eye with extreme disfavour the floating corpse of a drowned woman in the foreground. A few bracelets, coral necklaces, and other articles of jewellery, scattered around loosely, complete this remarkable picture.

It is one which, in some vague, unconscious way, symbolises, to my fancy, the character of a man. I have never been able to explain exactly why. I think I must have seen the picture in some illustrated volume when a baby, or my mother may have dreamed it before I was born.

As a child I was not handsome. When I consulted the triangular bit of looking-glass which I always carried with me, it showed a pale, sandy, and freckled face, shaded by locks like the colour of seaweed when the sun strikes it in deep water. My eyes were said to be indistinctive; they were a faint, ashen gray; but above them rose—my only beauty—a high, massive, domelike forehead, with polished temples, like door-knobs of the purest porcelain.

Our family was a family of governesses. My mother had been one, and my sisters had the same occupation. Consequently, when, at the age of thirteen, my eldest sister handed me the advertisement of Mr. Rawjester, clipped from that day's *Times*, I accepted it as my destiny. Nevertheless, a mysterious presentiment of an indefinite future haunted me in my dreams that night, as I lay upon my little snow-white bed. The next morning, with two bandboxes tied up in silk handkerchiefs, and a hair trunk, I turned my back upon Minerva Cottage for ever.

## CHAPTER II.

BLUNDERBORE HALL, the seat of James Rawjester, Esq., was encompassed by dark pines and funereal hemlocks on all sides. The wind sang weirdly in the turrets and moaned through the long-drawn avenues of the park. As I approached the house I saw several mysterious figures flit before the windows, and a yell of demoniac laughter answered my summons at the bell. While I strove to repress my gloomy forebodings, the housekeeper, a timid, scared-looking old woman, showed me into the library.

I entered, overcome with conflicting emotions. I was dressed in a narrow gown of dark serge, trimmed with black bugles. A thick green shawl was pinned across my breast. My hands were encased with black half-mittens worked with steel beads; on my feet were large pattens, originally the property of my deceased grandmother. I carried a blue cotton umbrella. As I passed before a mirror I could not help glancing at it, nor could I disguise from myself the fact that I was not handsome.

Drawing a chair into a recess, I sat down with folded hands, calmly awaiting the arrival of my master. Once or twice a fearful yell rang through the house, or the rattling of chains, and curses uttered in a deep, manly voice, broke upon the oppressive stillness. I began to feel my soul rising with the emergency of the moment.

"You look alarmed, miss. You don't hear anything, my dear, do you?" asked the housekeeper nervously.

"Nothing whatever," I remarked calmly, as a terrific scream, followed by the dragging of chairs and tables in the room above, drowned for a moment my reply. "It is the silence, on the contrary, which has made me foolishly nervous."

The housekeeper looked at me approvingly, and instantly made some tea for me.

I drank seven cups; as I was beginning the eighth, I heard a crash, and the next moment a man leaped into the room through the broken window.

## CHAPTER III.

THE crash startled me from my self-control. The housekeeper bent toward me and whispered—

"Don't be excited. It's Mr. Rawjester,—he prefers to come in sometimes in this way. It's his playfulness, ha! ha! ha!"

"I perceive," I said calmly. "It's the unfettered impulse of a lofty soul breaking the tyrannising bonds of custom." And I turned toward him.

He had never once looked at me. He stood with his back to the fire, which set off the herculean breadth of his shoulders. His face was dark and expressive; his under jaw squarely formed, and remarkably heavy. I was struck with his remarkable likeness to a gorilla.

As he absently tied the poker into hard knots with his

nervous fingers, I watched him with some interest. Suddenly he turned toward me—

"Do you think I'm handsome, young woman?"

"Not classically beautiful," I returned calmly; "but you have, if I may so express myself, an abstract manliness,—a sincere and wholesome barbarity which, involving as it does the naturalness"—— But I stopped, for he yawned at that moment,—an action which singularly developed the immense breadth of his lower jaw,—and I saw he had forgotten me. Presently he turned to the housekeeper—

"Leave us."

The old woman withdrew with a curtsey.

Mr. Rawjester deliberately turned his back upon me and remained silent for twenty minutes. I drew my shawl the more closely around my shoulders and closed my eyes.

"You are the governess?" at length he said.

"I am, sir."

"A creature who teaches geography, arithmetic, and the use of the globes—ha!—a wretched remnant of femininity,—a skimp pattern of girlhood with a premature flavour of tea-leaves and morality. Ugh!"

I bowed my head silently.

"Listen to me, girl!" he said sternly; "this child you have come to teach—my ward—is not legitimate. She is the offspring of my mistress,—a common harlot. Ah! Miss Mix, what do you think of me now?"

"I admire," I replied calmly, "your sincerity. A mawkish regard for delicacy might have kept this disclosure to yourself. I only recognise in your frankness that perfect community of thought and sentiment which should exist between original natures."

I looked up; he had already forgotten my presence, and was engaged in pulling off his boots and coat. This done, he sank down in an arm-chair before the fire, and ran the poker wearily through his hair. I could not help pitying him.

The wind howled dismally without, and the rain beat furiously against the windows. I crept toward him and seated myself on a low stool beside his cha.r.

Presently he turned, without seeing me, and placed his foot absently in my lap. I affected not to notice it. But he started and looked down.

"You here yet—Carrothead? Ah, I forgot. Do you speak French?"

"*Oui, Monsieur.*"

"*Taisez-vous!*" he said sharply, with singular purity of accent. I complied. The wind moaned fearfully in the chimney, and the light burned dimly. I shuddered in spite of myself. "Ah, you tremble, girl!"

"It is a fearful night."

"Fearful! Call you this fearful, ha! ha! ha! Look! you wretched little atom, look!" and he dashed forward, and leaping out of the window, stood like a statue in the pelting storm, with folded arms. He did not stay long, but in a few minutes returned by way of the hall chimney. I saw from the way that he wiped his feet on my dress that he had again forgotten my presence.

"You are a governess. What can you teach?" he asked, suddenly and fiercely thrusting his face in mine.

"Manners!" I replied calmly.

"Ha! teach *me!*"

"You mistake yourself," I said, adjusting my mittens. "Your manners require not the artificial restraint of society. You are radically polite; this impetuosity and ferociousness is simply the sincerity which is the basis of a proper deportment. Your instincts are moral; your better nature, I see, is religious. As St. Paul justly remarks—see chap. **6, 8, 9,** and **10**"——

He seized a heavy candlestick, and threw it at me. I dodged it submissively but firmly.

"Excuse me," he remarked, as his under jaw slowly relaxed. "Excuse me, Miss Mix—but I can't stand St. Paul! Enough—you are engaged."


## CHAPTER IV.

I FOLLOWED the housekeeper as she led the way timidly to my room. As we passed into a dark hall in the wing, I noticed that it was closed by an iron gate with a grating. Three of the doors on the corridor were likewise grated. A strange noise, as of shuffling feet and the howling of infuriated animals, rang through the hall. Bidding the housekeeper good-night, and taking the candle, I entered my bedchamber.

I took off my dress, and putting on a yellow flannel nightgown, which I could not help feeling did not agree with my complexion, I composed myself to rest by reading "Blair's Rhetoric" and "Paley's Moral Philosophy." I had just put out the light, when I heard voices in the corridor. I listened attentively. I recognised Mr. Raw-jester's stern tones.

"Have you fed No. 1?" he asked.

"Yes, sir," said a gruff voice, apparently belonging to a domestic.

"How's No. 2?"

"She's a little off her feed, just now, but will pick up in a day or two!"

"And No. 3?"

"Perfectly furious, sir. Her tantrums are ungovernable." "Hush!"

The voices died away, and I sank into a fitful slumber.

I dreamed that I was wandering through a tropical forest. Suddenly I saw the figure of a gorilla approaching me. As it neared me, I recognised the features of Mr. Rawjester. He held his hand to his side as if in pain. I saw that he had been wounded. He recognised me and called me by name, but at the same moment the vision changed to an Ashantee village, where, around the fire, a group of negroes were dancing and participating in some wild *Obi* festival. I awoke with the strain still ringing in my ears.

"Hokee-pokee wokee fum !"

"Good Heavens ! could I be dreaming? I heard the voice distinctly on the floor below, and smelt something burning. I arose, with an indistinct presentiment of evil, and hastily putting some cotton in my ears and tying a towel about my head, I wrapped myself in a shawl and rushed downstairs. The door of Mr. Rawjester's room was open. I entered.

Mr. Rawjester lay apparently in a deep slumber, from which even the clouds of smoke that came from the burning curtains of his bed could not rouse him. Around the room a large and powerful negress, scantily attired, with her head adorned with feathers, was dancing wildly, accompanying herself with bone castanets. It looked like some terrible *fetich*.

I did not lose my calmness. After firmly emptying the pitcher, basin, and slop-jar on the burning bed, I proceeded cautiously to the garden, and returning with the garden-engine, I directed a small stream at Mr. Rawjester.

At my entrance the gigantic negress fled. Mr. Rawjester yawned and woke. I explained to him, as he rose dripping from the bed, the reason of my presence. He did not seem to be excited, alarmed, or discomposed. He gazed at me curiously.

"So you risked your life to save mine, eh? you canary-coloured teacher of infants."

I blushed modestly, and drew my shawl tightly over my yellow flannel nightgown.

"You love me, Mary Jane,—don't deny it! This trembling shows it!" He drew me closely toward him, and said, with his deep voice tenderly modulated—

"How's her pooty tootens,—did she get her 'ittle tootens wet,—bess her?"

I understood his allusion to my feet. I glanced down and saw that in my hurry I had put on a pair of his old india-rubbers. My feet were not small or pretty, and the addition did not add to their beauty.

"Let me go, sir," I remarked quietly. "This is entirely improper; it sets a bad example for your child." And I firmly but gently extricated myself from his grasp. I approached the door. He seemed for a moment buried in deep thought.

"You say this was a negress?"

"Yes, sir."

"Humph, No. 1, I suppose?"

"Who is Number One, sir?"

"My *first*," he remarked, with a significant and sarcastic smile. Then, relapsing into his old manner, he threw his boots at my head, and bade me begone. I withdrew calmly.


## CHAPTER V.

My pupil was a bright little girl, who spoke French with a perfect accent. Her mother had been a French ballet-dancer, which probably accounted for it. Although she was only six years old, it was easy to perceive that she had been several times in love. She once said to me—

"Miss Mix, did you ever have the *grande* passion? Did you ever feel a fluttering here?" and she placed her hand upon her small chest, and sighed quaintly, "a kind of distaste for *bonbons* and *caromels*, when the world seemed as tasteless and hollow as a broken cordial drop."

"Then you have felt it, Nina?" I said quietly.

"Oh dear, yes. There was Buttons,—that was our page, you know,—I loved him dearly, but papa sent him away. Then there was Dick, the groom, but he laughed at me and I suffered misery!" and she struck a tragic French attitude. "There is to be company here to-morrow," she added, rattling on with childish *naïveté*, "and papa's sweet-heart—Blanche Marabout—is to be here. You know they say she is to be my mamma."

What thrill was this shot through me? But I rose calmly, and administering a slight correction to the child, left the apartment.

Blunderbore House, for the next week, was the scene of gaiety and merriment. That portion of the mansion closed with a grating was walled up, and the midnight shrieks no longer troubled me.

But I felt more keenly the degradation of my situation. I was obliged to help Lady Blanche at her toilet and help her to look beautiful. For what? To captivate him? Oh—no, no,—but why this sudden thrill and faintness? Did he really love her? I had seen him pinch and swear at her. But I reflected that he had thrown a candlestick at my head, and my foolish heart was reassured.

It was a night of festivity, when a sudden message obliged Mr. Rawjester to leave his guests for a few hours. "Make yourselves merry, idiots," he added, under his breath, as he passed me. The door closed and he was gone.

An half-hour passed. In the midst of the dancing a

shriek was heard, and out of the swaying crowd of fainting women and excited men a wild figure strode into the room. One glance showed it to be a highwayman, heavily armed, holding a pistol in each hand.

"Let no one pass out of this room!" he said, in a voice of thunder. "The house is surrounded and you cannot escape. The first one who crosses yonder threshold will be shot like a dog. Gentlemen, I'll trouble you to approach in single file, and hand me your purses and watches."

Finding resistance useless, the order was ungraciously obeyed.

"Now, ladies, please to pass up your jewellery and trinkets."

This order was still more ungraciously complied with. As Blanche handed to the bandit captain her bracelet, she endeavoured to conceal a diamond necklace, the gift of Mr. Rawjester, in her bosom. But, with a demoniac grin, the powerful brute tore it from its concealment, and administering a hearty box on the ear of the young girl, flung her aside.

It was now my turn. With a beating heart I made my way to the robber chieftain, and sank at his feet. "O sir, I am nothing but a poor governess, pray let me go."

"O ho! A governess? Give me your last month's wages, then. Give me what you have stolen from your master!" and he laughed fiendishly.

I gazed at him quietly, and said, in a low voice: "I have stolen nothing from you, Mr. Rawjester!"

"Ah, discovered! Hush! listen, girl!" he hissed, in a fierce whisper, "utter a syllable to frustrate my plans and you die; aid me, and "—— But he was gone.

In a few moments the party, with the exception of myself, were gagged and locked in the cellar. The next moment torches were applied to the rich hangings, and the house was in flames. I felt a strong hand seize me, and bear me out in the open air and place me up on the hillside, where I could overlook the burning mansion. It was Mr. Rawjester.

"Burn!" he said, as he shook his fist at the flames. Then sinking on his knees before me, he said hurriedly—

"Mary Jane, I love you; the obstacles to our union are or will be soon removed. In yonder mansion were confined my three crazy wives. One of them, as you know, attempted to kill me! Ha! this is vengeance! But will you be mine?"

I fell, without a word, upon his neck.

# 𝔐𝔯. 𝔐𝔦𝔡𝔰𝔥𝔦𝔭𝔪𝔞𝔫 𝔅𝔯𝔢𝔢𝔷𝔶.

*A NAVAL OFFICER.*

BY CAPTAIN M—RRY—T, R.N.

## CHAPTER I.

MY father was a north-country surgeon. He had retired, a widower, from her Majesty's navy many years before, and had a small practice in his native village. When I was seven years old he employed me to carry medicines to his patients. Being of a lively disposition, I sometimes amused myself, during my daily rounds, by mixing the contents of the different phials. Although I had no reason to doubt that the general result of this practice was beneficial, yet, as the death of a consumptive curate followed the addition of a strong mercurial lotion to his expectorant, my father concluded to withdraw me from the profession and send me to school.

Grubbins, the schoolmaster, was a tyrant, and it was not long before my impetuous and self-willed nature rebelled against his authority. I soon began to form plans of revenge. In this I was assisted by Tom Snaffle,—a school-fellow. One day Tom suggested—

"Suppose we blow him up. I've got two pounds of powder!"

"No, that's too noisy," I replied.

Tom was silent for a minute, and again spoke—

"You remember how you flattened out the curate, Pills! Couldn't you give Grubbins something—something to make him leathery sick—eh?"

A flash of inspiration crossed my mind. I went to the shop of the village apothecary. He knew me; I had often purchased vitriol, which I poured into Grubbins's inkstand to corrode his pens and burn up his coat-tail, on which he was in the habit of wiping them. I boldly asked for an ounce of chloroform. The young apothecary winked and handed me the bottle.

It was Grubbins's custom to throw his handkerchief over his head, recline in his chair and take a short nap during recess. Watching my opportunity, as he dozed, I managed to slip his handkerchief from his face and substitute my own, moistened with chloroform. In a few minutes he was insensible. Tom and I then quickly shaved his head, beard, and eyebrows, blackened his face with a mixture of vitriol and burnt cork, and fled. There was a row and scandal the next day. My father always excused me by asserting that Grubbins had got drunk,—but somehow found it convenient to procure me an appointment in her Majesty's navy at an early day.

## CHAPTER II.

An official letter, with the Admiralty seal, informed me that I was expected to join H. M. ship Belcher, Captain Boltrope, at Portsmouth, without delay. In a few days I presented myself to a tall, stern-visaged man, who was slowly pacing the leeward side of the quarter-deck. As I touched my hat he eyed me sternly—

"So ho! Another young suckling. The service is going to the devil. Nothing but babes in the cockpit and grannies in the board. Boatswain's mate, pass the word for Mr. Cheek!"

Mr. Cheek, the steward, appeared and touched his hat.

"Introduce Mr. Breezy to the young gentlemen. Stop! Where's Mr. Swizzle?"

"At the masthead, sir."

"Where's Mr. Lankey?"

"At the masthead, sir."

"Mr. Briggs?"

"Masthead, too, sir."

"And the rest of the young gentlemen?" roared the enraged officer.

"All masthead, sir."

"Ah!" said Captain Boltrope, as he smiled grimly, "under the circumstances, Mr. Breezy, you had better go to the masthead too."

## CHAPTER III.

AT the masthead I made the acquaintance of two youngsters of about my own age, one of whom informed me that he had been there three hundred and thirty-two days out of the year.

"In rough weather, when the old cock is out of sorts, you know, we never come down," added a young gentleman of nine years, with a dirk nearly as long as himself, who had been introduced to me as Mr. Briggs. "By the way, Pills," he continued, "how did you come to omit giving the captain a naval salute?"

"Why, I touched my hat," I said innocently.

"Yes, but that isn't enough, you know. That will do very well at other times. He expects the naval salute when you first come on board—greeny!"

I began to feel alarmed, and begged him to explain.

"Why, you see, after touching your hat, you should have touched him lightly with your forefinger in his waistcoat, so, and asked, 'How's his nibs?'—you see?"

"How's his nibs?" I repeated.

"Exactly. He would have drawn back a little, and then you should have repeated the salute remarking, 'How's his royal nibs?' asking cautiously after his wife and family, and requesting to be introduced to the gunner's daughter."

"The gunner's daughter?"

"The same; you know she takes care of us young gentlemen; now don't forget, Pillsy!"

When we were called down to the deck I thought it a good chance to profit by this instruction. I approached Captain Boltrope and repeated the salute without conscientiously omitting a single detail. He remained for a moment livid and speechless. At length he gasped out—

"Boatswain's mate?"

"If you please, sir," I asked tremulously, "I should like to be introduced to the gunner's daughter!"

"Oh, very good, sir!" screamed Captain Boltrope, rubbing his hands and absolutely capering about the deck with rage. "Oh, d—n you! Of course you shall! Oh, ho! the gunner's daughter! Oh, h—ll! this is too much! Boatswain's mate!" Before I well knew where I was, I was seized, borne to an eight-pounder, tied upon it and flogged!

## CHAPTER IV.

As we sat together in the cockpit, picking the weevils out of our biscuit, Briggs consoled me for my late mishap, adding that the "naval salute," as a custom, seemed just then to be honoured more in the *breach* than the observance. I joined in the hilarity occasioned by the witticism, and in a few moments we were all friends. Presently Swizzle turned to me—

"We have just been planning how to confiscate a keg of claret, which Nips, the purser, keeps under his bunk. The old nipcheese lies there drunk half the day, and there's no getting at it."

"Let's get beneath the state-room and bore through the deck, and so tap it," said Lankey.

The proposition was received with a shout of applause. A long half-inch auger and bit was procured from Chips, the carpenter's mate, and Swizzle, after a careful examination of the timbers beneath the wardroom, commenced operations. The auger at last disappeared, when suddenly there was a slight disturbance on the deck above. Swizzle withdrew the auger hurriedly; from its point a few bright red drops trickled.

"Huzza! send her up again!" cried Lankey.

The auger was again applied. This time a shriek was heard from the purser's cabin. Instantly the light was doused, and the party retreated hurriedly to the cockpit. A sound of snoring was heard as the sentry stuck his head into the door. "All right, sir," he replied in answer to the voice of the officer of the deck.

The next morning we heard that Nips was in the surgeon's hands, with a bad wound in the fleshy part of his leg, and that the auger had *not* struck claret.

## CHAPTER V.

"Now, Pills, you'll have a chance to smell powder," said Briggs as he entered the cockpit and buckled around his waist an enormous cutlass. "We have just sighted a French ship."

We went on deck. Captain Boltrope grinned as we touched our hats. He hated the purser. "Come, young gentlemen, if you're boring for French claret, yonder's a good quality. Mind your con, sir," he added, turning to the quartermaster, who was grinning.

The ship was already cleared for action. The men, in their eagerness, had started the coffee from the tubs and filled them with shot. Presently the Frenchman yawed, and a shot from a long thirty-two came skipping over the water. It killed the quartermaster and took off both of Lankey's legs. "Tell the purser our account is squared," said the dying boy, with a feeble smile.

The fight raged fiercely for two hours. I remember killing the French admiral, as we boarded, but on looking around for Briggs, after the smoke had cleared away, I was intensely amused at witnessing the following novel sight —

Briggs had pinned the French captain against the mast with his cutlass, and was now engaged, with all the hilarity of youth, in pulling the Captain's coat-tails between his legs, in imitation of a dancing-jack. As the Frenchman lifted his legs and arms, at each jerk of Briggs's, I could not help participating in the general mirth.

"You young devil, what are you doing?" said a stifled voice behind me. I looked up and beheld Captain Boltrope, endeavouring to calm his stern features, but the twitching around his mouth betrayed his intense enjoyment of the scene. "Go to the masthead—up with you, sir!" he repeated sternly to Briggs.

"Very good, sir," said the boy, coolly preparing to mount the shrouds. "Good-bye, Johnny Crapaud. Humph!" he added, in a tone intended for my ear, "a pretty way to treat a hero. The service is going to the devil!"

I thought so too.

## CHAPTER VI.

WE were ordered to the West Indies. Although Captain Boltrope's manner toward me was still severe, and even harsh, I understood that my name had been favourably mentioned in the despatches.

Reader, were you ever at Jamaica? If so, you remember the negresses, the oranges, Port Royal Tom—the yellow fever. After being two weeks at the station, I was taken sick of the fever. In a month I was delirious. During my paroxysms, I had a wild distempered dream of a stern face bending anxiously over my pillow, a rough hand smoothing my hair, and a kind voice saying —

"Bess his 'ittle heart! Did he have the naughty fever?" This face seemed again changed to the well-known stern features of Captain Boltrope.

When I was convalescent, a packet edged in black was put in my hand. It contained the news of my father's death, and a sealed letter which he had requested to be given to me on his decease. I opened it tremblingly. It read thus —

"MY DEAR BOY,—I regret to inform you that in all probability you are not my son. Your mother, I am grieved to say, was a highly improper person. Who your father

may be, I really cannot say, but perhaps the Honourable
Henry Boltrope, Captain R.N., may be able to inform you.
Circumstances over which I have no control have deferred
this important disclosure.

" YOUR STRICKEN PARENT."

And so Captain Boltrope was my father. Heavens!
Was it a dream? I recalled his stern manner, his obser-
vant eye, his ill-concealed uneasiness when in my presence.
I longed to embrace him. Staggering to my feet, I rushed
in my scanty apparel to the deck, where Captain Boltrope
was just then engaged in receiving the Governor's wife and
daughter. The ladies shrieked ; the youngest, a·beautiful
girl, blushed deeply. Heeding them not, I sank at his feet,
and, embracing them, cried—

"My father !"

" Chuck him overboard ! " roared Captain Boltrope.

"Stay," pleaded the soft voice, of Clara Maitland, the
Governor's daughter.

"Shave his head! he's a wretched lunatic !" continued
Captain Boltrope, while his voice trembled with excitement.

" No, let me nurse and take care of him," said the lovely
girl, blushing as she spoke. " Mamma, can't we take him
home ? "

The daughter's pleading was not without effect. In the
meantime I had fainted. When I recovered my senses I
found myself in Governor Maitland's mansion.

## CHAPTER VII.

THE reader will guess what followed. I fell deeply in love with Clara Maitland, to whom I confided the secret of my birth. The generous girl asserted that she had detected the superiority of my manner at once. We plighted our troth, and resolved to wait upon events.

Briggs called to see me a few days afterward. He said that the purser had insulted the whole cockpit, and all the midshipmen had called him out. But he added thoughtfully: "I don't see how we can arrange the duel. You see there are six of us to fight him."

"Very easily," I replied. "Let your fellows all stand in a row, and take his fire; that, you see, gives him six chances to one, and he must be a bad shot if he can't hit one of you; while, on the other hand, you see, he gets a volley from you six, and one of you'll be certain to fetch him."

"Exactly;" and away Briggs went, but soon returned to say that the purser had declined,—"like a d—d coward," he added.

But the news of the sudden and serious illness of Captain Boltrope put off the duel. I hastened to his bedside, but too late,—an hour previous he had given up the ghost.

I resolved to return to England. I made known the secret of my birth, and exhibited my adopted father's letter to Lady Maitland, who at once suggested my marriage with her daughter, before I returned to claim the property. We were married, and took our departure next day.

I made no delay in posting at once, in company with my wife and my friend Briggs, to my native village. Judge of my horror and surprise when my late adopted father came out of his shop to welcome me.

" Then you are not dead !" I gasped

" No, my dear boy."

" And this letter ? "

My father—as I must still call him—glanced on the paper, and pronounced it a forgery. Briggs roared with laughter. I turned to him and demanded an explanation.

" Why, don't you see, Greeny, it's all a joke,—a midshipman's joke ! "

" But "—— I asked.

" Don't be a fool. You've got a good wife,—be satisfied."

I turned to Clara, and was satisfied. Although Mrs. Maitland never forgave me, the jolly old Governor laughed heartily over the joke, and so well used his influence that I soon became, dear reader, Admiral Breezy, K.C.B.

# Guy Heavystone;

OR,

## "ENTIRE."

### *A MUSCULAR NOVEL.*

BY THE AUTHOR OF "SWORD AND GUN."

## CHAPTER I.

### "NEREI REPANDIROSTRUM INCURVICERVICUM PECUS."

A DINGY, swashy, splashy afternoon in October; a school-yard filled with a mob of riotous boys. A lot of us standing outside.

Suddenly came a dull, crashing sound from the school-room. At the ominous interruption I shuddered involuntarily, and called to Smithsye—

"What's up, Smithums?"

"Guy's cleaning out the fourth form," he replied.

At the same moment George de Coverly passed me, holding his nose, from whence the bright Norman blood streamed redly. To him the plebeian Smithsye laughingly—

"Cully! how's his nibs?"

I pushed the door of the schoolroom open. There are some spectacles which a man never forgets. The burning of Troy probably seemed a large-sized conflagration to the pious Æneas, and made an impression on him which he carried away with the feeble Anchises.

In the centre of the room, lightly brandishing the piston-rod of a steam-engine, stood Guy Heavystone alone. I say alone, for the pile of small boys on the floor in the corner could hardly be called company.

I will try and sketch him for the reader. Guy Heavystone was then only fifteen. His broad, deep chest, his sinewy and quivering flank, his straight pastern, showed him to be a thorough-bred. Perhaps he was a trifle heavy in the fetlock, but he held his head haughtily erect. His eyes were glittering but pitiless. There was a sternness about the lower part of his face,—the old Heavystone look, —a sternness, heightened, perhaps, by the snaffle-bit which, in one of his strange freaks, he wore in his mouth to curb his occasional ferocity. His dress was well adapted to his square-set and herculean frame. A striped knit under-shirt, close-fitting striped tights, and a few spangles set off his figure ; a neat Glengarry cap adorned his head. On it was displayed the Heavystone crest, a cock *regardant* on a dunghill *or*, and the motto, " Devil a better ! "

I thought of Horatius on the bridge, of Hector before the walls. I always make it a point to think of something classical at such times.

He saw me, and his sternness partly relaxed. Something like a smile struggled through his grim lineaments. It was like looking on the Jungfrau after having seen Mont Blanc,—a trifle, only a trifle less sublime and awful. Rest-ing his hand lightly on the shoulder of the head-master, who shuddered and collapsed under his touch, he strode toward me.

His walk was peculiar. You could not call it a stride. It was like the " crest-tossing Bellerophon,"—a kind of prancing gait. Guy Heavystone pranced toward me.

## CHAPTER II.

"Lord Lovel he stood at the garden gate,
A-combing his milk-white steed."

It was the winter of 186— when I next met Guy Heavystone. He had left the University and had entered the
79th "Heavies." "I have exchanged the gown for the
sword, you see," he said, grasping my hand, and fracturing
the bones of my little finger, as he shook it.

I gazed at him with unmixed admiration. He was
squarer, sterner, and in every way smarter and more
remarkable than ever. I began to feel toward this man as
Phalaster felt towards Phyrgino, as somebody must have felt
toward Archididasculus, as Boswell felt toward Johnson.

"Come into my den," he said, and lifting me gently by
the seat of my pantaloons he carried me upstairs and
deposited me, before I could apologise, on the sofa. I
looked around the room. It was a bachelor's apartment,
characteristically furnished in the taste of the proprietor.
A few claymores and battleaxes were ranged against the
wall, and a culverin, captured by Sir Ralph Heavystone,
occupied the corner, the other end of the room being taken
up by a light battery. Foils, boxing-gloves, saddles, and
fishing-poles lay around carelessly. A small pile of billets-
doux lay upon a silver salver. The man was not an
anchorite, nor yet a Sir Galahad.

I never could tell what Guy thought of women. "Poor
little beasts," he would often say when the conversation
turned on any of his fresh conquests. Then, passing his
hand over his marble brow, the old look of stern fixedness
of purpose and unflinching severity would straighten the
lines of his mouth, and he would mutter, half to himself,
"S'death!"

"Come with me to Heavystone Grange. The Exmoor Hounds throw off to-morrow. I'll give you a mount," he said, as he amused himself by rolling up a silver candlestick between his fingers. "You shall have *Cleopatra.* But stay," he added thoughtfully; "now I remember, I ordered *Cleopatra* to be shot this morning."

"And why?" I queried.

"She threw her rider yesterday and fell on him "——

"And killed him?"

"No. That's the reason why I have ordered her to be shot. I keep no animals that are not dangerous—I should add—*deadly!*" He hissed the last sentence between his teeth, and a gloomy frown descended over his calm brow.

I affected to turn over the tradesmen's bills that lay on the table, for, like all of the Heavystone race, Guy seldom paid cash, and said—

"You remind me of the time when Leonidas "——

"Oh, bother Leonidas and your classical allusions. Come!"

We descended to dinner.

### CHAPTER III.

"He carries weight, he rides a race,
'Tis for a thousand pound."

"THERE is Flora Billingsgate, the greatest coquette and hardest rider in the country," said my companion, Ralph Mortmain, as we stood upon Dingleby Common before the meet.

I looked up and beheld Guy Heavystone bending haughtily over the saddle, as he addressed a beautiful brunette. She was indeed a splendidly groomed and high-spirited woman. We were near enough to overhear the following conversation, which any high-toned reader will recognise as the common and natural expression of the higher classes.

"When Diana takes the field the chase is not wholly confined to objects *feræ naturæ*," said Guy, darting a significant glance at his companion. Flora did not shrink either from the glance or the meaning implied in the sarcasm.

"If I were looking for an Endymion, now"— she said archly, as she playfully cantered over a few hounds and leaped a five-barred gate.

Guy whispered a few words, inaudible to the rest of the party, and curvetting slightly, cleverly cleared two of the huntsmen in a flying leap, galloped up the front steps of the mansion, and dashing at full speed through the hall leaped through the drawing-room window and rejoined me, languidly, on the lawn.

"Be careful of Flora Billingsgate," he said to me, in low stern tones, while his pitiless eye shot a baleful fire. "*Gardez vous !*"

"*Gnothi seauton*," I replied calmly, not wishing to appear to be behind him in perception or verbal felicity.

Guy started off in high spirits. He was well carried. He and the first whip, a ten-stone man, were head and head at the last fence, while the hounds were rolling over their fox a hundred yards farther in the open.

But an unexpected circumstance occurred. Coming back, his chestnut mare refused a ten-foot wall. She reared and fell backward. Again he led her up to it lightly ; again she refused, falling heavily from the coping. Guy started to his feet. The old pitiless fire shone in his eyes ; the old stern look settled around his mouth. Seizing the mare by the tail and mane he threw her over the wall. She landed twenty feet on the other side, erect and trembling. Lightly leaping the same obstacle himself, he remounted her. She did not refuse the wall the next time.

## CHAPTER IV.

*" He holds him by his glittering eye."*

GUY was in the North of Ireland, cock-shooting. So
Ralph Mortmain told me, and also that the match between
Mary Brandagee and Guy had been broken off by Flora
Billingsgate. " I don't like those Billingsgates," said Ralph,
" they're a bad stock. Her father, Smithfield de Billingsgate, had an unpleasant way of turning up the knave from
the bottom of the pack. But *nous verrons ;* let us go and
see Guy."

The next morning we started for Fin-ma-Coul's Crossing.
When I reached the shooting-box, where Guy was entertaining a select company of friends, Flora Billingsgate
greeted me with a saucy smile.

Guy was even squarer and sterner than ever. His gusts
of passion were more frequent, and it was with difficulty
that he could keep an able-bodied servant in his family.
His present retainers were more or less maimed from
exposure to the fury of their master. There was a strange
cynicism, a cutting sarcasm in his address, piercing through
his polished manner. I thought of Timon, &c., &c.

One evening, we were sitting over our Chambertin, after
a hard day's work, and Guy was listlessly turning over
some letters, when suddenly he uttered a cry. Did you
ever hear the trumpeting of a wounded elephant ? It was
like that.

I looked at him with consternation. He was glancing
at a letter which he held at arm's length, and snorting, as
it were, at it as he gazed. The lower part of his face was
stern, but not as rigid as usual. He was slowly grinding
between his teeth the fragments of the glass he had just
been drinking from. Suddenly he seized one of his ser-

vants, and forcing the wretch upon his knees, exclaimed, with the roar of a tiger—

"Dog! why was this kept from me?"

"Why, please sir, Miss Flora said as how it was a reconciliation from Miss Brandagee, and it was to be kept from you where you would not be likely to see it,—and—and"——

"Speak, dog! and you"——

"I put it among your bills, sir!"

With a groan, like distant thunder, Guy fell swooning to the floor.

He soon recovered, for the next moment a servant came rushing into the room with the information that a number of the ingenuous peasantry of the neighbourhood were about to indulge that evening in the national pastime of burning a farmhouse and shooting a landlord. Guy smiled a fearful smile, without, however, altering his stern and pitiless expression.

"Let them come," he said calmly; "I feel like entertaining company."

We barricaded the doors and windows, and then chose our arms from the armoury. Guy's choice was a singular one: it was a landing net with a long handle, and a sharp cavalry sabre.

We were not destined to remain long in ignorance of its use. A howl was heard from without, and a party of fifty or sixty armed men precipitated themselves against the door.

Suddenly the window opened. With the rapidity of lightning, Guy Heavystone cast the net over the head of the ringleader, ejaculated "*Habet!*" and with a back stroke of his cavalry sabre severed the member from its trunk, and drawing the net back again, cast the gory head upon the floor, saying quietly—

" One."

Again the net was cast, the steel flashed, the net was withdrawn, and an ominous " Two ! " accompanied the head as it rolled on the floor.

" Do you remember what Pliny says of the gladiator ? " said Guy, calmly wiping his sabre. " How graphic is that passage commencing ' *Inter nos, &c.*' " The sport continued until the heads of twenty desperadoes had been gathered in. The rest seemed inclined to disperse. Guy incautiously showed himself at the door ; a ringing shot was heard, and he staggered back, pierced through the heart. Grasping the door-post in the last unconscious throes of his mighty frame, the whole side of the house yielded to that earthquake tremor, and we had barely time to escape before the whole building fell in ruins. I thought of Samson, the Giant Judge, &c., &c. ; but all was over.

**Guy** Heavystone had died as he had lived,—*hard.*

# John Jenkins;

OR,

## *THE SMOKER REFORMED.*

BY T. S. A—TH—R.

## CHAPTER I.

" ONE cigar a day ! " said Judge Boompointer.

"One cigar a day !" repeated John Jenkins, as with trepidation he dropped his half-consumed cigar under his work-bench.

"One cigar a day is three cents a day." remarked Judge Boompointer gravely ; "and do you know, sir, what one cigar a day, or three cents a day, amounts to in the course of four years ? "

John Jenkins, in his boyhood, had attended the village school, and possessed considerable arithmetical ability. Taking up a shingle which lay upon his work-bench, and producing a piece of chalk, with a feeling of conscious pride he made an exhaustive calculation.

" Exactly forty-three dollars and eighty cents," he replied, wiping the perspiration from his heated brow, while his face flushed with honest enthusiasm.

" Well, sir, if you saved three cents a day, instead of wasting it, you would now be the possesser of a new suit of clothes, an illustrated Family Bible, a pew in the church, a complete set of Patent Office Reports, a hymn-book, and a paid subscription to 'Arthur's Home Magazine,' which could be purchased for exactly forty-three dollars and eighty cents ; and," added the Judge, with increasing sternness, " if you calculate leap-year, which you seem to have strangely omitted, you have three cents more, sir ; *three cents more !* What would that buy you, sir?"

" A cigar," suggested John Jenkins ; but, colouring again deeply, he hid his face.

" No, sir," said the Judge, with a sweet smile of bene-volence stealing over his stern features ; " properly invested, it would buy you that which passeth all price. Dropped into the missionary-box, who can tell what heathen, now idly and joyously wantoning in nakedness and sin, might be brought to a sense of his miserable condition, and made, through that three cents, to feel the torments of the wicked?"

With these words the Judge retired, leaving John Jenkins buried in profound thought. " Three cents a day," he muttered. " In forty years I might be worth four hundred and thirty-eight dollars and ten cents,—and then I might marry Mary. Ah, Mary!" The young carpenter sighed, and drawing a twenty-five cent daguerreotype from his vest-pocket, gazed long and fervidly upon the features of a young girl in book muslin and a coral necklace. Then, with a resolute expression, he carefully locked the door of his work-shop and departed.

Alas ! his good resolutions were too late. We trifle with the tide of fortune which too often nips us in the bud and casts the dark shadow of misfortune over the bright lexicon of youth ! That night the half-consumed fragment of John Jenkins's cigar set fire to his work-shop and burned it up, together with all his tools and materials. There was no insurance.

## CHAPTER II.

### THE DOWNWARD PATH.

" THEN you still persist in marrying John Jenkins ? " queried Judge Boompointer, as he playfully, with paternal familiarity, lifted the golden curls of the village belle, Mary Jones.

"I do," replied the fair young girl, in a low voice, that resembled rock candy in its saccharine firmness,—"I do. He has promised to reform. Since he lost all his property by fire "——

" The result of his pernicious habit, though he illogically persists in charging it to me," interrupted the Judge.

"Since then," continued the young girl, "he has endeavoured to break himself off the habit. He tells me that he has substituted the stalks of the Indian ratan, the outer part of a leguminous plant called the smoking-bean, and the fragmentary and unconsumed remainder of cigars which occur at rare and uncertain intervals along the road, which, as he informs me, though deficient in quality and strength, are comparatively inexpensive." And blushing at her own eloquence, the young girl hid her curls on the Judge's arm.

"Poor thing !" muttered Judge Boompointer. "Dare I tell her all ? Yet I must."

"I shall cling to him," continued the young girl, rising with her theme, "as the young vine clings to some hoary ruin. Nay, nay, chide me not, Judge Boompointer. I will marry John Jenkins ! "

The Judge was evidently affected. Seating himself at the table, he wrote a few lines hurriedly upon a piece of paper, which he folded and placed in the fingers of the destined bride of John Jenkins.

"Mary Jones," said the Judge, with impressive earnestness, "take this trifle as a wedding gift from one who respects your fidelity and truthfulness. At the altar let it be a reminder of me." And covering his face hastily with a handkerchief, the stern and iron-willed man left the room. As the door closed, Mary unfolded the paper. It was an order on the corner grocery for three yards of flannel, a paper of needles, four pounds of soap, one pound of starch, and two boxes of matches!

"Noble and thoughtful man!" was all Mary Jones could exclaim, as she hid her face in her hands and burst into a flood of tears.

.     .     .     .     .     .     .

The bells of Cloverdale are ringing merrily. It is a wedding. "How beautiful they look!" is the exclamation that passes from lip to lip, as Mary Jones, leaning timidly on the arm of John Jenkins, enters the church. But the bride is agitated, and the bridegroom betrays a feverish nervousness. As they stand in the vestibule, John Jenkins fumbles earnestly in his vest-pocket. Can it be the ring he is anxious about? No. He draws a small brown substance from his pocket, and biting off a piece, hastily replaces the fragment and gazes furtively around. Surely no one saw him? Alas! the eyes of two of that wedding party saw the fatal act. Judge Boompointer shook his head sternly. Mary Jones sighed and breathed a silent prayer. Her husband chewed!

## CHAPTER III. AND LAST.

"WHAT! more bread?" said John Jenkins gruffly. "You're always asking for money for bread. D—nation! Do you want to ruin me by your extravagance?" and as he uttered these words he drew from his pocket a bottle of whisky, a pipe, and a paper of tobacco. Emptying the first at a draught, he threw the empty bottle at the head of his eldest boy, a youth of twelve summers. The missile struck the child full in the temple, and stretched him a lifeless corpse. Mrs. Jenkins, whom the reader will hardly recognise as the once gay and beautiful Mary Jones, raised the dead body of her son in her arms, and carefully placing the unfortunate youth beside the pump in the back-yard, returned with saddened step to the house. At another time, and in brighter days, she might have wept at the occurrence. She was past tears now.

"Father, your conduct is reprehensible!" said little Harrison Jenkins, the youngest boy. "Where do you expect to go when you die?"

"Ah!" said John Jenkins fiercely; "this comes of giving children a liberal education; this is the result of Sabbath schools. Down, viper!"

A tumbler thrown from the same parental fist laid out the youthful Harrison cold. The four other children had, in the meantime, gathered around the table with anxious expectancy. With a chuckle, the now changed and brutal John Jenkins produced four pipes, and filling them with tobacco, handed one to each of his offspring and bade them smoke. "It's better than bread!" laughed the wretch hoarsely.

Mary Jenkins, though of a patient nature, felt it her duty now to speak. "I have borne much, John Jenkins," she said. "But I prefer that the children should not smoke. It is an unclean habit, and soils their clothes. I ask this as a special favour!"

John Jenkins hesitated,—the pangs of remorse began to seize him.

"Promise me this, John!" urged Mary upon her knees.

"I promise!" reluctantly answered John.

" And you will put the money in a savings-bank ? "

" I will," repeated her husband; "and *I*'ll give up smoking, too."

" 'Tis well, John Jenkins ! " said Judge Boompointer, appearing suddenly from behind the door, where he had been concealed during this interview. " Nobly said ! my man. Cheer up ! I will see that the children are decently buried." The husband and wife fell into each other's arms. And Judge Boompointer, gazing upon the affecting spectacle, burst into tears.

**From** that day John Jenkins was an altered **man.**

# Fantine.

*AFTER THE FRENCH OF VICTOR HUGO.*

## PROLOGUE.

As long as there shall exist three paradoxes, a moral Frenchman, a religious atheist, and a believing sceptic; so long, in fact, as book-sellers shall wait—say twenty-five years—for a new gospel; so long as paper shall remain cheap and ink three *sous* a bottle, I have no hesitation in saying that such books as these are not utterly profitless.

VICTOR HUGO.

## I.

To be good is to be queer. What is a good man? Bishop Myriel.

My friend, you will possibly object to this. You will say you know what a good man is. Perhaps you will say your clergyman is a good man, for instance.

Bah! you are mistaken; you are an Englishman, and an Englishman is a beast.

Englishmen think they are moral when they are only serious. These Englishmen also wear ill-shaped hats, and dress horribly!

Bah! they are *canaille*.

Still, Bishop Myriel was a good man,—quite as good as you. Better than you, in fact.

One day M. Myriel was in Paris. This angel used to walk about the streets like any other man. He was not

proud, though fine-looking. Well, three *gamins de Paris*
called him bad names. Says one—

"Ah, *mon Dieu!* there goes a priest; look out for your
eggs and chickens!"

What did this good man do? He called to them kindly.

"My children," said he, "this is clearly not your fault.
I recognise in this insult and irreverence only the fault of
your immediate progenitors. Let us pray for your immediate progenitors."

They knelt down and prayed for their immediate progenitors.

The effect was touching.

The Bishop looked calmly around.

"On reflection," said he gravely, "I was mistaken; this
is clearly the fault of Society. Let us pray for Society."

They knelt down and prayed for Society.

The effect was sublimer yet. What do you think of
that? You, I mean.

Everybody remembers the story of the Bishop and
Mother Nez Retroussé. Old Mother Nez Retroussé sold
asparagus. She was poor; there's a great deal of meaning
in that word, my friend. Some people say "poor but
honest." I say, Bah!

Bishop Myriel bought six bunches of asparagus. This
good man had one charming failing; he was fond of
asparagus. He gave her a *franc* and received three *sous*
change.

The *sous* were bad,—counterfeit. What did this good
Bishop do? He said: "I should not have taken change
from a poor woman."

Then afterwards, to his housekeeper: "Never take
change from a poor woman."

Then he added to himself: "For the *sous* will probably
be bad."

## II.

WHEN a man commits a crime, society claps him in prison. A prison is one of the worst hotels imaginable. The people there are low and vulgar. The butter is bad, the coffee is green. Ah, it is horrible!

In prison, as in a bad hotel, a man soon loses, not only his morals, but what is much worse to a Frenchman, his sense of refinement and delicacy.

Jean Valjean came from prison with confused notions of Society. He forgot the modern peculiarities of hospitality. So he walked off with the Bishop's candlesticks.

Let us consider: candlesticks were stolen; that was evident. Society put Jean Valjean in prison; that was evident, too. In prison, Society took away his refinement; that is evident, likewise.

Who is Society?

You and I are Society.

My friend, you and I stole those candlesticks!

## III.

THE Bishop thought so, too. He meditated profoundly for six days. On the morning of the seventh he went to the Prefecture of Police.

He said: "Monsieur, have me arrested. I have stolen candlesticks."

The official was governed by the law of Society, and refused.

What did this Bishop do?

He had a charming ball and chain made, affixed to his leg, and wore it the rest of his life.

This is a fact!

## IV.

LOVE is a mystery.

A little friend of mine down in the country, at Auvergne, said to me one day : " Victor, Love is the world,—it contains everything."

She was only sixteen, this sharp-witted little girl, and a beautiful blonde. She thought everything of me.

Fantine was one of those women who do wrong in the most virtuous and touching manner. This is a peculiarity of French grisettes.

You are an Englishman, and you don't understand. Learn, my friend, learn. Come to Paris and improve your morals.

Fantine was the soul of modesty. She always wore high-neck dresses. High-neck dresses are a sign of modesty.

Fantine loved Tholmoyes. Why? My God! What are you to do? It was the fault of her parents, and she hadn't any. How shall you teach her? You must teach the parent if you wish to educate the child. How would you become virtuous?

Teach your grandmother !

## V.

WHEN Tholmoyes ran away from Fantine,—which was done in a charming, gentlemanly manner,—Fantine became convinced that a rigid sense of propriety might look upon her conduct as immoral. She was a creature of sensitiveness,—and her eyes were opened.

She was virtuous still, and resolved to break off the *liaison* at once.

So she put up her wardrobe and baby in a bundle. Child as she was, she loved them both. Then left Paris.

## VI.

FANTINE'S native place had changed.

M. Madeline—an angel, and inventor of jet-work—had been teaching the villagers how to make spurious jet.

This is a progressive age. Those Americans,—children of the West,—they make nutmegs out of wood.

I, myself, have seen hams made of pine, in the wigwams of those children of the forest.

But civilisation has acquired deception too. Society is made up of deception. Even the best French society.

Still there was one sincere episode.

Eh?

The French Revolution!

## VII.

M. MADELINE was, if anything, better than Myriel.

M. Myriel was a saint. M. Madeline a good man.

M. Myriel was dead. M. Madeline was living.

That made all the difference.

M. Madeline made virtue profitable. I have seen it written—

" Be virtuous and you will be happy."

Where did I see this written? In the modern Bible? No. In the Koran? No. In Rousseau? No. Diderot? No. Where then?

In a copy-book.

## VIII.

M. MADELINE was M. le Maire.

This is how it came about.

For a long time he refused the honour. One day an old woman, standing on the steps, said—

"Bah, a good mayor is a good thing.

"You are a good thing.

"Be a good mayor."

This woman was a rhetorician. She understood inductive ratiocination.


## IX.

WHEN this good M. Madeline, whom the reader will perceive must have been a former convict, and a very bad man, gave himself up to justice as the real Jean Valjean, about this same time, Fantine was turned away from the manufactory, and met with a number of losses from society. Society attacked her, and this is what she lost—

First her lover.

Then her child.

Then her place.

Then her hair.

Then her teeth.

Then her liberty.

Then her life.

What do you think of society after that? I tell you the present social system is a humbug.


## X.

THIS is necessarily the end of Fantine.

There are other things that will be stated in other volumes to follow. Don't be alarmed; there are plenty of miserable people left.

*Au revoir*—my friend.

# "La Femme."

## AFTER THE FRENCH OF M. MICHELET.

### I.

#### WOMEN AS AN INSTITUTION.

"IF it were not for women, few of us would at present be in existence." This is the remark of a cautious and discreet writer. He was also sagacious and intelligent.

Woman! Look upon her and admire her. Gaze upon her and love her. If she wishes to embrace you, permit her. Remember she is weak and you are strong.

But don't treat her unkindly. Don't make love to another woman before her face, even if she be your wife. Don't do it. Always be polite, even should she fancy somebody better than you.

If your mother, my dear Amadis, had not fancied your father better than somebody, you might have been that somebody's son. Consider this. Always be a philosopher, even about women.

Few men understand women. Frenchmen, perhaps, better than any one else. I am a Frenchman.

## II.

### THE INFANT.

SHE is a child—a little thing—an infant.

She has a mother and father. Let us suppose, for example, they are married. Let us be moral if we cannot be happy and free—they are married—perhaps—they love one another—who knows?

But she knows nothing of this; she is an infant—a small thing—a trifle!

She is not lovely at first. It is cruel, perhaps, but she is red, and positively ugly. She feels this keenly and cries. She weeps. Ah, my God, how she weeps! Her cries and lamentations now are really distressing.

Tears stream from her in floods. She feels deeply and copiously like M. Alphonse de Lamartine in his *Confessions.*

If you are her mother, Madame, you will fancy worms; you will examine her linen for pins, and what not. Ah, hypocrite! you, even *you*, misunderstand her.

Yet she has charming natural impulses. See how she tosses her dimpled arms. She looks longingly at her mother. She has a language of her own. She says, "goo goo," and "ga ga."

She demands something—this infant!

She is faint, poor thing. She famishes. She wishes to be restored. Restore her, Mother!

*It is the first duty of a mother to restore her child!*

## III.

### THE DOLL.

SHE is hardly able to walk; she already totters under the weight of a doll.

It is a charming and elegant affair. It has pink cheeks and purple-black hair. She prefers brunettes, for she has already, with the quick knowledge of a French infant, perceived she is a blonde, and that her doll cannot rival her. *Mon Dieu*, how touching! Happy child! She spends hours in preparing its toilet. She begins to show her taste in the exquisite details of its dress. She loves it madly, devotedly. She will prefer it to *bonbons*. She already anticipates the wealth of love she will hereafter pour out on her lover, her mother, her father, and finally, perhaps, her husband.

This is the time the anxious parent will guide these first outpourings. She will read her extracts from Michelet's "L'Amour," Rousseau's "Héloise," and the "Revue des deux Mondes."

## IV.

### THE MUD PIE.

SHE was in tears to-day.

She had stolen away from her *bonne* and was with some rustic infants. They had noses in the air, and large, coarse hands and feet.

They had seated themselves around a pool in the road, and were fashioning fantastic shapes in the clayey soil with their hands. Her throat swelled and her eyes sparkled with delight as, for the first time, her soft palms touched the plastic mud. She made a graceful and lovely pie. She stuffed it with stones for almonds and plums. She forgot everything. It was being baked in the solar rays, when madame came and took her away.

She weeps. It is night, and she is weeping still.

## V.

### THE FIRST LOVE

SHE no longer doubts her beauty. She is loved.

She saw him secretly. He is vivacious and sprightly. He is famous. He has already had an affair with Finfin, the *fille de chambre*, and poor Finfin is desolate. He is noble. She knows he is the son of Madame la Baronne Couturière. She adores him.

She affects not to notice him. Poor little thing! Hippolyte is distracted—annihilated—inconsolable and charming.

She admires his boots, his cravat, his little gloves—his exquisite pantaloons—his coat, and cane.

She offers to run away with him. He is transported, but magnanimous. He is wearied, perhaps. She sees him the next day offering flowers to the daughter of Madame la Comtesse Blanchisseuse.

She is again in tears.

She reads "Paul et Virginie." She is secretly transported. When she reads how the exemplary young woman laid down her life rather than appear *en déshabillé* to her lover, she weeps again. Tasteful and virtuous Bernardine de St. Pierre!—the daughters of France admire you!

All this time her doll is headless in the cabinet. The mud pie is broken on the road.

## VI.

### THE WIFE.

SHE is tired of loving and she marries.

Her mother thinks it, on the whole, the best thing. As the day approaches, she is found frequently in tears. Her mother will not permit the affianced one to see her, and he makes several attempts to commit suicide.

But something happens. Perhaps it is winter, and the water is cold. Perhaps there are not enough people present to witness his heroism.

In this way her future husband is spared to her. The ways of Providence are indeed mysterious. At this time her mother will talk with her. She will offer philosophy. She will tell her she was married herself.

But what is this new and ravishing light that breaks upon her? The toilet and wedding clothes ! She is in a new sphere.

She makes out her list in her own charming writing. Here it is. Let every mother heed it.*

.    .    .    .    .    .    .

She is married. On the day after, she meets her old lover. Hippolyte. He is again transported.

## VII.

### HER OLD AGE.

A FRENCHWOMAN never grows old.

* The delicate reader will appreciate the omission of certain articles for which English synonymes are forbidden.

# The Dweller of the Threshold.

### BY SIR ED—D L—TT—N B—LW—R.

## BOOK I.

### THE PROMPTINGS OF THE IDEAL.

IT was noon.   Sir Edward had stepped from his brougham and was proceeding on foot down the Strand.   He was dressed with his usual faultless taste, but in alighting from his vehicle his foot had slipped, and a small round disk of conglomerated soil, which instantly appeared on his high arched instep, marred the harmonious glitter of his boots. Sir Edward was fastidious.   Casting his eyes around, at a little distance he perceived the stand of a youthful boot-black.   Thither he sauntered, and carelessly placing his foot on the low stool, he waited the application of the polisher's art.   "'Tis true," said Sir Edward to himself, yet half aloud, "the contact of the Foul and the Disgusting mars the general effect of the Shiny and the Beautiful— and, yet, why am I here?   I repeat it, calmly and deliber-ately—-why am I here?   Ha!  Boy!"

The Boy looked up—his dark Italian eyes glanced intelligently at the Philosopher, and as with one hand he tossed back his glossy curls from his marble brow, and with the other he spread the equally glossy Day & Martin over the Baronet's boot, he answered in deep, rich tones "The Ideal is subjective to the Real.   The exercise of apperception gives a distinctiveness to idiocracy, which is, however, subject to the limits of ME. You are an admirer of the Beautiful, sir. You wish your boots blacked. The Beautiful is attainable by means of the Coin."

"Ah," said Sir Edward thoughtfully, gazing upon the almost supernal beauty of the Child before him; "you speak well. You have read ' Kant.' "

The Boy blushed deeply. He drew a copy of "Kant" from his blouse, but in his confusion several other volumes dropped from his bosom on the ground. The Baronet picked them up.

"Ah!" said the Philosopher, "what's this? ' Cicero's De Senectute,' at your age, too? 'Martial's Epigrams,' ' Cæsar's Commentaries.' What! a classical scholar?"

" E pluribus Unum. Nux vomica. Nil desperandum. Nihil fit!" said the Boy enthusiastically. The Philosopher gazed at the Child. A strange presence seemed to trans-fuse and possess him. Over the brow of the Boy glittered the pale nimbus of the Student.

"Ah, and ' Schiller's Robbers,' too?" queried the Philosopher.

"Das ist ausgespielt," said the Boy modestly.

"Then you have read my translation of ' Schiller's Ballads?'" continued the Baronet, with some show of interest.

"I have, and infinitely prefer them to the original," said the Boy, with intellectual warmth. "You have shown how in Actual life we strive for a Goal we cannot reach ; how in the Ideal the Goal is attainable, and there effort is victory. You have given us the Antithesis which is a key to the Remainder, and constantly balances before us the conditions of the Actual and the privileges of the Ideal."

"My very words," said the Baronet; "wonderful, won-derful!" and he gazed fondly at the Italian boy, who again resumed his menial employment.   Alas! the wings of the Ideal were folded.   The Student had been absorbed in the Boy.

But Sir Edward's boots were blacked, and he turned to depart.   Placing his hand upon the clustering tendrils that surrounded the classic nob of the infant Italian, he said softly, like a strain of distant music—

" Boy, you have done well.   Love the Good.   Protect the Innocent.   Provide for the Indigent.   Respect the Philosopher. . . . Stay!   Can you tell me what *is* The True, The Beautiful, The Innocent, The Virtuous?"

" They are things that commence with a capital letter," said the Boy promptly.

" Enough !   Respect everything that commences with a capital letter !   Respect ME !" and dropping a halfpenny in the hand of the boy, he departed.

The Boy gazed fixedly at the coin.   A frightful and instantaneous change overspread his features.   His noble brow was corrugated with baser lines of calculation.   His black eye, serpent-like, glittered with suppressed passion. Dropping upon his hands and feet, he crawled to the curbstone and hissed after the retreating form of the Baronet, the single word—

" Bilk !"

## BOOK II.

### IN THE WORLD.

" ELEVEN years ago," said Sir Edward to himself, as his brougham slowly rolled him toward the Committee Room : "just eleven years ago my natural son disappeared mysteriously.   I have no doubt in the world but that this little bootblack is he.   His mother died in Italy.   He resembles his mother very much. Perhaps I ought to provide for him. Shall I disclose myself? No! no! Better he should taste the sweets of Labour. Penury ennobles the mind and kindles the Love of the Beautiful. I will act to him, not like a Father, not like a Guardian, not like a Friend—but like a Philosopher!"

With these words, Sir Edward entered the Committee Room. His Secretary approached him. "Sir Edward, there are fears of a division in the House, and the Prime Minister has sent for you."

"I will be there," said Sir Edward, as he placed his hand on his chest and uttered a hollow cough!

No one who heard the Baronet that night, in his sarcastic and withering speech on the Drainage and Sewerage Bill, would have recognised the Lover of the Ideal and the Philosopher of the Beautiful. No one who listened to his eloquence would have dreamed of the Spartan resolution this iron man had taken in regard to the Lost Boy—his own beloved Lionel. None!

"A fine speech from Sir Edward to-night," said Lord Billingsgate, as arm-and-arm with the Premier, he entered his carriage.

"Yes! but how dreadfully he coughs!"

"Exactly. Dr. Bolus says his lungs are entirely gone; he breathes entirely by an effort of will, and altogether independent of pulmonary assistance."

"How strange!" and the carriage rolled away.

## BOOK III.

### THE DWELLER OF THE THRESHOLD.

" ADON AI, appear! appear ! "

And as the Seer spoke, the awful Presence glided out of Nothingness, and sat, sphinx-like, at the feet of the Alchemist.

" I am come ! " said the Thing.

" You should say, ' I have come,'—it's better grammar," said the Boy-Neophyte, thoughtfully accenting the substituted expression.

" Hush, rash Boy," said the Seer sternly. " Would you oppose your feeble knowledge to the infinite intelligence of the Unmistakable? A word, and you are lost for ever."

The Boy breathed a silent prayer, and handing a sealed package to the Seer, begged him to hand it to his father in case of his premature decease.

" You have sent for me," hissed the Presence, " Behold me, Apokatharticon,—the Unpronounceable. In me all things exist that are not already co-existent. I am the Unattainable, the Intangible, the Cause, and the Effect. In me observe the Brahma of Mr. Emerson ; not only Brahma himself, but also the sacred musical composition rehearsed by the faithful Hindoo. I am the real Gyges. None others are genuine."

And the veiled Son of the Starbeam laid himself loosely about the room, and permeated Space generally.

" Unfathomable Mystery," said the Rosicrucian in a low, sweet voice. " Brave Child with the Vitreous Optic · Thou who pervadest all things and rubbest against us without abrasion of the cuticle. I command thee, speak ! "

And the misty, intangible, indefinite Presence spoke.

## BOOK IV.

### MYSELF.

AFTER the events related in the last chapter, the reader will perceive that nothing was easier than to reconcile Sir Edward to his son Lionel, nor to resuscitate the beautiful Italian girl, who, it appears, was not dead, and to cause Sir Edward to marry his first and boyish love, whom he had deserted. They were married in St. George's, Hanover Square. As the bridal party stood before the altar, Sir Edward, with a sweet, sad smile, said in quite his old manner—

"The Sublime and Beautiful are the Real; the only Ideal is the Ridiculous and Homely. Let us always remember this. Let us through life endeavour to personify the virtues, and always begin 'em with a capital letter. Let us, whenever we can find an opportunity, deliver our sentiments in the form of roundhand copies. Respect the Aged. Eschew Vulgarity. Admire Ourselves. Regard the Novelist."

## 𝔑 𝔑.

*BEING A NOVEL IN THE FRENCH PARAGRAPHIC STYLE.*

—MADEMOISELLE, I swear to you that I love you.

—You who read these pages. You who turn your burning eyes upon these words—words that I trace—Ah, Heaven! the thought maddens me.

—I will be calm. I will imitate the reserve of the festive Englishman, who wears a spotted handkerchief which he calls a *Belchio*, who eats *biftek*, and caresses a bulldog. I will subdue myself like him.

—Ha! Poto-beer! All right—Goddam!

—Or, I will conduct myself as the free-born American—the gay Brother Jonathan! I will whittle me a stick. I will whistle to myself "Yankee Doodle," and forget my passion in excessive expectoration.

—Hoho!—wake snakes and walk chalks.

THE world is divided into two great divisions,—Paris and the provinces. There is but one Paris. There are several provinces, among which may be numbered England, America, Russia, and Italy.

N N. was a Parisian.

But N N. did not live in Paris. Drop a Parisian in the provinces, and you drop a part of Paris with him. Drop him in Senegambia, and in three days he will give you an *omelette soufflée*, or a *pâté de foie gras*, served by the neatest of Senegambian *filles*, whom he will call Mademoiselle. In three weeks he will give you an opera.

N N. was not dropped in Senegambia, but in San Francisco,—quite as awkward.

They find gold in San Francisco, but they don't understand gilding.

N N. existed three years in this place. He became bald on the top of his head, as all Parisians do. Look down from your box at the Opera Comique, Mademoiselle, and count the bald crowns of the fast young men in the pit. Ah—you tremble! They show where the arrows of love have struck and glanced off.

N N. was almost near-sighted, as all Parisians finally become. This is a gallant provision of Nature to spare them the mortification of observing that their lady friends grow old. After a certain age every woman is handsome to a Parisian.

One day, N N. was walking down Washington Street. Suddenly he stopped.

He was standing before the door of a mantuamaker. Beside the counter, at the farther extremity of the shop, stood a young and elegantly formed woman. Her face was turned from N N. He entered. With a plausible excuse, and seeming indifference, he gracefully opened conversation with the mantuamaker as only a Parisian can. But he had to deal with a Parisian. His attempts to view the features of the fair stranger by the counter were deftly combated by the shopwoman. He was obliged to retire.

N N. went home and lost his appetite. He was haunted by the elegant basque and graceful shoulders of the fair unknown, during the whole night.

The next day he sauntered by the mantuamaker. Ah! Heavens! A thrill ran through his frame, and his fingers tingled with a delicious electricity. The fair *inconnue* was there ! He raised his hat gracefully. He was not certain, but he thought that a slight motion of her faultless bonnet betrayed recognition. He would have wildly darted into the shop, but just then the figure of the mantuamaker appeared in the doorway.

—Did Monsieur wish anything?

—Misfortune! Desperation. N N. purchased a bottle of Prussic acid, a sack of charcoal, and a quire of pink note-paper, and returned home. He wrote a letter of fare-well to the closely-fitting basque, and opened the bottle of Prussic acid.

Some one knocked at his door. It was a Chinaman, with his weekly linen.

These Chinese are docile, but not intelligent. They are ingenious, but not creative. They are cunning in expe-dients, but deficient in tact. In love they are simply bar-barous. They purchase their wives openly, and not con-structively by attorney. By offering small sums for their sweethearts, they degrade the value of the sex.

Nevertheless, N N. felt he was saved. He explained all to the faithful Mongolian, and exhibited the letter he had written. He implored him to deliver it.

The Mongolian assented. The race are not cleanly or sweet-savoured, but N N. fell upon his neck. He embraced him with one hand, and closed his nostrils with the other. Through him, he felt he clasped the close-fitting basque.

The next day was one of agony and suspense. Evening came, but no Mercy. N N. lit the charcoal. But, to com-pose his nerves, he closed his door and first walked mildly up and down Montgomery Street. When he returned, he found the faithful Mongolian on the steps.

—All lity !

These Chinese are not accurate in their pronunciation They avoid the *r*, like the English nobleman.

N N. gasped for breath. He leaned heavily against the Chinaman.

—Then you have seen her, Ching Long?

—Yes. All lity. She cum. Top side of house.

The docile barbarian pointed up the stairs, and chuckled.

—She here—impossible! Ah, Heaven! do I dream?

—Yes. All lity,—top side of house. Good-bye, John.

This is the familiar parting epithet of the Mongolian. It is equivalent to our *au revoir*.

N N. gazed with a stupefied air on the departing servant.

He placed his hand on his throbbing heart. She here,—alone beneath this roof. O Heavens,—what happiness!

But how? Torn from her home. Ruthlessly dragged, perhaps, from her evening devotions, by the hands of a relentless barbarian. Could she forgive him?

He dashed frantically up the stairs. He opened the door.

She was standing beside his couch with averted face.

A strange giddiness overtook him. He sank upon his knees at the threshold.

—Pardon, pardon. My angel, can you forgive me?

A terrible nausea now seemed added to the fearful giddiness. His utterance grew thick and sluggish.

—Speak, speak, enchantress. Forgiveness is all I ask. My Love, my Life!

She did not answer. He staggered to his feet. As he rose, his eyes fell on the pan of burning charcoal. A terrible suspicion flashed across his mind. This giddiness—this nausea. The ignorance of the barbarian. This silence. O merciful heavens; she was dying!

He crawled toward her. He touched her. She fell forward with a lifeless sound upon the floor. He uttered a piercing shriek, and threw himself beside her.

·     ·     ·     ·     ·     ·     ·     ·

A file of gendarmes, accompanied by the *Chef* Burke, found him the next morning lying lifeless upon the floor. They laughed brutally—these cruel minions of the law—and disengaged his arm from the waist of the wooden dummy which they had come to reclaim from the mantua-maker.

Emptying a few bucketfuls of water over his form, they finally succeeded in robbing him, not only of his mistress, but of that Death he had coveted without her.

Ah! we live in a strange world, Messieurs.

# No Title.

### BY W—LK—E C—LL—NS.[1]

## PROLOGUE.

THE following advertisement appeared in the "Times" of the 17th of June 1845—

WANTED.—A few young men for a light genteel employment. Address             J. W., P. O.

In the same paper, of same date, in another column—

TO LET.—That commodious and elegant family mansion, No. 27 Limehouse Road, Pultneyville, will be rented low to a respectable tenant if applied for immediately, the family being about to remove to the Continent.

Under the local intelligence, in another column—

MISSING.—An unknown elderly gentleman a week ago left his lodgings in the Kent Road, since which nothing has been heard of him. He left no trace of his identity except a portmanteau containing a couple of shirts marked "209, WARD."

To find the connection between the mysterious disappearance of the elderly gentleman and the anonymous communication, the relevancy of both these incidents to the letting of a commodious family mansion, and the dead secret involved in the three occurrences, is the task of the writer of this history.

A slim young man with spectacles, a large hat, drab gaiters, and a note-book, sat late that night with a copy of the "Times" before him, and a pencil which he rattled nervously between his teeth in the coffee-room of the "Blue Dragon."

## CHAPTER I.

### MARY JONES'S NARRATIVE.

I AM upper housemaid to the family that live at No. 27 Limehouse Road, Pultneyville. I have been requested by Mr. Wilkey Collings, which I takes the liberty of here stating is a gentleman born and bred, and has some consideration for the feelings of servants, and is not above rewarding them for their trouble, which is more than you can say for some who ask questions and gets short answers enough, gracious knows, to tell what I know about them. I have been requested to tell my story in my own langwidge, though, being no schollard, mind cannot conceive. I think my master is a brute. Do not know that he has ever attempted to poison my missus,—which is too good for him, and how she ever came to marry him, heart only can tell,—but believe him to be capable of any such hatrosity. Have heard him swear dreadful because of not having his shaving-water at nine o'clock precisely. Do not know whether he ever forged a will or tried to get my missus' property, although, not having confidence in the man, should not be surprised if he had done so. Believe that there was always something mysterious in his conduct. Remember distinctly how the family left home to go abroad. Was putting up my back hair, last Saturday morning, when I heard a ring. Says cook, "That's missus' bell, and mind you hurry or the master 'ill know why." Says I, "Humbly thanking you, mem, but taking advice of them as is competent to give it, I'll take my time." Found missus dressing herself and master growling as usual. Says missus, quite calm and easy like, "Mary, we begin to pack to-day." "What for, mem?" says I, taken aback. "What's that hussy asking?" says master from the bedclothes quite savage like. "For the Continent—Italy," says missus— "Can you go, Mary?" Her voice was quite gentle and saintlike, but I knew the struggle it cost, and says I, "With *you*, mem, to India's torrid clime, if required, but with African Gorillas," says I, looking toward the bed, "never." "Leave the room," says master, starting up and catching of his bootjack. "Why, Charles!" says missus, "how you talk!" affecting surprise. "Do go, Mary," says she, slipping a half-crown into my hand. I left the room scorning to take notice of the odious wretch's conduct.

Cannot say whether my master and missus were ever legally married. What with the dreadful state of morals nowadays and them stories in the circulating libraries, innocent girls don't know into what society they might be obliged to take situations. Never saw missus' marriage certificate, though I have quite accidental-like looked in her desk when open, and would have seen it. Do not know of any lovers missus might have had. Believe she had a liking for John Thomas, footman, for she was always spiteful-like—poor lady—when we were together—though there was nothing between us, as cook well knows, and dare not deny, and missus needn't have been jealous. Have never seen arsenic or Prussian acid in any of the private drawers—but have seen paregoric and camphor. One of my master's friends was a Count Moscow, a Russian papist—which I detested.

## CHAPTER II.

### THE SLIM YOUNG MAN'S STORY.

I AM by profession a reporter, and writer for the press. I live at Pultneyville. I have always had a passion for the marvellous, and have been distinguished for my facility in tracing out mysteries, and solving enigmatical occurrences. On the night of the 17th June 1845, I left my office and walked homeward. The night was bright and starlight. I was revolving in my mind the words of a singular item I had just read in the " Times." I had reached the darkest portion of the road, and found myself mechanically repeating : " An elderly gentleman a week ago left his lodgings on the Kent Road," when suddenly I heard a step behind me.

I turned quickly, with an expression of horror in my face, and by the light of the newly risen moon beheld an elderly gentleman, with green cotton umbrella, approaching me. His hair, which was snow white, was parted over a broad, open forehead. The expression of his face, which was slightly flushed, was that of amiability verging almost upon imbecility. There was a strange, inquiring look about the widely opened mild blue eye,—a look that might have been intensified to insanity, or modified to idiocy. As he passed me, he paused and partly turned his face, with a gesture of inquiry. I see him still, his white locks blowing in the evening breeze, his hat a little on the back of his head, and his figure painted in relief against the dark blue sky.

Suddenly he turned his mild eye full upon me. A weak smile played about his thin lips. In a voice which had something of the tremulousness of age and the self-satisfied chuckle of imbecility in it, he asked, pointing to the rising moon, "Why?—Hush!"

He had dodged behind me, and appeared to be looking anxiously down the road. I could feel his aged frame shaking with terror as he laid his thin hands upon my shoulders and faced me in the direction of the supposed danger.

"Hush! did you not hear them coming?"

I listened; there was no sound but the soughing of the roadside trees in the evening wind. I endeavoured to reassure him, with such success that in a few moments the old weak smile appeared on his benevolent face.

"Why?—" But the look of interrogation was succeeded by a hopeless blankness.

"Why!" I repeated with assuring accents.

"Why," he said, a gleam of intelligence flickering over his face, "is yonder moon, as she sails in the blue empyrean, casting a flood of light o'er hill and dale, like— Why," he repeated, with a feeble smile, "is yonder moon, as she sails in the blue empyrean—" He hesitated,—stammered,—and gazed at me hopelessly, with the tears dripping from his moist and widely opened eyes.

I took his hand kindly in my own. "Casting a shadow o'er hill and dale," I repeated quietly, leading him up the subject, "like— Come, now."

"Ah!" he said, pressing my hand tremulously, "you know it?"

"I do. Why is it like—the—eh—the commodious mansion on the Limehouse Road?"

A blank stare only followed. He shook his head sadly. "Like the young men wanted for a light, genteel employment?"

He wagged his feeble old head cunningly.

"Or, Mr. Ward," I said, with bold confidence, "like the mysterious disappearance from the Kent Road?"

The moment was full of suspense.    He did not seem to hear me.    Suddenly he turned.

"Ha !"

I darted forward.    But he had vanished in the darkness.

## CHAPTER III.

### NO. 27 LIMEHOUSE ROAD.

IT was a hot midsummer evening.    Limehouse Road was deserted save by dust and a few rattling butchers' carts, and the bell of the muffin and crumpet man.    A commodious mansion, which stood on the right of the road as you enter Pultneyville, surrounded by stately poplars and a high fence surmounted by a *chevaux de frise* of broken glass, looked to the passing and footsore pedestrian like the genius of seclusion and solitude.    A bill announcing in the usual terms that the house was to let, hung from the bell at the servants' entrance.

As the shades of evening closed, and the long shadows of the poplars stretched across the road, a man carrying a small kettle stopped and gazed, first at the bill and then at the house.    When he had reached the corner of the fence, he again stopped and looked cautiously up and down the road.    Apparently satisfied with the result of his scrutiny, he deliberately sat himself down in the dark shadow of the fence, and at once busied himself in some employment, so well concealed as to be invisible to the gaze of passers-by. At the end of an hour he retired cautiously.

But not altogether unseen.    A slim young man, with spectacles and note-book, stepped from behind a tree as the retreating figure of the intruder was lost in the twilight, and transferred from the fence to his note-book the freshly stencilled inscription, " S—T—1860—X."

## CHAPTER IV.

### COUNT MOSCOW'S NARRATIVE.

I AM a foreigner. Observe ! To be a foreigner in England
is to be mysterious, suspicious, intriguing. M. Collins has
requested the history of my complicity with certain occurrences. It is nothing, bah ! absolutely nothing.

I write with ease and fluency. Why should I not write?
Tra la la ! I am what you English call corpulent. Ha,
ha ! I am a pupil of Macchiavelli. I find it much better
to disbelieve everything, and to approach my subject and
wishes circuitously, than in a direct manner. You have
observed that playful animal, the cat. Call it, and it does
not come to you directly, but rubs itself against all the
furniture in the room, and reaches you finally—and scratches.
Ah, ha, scratches ! I am of the feline species. People
call me a villain—bah !

I know the family, living No. 27 Limehouse Road. I
respect the gentleman,—a fine, burly specimen of your
Englishman,—and madame, charming, ravishing, delightful. When it became known to me that they designed
to let their delightful residence, and visit foreign shores, I
at once called upon them. I kissed the hand of madame. I
embraced the great Englishman. Madame blushed slightly.
The great Englishman shook my hand like a mastiff.

I began in that dexterous, insinuating manner, of which
I am truly proud. I thought madame was ill. Ah, no. A
change, then, was all that was required. I sat down at the
piano and sang. In a few minutes madame retired. I was
alone with my friend.

Seizing his hand, I began with every demonstration of
courteous sympathy. I do not repeat my words, for my

intention was conveyed more in accent, emphasis, and manner, than speech. I hinted to him that he had another wife living. I suggested that this was balanced—ha !—by his wife's lover. That, possibly, he wished to fly ; hence the letting of his delightful mansion. That he regularly and systematically beat his wife in the English manner, and that she repeatedly deceived him. I talked of hope, of consolation, of remedy. I carelessly produced a bottle of strychnine and a small vial of stramonium from my pocket, and enlarged on the efficiency of drugs. His face, which had gradually become convulsed, suddenly became fixed with a frightful expression. He started to his feet, and roared " You d——d Frenchman ! "

I instantly changed my tactics, and endeavoured to embrace him. He kicked me twice, violently. I begged permission to kiss madame's hand. He replied by throwing me downstairs.

I am in bed with my head bound up, and beaf-steaks upon my eyes, but still confident and buoyant. I have not lost faith in Macchiavelli. Tra la la ! as they sing in the opera. I kiss everybody's hands.

## CHAPTER V.

### DR. DIGGS'S STATEMENT.

My name is David Diggs. I am a surgeon, living at No. 9 Tottenham Court. On the 15th of June 1854, I was called to see an elderly gentleman lodging on the Kent Road. Found him highly excited, with strong febrile symptoms, pulse 120, increasing. Repeated incoherently what I judged to be the popular form of a conundrum. On closer examination found acute hydrocephalus and both lobes of the brain rapidly filling with water. In consultation with an eminent phrenologist, it was further discovered that all the organs were more or less obliterated, except that of Comparison. Hence the patient was enabled to only distinguish the most common points of resemblance between objects, without drawing upon other faculties, such as Ideality or Language, for assistance. Later in the day found him sinking,—being evidently unable to carry the most ordinary conundrum to a successful issue. Exhibited Tinct. Val., Ext. Opii, and Camphor, and prescribed quiet and emollients. On the 17th the patient was missing.

## CHAPTER LAST.

### STATEMENT OF THE PUBLISHER.

On the 18th of June, Mr. Wilkie Collins left a roll of manuscript with us for publication, without title or direction, since which time he has not been heard from. In spite of the care of the proof-readers, and valuable literary assistance, it is feared that the continuity of the story has been destroyed by some accidental misplacing of chapters during its progress. How and what chapters are so misplaced, the publisher leaves to an indulgent public to discover.

# 𝕳𝖆𝖓𝖉𝖘𝖔𝖒𝖊 𝖎𝖘 𝖆𝖘 𝕳𝖆𝖓𝖉𝖘𝖔𝖒𝖊 𝕯𝖔𝖊𝖘.

BY CH—S R—DE.

## CHAPTER I.

THE Dodds were dead. For twenty years they had slept under the green graves of Kittery churchyard. The town folk still spoke of them kindly. The keeper of the alehouse, where David had smoked his pipe, regretted him regularly, and Mistress Kitty, Mrs. Dodd's maid, whose trim figure always looked well in her mistress's gowns, was inconsolable. The Hardins were in America. Raby was aristocratically gouty ; Mrs. Raby, religious. Briefly, then, we have disposed of—

1. Mr. and Mrs. Dodds (dead).

2. Mr. and Mrs. Hardin (translated).

3. Raby, *baron et femme.* (Yet I don't know about the former ; he came of a long-lived family, and the gout is an uncertain disease.)

We have active at the present writing (*place aux dames*)—

1. Lady Caroline Coventry, niece of Sir Frederick.

2. Faraday Huxley Little, son of Henry and Grace Little, deceased.

*Sequitur* to the above, A HERO AND HEROINE.

## CHAPTER II.

ON the death of his parents, Faraday Little was taken to Raby Hall. In accepting his guardianship, Mr. Raby struggled stoutly against two prejudices: Faraday was plain-looking and sceptical.

" Handsome is as handsome does, sweetheart," pleaded Jael, interceding for the orphan with arms that were still beautiful. " Dear knows, it is not his fault if he does not look like—his father," she added with a great gulp. Jael was a woman, and vindicated her womanhood by never en_tirely forgiving a former rival.

" It's not that alone, madam," screamed Raby, " but, d—m it, the little rascal's a scientist,—an atheist, a radical, a scoffer! Disbelieves in the Bible, ma'am; is full of this Darwinian stuff about natural selection and descent. Descent, forsooth ! In my day, madam, gentlemen were content to trace their ancestors back to gentlemen, and not to—monkeys ! "

" Dear heart, the boy is clever," urged Jael.

" Clever ! " roared Raby ; " what does a gentleman want with cleverness ? "

## CHAPTER III.

YOUNG Little *was* clever. At seven he had constructed a telescope ; at nine, a flying-machine. At ten he saved a valuable life.

Norwood Park was the adjacent estate,—a lordly domain dotted with red deer and black trunks, but scrupulously kept with gravelled roads as hard and blue as steel. There

Little was strolling one summer morning, meditating on a new top with concealed springs. At a little distance before him he saw the flutter of lace and ribbons. A young lady, a very young lady,—say of seven summers,—tricked out in the crying abominations of the present fashion, stood beside a low bush. Her nursery-maid was not present, possibly owing to the fact that John the footman was also absent.

Suddenly Little came towards her. " Excuse me, but do you know what those berries are ? " He was pointing to the low bush filled with dark clusters of shining—suspiciously shining—fruit.

" Certainly ; they are blueberries."

" Pardon me ; you are mistaken. They belong to quite another family."

Miss Impudence drew herself up to her full height (exactly three feet nine and a half inches), and, curling an eighth of an inch of scarlet lip, said, scornfully, " *Your* family, perhaps."

Faraday Little smiled in the superiority of boyhood over girlhood.

"I allude to the classification. That plant is the belladonna, or deadly nightshade. Its alkaloid is a narcotic poison."

Sauciness turned pale. " I—have—just—eaten—some !" And began to whimper. "Oh dear, what shall I do?" Then did it, *i.e.*, wrung her small fingers and cried.

" Pardon me one moment." Little passed his arm around her neck, and with his thumb opened widely the patrician-veined lids of her sweet blue eyes. "Thank Heaven, there is yet no dilation of the pupil; it is not too late !" He cast a rapid glance around. The nozzle and about three feet of garden hose lay near him.

" Open your mouth, quick ! "

It was a pretty, kissable mouth. But young Little meant

business.  He put the nozzle down her pink throat as far as it would go.

" Now, don't move."

He wrapped his handkerchief around a hoop-stick. Then he inserted both in the other end of the stiff hose. It fitted snugly.  He shoved it in and then drew it back.

Nature abhors a vacuum.  The young patrician was as amenable to this law as the child of the lowest peasant.

She succumbed.  It was all over in a minute.  Then she burst into a small fury.

"You nasty, bad—*ugly* boy."

Young Little winced, but smiled.

"Stimulants," he whispered to the frightened nursery-maid who approached ; "good evening."   He was gone.

## CHAPTER IV.

THE breach between young Little and Mr. Raby was slowly widening.   Little found objectionable features in the Hall.   " This black oak ceiling and wainscoting is not as healthful as plaster; besides, it absorbs the light.   The bed-room ceiling is too low ; the Elizabethan architects knew nothing of ventilation.   The colour of that oak panelling which you admire is due to an excess of carbon and the exuvia from the pores of your skin "——

"Leave the house," bellowed Raby, " before the roof falls on your sacrilegious head ! "

As Little left the house, Lady Caroline and a handsome boy of about Little's age entered.   Lady Caroline recoiled, and then—blushed.   Little glared ; he instinctively felt the presence of a rival.

## CHAPTER V.

LITTLE worked hard.   He studied night and day.   **In five**
years he became a lecturer, then a professor.

He soared as high as the clouds, he dipped as low as the
cellars of the London poor.   He analysed the London fog,
and found it two parts smoke, one disease, one unmention-
able abominations.   He published a pamphlet, which was
violently attacked.   Then he knew he had done something.

But he had not forgotten Caroline.   He was walking one
day in the Zoological Gardens and he came upon a pretty
picture,—flesh and blood too.

Lady Caroline feeding buns to the bears !   An exquisite
thrill passed through his veins.   She turned her sweet face
and their eyes met.   They recollected their first meeting
seven years before, but it was his turn to be shy and timid.
Wonderful power of age and sex !   She met him with perfect self-possession.

" Well meant, but indigestible I fear " (he alluded to the
buns).

" A clever person like yourself can easily correct that "
(she, the slyboots, was thinking of something else).

In a few moments they were chatting gaily.   Little
eagerly descanted upon the different animals ; she listened
with delicious interest.   An hour glided delightfully away.

After this sunshine, clouds.

To them suddenly entered Mr. Raby and a handsome
young man.   The gentlemen bowed stiffly and looked
vicious,—as they felt.   The lady of this quartette smiled
amiably, as she did not feel.

" Looking at your ancestors, I suppose," said Mr. Raby,
pointing to the monkeys ; "we will not disturb you.   Come.'
And he led Caroline away.

Little was heart-sick. He dared not follow them. But an hour later he saw something which filled his heart with bliss unspeakable.

Lady Caroline, with a divine smile on her face, feeding the monkeys !

## CHAPTER VI.

ENCOURAGED by love, Little worked hard upon his new flying-machine. His labours were lightened by talking of the beloved one with her French maid Thérèse, whom he had discreetly bribed. Mademoiselle Thérèse was venal, like all her class, but in this instance I fear she was not bribed by British gold. Strange as it may seem to the British mind, it was British genius, British eloquence, British thought, that brought her to the feet of this young *savan.*

" I believe," said Lady Caroline, one day, interrupting her maid in a glowing eulogium upon the skill of " M. Leetell,"—" I believe you are in love with this Professor." A quick flush crossed the olive cheek of Thérèse, which Lady Caroline afterward remembered.

The eventful day of trial came. The public were gathered, impatient and scornful as the pig-headed public are apt to be. In the open area a long cylindrical balloon, in shape like a Bologna sausage, swayed above the machine, from which, like some enormous bird caught in a net, it tried to free itself. A heavy rope held it fast to the ground.

Little was waiting for the ballast, when his eye caught Lady Caroline's among the spectators. The glance was appealing. In a moment he was at her side.

" I should like so much to get into the machine," said the arch-hypocrite demurely.

"Are you engaged to marry young Raby," said Little bluntly.

"As you please," she said with a courtesy; "do I take this as a refusal?"

Little was a gentleman. He lifted her and her lapdog into the car.

"How nice! it won't go off?"

"No, the rope is strong, and the ballast is not yet in."

A report like a pistol, a cry from the spectators, a thousand hands stretched to grasp the parted rope, and the balloon darted upward.

Only one hand of that thousand caught the rope,—Little's! But in the same instant the horror-stricken spectators saw him whirled from his feet and borne upward, still clinging to the rope, into space.


## CHAPTER VII.*

LADY CAROLINE fainted. The cold, watery nose of her dog on her cheek brought her to herself. She dared not look over the edge of the car; she dared not look up to the bellowing monster above her, bearing her to death. She threw herself on the bottom of the car, and embraced the only living thing spared her,—the poodle. Then she cried. Then a clear voice came apparently out of the circumambient air—

"May I trouble you to look at the barometer?"

She put her head over the car. Little was hanging at the end of a long rope. She put her head back again.

In another moment he saw her perplexed, blushing face over the edge,—blissful sight.

* The right of dramatisation of this and succeeding chapters is reserved by the writer.

"Oh, please don't think of coming up! Stay there, do!"

Little stayed. Of course she could make nothing out of the barometer, and said so. Little smiled.

"Will you kindly send it down to me?"

But she had no string or cord. Finally she said, "Wait a moment."

Little waited. This time her face did not appear. The barometer came slowly down at the end of—a stay-lace.

The barometer showed a frightful elevation. Little looked up at the valve and said nothing. Presently he heard a sigh. Then a sob. Then, rather sharply—

"Why don't you do something?"

## CHAPTER VIII.

LITTLE came up the rope hand over hand. Lady Caroline crouched in the farther side of the car. Fido, the poodle, whined. "Poor thing," said Lady Caroline, "it's hungry."

"Do you wish to save the dog?" said Little.

"Yes."

"Give me your parasol."

She handed Little a good-sized affair of lace and silk and whalebone. (None of your "sunshades.") Little examined its ribs carefully.

"Give me the dog."

Lady Caroline hurriedly slipped a note under the dog's collar, and passed over her pet.

Little tied the dog to the handle of the parasol and launched them both into space. The next moment they were slowly, but tranquilly, sailing to the earth.

"A parasol and a parachute are distinct, but not different. Be not alarmed, he will get his dinner at some farmhouse."

"Where are we now?"

"That opaque spot you see is London fog. Those twin clouds are North and South America. Jerusalem and Madagascar are those specks to the right."

Lady Caroline moved nearer; she was becoming interested. Then she recalled herself, and said freezingly, "How are we going to descend?"

"By opening the valve."

"Why don't you open it then?"

"BECAUSE THE VALVE-STRING IS BROKEN!"

## CHAPTER IX.

LADY CAROLINE fainted. When she revived it was dark. They were apparently cleaving their way through a solid block of black marble. She moaned and shuddered.

"I wish we had a light."

"I have no lucifers," said Little. "I observe, however, that you wear a necklace of amber. Amber under certain conditions becomes highly electrical. Permit me."

He took the amber necklace and rubbed it briskly. Then he asked her to present her knuckle to the gem. A bright spark was the result. This was repeated for some hours. The light was not brilliant, but it was enough for the purposes of propriety, and satisfied the delicately minded girl.

Suddenly there was a tearing, hissing noise and a smell of gas. Little looked up and turned pale. The balloon, at what I shall call the pointed end of the Bologna sausage, was evidently bursting from increased pressure. The gas was escaping, and already they were beginning to descend. Little was resigned but firm.

"If the silk gives way, then we are lost. Unfortunately I have no rope nor material for binding it."

The woman's instinct had arrived at the same conclusion sooner than the man's reason. But she was hesitating over a detail.

"Will you go down the rope for a moment?" she said, with a sweet smile.

Little went down. Presently she called to him. She held something in her hand,—a wonderful invention of the seventeenth century, improved and perfected in this : a pyramid of sixteen circular hoops of light yet strong steel, attached to each other by cloth bands.

With a cry of joy Little seized them, climbed to the balloon, and fitted the elastic hoops over its conical end. Then he returned to the car.

"We are saved."

Lady Caroline, blushing, gathered her slim but antique drapery against the other end of the car.

## CHAPTER X.

THEY were slowly descending. Presently Lady Caroline distinguished the outlines of Raby Hall. "I think I will get out here," she said.

Little anchored the balloon, and prepared to follow her.

"Not so, my friend," she said, with an arch smile. "We must not be seen together. People might talk. Farewell."

Little sprang again into the balloon and sped away to America. He came down in California, oddly enough in front of Hardin's door, at Dutch Flat. Hardin was just examining a specimen of ore.

"You are a scientist; can you tell me if that is worth anything?" he said, handing it to Little.

Little held it to the light. "It contains ninety per cent of silver."

Hardin embraced him. "Can I do anything for you, and why are you here?"

Little told his story. Hardin asked to see the rope. Then he examined it carefully.

"Ah, this was cut, not broken!"

"With a knife?" asked Little.

"No. Observe both sides are equally indented. It was done with a *scissors!*"

"Just Heaven!" gasped Little. "Thérèse!"


## CHAPTER XI.

LITTLE returned to London. Passing through London one day he met a dog-fancier. "Buy a nice poodle, sir?"

Something in the animal attracted his attention. "Fido!" he gasped.

The dog yelped.

Little bought him. On taking off his collar a piece of paper rustled to the floor. He knew the handwriting and kissed it. It ran—


"TO THE HONOURABLE AUGUSTUS RABY,—I cannot marry you. If I marry any one" (sly puss) "it will be the man who has twice saved my life,—Professor Little.

"CAROLINE COVENTRY."

And she did.

# Lothaw;

OR,

## *THE ADVENTURES OF A YOUNG GENTLEMAN IN SEARCH OF A RELIGION.*

BY MR. BENJAMINS.

## CHAPTER I.

" I REMEMBER him a little boy," said the Duchess. " His mother was a dear friend of mine; you know she was one of my bridesmaids."

" And you have never seen him since, mamma ? " asked the oldest married daughter, who did not look a day older than her mother.

" Never; he was an orphan shortly after. I have often reproached myself, but it is so difficult to see boys."

This simple yet first-class conversation existed in the morning-room of Plusham, where the mistress of the pala-tial mansion sat involved in the sacred privacy of a circle of her married daughters. One dexterously applied golden knitting-needles to the fabrication of a purse of floss silk of the rarest texture, which none who knew the almost fabu-lous wealth of the Duke would believe was ever destined to hold in its silken meshes a less sum than £1,000,000 ; another adorned a slipper exclusively with seed pearls; a third emblazoned a page with rare pigments and the finest quality of gold leaf. Beautiful forms leaned over frames glowing with embroidery, and beautiful frames leaned over forms inlaid with mother-of-pearl. Others, more remote, occasionally burst into melody as they tried the passages of a new and exclusive air given to them in MS. by some titled and devoted friend, for the private use of the aristocracy alone, and absolutely prohibited for publication.

The Duchess, herself the superlative of beauty, wealth, and position, was married to the highest noble in the Three Kingdoms. Those who talked about such matters said that their progeny were exactly like their parents,— a peculiarity of the aristocratic and wealthy. They all looked like brothers and sisters, except their parents, who, such was their purity of blood, the perfection of their manners, and the opulence of their condition, might have been taken for their own children's elder son and daughter. The daughters, with one exception, were all married to the highest nobles in the land. That exception was the Lady Coriander, who, there being no vacancy above a marquis and a rental of £1,000,000, waited. Gathered around the refined and sacred circle of their breakfast-table, with their glittering coronets, which, in filial respect to their father's Tory instincts and their mother's Ritualistic tastes, they always wore on their regal brows, the effect was dazzling as it was refined. It was this peculiarity and their strong family resemblance which led their brother-in-law, the good-humoured St. Addlegourd, to say that, "'Pon my soul, you know, the whole precious mob looked like a ghastly pack of court cards, you know." St. Addlegourd was a radical. Having a rent-roll of £15,000,000, and belonging to one of the oldest families in Britain, he could afford to be.

"Mamma, I've just dropped a pearl," said the Lady Coriander, bending over the Persian hearthrug.

"From your lips, sweet friend," said Lothaw, who came of age and entered the room at the same moment.

"No, from my work. It was a very valuable pearl, mamma; papa gave Isaacs and Sons £50,000 for the two."

"Ah, indeed," said the Duchess, languidly rising; "let us go to luncheon."

"But, your Grace," interposed Lothaw, who was still quite young, and had dropped on all-fours on the carpet in search of the missing gem, "consider the value"——

"Dear friend," interposed the Duchess, with infinite tact, gently lifting him by the tails of his dress-coat, "I am waiting for your arm."

## CHAPTER II.

LOTHAW was immensely rich. The possessor of seventeen castles, fifteen villas, nine shooting-boxes, and seven town houses, he had other estates of which he had not even heard.

Everybody at Plusham played croquet, and none badly. Next to their purity of blood and great wealth, the family were famous for this accomplishment. Yet Lothaw soon tired of the game, and after seriously damaging his aristo-cratically large foot in an attempt to "tight croquet" the Lady Aniseed's ball, he limped away to join the Duchess.

"I'm going to the hennery," she said.

"Let me go with you, I dearly love fowls—broiled," he added thoughtfully.

"The Duke gave Lady Montairy some large Cochins the other day," continued the Duchess, changing the subject with delicate tact.

> "Lady Montairy
> Quite contrary,
> How do your Cochins grow?"

sang Lothaw gaily.

The Duchess looked shocked. After a prolonged silence Lothaw abruptly and gravely said—

"If you please, ma'am, when I come into my property I should like to build some improved dwellings for the poor, and marry Lady Coriander."

"You amaze me, dear friend, and yet both your aspirations are noble and eminently proper," said the Duchess; "Coriander is but a child,—and yet," she added, looking graciously upon her companion, "for the matter of that, so are you."

## CHAPTER III.

MR. PUTNEY GILES'S was Lothaw's first grand dinner-party. Yet, by carefully watching the others, he managed to acquit himself creditably, and avoided drinking out of the finger-bowl by first secretly testing its contents with a spoon. The conversation was peculiar and singularly interesting.

"Then you think that monogamy is simply a question of the thermometer?" said Mrs. Putney Giles to her companion.

"I certainly think that polygamy should be limited by isothermal lines," replied Lothaw.

"I should say it was a matter of latitude," observed a loud talkative man opposite. He was an Oxford Professor with a taste for satire, and had made himself very obnoxious to the company, during dinner, by speaking disparagingly of a former well-known Chancellor of the Exchequer,—a great statesman and brilliant novelist,—whom he feared and hated.

Suddenly there was a sensation in the room; among the females it absolutely amounted to a nervous thrill. His Eminence, the Cardinal, was announced. He entered with great suavity of manner, and after shaking hands with everybody, asking after their relatives, and chucking the more delicate females under the chin with a high-bred grace peculiar to his profession, he sat down, saying, "And how do we all find ourselves this evening, my dears?" in several different languages, which he spoke fluently.

Lothaw's heart was touched. His deeply religious convictions were impressed. He instantly went up to this gifted being, confessed, and received absolution. "To-morrow," he said to himself, "I will partake of the communion, and endow the Church with my vast estates. For the present I'll let the improved cottages go."

## CHAPTER IV.

As Lothaw turned to leave the Cardinal, he was struck by a beautiful face. It was that of a matron, slim but shapely as an Ionic column. Her face was Grecian, with Corinthian temples; Hellenic eyes that looked from jutting eyebrows, like dormer-windows in an Attic forehead, completed her perfect Athenian outline. She wore a black frock-coat tightly buttoned over her bloomer trousers, and a standing collar.

"Your lordship is struck by that face," said a social parasite.

"I am; who is she?"

"Her name is Mary Ann. She is married to an American, and has lately invented a new religion."

"Ah!" said Lothaw eagerly, with difficulty restraining himself from rushing toward her.

"Yes; shall I introduce you?"

Lothaw thought of Lady Coriander's High Church proclivities, of the Cardinal, and hesitated: "No, I thank you, not now."

## CHAPTER V.

LOTHAW was maturing. He had attended two womans' rights conventions, three Fenian meetings, had dined at White's, and had danced *vis-à-vis* to a prince of the blood, and eaten off gold plates at Crecy House.

His stables were near Oxford, and occupied more ground than the University. He was driving over there one day, when he perceived some rustics and menials endeavouring to stop a pair of runaway horses attached to a carriage in which a lady and gentleman were seated. Calmly awaiting the termination of the accident, with high-bred courtesy Lothaw forebode to interfere until the carriage was overturned, the occupants thrown out, and the runaways secured by the servants, when he advanced and offered the lady the exclusive use of his Oxford stables.

Turning upon him a face whose perfect Hellenic details he remembered, she slowly dragged a gentleman from under the wheels into the light and presented him with ladylike dignity as her husband, Major-General Camperdown, an American.

"Ah," said Lothaw carelessly, "I believe I have some land there. If I mistake not, my agent, Mr. Putney Giles, lately purchased the State of—Illinois—I think you call it."

"Exactly. As a former resident of the city of Chicago, let me introduce myself as your tenant."

Lothaw bowed graciously to the gentleman, who, except that he seemed better dressed than most Englishmen, showed no other signs of inferiority and plebeian extraction.

"We have met before," said Lothaw to the lady as she

leaned on his arm, while they visited his stables, the University, and other places of interest in Oxford. "Pray tell me, what is this new religion of yours?"

"It is Woman Suffrage, Free Love, Mutual Affinity, and Communism. Embrace it and me."

Lothaw did not know exactly what to do. She, however, soothed and sustained his agitated frame and sealed with an embrace his speechless form. The General approached and coughed slightly with gentlemanly tact.

"My husband will be too happy to talk with you further on this subject," she said with quiet dignity, as she regained the General's side. "Come with us to Oneida. Brook Farm is a thing of the past."

## CHAPTER VI.

As Lothaw drove toward his country-seat, "The Mural Enclosure," he observed a crowd, apparently of the working class, gathered around a singular-looking man in the picturesque garb of an Ethiopian serenader. "What does he say?" inquired Lothaw of his driver.

The man touched his hat respectfully and said, "My Mary Ann."

"'My Mary Ann!'" Lothaw's heart beat rapidly. Who was this mysterious foreigner? He had heard from Lady Coriander of a certain Popish plot; but could he connect Mr. Camperdown with it?

The spectacle of two hundred men at arms who advanced to meet him at the gates of "The Mural Enclosure" drove all else from the still youthful and impressible mind of Lothaw. Immediately behind them, on the steps of the baronial halls, were ranged his retainers, led by the chief cook and bottle-washer, and head crumb-remover. On either side were two

companies of laundry-maids, preceded by the chief crimper
and fluter, supporting a long Ancestral Line, on which
depended the family linen, and under which the youthful
lord of the manor passed into the halls of his fathers.
Twenty-four scullions carried the massive gold and silver
plate of the family on their shoulders, and deposited it at
the feet of their master. The spoons were then solemnly
counted by the steward, and the perfect ceremony ended.

Lothaw sighed. He sought out the gorgeously gilded
"Taj," or sacred mausoleum erected to his grandfather in
the second story front room, and wept over the man he did
not know. He wandered alone in his magnificent park,
and then, throwing himself on a grassy bank, pondered on
the Great First Cause, and the necessity of religion. " I
will send Mary Ann a handsome present," said Lothaw
thoughtfully.

## CHAPTER VII.

" Each of these pearls, my lord, is worth fifty thousand
guineas," said Mr. Amethyst, the fashionable jeweller, as he
lightly lifted a large shovelful from a convenient bin behind
his counter.

"Indeed," said Lothaw carelessly, " I should prefer' to
see some expensive ones."

"Some number sixes, I suppose," said Mr. Amethyst,
taking a couple from the apex of a small pyramid that lay
piled on the shelf. " These are about the size of the
Duchess of Billingsgate's, but they are in finer condition.
The fact is, her Grace permits her two children, the Mar
quis of Smithfield and the Duke of St. Giles,—two sweet
pretty boys, my lord,—to use them as marbles in their
games. Pearls require some attention, and I go down there

regularly twice a week to clean them. Perhaps your lord-ship would like some ropes of pearls?"

"About half a cable's length," said Lothaw shortly, "and send them to my lodgings."

Mr. Amethyst became thoughtful. "I am afraid I have not the exact number—that is—excuse me one moment. I will run over to the Tower and borrow a few from the crown jewels." And before Lothaw could prevent him, he seized his hat and left Lothaw alone.

His position certainly was embarrassing. He could not move without stepping on costly gems which had rolled from the counter; the rarest diamonds lay scattered on the shelves; untold fortunes in priceless emeralds lay within his grasp. Although such was the aristocratic purity of his blood and the strength of his religious convictions that he probably would not have pocketed a single diamond, still he could not help thinking that he might be accused of taking some. "You can search me, if you like," he said when Mr. Amethyst returned; "but I assure you, upon the honour of a gentleman, that I have taken nothing."

"Enough, my lord," said Mr. Amethyst, with a low bow; "we never search the aristocracy."

## CHAPTER VIII.

As Lothaw left Mr. Amethyst's, he ran against General Camperdown. "How is Mary Ann?" he asked hurriedly.

"I regret to state that she is dying," said the General, with a grave voice, as he removed his cigar from his lips, and lifted his hat to Lothaw.

"Dying!" said Lothaw incredulously.

"Alas, too true!" replied the General. "The engage-ments of a long lecturing season, exposure in travelling by railway during the winter, and the imperfect nourishment afforded by the refreshments along the road, have told on her delicate frame. But she wants to see you before she dies. Here is the key of my lodging. I will finish my cigar out here."

Lothaw hardly recognised those wasted Hellenic outlines as he entered the dimly lighted room of the dying woman. She was already a classic ruin,—as wrecked and yet as perfect as the Parthenon. He grasped her hand silently.

"Open-air speaking twice a week, and saleratus bread in the rural districts, have brought me to this," she said feebly; "but it is well. The cause progresses. The tyrant man succumbs."

Lothaw could only press her hand.

"Promise me one thing. Don't—whatever you do—become a Catholic."

"Why?"

"The Church does not recognise divorce. And now embrace me. I would prefer at this supreme moment to introduce myself to the next world through the medium of the best society in this. Good-bye. When I am dead, be good enough to inform my husband of the fact."

## CHAPTER IX.

LOTHAW spent the next six months on an Aryan island, in an Aryan climate, and with an Aryan race.

"This is an Aryan landscape," said his host, "and that is a Mary Ann statue." It was, in fact, a full-length figure in marble of Mrs. General Camperdown!

"If you please, I should like to become a Pagan," said Lothaw, one day, after listening to an impassioned discourse on Greek art from the lips of his host.

But that night, on consulting a well-known spiritual medium, Lothaw received a message from the late Mrs. General Camperdown, advising him to return to England. Two days later he presented himself at Plusham.

"The young ladies are in the garden," said the Duchess. "Don't you want to go and pick a rose?" she added with a gracious smile, and the nearest approach to a wink that was consistent with her patrician bearing and aquiline nose.

Lothaw went and presently returned with the blushing Coriander upon his arm.

"Bless you, my children," said the Duchess. Then turning to Lothaw, she said: "You have simply fulfilled and accepted your inevitable destiny. It was morally impossible for you to marry out of this family. For the present, the Church of England is safe."

# The Haunted Man.

*A CHRISTMAS STORY.*

BY CH—R—S D—CK—N—S.

## PART I.

### THE FIRST PHANTOM.

DON'T tell me that it wasn't a knocker. I had seen it often enough, and I ought to know. So ought the three-o'clock beer, in dirty high-lows, swinging himself over the railing, or executing a demoniacal jig upon the doorstep; so ought the butcher, although butchers as a general thing are scornful of such trifles; so ought the postman, to whom knockers of the most extravagant description were merely human weaknesses, that were to be pitied and used. And so ought, for the matter of that, &c., &c., &c.

But then it was *such* a knocker. A wild, extravagant, and utterly incomprehensible knocker. A knocker so mysterious and suspicious that Policeman X 37, first coming upon it, felt inclined to take it instantly in custody, but compromised with his professional instincts by sharply and sternly noting it with an eye that admitted of no nonsense, but confidently expected to detect its secret yet. An ugly knocker; a knocker with a hard, human face, that was a type of the harder human face within. A human face that held between its teeth a brazen rod. So hereafter, in the mysterious future should be held, &c., &c.

But if the knocker had a fierce human aspect in the glare of day, you should have seen it at night, when it peered out of the gathering shadows and suggested an ambushed figure; when the light of the street lamps fell upon it, and wrought a play of sinister expression in its hard outlines; when it seemed to wink meaningly at a shrouded figure who, as the night fell darkly, crept up the steps and passed into the mysterious house; when the swinging door disclosed a black passage into which the figure seemed to lose itself and become a part of the mysterious gloom; when the night grew boisterous and the fierce wind made furious charges at the knocker, as if to wrench it off and carry it away in triumph. Such a night as this.

It was a wild and pitiless wind. A wind that had commenced life as a gentle country zephyr, but wandering through manufacturing towns had become demoralised, and reaching the city had plunged into extravagant dissipation and wild excesses. A roistering wind that indulged in Bacchanalian shouts on the street corners, that knocked off the hats from the heads of helpless passengers, and then fulfilled its duties by speeding away, like all young prodigals, —to sea.

He sat alone in a gloomy library listening to the wind that roared in the chimney. Around him novels and story-books were strewn thickly; in his lap he held one with its pages freshly cut, and turned the leaves wearily until his eyes rested upon a portrait in its frontispiece. And as the wind howled the more fiercely, and the darkness without fell blacker, a strange and fateful likeness to that portrait appeared above his chair and leaned upon his shoulder. The Haunted Man gazed at the portrait and sighed. The figure gazed at the portrait and sighed too.

"Here again?" said the Haunted Man.

" Here again," it repeated in a low voice.

" Another novel ? "

" Another novel."

" The old story ? "

" The old story."

" I see a child," said the Haunted Man, gazing from the pages of the book into the fire,—" a most unnatural child, a model infant. It is prematurely old and philosophic. It dies in poverty to slow music. It dies surrounded by luxury to slow music. It dies with an accompaniment of golden water and rattling carts to slow music. Previous to its decease it makes a will; it repeats the Lord's Prayer, it kisses the ' boofer lady.' That child "——

" Is mine," said the phantom.

" I see a good woman, undersized. I see several charming women, but they are all undersized. They are more or less imbecile and idiotic, but always fascinating and undersized. They wear coquettish caps and aprons. I observe that feminine virtue is invariably below the medium height, and that it is always simple and infantine. These women "——

" Are mine."

" I see a haughty, proud, and wicked lady. She is tall and queenly. I remark that all proud and wicked women are tall and queenly. That woman "——

" Is mine," said the phantom, wringing his hands.

" I see several things continually impending. I observe that whenever an accident, a murder, or death is about to happen, there is something in the furniture, in the locality, in the atmosphere, that foreshadows and suggests it years in advance. I cannot say that in real life I have noticed it,—the perception of this surprising fact belongs "——

" To me ! " said the phantom. The Haunted Man continued, in a despairing tone—

" I see the influence of this in the magazines and daily

papers; I see weak imitators rise up and enfeeble the world with senseless formula. I am getting tired of it. It won't do, Charles! it won't do!" and the Haunted Man buried his head in his hands and groaned. The figure looked down upon him sternly: the portrait in the frontispiece frowned as he gazed.

"Wretched man," said the phantom, "and how have these things affected you?"

"Once I laughed and cried, but then I was younger. Now, I would forget them if I could."

"Have then your wish. And take this with you, man whom I renounce. From this day henceforth you shall live with those whom I displace. Without forgetting me, 'twill be your lot to walk through life as if we had not met. But first you shall survey these scenes that henceforth must be yours. At one to-night, prepare to meet the phantom I have raised. Farewell!"

The sound of its voice seemed to fade away with the dying wind, and the Haunted Man was alone. But the firelight flickered gaily, and the light danced on the walls, making grotesque figures of the furniture.

"Ha, ha!" said the Haunted Man, rubbing his hands gleefully; "now for a whisky punch and a cigar."


## PART II.

### THE SECOND PHANTOM.

ONE! The stroke of the far-off bell had hardly died before the front door closed with a reverberating clang. Steps were heard along the passage; the library door swung open of itself, and the Knocker—yes, the Knocker—slowly strode into the room. The Haunted Man rubbed his eyes,—no! there could be no mistake about it,—it was the Knocker's face, mounted on a misty, almost imperceptible body. The brazen rod was transferred from its mouth to its right hand, where it was held like a ghostly truncheon.

"It's a cold evening," said the Haunted Man.

"It is," said the Goblin, in a hard, metallic voice.

"It must be pretty cold out there," said the Haunted Man, with vague politeness. "Do you ever—will you—take some hot water and brandy?"

"No," said the Goblin.

"Perhaps you'd like it cold, by way of change?" continued the Haunted Man, correcting himself, as he remembered the peculiar temperature with which the Goblin was probably familiar.

"Time flies," said the Goblin coldly. "We have no leisure for idle talk. Come!" He moved his ghostly truncheon toward the window, and laid his hand upon the other's arm. At his touch the body of the Haunted Man seemed to become as thin and incorporeal as that of the Goblin himself, and together they glided out of the window into the black and blowy night.

In the rapidity of their flight the senses of the Haunted Man seemed to leave him. At length they stopped suddenly.

"What do you see?" asked the Goblin.

"I see a battlemented mediæval castle. Gallant men in mail ride over the drawbridge, and kiss their gauntleted fingers to fair ladies, who wave their lily hands in return. I see fight and fray and tournament. I hear roaring heralds bawling the charms of delicate women, and shamelessly proclaiming their lovers. Stay. I see a Jewess about to leap from a battlement. I see knightly deeds, violence, rapine, and a good deal of blood. I've seen pretty much the same at Astley's."

"Look again."

" I see purple moors, glens, masculine women, bare-legged
men, priggish book-worms, more violence, physical excellence, and blood. Always blood,—and the superiority of
physical attainments."

" And how do you feel now?" said the Goblin.

The Haunted Man shrugged his shoulders. " None the
better for being carried back and asked to sympathise with
a barbarous age."

The Goblin smiled and clutched his arm; they again
sped rapidly away through the black night and again halted.

" What do you see?" said the Goblin.

" I see a barrack room, with a mess table, and a group
of intoxicated Celtic officers telling funny stories, and giving
challenges to duel. I see a young Irish gentleman capable
of performing prodigies of valour. I learn incidentally that
the acme of all heroism is the cornetcy of a dragoon regiment. I hear a good deal of French ! No, thank you,"
said the Haunted Man hurriedly, as he stayed the waving
hand of the Goblin ; " I would rather *not* go to the Peninsula,
and don't care to have a private interview with Napoleon."

Again the Goblin flew away with the unfortunate man,
and from a strange roaring below them he judged they were
above the ocean. A ship hove in sight, and the Goblin
stayed its flight. " Look," he said, squeezing his companion's arm.

The Haunted Man yawned. " Don't you think, Charles,
you're rather running this thing into the ground? Of
course it's very moral and instructive, and all that. But
ain't there a little too much pantomime about it ? Come
now ! "

" Look ! " repeated the Goblin, pinching his arm malevolently. The Haunted Man groaned.

" Oh, of course, I see her Majesty's ship Arethusa. Of
course I am familiar with her stern First Lieutenant, her

eccentric Captain, her one fascinating and several mischievous midshipmen. Of course I know it's a splendid thing to see all this, and not to be seasick. Oh, there the young gentlemen are going to play a trick on the purser. For God's sake, let us go," and the unhappy man absolutely dragged the Goblin away with him.

When they next halted, it was at the edge of a broad and boundless prairie, in the middle of an oak opening.

"I see," said the Haunted Man, without waiting for his cue, but mechanically, and as if he were repeating a lesson which the Goblin had taught him,—"I see the Noble Savage. He is very fine to look at! But I observe under his war-paint, feathers, and picturesque blanket, dirt, disease, and an unsymmetrical contour. I observe beneath his inflated rhetoric deceit and hypocrisy; beneath his physical hardihood, cruelty, malice, and revenge. The Noble Savage is a humbug. I remarked the same to Mr. Catlin."

"Come," said the phantom.

The Haunted Man sighed, and took out his watch. "Couldn't we do the rest of this another time?"

"My hour is almost spent, irreverent being, but there is yet a chance for your reformation. Come!"

Again they sped through the night, and again halted. The sound of delicious but melancholy music fell upon their ears.

"I see," said the Haunted Man, with something of interest in his manner,—"I see an old moss-covered manse beside a sluggish, flowing river. I see weird shapes : witches, Puritans, clergymen, little children, judges, mesmerised maidens, moving to the sound of melody that thrills me with its sweetness and purity. But, although carried along its calm and evenly flowing current, the shapes are strange and frightful : an eating lichen gnaws at the heart of each. Not only the clergymen, but witch, maiden, judge, and Puritan, all wear Scarlet Letters of some kind burned upon their hearts. I am fascinated and thrilled, but I feel a morbid sensitiveness creeping over me. I—I beg your pardon." The Goblin was yawning frightfully. "Well, perhaps we had better go."

"One more, and the last," said the Goblin.

They were moving home. Streaks of red were beginning to appear in the eastern sky. Along the banks of the blackly flowing river by moorland and stagnant fens, by low houses, clustering close to the water's edge, like strange mollusks crawled upon the beach to dry; by misty black barges, the more misty and indistinct seen through its mysterious veil the river fog was slowly rising. So rolled away and rose from the heart of the Haunted Man, &c., &c.

They stopped before a quaint mansion of red brick. The Goblin waved his hand without speaking.

"I see," said the Haunted Man, "a gay drawing-room. I see my old friends of the club, of the college, of society, even as they lived and moved. I see the gallant and unselfish men, whom I have loved, and the snobs whom I have hated. I see strangely mingling with them, and now and then blending with their forms, our old friends Dick Steele, Addison, and Congreve. I observe, though, that these gentlemen have a habit of getting too much in the way. The royal standard of Queen Anne, not in itself a beautiful ornament, is rather too prominent in the picture. The long galleries of black oak, the formal furniture, the old portraits, are picturesque, but depressing. The house is damp. I enjoy myself better here on the lawn, where they are getting up a Vanity Fair. See, the bell rings, the curtain is rising, the puppets are brought out for a new play. Let me see."

The Haunted Man was pressing forward in his eagerness, but the hand of the Goblin stayed him, and pointing
to his feet he saw, between him and the rising curtain, a
new-made grave. And bending above the grave in passionate grief, the Haunted Man beheld the phantom of
the previous night.

.    .    .    .    .

The Haunted Man started, and—woke. The bright
sunshine streamed into the room. The air was sparkling
with frost. He ran joyously to the window and opened it.
A small boy saluted him with "Merry Christmas." The
Haunted Man instantly gave him a Bank of England note.
"How much like Tiny Tim, Tom, and Bobby that boy
looked,—bless my soul, what a genius this Dickens has !"

A knock at the door, and Boots entered.

"Consider your salary doubled instantly. Have you
read ' David Copperfield ? '"

" Yezzur."

" Your salary is quadrupled. What do you think of the
' Old Curiosity Shop ? '"

The man instantly burst into a torrent of tears, and then
into a roar of laughter.

" Enough ! Here are five thousand pounds. Open a
porter-house, and call it ' Our Mutual Friend.' Huzza !
I feel so happy !" And the Haunted Man danced about
the room.

And so, bathed in the light of that blessed sun, and yet
glowing with the warmth of a good action, the Haunted
Man, haunted no longer, save by those shapes which make
the dreams of children beautiful, reseated himself in his
chair, and finished "Our Mutual Friend."

# The Hoodlum Band;

OR,

## *THE BOY CHIEF, THE INFANT POLITICIAN, AND THE PIRATE PRODIGY.*

## CHAPTER I.

IT was a quiet New England village. Nowhere in the valley of the Connecticut the autumn sun shone upon a more peaceful, pastoral, manufacturing community. The wooden nutmegs were slowly ripening on the trees, and the white-pine hams for Western consumption were gradually rounding into form under the deft manipulation of the hardy American artisan. The honest Connecticut farmer was quietly gathering from his threshing-floor the shoe-pegs, which, when intermixed with a fair proportion of oats, offered a pleasing substitute for fodder to the effete civilisations of Europe. An almost Sabbath-like stillness prevailed. Doemville was only seven miles from Hartford, and the surrounding landscape smiled with the conviction of being fully insured.

Few would have thought that this peaceful village was the home of the three young heroes whose exploits would hereafter—but we anticipate.

Doemville Academy was the principal seat of learning in the county. Under the grave and gentle administration of

the venerable Doctor Context, it had attained just popu-
larity. Yet the increasing infirmities of age obliged the
doctor to relinquish much of his trust to his assistants, who,
it is needless to say, abused his confidence. Before long
their brutal tyranny and deep laid malevolence became
apparent. Boys were absolutely forced to study their
lessons. The sickening fact will hardly be believed, but
during school-hours they were obliged to remain in their
seats with the appearance, at least, of discipline. It is
stated by good authority that the rolling of croquet balls
across the floor during recitation was objected to, under
the fiendish excuse of its interfering with their studies.
The breaking of windows by base-balls, and the beating of
small scholars with bats, was declared against. At last,
bloated and arrogant with success, the under-teachers threw
aside all disguise, and revealed themselves in their true
colours. A cigar was actually taken out of a day-scholar's
mouth during prayers! A flask of whisky was dragged
from another's desk, and then thrown out of the window.
And finally, Profanity, Hazing, Theft, and Lying were
almost discouraged.

Could the youth of America, conscious of their power,
and a literature of their own, tamely submit to this
tyranny? Never! We repeat it firmly. Never! We
repeat it to parents and guardians. Never! But the
fiendish tutors, chuckling in their glee, little knew what
was passing through the cold, haughty intellect of Charles
Francis Adams Golightly, aged ten; what curled the lip of
Benjamin Franklin Jenkins, aged seven; or what shone in
the bold, blue eyes of Bromley Chitterlings, aged six and
a half, as they sat in the corner of the playground at recess.
Their only other companion and confidant was the negro
porter and janitor of the school, known as "Pirate Jim."

Fitly, indeed, was he named, as the secrets of his early

wild career—confessed freely to his noble young friends—
plainly showed. A slaver at the age of seventeen, the
ringleader of a mutiny on the African coast at the age of
twenty, a privateersman during the last war with England,
the commander of a fire-ship and its sole survivor at twenty-
five, with a wild, intermediate career of unmixed piracy,
until the Rebellion called him to Civil Service again as a
blockade runner, and peace and a desire for rural repose
led him to seek the janitorship of the Doemville Academy,
where no questions were asked and references not exchanged—he was, indeed, a fit mentor for our daring youth.
Although a man whose days had exceeded the usual space
allotted to humanity, the various episodes of his career footing his age up to nearly one hundred and fifty-nine years,
he scarcely looked it, and was still hale and vigorous.

"Yes," continued Pirate Jim critically; "I don't think
he was any bigger nor you, Master Chitterlings, if as big,
when he stood on the fork'stle of my ship and shot the
captain o' that East Injyman dead. We used to call him
little Weevils, he was so young-like. But, bless your
hearts, boys! he wa'n't anything to Little Sammy Barlow,
ez once crep' up inter the captain's state-room on a
Rooshin frigate, stabbed him to the heart with a jack-knife,
then put on the captain's uniform and his cocked hat, took
command of the ship, and fout her hisself."

"Wasn't the captain's clothes big for him?" asked B.
Franklin Jenkins anxiously.

The janitor eyed young Jenkins with pained dignity.

"Didn't I say the Rooshin captain was a small, a very
small, man? Rooshins is small, likewise Greeks."

A noble enthusiasm beamed in the faces of the youthful
heroes.

"Was Barlow as large as me?" asked C. F. Adams
Golightly, lifting his curls from his Jove-like brow.

"Yes; but, then, he hed hed, so to speak, experiences. It was allowed that he had pizened his schoolmaster afore he went to sea. But it's dry talking, boys."

Golightly drew a flask from his jacket and handed it to the janitor. It was his father's best brandy. The heart of the honest old seaman was touched.

"Bless ye, my own pirate boy!" he said, in a voice suffocating with emotion.

"I've got some tobacco," said the youthful Jenkins, "but it's fine cut; I use only that now."

"I kin buy some plug at the corner grocery," said Pirate Jim, "only I left my portmoney at home."

"Take this watch," said young Golightly; "'tis my father's. Since he became a tyrant and usurper, and forced me to join a corsair's band, I've begun by dividing the property."

"This is idle trifling," said young Chitterlings wildly. "Every moment is precious. Is this an hour to give to wine and wassail? Ha, we want action—action! We must strike the blow for freedom to-night—ay, this very night. The scow is already anchored in the mill-dam freighted with provisions for a three months' voyage. I have a black flag in my pocket. Why, then, this cowardly delay?"

The two elder youths turned with a slight feeling of awe and shame to gaze on the glowing cheeks, and high, haughty crest of their youngest comrade—the bright, the beautiful Bromley Chitterlings. Alas! that very moment of forgetfulness and mutual admiration was fraught with danger. A thin, dyspeptic, half-starved tutor approached.

"It is time to resume your studies, young gentlemen," he said, with fiendish politeness.

They were his last words on earth.

"Down, Tyrant!" screamed Chitterlings.

"Sic him—I mean *sic semper tyrannis!*" said the classical Golightly.

A heavy blow on the head from a base-ball bat, and the rapid projection of a base-ball against his empty stomach, brought the tutor a limp and lifeless mass to the ground. Golightly shuddered. Let not my young readers blame him too rashly. It was his first homicide.

"Search his pockets," said the practical Jenkins.

They did so, and found nothing but a Harvard Triennial Catalogue.

"Let us fly," said Jenkins

"Forward to the boats!" cried the enthusiastic Chitterlings.

But C. F. Adams Golightly stood gazing thoughtfully at the prostrate tutor.

"This," he said calmly, "is the result of a too free government and the common-school system. What the country needs is reform. I cannot go with you, boys."

"Traitor!" screamed the others.

C. F. A. Golightly smiled sadly.

"You know me not. I shall not become a pirate—but a Congressman!"

Jenkins and Chitterlings turned pale.

"I have already organised two caucuses in a base-ball club, and bribed the delegates of another. Nay, turn not away. Let us be friends, pursuing through various ways one common end. Farewell!" They shook hands.

"But where is Pirate Jim?" asked Jenkins.

"He left us but for a moment to raise money on the watch to purchase armament for the scow. Farewell!"

And so the gallant, youthful spirits parted, bright with the sunrise of hope.

That night a conflagration raged in Doemville. The Doemville Academy, mysteriously fired, first fell a victim to the devouring element. The candy shop and cigar store, both holding heavy liabilities against the academy, quickly followed. By the lurid gleams of the flames, a long, low, sloop-rigged scow, with every mast gone except one, slowly worked her way out of the mill-dam towards the Sound. The next day three boys were missing—C. F. Adams Golightly, B. F. Jenkins, and Bromley Chitterlings. Had they perished in the flames? Who shall say? Enough that never more under these names did they again appear in the homes of their ancestors.

Happy, indeed, would it have been for Doemville had the mystery ended here. But a darker interest and scandal rested upon the peaceful village. During that awful night the boarding-school of Madame Brimborion was visited stealthily, and two of the fairest heiresses of Connecticut— daughters of the president of a savings bank and insurance director—were the next morning found to have eloped. With them also disappeared the entire contents of the Savings Bank, and on the following day the Flamingo Fire Insurance Company failed.

## CHAPTER II.

LET my young readers now sail with me to warmer and more hospitable climes. Off the coast of Patagonia a long, low, black schooner proudly rides the seas, that break softly upon the vine-clad shores of that luxuriant land. Who is this that, wrapped in Persian rugs, and dressed in the most expensive manner, calmly reclines on the quarter-deck of the schooner, toying lightly ever and anon with the luscious fruits of the vicinity, held in baskets of solid gold by Nubian slaves? or at intervals, with daring grace, guides an ebony velocipede over the polished black walnut decks, and in and out the intricacies of the rigging? Who is it?

well may be asked. What name is it that blanches with
terror the cheeks of the Patagonian navy? Who but the
Pirate Prodigy—the relentless Boy Scourer of Patagonian
seas? Voyagers slowly drifting by the Silurian beach,
coasters along the Devonian shore, still shudder at the
name of Bromley Chitterlings—the Boy Avenger, late of
Hartford, Connecticut.

It has been often asked by the idly curious, Why,
Avenger, and of what? Let us not seek to disclose the
awful secret hidden under that youthful jacket. Enough
that there may have been that of bitterness in his past life
that they

"Whose soul would sicken o'er the heaving wave,"

or "whose soul would heave above the sickening wave,"
did not understand. Only one knew him, perhaps too
well—a queen of the Amazons taken prisoner off Terra del
Fuego a week previous. She loved the Boy Avenger.
But in vain; his youthful heart seemed obdurate.

"Hear me," at last, he said, when she had for the
seventh time wildly proffered her hand and her kingdom in
marriage, "and know once and for ever why I must decline
your flattering proposal. I love another."

With a wild, despairing cry she leaped into the sea, but
was instantly rescued by the Pirate Prodigy. Yet, even in
that supreme moment, such was his coolness, that on his
way to the surface he captured a mermaid, and placing her
in charge of his steward, with directions to give her a state-
room, with hot and cold water, calmly resumed his place
by the Amazon's side. When the cabin door closed on his
faithful servant, bringing champagne and ices to the
interesting stranger, Chitterlings resumed his narrative with
a choking voice—

"When I first fled from the roof of a tyrannical parent

I loved the beautiful and accomplished Eliza J. Sniffen. Her father was president of the Working-men's Savings' Bank, and it was perfectly understood that in the course of time the entire deposits would be his. But, like a vain fool, I wished to anticipate the future, and in a wild moment persuaded Miss Sniffen to elope with me; and with the entire cash assets of the bank, we fled together." He paused, overcome with emotion. " But fate decreed it otherwise. In my feverish haste, I had forgotten to place among the stores of my pirate craft that peculiar kind of chocolate caromel to which Eliza Jane was most partial. We were obliged to put into New Rochelle on the second day out, to enable Miss Sniffen to procure that delicacy at the nearest confectioner's, and match some zephyr worsteds at the first fancy shop. Fatal mistake. She went—she never returned !" In a moment he resumed, in a choking voice, " After a week's weary waiting, I was obliged to put to sea again, bearing a broken heart and the broken bank of her father. I have never seen her since."

"And you still love her?" asked the Amazon queen excitedly.

"Ay, for ever !"

"Noble youth. Here, take the reward of thy fidelity, for know, Bromley Chitterlings, that I am Eliza Jane. Wearied with waiting, I embarked on a Peruvian Guano ship—but it's a long story, dear."

"And altogether too thin," said the Boy Avenger, fiercely releasing himself from her encircling arms. "Eliza Jane's age, a year ago, was only thirteen, and you are forty, if a day."

"True," she returned sadly, "but I have suffered much, and time passes rapidly, and I've grown. You would scarcely believe that this is my own hair."

"I know not," he replied, in gloomy abstraction.

"Forgive my deceit," she returned.   "If you are affianced to another, let me at least be—a mother to you."

The Pirate Prodigy started, and tears came to his eyes. The scene was affecting in the extreme.  Several of the oldest seamen—men who had gone through scenes of suffering with tearless eyes and unblanched cheeks—now retired to the spirit room to conceal their emotion.  A few went into caucus in the forecastle, and returned with the request that the Amazonian queen should hereafter be known as the "Queen of the Pirates' Isle."

"Mother!" gasped the Pirate Prodigy.

"My son!" screamed the Amazonian queen.

They embraced.  At the same moment a loud flop was heard on the quarter-deck.  It was the forgotten mermaid, who, emerging from her state-room, and ascending the companion-way at that moment, had fainted at the spectacle.  The Pirate Prodigy rushed to her side with a bottle of smelling-salts.

She recovered slowly.  "Permit me," she said, rising with dignity, "to leave the ship.  I am unaccustomed to such conduct."

"Hear me—she is my mother!"

"She certainly is old enough to be," replied the mermaid; "and to speak of that being her own hair," she said, as she rearranged with characteristic grace, a comb, and a small hand-mirror, her own luxuriant tresses.

"If I couldn't afford any other clothes, I might wear a switch, too!" hissed the Amazonian queen.  "I suppose you don't dye it on account of the salt water?  But perhaps you prefer green, dear?"

"A little salt water might improve your own complexion, love."

"Fishwoman!" screamed the Amazonian queen.

"Bloomerite!" shrieked the mermaid.

In another instant they had seized each other.

"Mutiny! Overboard with them!" cried the Pirate Prodigy, rising to the occasion, and casting aside all human affection in the peril of the moment.

A plank was brought and the two women placed upon it.

"After you, dear," said the mermaid significantly to the Amazonian queen; "you're the oldest."

"Thank you!" said the Amazonian queen, stepping back. "Fish is always served first."

Stung by the insult, with a wild scream of rage the mermaid grappled her in her arms and leaped into the sea.

As the waters closed over them for ever, the Pirate Prodigy sprang to his feet. "Up with the black flag, and bear away for New London," he shouted in trumpet-like tones. "Ha! ha! Once more the Rover is free!"

Indeed it was too true. In that fatal moment he had again loosed himself from the trammels of human feeling and was once more the Boy Avenger.

## CHAPTER III.

AGAIN I must ask my young readers to mount my hippogriff and hie with me to the almost inaccessible heights of the Rocky Mountains. There, for years, a band of wild and untamable savages, known as the Pigeon Feet, had resisted the blankets and Bibles of civilisation. For years the trails leading to their camp were marked by the bones of teamsters and broken waggons, and the trees were decked with the dying scalp-locks of women and children. The boldest of military leaders hesitated to attack them in their fortresses, and prudently left the scalping-knives, rifles, powder, and shot provided by a paternal government for their welfare lying on the ground a few miles from their encampment, with the request that they were not to be used until the military had safely retired. Hitherto, save an occasional incursion into the territory of the Knock-knees, a rival tribe, they had limited their depredations to the vicinity.

But lately a baleful change had come over them. Acting under some evil influence, they now pushed their warfare into the white settlements, carrying fire and destruction with them. Again and again had the Government offered them a free pass to Washington and the privilege of being photographed, but under the same evil guidance they refused. There was a singular mystery in their mode of aggression. Schoolhouses were always burned, the schoolmasters taken into captivity, and never again heard from. A palace car on the Union Pacific Railway, containing an excursion party of teachers *en route* to San Francisco, was surrounded, its inmates captured, and—their vacancies in the school catalogue never again filled. Even a board of educational examiners, proceeding to Cheyenne, were taken prisoners, and obliged to answer questions they themselves had proposed, amidst horrible tortures. By degrees these atrocities were traced to the malign influence of a new chief of the tribe. As yet little was known of him but through his baleful appellations, "Young Man who Goes for His Teacher," and "He lifts the Hair of the School Marm." He was said to be small and exceedingly youthful in appearance. Indeed, his earlier appellative, "He Wipes His Nose on His Sleeve," was said to have been given to him to indicate his still boy-like habits.

It was night in the encampment and among the lodges of the Pigeon Toes. Dusky maidens flitted in and out among the camp-fires like brown moths, cooking the toothsome buffalo-hump, frying the fragrant bear's-meat, and stewing the esculent bean for the braves. For a few favoured ones sput grasshoppers were reserved as a rare delicacy, although the proud Spartan soul of their chief scorned all such luxuries.

He was seated alone in his wigwam, attended only by the gentle Mushymush, fairest of the Pigeon Feet maidens. Nowhere were the characteristics of her great tribe more plainly shown than in the little feet that lapped over each other in walking. A single glance at the chief was sufficient to show the truth of the wild rumours respecting his youth. He was scarcely twelve, of proud and lofty bearing, and clad completely in wrappings of various-coloured scalloped cloths, which gave him the appearance of a somewhat extra-sized penwiper. An enormous eagle's feather, torn from the wing of a bald eagle who once attempted to carry him away, completed his attire. It was also the memento of one of his most superhuman feats of courage. He would undoubtedly have scalped the eagle but that nature had anticipated him.

"Why is the Great Chief sad?" said Mushymush softly. "Does his soul still yearn for the blood of the palefaced teachers? Did not the scalping of two professors of geology in the Yale exploring party satisfy his warrior's heart yesterday? Has he forgotten that Gardener and King are still to follow? Shall his own Mushymush bring him a botanist to-morrow? Speak, for the silence of my brother lies on my heart like the snow on the mountain and checks the flow of my speech."

Still the proud Boy Chief sat silent. Suddenly he said "Hist!" and rose to his feet. Taking a long rifle from the ground he adjusted its sight. Exactly seven miles away on the slope of the mountain the figure of a man was seen walking. The Boy Chief raised the rifle to his unerring eye and fired. The man fell.

A scout was despatched to scalp and search the body. He presently returned.

" Who was the paleface?" eagerly asked the chief.

"A life insurance agent."

A dark scowl settled on the face of the chief.

" I thought it was a book pedlar."

" Why is my brother's heart sore against the book pedlar?" asked Mushymush.

" Because," said the Boy Chief fiercely, " I am again without my regular dime novel—and I thought he might have one in his pack. Hear me, Mushymush. The United States mails no longer bring me my *Young America* or my *Boys' and Girls' Weekly.* I find it impossible, even with my fastest scouts, to keep up with the rear of General Howard, and replenish my literature from the sutler's waggon. Without a dime novel or a *Young America*, how am I to keep up this Injin business?"

Mushymush remained in meditation a single moment. Then she looked up proudly.

" My brother has spoken. It is well. He shall have his dime novel. He shall know the kind of hair-pin his sister Mushymush is."

And she arose and gambolled lightly as the fawn out of his presence.

In two hours she returned. In one hand she held three small flaxen scalps, in the other "The Boy Marauder," complete in one volume, price ten cents.

" Three palefaced children," she gasped, " were reading it in the tail end of an emigrant waggon. I crept up to them softly. Their parents are still unaware of the accident," and she sank helpless at his feet.

" Noble girl!" said the Boy Chief, gazing proudly on her prostrate form; " and these are the people that a military despotism expects to subdue!"

## CHAPTER IV.

BUT the capture of several waggon-loads of commissary whisky, and the destruction of two tons of stationery intended for the general commanding, which interfered with his regular correspondence with the War Department, at last awakened the United States military authorities to active exertion. A quantity of troops were massed before the Pigeon Feet encampment, and an attack was hourly imminent.

"Shine your boots, sir?"

It was the voice of a youth in humble attire, standing before the flap of the commanding general's tent.

The general raised his head from his correspondence.

"Ah," he said, looking down on the humble boy, "I see; I shall write that the appliances of civilisation move steadily forward with the army. Yes," he added, "you may shine my military boots. You understand, however, that to get your pay you must first"——

"Make a requisition on the commissary-general, have it certified to by the quartermaster, countersigned by the post-adjutant, and submitted by you to the War Department"——

"And charged as stationery," added the general gently. "You are, I see, an intelligent and thoughtful boy. I trust you neither use whisky, tobacco, nor are ever profane?"

"I promised my sainted mother"——

"Enough! Go on with your blacking; I have to lead the attack on the Pigeon Feet at eight precisely. It is now half-past seven," said the general, consulting a large kitchen clock that stood in the corner of his tent.

The little bootblack looked up: the general was absorbed in his correspondence. The bootblack drew a tin putty-blower from his pocket, took unerring aim, and nailed in a single shot the minute-hand to the dial. Going on with his blacking, yet stopping ever and anon to glance over the general's plan of campaign, spread on the table before him, he was at last interrupted by the entrance of an officer.

"Everything is ready for the attack, general. It is now eight o'clock."

"Impossible ! It is only half-past seven."

"But my watch, and the watches of the staff"——

"Are regulated by my kitchen clock, that has been in my family for years. Enough ! it is only half-past seven."

The officer retired ; the bootblack had finished one boot. Another officer appeared.

"Instead of attacking the enemy, general, we are attacked ourselves. Our pickets are already driven in."

"Military pickets should not differ from other pickets," said the bootblack modestly. "To stand firmly they should be well driven in."

"Ha ! there is something in that," said the general thoughtfully. "But who are you, who speak thus?"

Rising to his full height, the bootblack threw off his outer rags, and revealed the figure of the Boy Chief of the Pigeon Feet.

"Treason !" shrieked the general ; "order an advance along the whole line."

But in vain. The next moment he fell beneath the tomahawk of the Boy Chief, and within the next quarter of an hour the United States army was dispersed. Thus ended the battle of Bootblack Creek.

## CHAPTER V.

AND yet the Boy Chief was not entirely happy. Indeed, at times he seriously thought of accepting the invitation extended by the Great Chief at Washington immediately after the massacre of his soldiers, and once more revisiting the haunts of civilisation. His soul sickened in feverish inactivity; schoolmasters palled on his taste; he had introduced base-ball, blind hooky, marbles, and peg-top among his Indian subjects, but only with indifferent success. The squaws persisted in boring holes through the china alleys and wearing them as necklaces; his warriors stuck pikes in their base-ball bats, and made war-clubs of them. He could not but feel, too, that the gentle Mushymush, although devoted to her paleface brother, was deficient in culinary education. Her mince pies were abominable; her jam far inferior to that made by his Aunt Sally of Doemville. Only an unexpected incident kept him equally from the extreme of listless Sybaritic indulgence or of morbid cynicism. Indeed, at the age of twelve, he already had become disgusted with existence.

He had returned to his wigwam after an exhausting buffalo-hunt, in which he had slain two hundred and seventy-five buffalos with his own hand, not counting the individual buffalo on which he had leaped, so as to join the herd, and which he afterward led into the camp a captive and a present to the lovely Mushymush. He had scalped two express riders, and a correspondent of the *New York Herald;* had despoiled the Overland Mail Stage of a quantity of vouchers which enabled him to draw double rations from the Government, and was reclining on a bearskin smoking and thinking of the vanity of human endeavour, when a scout entered, saying that a paleface youth had demanded access to his person.

"Is he a commissioner? If so, say that the red man is rapidly passing to the happy hunting-grounds of his fathers, and now desires only peace, blankets, and ammunition; obtain the latter, and then scalp the commissioner."

"But it is only a youth who asks an interview."

"Does he look like an insurance agent? If so, say that I have already policies in three Hartford companies. Meanwhile prepare the stake, and see that the squaws are ready with their implements of torture."

The youth was admitted; he was evidently only half the age of the Boy Chief. As he entered the wigwam, and stood revealed to his host, they both started. In another moment they were locked in each other's arms.

"Jenky, old boy!"

"Bromley, old fel!"

B. F. Jenkins, for such was the name of the Boy Chief, was the first to recover his calmness. Turning to his warriors he said proudly—

"Let my children retire while I speak to the agent of our Great Father in Washington. Hereafter no latch-keys will be provided for the wigwams of the warriors. The practice of late hours must be discouraged."

"How!" said the warriors, and instantly retired.

"Whisper!" said Jenkins, drawing his friend aside; "I am known here only as the Boy Chief of the Pigeon Toes."

"And I," said Bromley Chitterlings proudly, "am known everywhere as the Pirate Prodigy—the Boy Avenger of the Patagonian coast."

"But how came you here?"

"Listen! My pirate brig, the *Lively Mermaid*, now lies at Meiggs's wharf in San Francisco, disguised as a Mendicino lumber vessel. My pirate crew accompanied me here in a palace car from San Francisco."

"It must have been expensive," said the prudent Jenkins.

"It was, but they defrayed it by a collection from the other passengers—you understand. The papers will be full of it to-morrow. Do you take in the *New York Sun?*"

"No; I dislike their Indian policy. But why are you here?"

"Hear me, Jenk! 'Tis a long and a sad story. The lovely Eliza J. Sniffen, who fled with me from Doemville, was seized by her parents and torn from my arms at New Rochelle. Reduced to poverty by the breaking of the savings bank of which he was president—a failure to which I largely contributed, and the profits of which I enjoyed—I have since ascertained that Eliza Jane Sniffen was forced to become a schoolmistress, departed to take charge of a seminary in Colorado, and since then has never been heard from."

Why did the Boy Chief turn pale, and clutch at the tent-pole for support? Why, indeed?

"Eliza Jane Sniffen," gasped Jenkins, "aged fourteen, red-haired, with a slight tendency to strabismus?"

"The same."

"Heaven help me! She died by my mandate!"

"Traitor!" shrieked Chitterlings, rushing at Jenkins with a drawn poniard.

But a figure interposed. The slight girlish form of Mushymush with outstretched hands stood between the exasperated Pirate Prodigy and the Boy Chief.

"Forbear," she said sternly to Chitterlings; "you know not what you do."

The two youths paused.

"Hear me," she said rapidly. "When captured in a confectioner's shop at New Rochelle, E. J. Sniffen was taken back to poverty. She resolved to become a schoolmistress. Hearing of an opening in the West, she proceeded to Colorado to take exclusive charge of the *pensionnat* of Mdme. Choflie, late of Paris. On the way thither she was captured by the emissaries of the Boy Chief"——

"In consummation of a fatal vow I made, never to spare educational instructors," interrupted Jenkins.

"But in her captivity," continued Mushymush, "she managed to stain her face with poke-berry juice, and mingling with the Indian maidens was enabled to pass for one of the tribe. Once undetected, she boldly ingratiated herself with the Boy Chief—how honestly and devotedly he best can tell—for I, Mushymush, the little sister of the Boy Chief, am Eliza Jane Sniffen."

The Pirate Prodigy clasped her in his arms. The Boy Chief, raising his hand, ejaculated—

"Bless you, my children!"

"There is but one thing wanting to complete this re-union," said Chitterlings, after a pause, but the hurried entrance of a scout stopped his utterance.

"A commissioner from the Great Father in Washington."

"Scalp him!" shrieked the Boy Chief; "this is no time for diplomatic trifling."

"We have, but he still insists upon seeing you, and has sent in his card."

The Boy Chief took it, and read aloud, in agonised accents—

"Charles Francis Adams Golightly, late page in United States Senate, and acting commissioner of United States."

In another moment, Golightly, pale, bleeding and, as it were, prematurely bald, but still cold and intellectual, entered the wigwam. They fell upon his neck and begged his forgiveness.

"Don't mention it," he said quietly; "these things must and will happen under our present system of government. My story is brief. Obtaining political influence through caucuses, I became at last page in the Senate. Through the exertions of political friends, I was appointed clerk to the commissioner whose functions I now represent. Know-ing through political spies in your own camp who you were, I acted upon the physical fears of the commissioner, who was an ex-clergyman, and easily induced him to deputise me to consult with you. In doing so, I have lost my scalp, but as the hirsute signs of juvenility have worked against my political progress I do not regret it.  As a partially bald young man I shall have more power.  The terms that I have to offer are simply this : you can do everything you want, go anywhere you choose, if you will only leave this place.  I have a hundred-thousand-dollar draft on the United States Treasury in my pocket at your immediate disposal."

"But what's to become of me ? " asked Chitterlings.

"Your case has already been under advisement.  The Secretary of State, who is an intelligent man, has determined to recognise you as *de jure* and *de facto* the only loyal representative of the Patagonian Government.  You may safely proceed to Washington as its envoy extraordinary. I dine with the secretary next week."

" And yourself, old fellow ? "

" I only wish that twenty years from now you will recognise by your influence and votes the rights of C. F. A. Golightly to the presidency."

And here ends our story.  Trusting that my dear young friends may take whatever example or moral their respective parents and guardians may deem fittest from these pages, I hope in future years to portray further the career of those three young heroes I have already introduced in the spring-time of life to their charitable consideration.

**THE END.**